# J.A. Konrath and Ann Voss Peterson

THOMAS & MERCER

Text copyright © 2013 J.A. Konrath and Ann Voss Peterson

All rights reserved.

Printed in the United States of America.

No part of this book may be reproduced, or stored in a retrieval system, or transmitted in any form or by any means, electronic, mechanical, photocopying, recording, or otherwise, without express written permission of the publisher.

Published by Thomas & Mercer

PO Box 400818

Las Vegas, NV 89140

ISBN-13: 9781612185149

ISBN-10: 1612185142

Library of Congress Control Number: 2012921113

*The only thing more dangerous than being her enemy is being her ally...*

# AUTHORS' INTRODUCTION

*Three* was written as a standalone thriller and requires no prior knowledge of either Peterson's or Konrath's respective bodies of work. But it is the third novel in the Codename: Chandler trilogy. It is also preceded by several other works featuring many of the characters who inhabit this novel.

In the Kindle book edition of *Three*, the reader will come across occasional hyperlinks when a character first appears. Clicking on this underscored text will take the reader to a brief description of the character and the work they appear in, for those interested in getting more information, clarity, or explanations of past events. These links, however, are in no way necessary to understanding and enjoying the *Three* story line.

Our goal is to provide the reader with a complete picture of the many novellas and novels that compose our interconnected body of fiction, and the e-book format has given us the opportunity to unify our works in a way that has been impossible in the print world.

We hope this state-of-the-art feature enhances your enjoyment of *Three*.

# Chandler

*"The enemy of your enemy is not always your friend,"*
*The Instructor said. "But sometimes she can be useful."*

"We need to hide somewhere, plan our next move," Hammett said. "He'll be looking for us."

Hammett was naked and handcuffed to the porch railing, the falling drizzle beading up on her skin, washing away dirt and leaves. Though she was my identical twin and had identical training, her body wasn't quite the same as mine. Her hair was longer, darker. Her multiple scars were in different places. Her stomach muscles were a bit more sculpted. And for some strange reason—I have no idea how—she seemed to be a cup size larger.

I wondered if I'd made the right choice letting her live. Something I'm sure I would always wonder. But we needed the information Hammett had, which made her more of an asset than a liability.

For now. Barely.

"No shit," Fleming said. She was also my sister, another twin, and had more scars than Hammett and I combined. Fleming backed up her wheelchair on the porch until she was under the awning and out of the weather. She met my eyes, her face stern. "But once you've assassinated the president of the United States, your options narrow."

*No shit* was right. I hadn't wanted to kill him. Wouldn't have if I could have saved those I cared about any other way. But what was done was done. I was the fifth presidential assassin in American history, part of a very select collection of scum.

But it got worse.

Evidence against me also implicated Fleming, and even more interestingly, Hammett—the woman I hated as much as the man who'd forced me to commit this crime.

We were in this mess together. And there didn't seem to be any way out of it.

"The Instructor knows all of my safe houses," Hammett said. "And if he hacked into your network, he knows yours as well."

"He didn't hack me," Fleming said. She folded her arms across her chest. Defensiveness, or fear.

"Are you sure?" Hammett asked. "One hundred fucking percent sure? Because if you aren't, he'll be waiting for us when we get there, dumbass. Why don't you try using that high IQ of yours for something other than inventing exploding phones?"

Fleming didn't answer.

We were at a farmhouse on the outskirts of tiny Lake Loyal, Wisconsin. It belonged to a man I thought I loved who didn't love me back. He was gone.

"Let's work on not speaking until asked a direct question," I warned Hammett. "I could still take you back to the woods."

She rolled her eyes. "Whatever you say, Chandler. Or can I call you Lee Harvey?"

The man standing next to Fleming, a former gymnast turned former mob enforcer named Tequila, stared at Hammett.

"Should have killed her," he said.

"Big talk from such a little man," Hammett said. Then she smiled, a scary imitation of coquettish, sticking out her chest and wiggling. "Like what you see? I know you do."

"Seen it," Tequila said, placing his hand on Fleming's shoulder and squeezing. "But when I did, it was sexy."

I held a bag with my previously worn, stained clothes, which I tossed at Hammett. "Are you sure The Instructor knows our safe houses?" I asked.

She caught the bag in her handcuffed hands. The vixen disappeared, replaced by the stone-cold hit woman. "It's scary how much he knows," Hammett said. "The guy is plugged into everything. We check into a bed-and-breakfast in Durango, Colorado, without Internet or phone service, he'll know. And we're not exactly inconspicuous." Hammett cast a quick look at Fleming, lowering her eyes to my sister's wheelchair.

I chewed my lower lip, thinking. When someone like The Instructor had the means, and the notion, to find you, there weren't many places to hide. Even in this remote location in the woods, with plenty of tree cover, we shouldn't have been outside. I could almost feel the spy satellites staring down at me from low Earth orbit.

The Instructor hadn't publicly revealed his evidence of my guilt—a video of my pressing the button that killed the president—and there was no telling when he'd play that card. Life was difficult for those on the top of the government's Most Wanted list. I knew. I'd killed my share of them.

To really, truly disappear, you had to erase your trail, erase your identity, then go where no one knows you or expects you to go. It would be tricky, especially with Fleming. Maybe we could drop off the grid by vanishing into the woods, or the mountains, or the desert, but that didn't serve our ultimate purpose. Unless we wanted to be hunted our whole lives, we needed to find, and kill, the ones hunting us. That meant we needed access to certain things: weapons, communications, computers, transportation, cash, disguises, and ultimately new IDs. Things that left trails rather than erased them. And if our safe houses were compromised, so were our contacts, and anyone who'd ever assisted any of us on a mission would be under surveillance.

This was going to be tough. But things would get even tougher.

"Is there any place we can go that no one knows about?" Hammett asked. "A place that's never been spoken about on the phone? Never mentioned in an e-mail? Someplace so far off the grid that no eye in the sky has noticed it?"

"Tall order," Fleming said to Hammett. "You know of any?"

"Maybe one or two. But would you trust me?"

Fleming and I said, "Hell no," at the same time. Then we looked at each other, and I guessed she was thinking what I was thinking.

There *was* one place that was safe. Only three people knew about it: Fleming, me, and the girl we'd hidden there. The journey would be risky, but once we arrived we'd be virtually invisible while we regrouped and plotted our next move.

"OK," I said. "We're going to need a vehicle, ammo, supplies."

Tequila shrugged. "I've only got a few hundred bucks left."

I stared at the man who had helped me beyond words, whom I now thought of as a friend.

"Your employment has been terminated, amigo. Go back home."

His shrug turned into something else, a cross between disappointment and disapproval.

"You sure?"

"You've done enough, and this isn't your fight. Things are going to get really hot, and you don't want to be a part of that." I held out my hand. "Thanks. For everything."

He shook my hand with conviction and warmth. "My pleasure, Chandler."

"Give Fleming your bank wiring info. I'll pay you what I owe you in the next few days."

"Be safe," he said. Then he released my hand and looked at Fleming. "Can I trust you with my bank information?"

"Only one way to find out," Fleming said, her lips curling in a smile. "Share it, then try to get the information out of me."

"Sounds like a challenge."

He opened the door, then pushed Fleming back into the house. I also wanted to get out of the rain, but I didn't have any burning desire to listen to them say good-bye to each other. Especially since I knew what it would entail. So instead I stood out there, getting more and more drenched, watching my evil sister try to put on pants with both hands handcuffed around the stair railing.

"Get on your knees," I said.

"Kinky. Especially since we're related."

I gave her a look that said I wasn't kidding. Hammett knelt in the mud, and I came behind her and pressed my chest against her back, letting her take most of my weight. Then I uncuffed her left hand and placed the Skorpion submachine gun against the back of her head.

"Can you get dressed without forcing me to kill you?"

"I guess we'll see."

I eased back, and Hammett stood up. After a prerequisite tough-girl stare to prove she wasn't afraid, she got dressed in my dirty clothes. When she was finished, she dutifully locked her hands back together in front of her.

"This sweater smells. And it's ugly. Who taught you how to shop?"

"Some of us didn't do so well with our adopted parents," I said, thinking of the bastard who'd adopted me at age eleven after my first adoptive parents died.

Something dark passed over Hammett's eyes, and she surprised me by not replying. The rain kept coming. Not a heavy downpour, but a slow, stinging drizzle that pattered on the leaves and clicked against the windowpanes. It took longer to do the job, but it got you just as wet. Death by a thousand cuts.

"So now what?" Hammett eventually said. "We stand out here and get wetter and wetter while those two bump uglies?"

"Up the stairs."

I marched Hammett into the house, to the kitchen, and sat her at the table. In the fridge I found a loaf of bread, some mustard, cheddar cheese slices, and a package of deli ham. There was also a tomato, but that would involve slicing, and I didn't want Hammett anywhere near a knife.

I made myself a sandwich, then kept my hand on the Skorpion while Hammett assembled one for herself.

"What?" she said, grinning. "I'm going to kill you with this cheese?"

"It *is* sharp cheddar."

For a moment, neither of us said anything. And then it happened.

She laughed, and so did I.

Not what I was expecting. I hated this woman. She'd done things to me, to Fleming, and to the world that were unspeakable and unforgivable. Sharing a joke wasn't something you were supposed to do with the enemy.

I stopped laughing, ate my sandwich warily. Hammett finished hers first and went for seconds. Then the groaning started.

Fleming first. Then Tequila. Fleming's rose in pitch until the groans became squeals then whimpers.

"Jesus," Hammett said. "Do I sound like that?"

It was the same thing I'd wondered the first time I heard Fleming and Tequila go at it.

"Probably," I admitted, afraid we were all more alike than I wanted to believe.

"I don't see how she can go on living with her legs messed up like that."

"She seems to be coping OK."

"I would have eaten a bullet."

"That's still an option."

Hammett rolled her eyes, taking another bite of sandwich. "Can you cut the threats already? I know why you didn't kill me."

I didn't want to have this conversation. "You can help us find The Instructor."

"Yes. But that's not the main reason."

She was right. But I didn't have any desire to admit it.

"The Instructor videotaped your little speech, where you pressed the destruct code on that cell phone," Hammett said. "That code blew up the president's phone, probably blowing his head off. The Instructor also has the phone you used, with your fingerprints. Which are also my fingerprints, thanks to the bizarre genetic fuckup of our birth. Once The Instructor makes that video public, we're going to be hunted to the far corners of the earth."

"So we kill him first," I said.

"And if we don't, you kill me. Leave my body someplace public. I take the fall for the murder you committed. A perfect patsy. Prints match. Face matches. No more being hunted."

She took another bite. I didn't say anything. There was nothing to say. Hammett was correct. If things got too hot, I wouldn't hesitate to kill her to throw the trail off Fleming and me.

And I knew Hammett felt the same way about the two of us.

"I could always kill you now," I said. "Keep your body on ice."

"Wicked. It's such a shock your boy toy left you, when you have thoughts like that. Did you really believe people like us could have a relationship with a civilian?"

"That's none of your business." I had a quarter of sandwich left, but was no longer hungry. I set it on the table. "And I'm not like you."

Tequila must have changed his angle or his tempo, because Fleming's squeals became full-blown screams.

"I heard your little breakup scene," Hammett said. She fluttered her eyelids and said, *"Oh, Lund, why can't you be with me?"*

"Careful," I said.

Hammett changed her voice, making it lower to imitate Lund. *"The man guarding the truck. I watched you slit his throat. I saw..."*

She played me again. *"If he saw us, he would have shot us."*

Lund again. *"It's not that."*

Me. *"Then what is it? I don't understand."*

"Shut up," I told her.

But Hammett went on. *"I saw your face when you killed him. There was...nothing there."*

"Enough." I stood up, and without thinking I raised the Skorpion.

Hammett didn't stop, still quoting Lund verbatim. *"Your eyes, they were flat, dead, as if killing him was nothing more to you than swatting a mosquito. You ended a man's life, and you felt nothing at all."*

She grinned, and said in her own voice, "Kinda like now."

I almost pulled the trigger. Instead, I lashed out and slapped Hammett across the face, only turning my fist into a flat palm at the last possible moment.

Hammett's head reared back, and then she looked at me with amusement as her cheek blossomed red.

"And you seriously wonder why he left you?" she asked.

I searched my mind for some reply, some retort, but came up blank.

"You're a weapon, Chandler. Trained by the government to murder without mercy or guilt. You'll hurt, maim, torture, and kill both the guilty and the innocent to complete your mission. You think you hate me? Wake up, sister. We're the same. You want someone to hate, take a good, long look in the mirror."

I wanted to hit her again. To hit her over and over until her face was so bloody it no longer looked like mine.

But summoning up some Herculean self-control, I managed to sit back down. "I'm not like you."

"Well," Hammett said, reaching for the bread. "I guess we'll have to wait and see."

# The White House

President J. Phillip Ratzenberger sat behind the Resolute desk in the Oval Office, running his palm across the mirror-polished surface. It seemed to tingle and vibrate beneath his fingertips, causing goose bumps to stand at attention all up his arm. Ratzenberger's throat was dry, his ears red and hot.

It was better than touching a beautiful woman.

He had worked his whole life to get this moment. And though it came as the result of a tragedy rather than an election, Ratzenberger felt that he'd earned it. More than that, he *deserved* to be president. Especially now. More than ever, his country needed a strong, dedicated leader. Someone to ensure America's dominance of the world—politically, industrially, militarily, economically.

Chaz, the White House cat, slunk up and stared at Ratzenberger, emitting a sour meow that sounded more like a *meep*, completely spoiling the mood. The president scowled, hitting the intercom button on the desk.

"The damn cat is in my office. Get it out of here."

Mullins, one of his Secret Service drones, came into the office and quickly located and snatched up the cat, which immediately began purring.

"Tell my wife if it gets in here again, I'll have you boys shoot it."

"Yes, sir."

"You'd do that, right? If I ordered you to?"

"My duty is to protect you, Mr. President."

"That animal destroys my peace of mind. If you killed it, you'd be protecting my ability to ably run this country."

"Yes, sir."

Mullins turned to leave, and Ratzenberger made a note to have him replaced. On the far wall, CNN showed what seemed to be an endless loop of his predecessor's body being wheeled out of the press room on a gurney, an image that had been seen by billions of people and in less than twenty-four hours had become as iconic as the Zapruder film of Kennedy's assassination. As the gurney was hurried out, the bloodstain under the white sheet doubled, then tripled in size, sticking to what was left of the former president's head, molding to its disfigured outline.

An apt image, considering the bloodshed to come. Rivers of blood across the hemisphere...

The phone rang, startling Ratzenberger out of his reverie. He snatched it up, slapping the receiver to his ear.

"This is the vice—" No. Wrong. "This is the president."

"It's me."

Ratzenberger frowned. It was the man who had orchestrated his predecessor's demise. The one who was helping him implement his current plan for the USA. The previous president hadn't liked the man. He was too smart. Too plugged in. And too sure of his power. But Ratzenberger needed him, and owed him, and he had to play nice for the time being.

"Have you found them yet?" Ratzenberger asked.

"We're working on it, Mr. President."

"Where is the science team?"

"En route. I need funding."

"You have funding."

"I need more."

"I'll inform the DOD. As long as it's a reasonable number, you'll get it."

"How's the new office?"

"Hmm?" Odd thing to say. "It's...it's magnificent."

"I'll be in touch."

The man who called himself The Instructor hung up, leaving the most powerful man in the free world wondering if he were indeed the most powerful.

# Fleming

*"There will be times when you need money," The Instructor said. "The ends justify the means."*

Fleming was sore all over, some of it good, most of it not. Her legs—scarred and useless and with more metal pins than bones—were the main source of her pain, and she also had other aches that competed. But the parts that ached from the recent, vigorous session of lovemaking with Tequila were enough to make Fleming feel almost normal. At least for the moment.

"I like you," she said afterward, snuggling up to his naked body, even managing to hook a useless leg over his. It was as intimate a thing as she'd ever said to a man in—well—ever.

"I like you, too. You sure you want to send me away?"

"The three of us—me and my sisters...We're probably all going to die within the next few days."

Tequila said nothing for several seconds. When he spoke, his voice was as soft as she'd ever heard it. "I know."

"And I...I wouldn't like seeing you die. Or having you watch me die."

He drew his finger up Fleming's bare back, letting his hand come to rest on the nape of her neck. "Are you scared?" he asked.

A silly question. Fleming, Chandler, and Hammett were about to be hunted as the assassins of the president of the United

States. As soon as The Instructor released the video, they'd be the most wanted fugitives in the world. Every government agency on the planet, every private contractor, would be after them. Who wouldn't be scared?

And yet, Fleming wasn't.

"No," she said.

"Tired of living?"

"Not that. These past few days, I faced death so many times, I think I've resigned myself to it."

Tequila pulled his arm away, sat up in bed, swinging his legs over the side.

"Years ago, I lost my sister," he said. "I felt the same way. Went after the men who did it and figured there was no way I'd survive. So I just accepted the inevitable. Except…"

Fleming felt like reaching out, touching him. But she kept her hands to herself. "Except what?"

"Except I didn't die."

"How'd that work out for you?" She meant it to be a playful question, but Tequila didn't answer.

"Be careful what you wish for," he eventually said. "Because you may not get it."

"I don't understand."

"The bad parts. They aren't what makes life unbearable."

"What does?"

Tequila frowned. "The good parts."

Fleming understood. If you have nothing to lose, you can't be hurt. But once you have something to lose…

Tequila rolled away, finding his boxer-briefs on the floor next to the bed. Fleming watched him.

She really did like Tequila, but it wasn't love. Asking him to leave was regrettable, but it was a courtesy from one professional to another, not a heartbreak. Fleming wasn't sure she even knew what heartbreak was. After the accident, she resigned herself to living alone, growing old alone. She would never have a family. She would never have a man she had more than a passing affection for. And after the last few days, she accepted that she wouldn't live through next week.

Strange that she could be so calm about it.

"You're older than me," Fleming said.

"By a lot."

"So…"

"So what made me go on living?"

Fleming nodded.

"No one is good enough to kill me," Tequila said. "And I'm too chicken shit to end things myself."

"Chicken shit?" She'd heard few things so ridiculous. "I don't think you have a chicken shit bone in your body."

"Then what is it?"

"I don't know." Fleming thought about the choice she'd faced in the black site prison, holding a scalpel to her own throat. She should have taken her life to protect the secrets she knew. If she had, the president would still be alive. And Chandler, along with Hammett, wouldn't be facing almost certain death now. Yet, somewhat ironically, at the time it was her desperation to save Chandler that made Fleming determined to live.

"Maybe it's sheer stubbornness," she said, looking at Tequila's back. "Or curiosity."

"Curiosity?"

"Life is filled with unexpected turns, and you want to find out what happens next."

Tequila raised an eyebrow. "Could be. Are you curious?"

Fleming made sure she weighed the question before answering. "Yes."

"Then watch your ass out there," he said, leaning over and giving her a smack on the rump, followed by a tiny kiss on the cheek.

He finished dressing and walked out of the bedroom. Fleming flopped over, graceful as a beached fish, locating her panties and awkwardly threading her ruined legs into them. Her pants were next, a pair of loose-fitting khakis. Usually, during the ordeal of dressing, Fleming lamented her clothing, chosen for convenience over looks. She hadn't bothered to wear cute jeans since the accident. Her Diane von Furstenberg boots had scuffs on the toes, but the soles were factory-fresh, and except for those boots, she'd taken to buying footwear with low or no heels because they kept catching on her chair. She couldn't remember the last time she wore a dress.

But as she put on her clothes, Fleming didn't focus on her disability, or her appearance. Instead she thought about what Tequila said, about how the good parts in life made it unbearable. Was that why she had no friends? Was that the reason she kept men at arm's length?

If so, was that the person she wanted to be?

Fleming allowed herself a grin. Self-awareness on the way to the gallows didn't do a girl much good.

She crawled her arms into her shirt and then awkwardly plopped into her wheelchair, which had recently been pimped out above factory standards, having been reinforced and fitted with hidden weapon compartments. When Fleming rolled into the kitchen, Tequila was there with Chandler and Hammett, making two ham and cheese sandwiches. He handed her one, and she took a bite. Too much mustard, but delicious just the same. She hadn't realized how hungry she was.

"The plan is for Tequila to take us into Baraboo," Chandler said. "We secure a vehicle and essential supplies, and then drive east." Then she frowned. "The problem is money. If The Instructor has hacked us, or already has physical and electronic surveillance in place, we can't go to any known contacts or drops."

Fleming knew Chandler had cash stashed around Chicago and the suburbs, as well as in various parts of the country and the world. Hammett had the same training. Fleming also had various stashes in various locations, including several Swiss banks. But those sites could be compromised, and wiring money would involve picking it up, which left electronic trails. If The Instructor had the entire Department of Defense behind him, Fleming couldn't be sure they could get money without tripping some alert, even if they were in and out fast. It would probably be safer to rob a bank.

The thought brought a smile to her face. Wiping some mustard off her lips with the back of her hand, she said, "How do you girls feel about armed robbery?"

\*\*\*

When they arrived in Baraboo in Tequila's truck a half hour later, he dropped them off at a busy shopping center, in an empty corner of the parking lot. After gently setting Fleming down in her wheelchair, Tequila held out his hand.

"If you survive this, maybe you can look me up."

She took his hand in hers and shook it once, warmly. "I might just do that."

Then he nodded at Chandler, got into his truck, and drove off. No passionate kiss good-bye. No promise to keep in touch. That was how professionals worked. And that was fine with Fleming. She liked Tequila, as a business associate, and as a lover. She liked him a lot, in fact. But even if she ever chose to quit the business, she could never have anything long-term or serious with Tequila.

After all, the guy was a stone-cold killer.

"So, what's the deal?" Hammett asked. The light drizzle was matting down her hair. "You gonna keep me cuffed forever? Or do we reach a point where we start trusting one another?"

"I vote for cuffed forever," Fleming said. "I'd also add *gagged*."

Chandler frowned. "The robbery is a two-person job, plus a wheelman."

"And you're the wheelman," Hammett said, staring at Fleming's chair. "For obvious reasons."

Fleming's face pinched. She didn't trust Hammett. There were rules in this business, and Hammett had broken them. At the same time, an unloaded pistol didn't do anyone much good. You either loaded it with intent to shoot or ditched it. They needed to use Hammett or get rid of her.

"Sis?" Chandler asked.

"Uncuff her," Fleming said. "She tries anything, I'll kill her."

"Don't be so mean," Hammett said. "They might kick you out of the Special Olympics."

Fleming hit the left lever on her chair, and the side panel opened up and instantly pressed a spring-loaded 9mm handgun into her palm. "My favorite event is the Bitch Shoot," she said. "Wanna see me go for the gold?"

"Try to steal a vehicle without killing each other," Chandler said, tossing Hammett the handcuff keys. "Find one with a trailer hitch. I'm getting supplies."

She headed off toward the supermarket. Hammett eyed the gun, then looked at Fleming. "I'm guessing we're looking for a van and not a subcompact," she said. "Unless we can origami your legs and chair into the trunk."

Fleming saw the amusement in Hammett's eyes, and wondered if it was a deliberate provocation, or just good-natured ball-busting.

"No reaction?" Hammett asked while removing the cuffs. "When you fell, did it also shatter your sense of humor?"

Fleming scowled. "Maybe I lost it a few days ago, when your partner was breaking my fingers."

Hammett rubbed her wrist. "Seriously? That's your beef? That my partner broke your fingers? I figured you'd be used to broken bones at this point."

Fleming cocked the nine. "I should do the world a favor and end you right now."

Hammett sighed dramatically, then stuck out her little finger and held it in front of Fleming. "Here. If it'll make you stop acting like a baby, go ahead and break it."

Fleming searched her sister's face for some sort of deception. She didn't see any. But if this wasn't a trick, what was it? Was this psychopath actually serious?

"C'mon," Hammett said, wiggling the pinkie. "You gonna do it or not?"

"You want me to break your finger?"

"No, pinhead, I don't want you to break my finger. But if we're going to work together, I don't want you holding a grudge.

Christ, I waterboarded Chandler, and she's not acting as pissy as you are."

"I'm not like you, Hammett. I don't get off on hurting people."

Hammett smiled coyly. "Are you sure? Think about how much trouble and pain I've caused you and her. All the hell you've gone through, because of me. Wouldn't you feel better if you—*HOLYMOTHERFUCKINGSHIT!*"

Fleming released Hammett's pinkie, now bent at a wrong angle, and brought the gun up in case Hammett tried to retaliate.

"I gotta admit it," Fleming said. "That felt pretty good."

Hammett let out a sound that was part hysterical laugh, part agonized groan. Her pinkie stuck out ninety degrees, almost like a hitchhiker's thumb.

"OK, sis. Ha ha ha. Good times." Her teeth were grinding together in the world's most pained smile. "Now snap it back into place."

"It's going to hurt."

"Just do it."

Fleming tucked the gun away, then grasped the pinkie again and reversed her previous action, feeling the phalange bones grind together. Hammett fell to one knee, made a fist with her free hand, and hit herself in the thigh several times in rapid succession. A woman pushing a stroller walked past, averting her eyes when Fleming stared at her. Hammett made a gagging sound and then threw up in the parking lot.

"Wow," Hammett said, spitting. "That hurts like hell."

"Never broke a finger before?"

"Plenty. On other people. Never one of mine. Got any of that Demerol left?"

"I think so."

"How about you give me a shot, then we find a van to steal?"

Surprisingly, a lot of the animosity Fleming had felt moments ago toward Hammett was gone. She still didn't trust her, but the resentment had abated. At least for now.

"OK." Fleming dug into the compartment under her seat and took out the first-aid kit. She gave Hammett an injection in her pinkie. "It's not a lot. You'll still have use of your hand."

"Cool. Thanks." Hammett gave her fingers a slow wiggle, then cleared her throat. "So, that Tequila dude. Sounded like he rocked your world. I'm surprised you aren't hoarse."

Even though Hammett was her sister, Fleming didn't feel the need to engage in sister talk with a maniac. "Let's keep our relationship professional, Hammett."

"Fine. So, one professional to another, how good was he in the sack?"

Now Fleming actually had to force herself not to smile. "He can hold a handstand while doing a split."

"Impressive. But what good is that?"

Fleming stared at Hammett for several seconds, then finally gave in and shared the details.

Hammett's eyes went wide. "Oh. My. God. And you let him go? I would have chained him up in my basement and kept him forever."

Fleming couldn't tell if Hammett was serious or not, and decided she probably was. She handed Hammett a packet of ibuprofen, then tucked away the kit and took out a toolbox. "You want to do the van or the plates?"

"I'll get the vehicle. You're already at the perfect height to take off plates."

"Fine. No collateral damage. You can steal a van. But don't kill anyone."

"You really think I'm that unhinged?"

"You tried to nuke London," Fleming said evenly.

"I was in a bad mood that day."

"No civilians, Hammett."

"You think they're going to just hand over their rides? What am I supposed to do with them if they say no?"

"Something else. I dunno. Ask them to dance and take the car when they're not looking. I don't care. Figure something out. Just no deaths."

"You got it, sis. I promise I'll adhere to your strict moral code while committing grand theft auto."

Hammett headed off in the direction of the shops, and Fleming rolled into the lot, feeling very much like she'd just signed a deal with the devil.

# Hammett

*"Enemies change, and allies change," said The Instructor. "You don't owe loyalty to the past. Loyalty is for the present."*

Even though she ached in too many places to count, had failed miserably on her last two missions, was betrayed by her employer, and would be given a death sentence by the United States government, Hammett felt pretty good. Somehow she had avoided getting killed so far, the rain had stopped, and even though she'd switched sides, at least her new partners were competent.

Hammett had worked with her other four sisters—originally Hammett, Chandler, Fleming, and the other four had been septuplets—and they had been, without a doubt, the best team she'd ever been a part of. Unfortunately, Chandler had killed the other four. But now that Hammett was working with Chandler and Fleming, she felt the same kind of thrill. The three of them were what was left of the best of the best; they had the same training, the same DNA, and they all thought a lot alike.

Hammett decided she was going to enjoy her time with her sisters, up until the inevitable moment she'd be forced to kill them. But until that point, they shared the same goal, and had to function as a unit.

She walked the parking lot, shopping for her new vehicle.

Many times in her line of work, and a few times in her personal life when she couldn't get a cab, Hammett had stolen vehicles. Hot-wiring was a lot more complicated than it was portrayed in the movies, and with newer-model cars it was often impossible. Carjacking often put the law on your tail in relatively short order. The easiest and smartest way to steal a car was to obtain the keys and get a good head start before the owner knew it was missing.

Or to just kill the owner. But Fleming was being a wimp about that.

Hammett could probably kill someone and Fleming wouldn't know, but that was a risky avenue to go down. Hammett needed her new teammates to trust her, at least a little, and that meant staying true to her word. In this business, you were only as good as your promise. So Hammett intended to not give them any reason to mistrust her, until she inevitably betrayed them and killed them both.

She prowled the parking lot until she found the perfect mark—a woman in a recent-model SUV, her Nine West purse remaining open after she dropped her keys into it.

Hammett opened her eyes wide and swiped a finger across her corneas. Then she stuck a fingernail up her nose, scratching the fragile mucus membranes. Once in character, she ran at the woman, bumping her from behind and knocking her purse free.

Hammett rolled across the parking lot, landing near the purse. Tears were streaming down her face, and blood flowed from her nostril and dribbled over her lips.

"Hey!" The mark looked angry and confused before spotting Hammett on the ground. "Oh my God, are you OK?"

"My ex," Hammett said, making her voice quiver. "He's after me. He's coming!"

She pointed behind her. The woman turned to look. Hammett took her car keys, and the woman's wallet as well. Then she snapped the handbag closed.

"I don't see him," the woman said, turning back around. "Do you need help? Should I call the police?"

"No! The police won't help. I…I gotta go."

Hammett took off, sprinting across the parking lot, pinching her nostrils. When the bleeding stopped, she ducked into an

L.L.Bean. Used to shopping quickly, Hammett picked out some black steel-toed hiking boots, black rain pants, wool socks, a gray T-shirt, and a bulky gray sweater. She bought them all, along with some strawberry lip balm from the checkout line display, paying with the woman's credit card. After changing in the bathroom, she went to pick up her new SUV.

Fleming was already there, switching out the plates in the front.

"Not bad," Fleming said. "I swapped tags with an out-of-state SUV, so it'll take some time to sort out."

Hammett nodded, then handed Fleming the lip balm.

"What is this?" Fleming asked.

"It's lip balm."

"What's it for?"

"You put it on your lips when they're chapped. Duh."

"I meant why are you giving it to me?"

"Your lips are chapped."

Fleming raised a hand, touching her lips, and Hammett spotted Chandler heading toward them with two huge bags of supplies.

"You guys work out your differences?" Chandler asked.

Hammett said, "She broke my pinkie, and I bought her some Chapstick."

If Chandler found the comment odd, she didn't show it. Nor did she acknowledge Hammett's new outfit, which was much more stylish and flattering and far less smelly than the one she'd given her sister back at the farmhouse.

"This our vehicle?"

Hammett dangled the keys. Chandler took them, and they loaded the bags and Fleming into the SUV, followed by her wheelchair.

"I know a place in Milwaukee, perfect to knock over," Hammett said. "Should net at least fifty K."

They headed east as Hammett laid out the details. When she checked the rearview, she caught Fleming putting on some lip balm.

*Good. Fleming is letting her guard down a bit.*
Hammett allowed herself a small grin.
*Now to get Chandler to do the same.*

# Chandler

*"When things go wrong," The Instructor said, "bail out."*

A mile away from our target, I traded seats with Fleming, letting her drive using her aluminum forearm crutch to work the pedals.

During the two-hour drive, Hammett had kept busy sawing off the stocks and barrels of the two Mossberg 12-gauge shotguns I'd bought at Walmart using the hacksaw and C-clamps I'd also bought at Walmart. It hadn't been an easy task, especially with her broken finger, but she'd done it without complaint. Other supplies included a half-dozen prepaid disposable cell phones, three buck knives, and a giant bottle of Advil. I passed it all around.

Fleming circled the block once, while Hammett and I hunkered down by the side door, weapons in hands.

"If we're not in and out in thirty seconds," I said to Fleming, "keep waiting."

She patted the Skorpion submachine gun in her lap. "I'm not going anywhere. Take all the time you need."

I stared at Hammett until she noticed me and stared back.

"What?"

"No killing," I told her.

"Are you kidding? These guys signed on for this. Goes with the territory."

"You heard me."

"So if they shoot at us, what do you want me to do? Bat my eyelashes and flirt?"

"Wound," I said.

She made a face. "You two could take the fun out of a clown orgy, you know that?"

The SUV eased to a stop. I brought up my Mossberg. Six shells in the tube and one in the chamber. I had extras in my pockets, but if we needed to reload we'd done something very wrong.

"In and out, you clear the door and the civilians, I'll hit the safe," I said. "On three. One…"

"Three!" Hammett opened her door and leaped out of the vehicle. I ran after her, and within four steps she'd shot both men guarding the front entrance, the Mossberg booming, buckshot tattooing blood into the walls.

Both shots were low, ripping through legs and feet, and as Hammett barreled through the front door, I attended to the guards and removed their guns and cell phones, shoving them into my backpack as they writhed and swore and moaned in pain.

"Don't do the crime if you can't do the time," I told one of them, a black guy who couldn't have been older than eighteen. "This ain't a game for kiddies."

I followed Hammett inside, where she fired off two more rounds, one at a third guard, the other into a wall, yelling for everyone to get down.

They moved as fast as stoned people could.

I hadn't initially liked the idea of robbing drug dealers. A bank would have been safer, the guards and patrons more predictable. But banks had cameras and hitting one was a federal offense, which would risk putting the FBI on our tails. Crack dealers wouldn't chase us cross-country. Hell, after being robbed by two women, they wouldn't even admit what happened to their homies for fear of losing face.

I disarmed the third soldier, a pudgy, mean-looking kid around twenty, whom Hammett had shot in the groin. He didn't resist, too busy clutching himself and screaming a mantra that consisted of repeating the word *bitch* over and over.

The house was dim and shabby. Those who weren't passed out on the filthy sofas were on the floor, ducking, begging, or attempting to crawl out the front door unnoticed. I scanned the room for weapons, noting the position of every person's hands. It smelled like body odor and crack smoke and desperation, with the newly introduced odors of blood and gunpowder mingling in.

There were gunshots—low caliber—deeper inside the house. Satisfied that no one from this room was in any shape to cause us trouble, I headed into the adjoining kitchen, following the path Hammett had gone, both hands steel-tight on my weapon, as if someone was trying to take it from me. An older man sat at a dirty Formica-topped table. As I moved past, I caught movement from the corner of my eye, the guy reaching into his jacket. I swung the barrel around and almost fired, before I saw it was a crack pipe.

I guess everyone had their priorities.

I blew out a breath, trying to reel myself in. I felt jumpy, out of my element. My heart rate raced, on the edge of being too fast. My palms were damp on my shotgun. The reaction was so unlike me. I had performed many operations more stressful than this one. I had nerves of ice.

I tried to control my breathing, slow my vitals with techniques I'd honed over the years, but the foul smoke constricted my throat and made deep breathing difficult. My heart beat, too fast, and I could hear the thrum in my ears.

Two more shotgun blasts from Hammett's Mossberg, coming from above.

I found stairs leading to the second floor and took them two at a time, my legs feeling heavy. I was exhausted—all of us were— but I had deep reserves. That said, even the deepest wells eventually run dry, and the last week had been hell. Knocking over a drug house in a neighborhood populated by gangbangers who wear guns like bling wasn't a good time to run out of steam.

At the top of the staircase, I dropped to one knee, shotgun extended, sighting down the hallway. As with many older houses, the hall was long and narrow, what cops liked to call a vertical coffin. If anyone came down that hall, I'd have them as trapped as a fake duck in a shooting gallery. But the same dynamic applied to me. Rooms flanked either side, and in any doorway a gunman could be waiting on my next move. I'd have to be fast, or I'd be dead.

Burned gunpowder stuck in my throat and choked the air, the overhead light too dim to cut the haze. Shouting boomed from a room at the end of the hall. Taking advantage of the distraction, I gathered my legs under me and sprang into the hall. I sprinted its length, catching glimpses of darkened rooms and vacant doorways from the corner of my eye. Reaching the source of the commotion, I whipped around the doorjamb and entered the room low, catching peripheral movement to my left. I snapped my head around and focused on Hammett, who stood with her weapon raised, the sawed-off barrel pointing straight at me.

I brought my shotgun up—*that double-crossing…!*—but she was faster, and before I could finish the thought, she fired.

The *boom!* punched my ears so loud it vibrated in my fillings. I felt a warm tug on my thigh but not the instant death I'd been expecting. I fired as I went to the floor, Hammett getting in under the blast and rolling up to me, one of her hands knocking my shotgun away while the other pressed her hot barrel to my neck, searing my skin.

I reached up, clawing at her eyes. Hammett leaned back and used the gun to push my chin to the left. There in the shadows a gangbanger twitched in a puddle of his own pooling blood, eyes open and vacant, a .45 still clenched in his fist.

Hammett yelled something my stunned ears weren't able to hear, but I didn't have to know what she said to add two and two together. She hadn't been shooting at me—she'd taken out the guy behind me. Maybe he'd been behind the door. Maybe he'd followed me into the room, and I'd somehow missed it. But whatever had happened, he'd almost killed me.

My psychotic sister had saved my life, and I had almost shot her in response.

I met her eyes and nodded, letting her know I got it, and immediately she had her hand on my shirt and was pulling me to my feet. I checked my thigh, saw my pants were pockmarked with four spots of blood where buckshot had tagged me.

No pain yet, but it would come.

The safe was in the corner of the room, as Hammett had pre-dicted. A medium-size Sentry model, under a painting of a cruci-fied black Jesus. Not waiting for me, Hammett started working the combination dial, leaving me to cover the door. After twenty seconds, the Sentry remained locked.

"There a problem?" I asked, my ears still ringing.

"They might have changed the combination. It's been over a year."

The whole reason we'd chosen this spot was because Hammett had once taken a job where she'd been required to get informa-tion from one of the Midwest's top gang leaders.

*"After a few hours with me, he told me his whole life story,"* Hammett had said. *"Every woman he'd slept with. Every crime he'd committed. The locations of seventeen drug houses, along with combinations to all of their safes."*

"Maybe you're mixing it up with another location," I said.

"Not possible."

"Give me a break. Everyone can make mistakes."

"Not me. Eidetic memory."

"You still could have mixed—"

"There we go."

The safe door opened, and I was left wondering why Hammett and I shared the same features down to our fingerprints, but she had a photographic memory and I didn't.

She pulled a plastic Walmart bag from her pocket and began stuffing it with bundles of money, each banded with a bank strip that indicated denomination. Hammett left the stacks of singles, but did take a nickel-plated .357 and a Rolex with a gold bracelet. Then we were moving again, through the hall, down the stairs, and out the door where Fleming still waited.

The streets were fairly empty, and the few people on the side-walk looked in any direction but at us, probably sensing things weren't quite right. I listened for police sirens, didn't hear any. Nice neighborhood.

We piled into the backseat, and Fleming took off at a quick clip. I was reaching for my seat belt when Hammett's shotgun was once again pressed against my neck.

"You ever shoot at me again, I end you," she said.

I met her eyes. Hard colliding with hard. The mistake had been mine in the drug house, but hell if I was going to flip over and show my belly. Not to Hammett.

"End me? How many times have you tried? Yet I'm still here, bitch."

The SUV stopped and Fleming's Skorpion appeared at Hammett's temple. "Put it down, Hammett."

"Your dumbass sister almost killed me," Hammett said, her upper lip in a snarl.

"Now," Fleming ordered.

Hammett lowered her gun, keeping her eyes on mine. "Don't you know how to clear a room, rookie? Check behind the goddamn door next time."

She was right. Fatigue, or just plain bad judgment, had almost gotten me killed. Hammett had saved my life. But there was no way I was going to thank her. Ever.

"Chandler's hit," Fleming said, peering over the seat at my leg. She tucked away the Skorpion and replaced it with a first-aid kit, holding it out to Hammett. Then she shifted the SUV into gear again, turned on the dome light in back, and joined the weak flow of traffic.

Without further comment, Hammett opened the kit and removed some scissors, then sliced through my pants where I'd been shot. She wiped away the blood with gauze, and I stared down at the four puncture marks.

"No bleeders," Hammett said. Her voice had lost all the anger and sarcasm. "Missed the femoral artery. I can get these out."

She numbed me with Demerol, poured on a bottle of alcohol, then went to work with the needle-nose tweezers. I closed my eyes and tried to relax—which is, of course, impossible to do when someone's digging buckshot out of your leg.

"Had to do this to myself, once," Hammett said. "Beijing. Didn't have tweezers, so I filed down a pair of chopsticks. Got a nasty infection. I saw some antibiotics in that duffel the shrimp left us, so when we're done, take a few. Tough to function with a fever."

I didn't like Hammett's conversational tone. A minute ago, she'd had a gun to my neck. Now she wanted to be chummy and chitchat. And I had an idea why.

At Hydra, the secret government agency for which we'd all once worked, I'd had a psychology instructor named Albrecht, who'd explained in excruciating detail how to verbally manipulate others. It was partly what you said, and partly how you said it, with tone and inflection and body language. I learned how to flirt and channel my inner femme fatale. I learned how to be commanding, to make people want to follow my orders. I learned how to be completely nonthreatening, an instant best friend.

"Cut the bullshit," I told Hammett. "I took the same classes you did."

"Ease up, killer. Just trying to distract you from the pain."

I opened my eyes to stare at her. "I'm never going to trust you, Hammett. Never. Let that play through your eidetic head next time you're trying to con me into liking you."

Hammett didn't get angry. If anything, she appeared thoughtful. "There are things I've done that you haven't. Lines I've crossed that you believe you never would. And that makes me a monster in your eyes. At the same time, you kill people for the government, but you think you still have some morals left. That makes you a hypocrite in my eyes. A hypocrite, and a coward who is afraid to let her nature take her where it wants to go."

I kept my expression neutral. "That gang leader, the one you tortured to get the safe combination. Did you enjoy hurting him?"

"Among his many sources of income was kiddie porn. Distributing and producing."

"So he was a scumbag. My question was, did you enjoy making him suffer?"

Hammett withdrew the tweezers, which gripped some lead shot. She stared at it, as if it held the answer to the meaning of life.

"So what you're saying, Chandler, is that torturing someone isn't wrong. You're saying it is only wrong if the torturer enjoys it. And you don't think that's hypocritical?"

"I think you're sick in the head."

Hammett tossed the BB over her shoulder, then went back to work on my leg. "The only difference between me, you, and Christopher Reeve up there in the driver's seat is nurture. By nature, we're just three copies of the same DNA. So if you want to judge me, walk a mile in my shoes and remember that there but for the grace of God, go you."

She jabbed me with the tweezers again, and I squeezed my eyes closed and set my jaw and tensed until it was over.

\*\*\*

I woke up in daylight, stretched across the backseat, a blanket over me and a pillow behind my neck. The vehicle smelled like coffee and bacon, and Hammett, in the passenger seat, was rattling off a string of numbers to Fleming, who still drove.

"One, six, four, two, zero, one, nine, eight, nine. Is that a thousand?"

"Yeah," Fleming said. "Can you do the next thousand?"

"Never memorized it that far."

Fleming laughed. "Puny mind. They're three, eight, zero, nine, five, two—"

"I smell coffee," I said.

"Oh, good morning, Chandler," Fleming said. "I'm reciting pi to two thousand digits. Hammett has only memorized the first thousand. How many do you know?"

"I know three point one four. Is there coffee left?"

Hammett passed me a paper cup bearing the insignia of a fast-food joint. I sipped from the plastic lid. Still warm.

"That's all you know?" Fleming asked.

"Pi doesn't hold the same appeal to me as it apparently does to you two. I smell bacon."

Hammett gave me a wrapped egg sandwich, then reached out to feel my head. I managed to avoid flinching.

"No fever. Your leg stiff?"

My whole body was stiff. But I said, "It's fine. Where are we?"

"Just passed Syracuse. Gotta pee?"

I tuned in to my bladder. "Yeah."

"You guys ever had to drink your own urine?" Hammett asked.

I frowned, my cheeks filled with bitter coffee.

"I built a solar still once, to desalinate seawater," Fleming said. "Chandler?"

"My own?" I asked, deadpan.

After a pause, Hammett and Fleming began to laugh. I also felt a smile threatening to break, and hid it with another sip off coffee.

"Three days," Hammett said. "No water. Op went bad. Stuck in a desert. Hundred-and-five-degree heat."

"So you drank your own pee?" Fleming asked.

"No. I drank snake blood."

"Really? What did it taste like?"

Hammett hesitated, then said, "Pee."

They laughed again, which annoyed me. Could have been a jealousy issue. I'd been bonding with Fleming over these past few days, and maybe I didn't want to share her with Hammett. Could have been a trust issue, since I knew Hammett would kill both of us with zero provocation. Or maybe I was just in a bad mood because I hurt all over.

So I ate my sandwich and didn't contribute to their conversation, which rambled on about all the gross things they'd eaten in the name of survival, and when we stopped at a gas station, I limped out of the vehicle with the first-aid kit and hobbled into a filthy stall where I cleaned and redressed all of my various injuries.

I was a mess. If I stayed in this business for the next five years without managing to get killed, I wouldn't have an unscarred patch of skin on me.

Recently, I'd thought about quitting. I had money tucked away that would tide me over for a while. I'd have to find work eventually, but it could be legitimate work, not wet work. No more killing people. No more being shot. No more wondering what life would be like as a civilian.

Could be boring. But bored and alive surely trumped being tortured and killed, which was how things would likely end up for me.

Of course, I couldn't quit until the current situation had been dealt with. I wasn't sure how far up the chain of command it went, but at the very least The Instructor had to die. Until that happened, I'd be a target.

I swallowed some ibuprofen, looked at the beaten dog in the bathroom mirror, did a pathetic finger comb, then went back to the SUV.

Hammett had her hip on the fender. She was smoking a cigar, one of those cheroots that Clint Eastwood made popular in old westerns. Her gaze was someplace else. A big No Smoking sign was on the gas pump next to her.

"I can justify every single thing I've ever done," she said without looking at me.

"Everyone can. That's the problem. Lots of people justifying actions when they should be questioning them."

"As if you're any different."

I didn't know what to say to that, so I said nothing at all.

She took another puff, flicked the remainder into the parking lot, then looked at me. "Front seat or back?"

"Back."

Hammett opened the car door, then paused. "You think I have no regrets. You're wrong. I don't regret killing anybody. I regret I didn't start killing sooner." She got into the passenger seat without explaining herself, and a big part of me was relieved she didn't. Whatever Hammett's story was, I had a good feeling I didn't want to hear it.

I climbed into the backseat, stretched out, and promptly fell asleep. I slept until Fleming woke me up again, saying we'd arrived in Maine.

# Years Ago…

Her codename was Hammett, but her adoptive parents had named her Betsy.

She lived in a middle-class house in a middle-class neighborhood with her dog, Max, and her sister, Rebecca. Rebecca was two years older, and everything Betsy wanted to be. Taller. Stronger. Fearless. Confident. Outgoing. Rebecca did well in school and was liked by her teachers and the other children. Betsy was the opposite. Shy, withdrawn, confused. She sometimes cried for no discernible reason. The only friends Betsy had were Rebecca's, and Betsy knew they only played with her because Rebecca forced them to.

On Rebecca's twelfth birthday, while Mother was at the store buying ingredients to make the cake, Father called the girls into his room and told them they were adopted.

"It's OK," he said. "I'm not your real dad, but I still love you very much. Don't be afraid. It's OK. I love you so much, Rebecca. It's OK."

He kept saying, "It's OK," over and over, as he took off his clothes and did things to Rebecca while Betsy watched.

Afterward, he gave them twenty dollars and told them not to tell Mother because it was their special secret.

Rebecca and Betsy kept that special secret, even though Father did it again and again. Eventually, the girls saved up $500, and after one of Father's nightly visits, they snuck out of the house and rode their bikes to a bar that Father said was a bad place and they went inside and walked over to a mean-looking man who was in the corner drinking by himself. He had a tattoo of a devil on the back of his hand. Rebecca offered him all their money to kill Father.

The man agreed, but when they went out into the parking lot, he punched Rebecca in the face and took her money and rode off on his motorcycle, which had naked women painted on the gas tank.

It took another year for the girls to save up $500. When they did, they went to a boy in school named Mick. Mick was in a gang and had been arrested many times. He sold them a gun.

On Rebecca's fourteenth birthday, Mother went to the store to buy ingredients for her birthday cake, and Rebecca shot Father twice in the back of the head while he was watching TV. She took the gun to the bad bar, and she and Betsy hid in the bushes until the man who stole their money showed up. They put the gun in the man's saddlebag on his motorcycle. Then she and Betsy called the police.

The man with the devil tattoo was arrested for murder, abduction, and sexual assault. Rebecca described, in great detail, the things the man had done to her after she saw him kill Father.

A month later, Rebecca and Betsy joined Mick's gang.

Fifteen years later, Betsy was killing people for Uncle Sam.

# Chandler

*"You don't have to like someone to trust them," said The Instructor. "And sometimes if the situation is dire enough, you don't even have to trust them to trust them."*

I had a twenty-foot Maritime Challenger Classic on a trailer in a Portland, Maine, storage locker. It was registered under a name I used for nothing else, the rent paid in advance via money orders made out to cash. I'd kept this boat and the island we were headed to completely under the radar, and the only other people on earth who knew they existed were Fleming and a girl named Julie.

We put in at a dock near the mouth of the Kennebec River. After we loaded everything from the SUV into the boat, Fleming slipped behind its wheel and Hammett stripped to her undies. I backed the boat into the water, and Hammett waded into the frigid water after it, uncranking the winch and letting the craft float free.

I pulled the SUV into the parking lot near the launch site and unhitched the trailer, putting a lock on the wheel. Then I drove upriver until I found a remote area, not all that hard to come by in rural Maine. After wiping the vehicle down, inside and out, I hiked to the pier. My sisters had already docked the boat. As far as I could see, their only company was a flock of gulls and encroaching fog. I climbed into the vessel, released the mooring line, and settled behind Fleming on one of the built-in bench seats flanking the engine. As she motored down the river, I eyed Hammett, whose head was now covered by a reusable canvas grocery sack.

"I like the new look," I said, directing the comment to Fleming more than Hammett.

"I found it in the back of the SUV," Fleming said. "Thought it wise she didn't know exactly where we were going."

Apparently, despite their chumminess on the road trip from Wisconsin, Fleming still harbored reservations about trusting Hammett.

I had to admit I was relieved. "Good thinking. I'm also getting tired of seeing her face."

Fleming turned, giving me a little smile.

"This bag smells like ass," Hammett said, her voice muffled by the canvas. "Did you guys go shopping for ass somewhere?"

We didn't answer, but my mood brightened a bit.

"If I'm seasick, will you take the damn bag off? Or do I have to wear my puke?"

"I vote for wearing it," I said.

"Glad you think it's funny. Also, you both are morons. I know where we left shore, know how fast this motor can go, can keep time in my head, and even in the fog, I can feel the sun on my skin so I know our direction. Wherever you're taking me, I'll be able to find it again, even if I'm still wearing this stupid sack."

"Shit, she's right." Fleming patted her shoulder. "Go ahead and take it off, Hammett. It was a dumb idea."

And our brief moment of anti-Hammett camaraderie was gone. Just that fast.

I stared at the back of Fleming's head. I knew she was angry that I'd assassinated the president. I couldn't blame her for that. But each time she played her bonding game with Hammett and cut me out, I couldn't help feeling eleven years old. The new kid in a new school who once again thought she'd found a friend, a confidant, a sister, only to discover herself alone and despised in the end.

Hammett threw the bag onto the bottom of the boat and whipped her hair around. "So what is this place? A swanky vacation spot you want to keep for yourselves?"

I didn't like Hammett asking about the island, and I wasn't ready to tell her the whole truth. But saying nothing would just pique her interest. I needed to throw her something.

"A safe house The Instructor doesn't know about."

"Convenient."

"No," I said. "Prepared."

Fog thickened the nearer we drew to the ocean, the still air carrying the type of dank chill that reached one's bones and the strong scent of saltwater fish. The Demerol shots I'd had no longer held back the pain in my leg, although with every other inch of my body hurting, too, the aches blended until it was hard to tell one from another.

We reached the river's mouth in silence, and after passing a Civil War–era fort and long sand beach, we motored out into the Atlantic. Waves churned under the boat, swaying us side to side. We moved past small islands dotting the steel-gray water, all uninhabited, the scrubby vegetation stunted by salt and cold. After fifteen minutes our destination loomed ahead like a boulder plopped into the surf. Larger than the other islands, it sported a lighthouse on its crest, idle and dark in the murk, more modern means of navigation having replaced the need for its beacon.

I'd always found the area beautiful, although today it was difficult to see much through the fog blanket. Seagulls screeched in the air, though all I could spot was a flash of white wings here and there. The roar of waves battering sheer rock faces on three of the island's sides nearly drowned out the drone of our boat's engine, and the distant moan of a foghorn made the air shudder.

Fleming guided the boat to the island's minimal dock. Situated on the only sloping side of the island, the dock and shack of a boathouse were connected to the lighthouse by a tramway designed to transport cargo up the steep hill. Resembling those used in old coal mines, the tram system had been built by the lighthouse keeper a hundred years ago, and it looked its age. A diesel-powered hoisting engine pulled the simple car up the rust-covered tracks, a walkway following alongside. Today both tracks and walkway seemed to reach into the mist, as if they led nowhere at all.

While Fleming finished tying off to a salt-encrusted pylon, I started unloading, and Hammett smoothed her hair with a hand while taking in the scenery.

"This is it? I really have to introduce you two to some better vacation spots."

"Start your vacation by helping unload the boat."

She gave an eye-roll, but got to work.

I pulled Fleming's wheelchair from the boat first. Heavier than any normal chair due to its many modifications, it strained my back and arms as I managed to wrestle it up a set of wooden steps and into the waiting tram car, which was basically a large wooden pallet on iron wheels. Hammett and I emptied the boat of food, ammo, and other supplies, Fleming handing us the bags. Then I took the weapons, Hammett gathered Fleming piggyback style, and the three of us trudged up the rickety wooden path.

A small engine house sat at the top of the tracks. A tiny framed structure, it held the tram's hoisting engine as well as a small security camera I'd installed under one of the eaves. Focused on the top of the walkway, the camera was activated by a motion sensor at the boathouse. Since the lighthouse was surrounded by sheer cliffs on three sides and the only way up was the tram and walkway, the system ensured no visitors would arrive unseen.

I used the electric ignition switch to start the old diesel engine, and it began to wind the cable around its main pulley, sputtering and choking and threatening to explode at any moment. When the tram reached the top forty steep meters later, Hammett lowered Fleming into her wheelchair, and we all took a load of supplies and set out along the winding paved path for the lighthouse.

Perched on the highest point of the island, the classic white cylindrical tower with its attached redbrick keeper's house looked as if it were straight from a postcard. Fifty feet off the ground and another fifty above the breakers, the beacon could be seen for miles on the open sea back when it was in use.

At our approach, a dog's bark pierced the ceaseless rhythm of the waves, and a dark brown mutt with oversize ears bounded down the shallow steps of the one-bedroom house. He ran to me first, jamming his face in my crotch and taking a good sniff.

I pushed him away and ruffled his ears. "Hiya, Kirk."

As the dog went on to check out my sisters, I focused on the keeper's place and the slender blonde standing in the doorway.

She looked good, if a bit pale, wearing a thick sweater, jeans, and the Adirondack jacket I had bought her a year ago. With blond hair reaching halfway down her back, she was beautiful enough to turn many a male head.

But around here there were no male heads to turn.

"Chandler?" she said, searching our three identical faces.

"Julie." I closed the few feet between us and engulfed her in a hug.

She hugged me back, hard. "I didn't think you were coming until winter."

I wasn't sure how much I wanted to tell Julie about our situation. With all she'd been through in her young life, I hesitated to add to her burden. "We thought we'd surprise you."

She gave me a sideways look. Not quite buying it.

"It's complicated. All I can tell you is that we need a place to stay for a while."

Julie nodded, and glanced at Fleming and Hammett, the other two parts of the *we*.

"These are my sisters." I made introductions.

Looking past me, she gave Fleming and Hammett a smile and they exchanged hellos.

"I didn't know you had sisters," Julie said, bringing her attention back to me.

"Last time I saw you, I didn't know either."

While Fleming had been my handler during the op when I'd met Julie, I'd only known her as Jacob, an electronically disguised voice on the phone. Back then I had no clue I had a sister, let alone six identical ones.

"Cool dog," Hammett said.

"Chandler gave him to me when he was a puppy. His name is Kirk."

"Nice to meet you, Kirk."

Hammett dropped to a knee. Setting the ammo and bags of food she carried on the grass, she held out an open palm. Kirk gave it a sniff and lowered his head to be petted, just as he did with me. Apparently Kirk didn't discriminate when it came to receiving affection. And here I thought dogs were supposed to have a keen sense about people.

Julie took me aside, whispering in my ear, "Chandler, bringing them here was—"

"I know. We didn't have a choice, Julie."

"But—"

A strange sound came from the house: a faint, electronic warble that took me a few seconds to recognize. I shifted the duffel and raised the Skorpion. "The alarm."

"Alarm?" Hammett echoed. She seemed unduly preoccupied with the canine.

"From the boathouse. Someone's here. Inside. Everyone. Now."

Fleming shouldered her shotgun, scanning the fog.

Julie grabbed Hammett's dropped bags and Kirk's collar and started pulling him toward the house.

Hammett didn't move. "Give me a gun. I'll go down, see what's up."

"There's a camera on the engine house. If they come up the hill, we'll be able to see who's there from the main house."

"If we have to fight, we should take it to them. Up here we have nowhere to run."

It could be anyone at the pier, some innocent boater seeing our rig at the dock and letting their curiosity get the better of them. Or it could be something more ominous. Either way, I didn't want Hammett wandering around by herself. I wanted to know where she was and what she was doing. "Get in the house."

"Damn it, Chandler. Give me the Skorpion."

"You have that .357 from the safe."

Her hand moved to the small of her back, where I knew she had the pistol. "I'd like something a little better at a distance."

"Get in the house. Then we'll talk about the best use for our weaponry."

"What, are you afraid I'm going to sell you out to the first bidder?"

She had saved my ass in Milwaukee, so it didn't seem that was part of her immediate agenda, but since I wasn't sure what her agenda was, better to be safe than dead.

"If I see you even consider it, I want to be close enough to kill you myself."

"Love you, too, sis. But you're making a mistake."

"Get in the damn house."

Picking up my bags, she finally started for the porch. Halfway up the steps, Kirk gave a low growl, the fur on his back rising. And then I heard it as well: the rhythmic beat of helicopter blades.

Oh, hell.

"Help Fleming up those steps."

I scanned the sky, seeing a blanket of gray fog and nothing more. Whoever was flying in this soup had to be doing it under instrument flight rules, or IFR, using their cockpit controls to guide them since the fog had limited visual flight. That left out the majority of helicopters and pilots. This was no innocent flyby. This was a well-trained pilot, here for a reason.

And I'd bet that boat at the dock was no pleasure trip either. *Damn it.*

I heard Hammett mount the steps above me, Fleming's chair thunking up with her. I backed up the steps, sweeping the area with eyes and submachine gun and followed them into the house.

Hammett was waiting for me in the kitchen, hands on her hips. "So you'd rather let everyone get shot than tell me what's going on?"

I leveled the Skorpion on her. "How did he find us?"

"How should I know?"

"You told him."

"And how would I have done that? Telepathy?"

The facts seemed obvious. "No one followed us, and now suddenly they're here."

Her face was pinched. "What's wrong with you? It wasn't me. Maybe they did follow, and you just didn't see them. God knows you can't hang that one on me, since you bagged my head for part of the trip."

I shook off the suggestion, but my stomach gave an uncomfortable roll. Had someone followed us and I missed it? In my need to hide from The Instructor, had I led him to Julie's door?

I lowered my weapon and scanned the fog outside. I couldn't see the helicopter, but there was only one place for it to land on the island. Unless it didn't land. I'd exited many a hovering helicopter, using a zip line or BASE jump chute. I had no way to know how many operatives might be out there, or what direction they would come from.

I checked the security monitor on the countertop next to the microwave. At first, the view down the walkway showed nothing but more gray fog. Then two figures appeared, one male, one female.

The man was Asian, built like Arnold Schwarzenegger before politics made him soft. But this man was a far cry from movie-star pretty. A scar snaked across his throat, gnarled and swollen like an earthworm lying on pavement after a summer storm. He also had several scarred patches on his dome that his crew cut didn't fill in. Frankenstein's monster came to mind.

The woman was in her twenties, emaciated looking, wearing a black T-shirt with the arms ripped off, no jacket of any kind. Dark hair draped from a side part over her left eye, the right side short enough to show scalp. But the most striking thing about her were the black lines slashing her pale skin, all the way from her wrists to her upper arms, some kind of artless tattoos.

Both were ready for war, Heckler & Koch UMP submachine guns at the ready, shotgun holsters on their shoulders, flak jackets webbed with ammo clips and grenades.

"Now will you give me the damn Skorpion?" asked Hammett.

Judging from the sound, the helicopter hovered on the opposite side of the house. In this weather and with us sheltered inside, it would have a tough time engaging us from the air, but I doubted that was the plan. There would be more pros, like the two trudging up the hill, and they would be in position soon.

If they were here to catch us, we wouldn't make it easy for them. If they were here to kill us, there wasn't much we could do about it. But at the very least, we could go down swinging.

I handed the machine gun to Hammett. "You need to—"

"I know, I know. If I fuck up, you'll kill me, blah blah blah." She checked the weapon, splitting her attention between the security camera and the murk outside. "You're a goddamn broken record."

"You need to stay here," I finished.

Hammett glanced at me, her face twisting up as if she smelled something unpleasant.

"I mean it, Hammett."

"You want me to hang around and play Alamo? You're a shitty team leader, you know that?"

But she didn't move from the door.

Not sure which mistake I was making from this multiple-choice test of screwups, I headed to the back of the house. I found

Fleming in the kitchen. She'd upended Julie's little table and was now hunkered down behind it in her chair, keeping watch through the windows at the back of the house, shotgun ready.

"Side of my chair," she said, tilting her chin at the second shotgun tucked along her thigh.

I armed myself with a Mossberg and filled her in on the two approaching from the dock.

"I think Hammett gave us away somehow," I added at the end.

"There are other ways The Instructor could have known about this place." Fleming gave me a neutral glance. "Could have been you, not Hammett."

Fleming's words stung, as if she had taken Hammett's side over mine. But I was being stupid, and this time I had the grace to know it. Or maybe I just didn't have time to be petty.

"I know we trust each other, so what are you saying?"

"The Instructor could have been tracking you the night you brought Julie here."

It only took me a second to see where Fleming was going. "The chip."

My sisters and I all had tracking chips implanted right below our belly buttons during our training under The Instructor, and none of us had a clue they were there until a week ago. The three of us had removed them since and had the still-painful incisions to show for it, but that didn't change the fact that The Instructor could have noted my unscheduled visits to this remote island.

I felt queasy. "There's a helicopter on the other side of us."

She nodded. "Know how many are coming for dinner?"

"No. I only installed the one camera. I figured a sky approach would be obvious. Didn't take the damn fog into account."

"At least we have something."

I knew she was trying to ease my mind, but it didn't work. I'd screwed up. Shitty team leader, indeed.

I found Julie with Kirk. She was standing ramrod straight in the middle of her bedroom. The closet-size space featured a wide window, putting her in clear view of anyone outside.

"They're here, aren't they?" she said, trying to choke back tears. "It's starting all over again."

I slipped my free arm around her trembling shoulders. "They aren't here for you, honey. They want us. Now come away from the window."

"I just don't think I can take…"

"Come on, Julie." I guided her out and down the hall. "You're going to hide. We'll take care of this."

"Chandler, if they shoot me…your sisters…oh God."

The nightmare scenario flashed through my mind. A stray bullet, Julie's blood spreading in a pool on the floorboards…

"I'm not going to let that happen. I have a place in mind that's safe."

I steered her through the galley-like utility room and into the lighthouse. Once we were inside the stone-and-mortar silo, I coaxed her to the far side of the spiral stairs and lowered her into a crouch on the floor, her back against the curved wall.

"See? Here the bullets can't reach you."

She nodded quickly.

"Don't cry, all right? No crying."

She nodded again.

I brushed her hair away from her eyes. Remarkably, they were still dry. Good girl. "I'm going to leave now. I want you to stay here, hide here, and don't come out no matter what happens. Understand?"

"Yes."

Kirk had followed us, and he spooned his body into Julie and leaned against her leg.

"See? Kirk's here. You aren't alone."

Julie nodded and moved a hand to the dog's head.

"You're going to be OK, honey. I promise."

"I'm not worried about me."

"The rest of us are old pros at this." I smiled, forcing confidence I didn't feel.

Julie didn't smile back, didn't answer except for a tremble to her lower lip. She hugged her dog and rocked slightly.

"You shouldn't have come, Chandler."

"I'm sorry about this, Julie. I really am."

"It isn't you. It's me. People shouldn't be around me. I'm poison."

"Come on, Julie. Don't say that. I know you. You're brave. You can do this. You've gone through worse."

I hoped the words conveyed how much I'd come to care for her over the years, and how very impressed I was with how she'd handled all that had happened to her and still managed to stay as sweet as the girl I'd first met.

"I'm trying. I just…"

"I know. I'll take care of this."

She nodded.

"Have I ever let you down before?"

"No."

"And I won't now. But you need to stay here. Stay hidden. OK?"

"OK."

"Good girl." I engulfed her in a quick hug.

"Thanks, Chandler. I don't know what I'd do without you."

Her words burned. Whether The Instructor had followed us today or noted my movements in the past, it didn't matter. His people were here because of me. And although Julie saw me as her savior, I knew the truth.

By coming here I'd put her in danger.

Swallowing the thick feeling in my throat, I returned to the living room. It was a charming room, just like the rest of the keeper's house. Wood floors, crown molding, and furnished with an eclectic jumble of pieces ranging from valuable antiques to pressboard. Throughout the years, I'd brought Julie items to spruce up the place: a hand-woven rug, throw pillows, paint. But the special touches, she'd done herself. Charcoal sketches in weathered wood frames on the walls, vases of dried flowers, a mosaic of seashells made into a side table.

She'd put a lot of time into the place, but then, she had nothing but time. Solitary, lonely time. I'd been feeling bad about that while coming in on the boat, but now I wished more than anything that we'd stayed away. Time alone reading books and making crafts was safer than houseguests like us.

Hammett was still positioned near the door, and I was somewhat surprised to see her there.

"How far have they gotten?"

"They stopped at the top of the hill, next to the camera. They're communicating with someone. Too bad your camera doesn't have audio."

"But lucky that you know how to read lips."

Hammett shot me a sly smile, then mouthed, "Damn right, fearless leader."

"What did they say?"

"Nightfall. I assume that refers to when they'll storm the house." Logical assumption. "What else?"

"I caught names. Someone named Scarlett is calling the shots, it seems. Rhett, Earnshaw, and Heathcliff are in play."

"Characters from classic novels?" I had an uneasy feeling that I couldn't nail down.

"I could be off."

She could. A lot of phonemes share the same facial and mouth position. It's up to the soft palate and tongue to differentiate those sounds, and of course their positions can't be seen. But coming up with four names that all adhered to a common theme was too much of a coincidence.

"Codenames."

"No shit. I get where Scarlett and Rhett come from. I saw the movie. But you got me on the others. I never read any of that gothic crap when I was a kid."

As minor as it was, I enjoyed knowing something Hammett didn't. "In Emily Brontë's novel *Wuthering Heights*, Heathcliff's love is Catherine Earnshaw."

"How about the name Tristan? That's what the emo chick is calling Mr. Behemoth."

I shook my head. It had been a while.

"Tristan and Isolde were tragic lovers," Fleming shouted from the kitchen.

Hammett nodded. "That was it. Izzy. It looked like he called her Izzy."

Something still nagged at me, just out of reach. "So we have a bunch of fictional tragic lovers after us."

"At least you have something in common with them." Hammett grinned.

I ignored her. I had it, the elusive connection. "Remember the Jamaican guy at the ammo plant in Wisconsin?"

Hammett nodded. "The Instructor brought him in, didn't tell me."

I'd killed him, cut his throat with his own razor blade. "His name was Rochester."

Hammett stared at me blankly.

"Rochester and Jane are from the novel *Jane Eyre*. But their story wasn't tragic. They got together at the end."

Hammett rolled her eyes. "Now you ruined it for me. Ever heard of issuing a spoiler alert?"

"At least in this world, Rochester came to a tragic end."

"Did you see *Sixth Sense*? Bruce Willis?"

"No. Why?"

"He died at the beginning. He's a ghost the whole movie."

"Why are you telling me this?"

"And Darth Vader is Luke's father. Spoilers suck, don't they?"

"Whatever."

"And Soylent Green is people."

I knew Hammett was talking out of nervous bravado, so I didn't mind much. In pressure situations, everyone had their own quirks.

I had a thought. "Did anyone mention Jane?"

"Not that I caught."

"So there are six. Seven including Rochester."

"Seven," Hammett said. "We were seven, too."

She was right. My sisters and I totaled seven. We'd been trained separately at Hydra, and training had taken a long time.

But Rochester had also been trained by The Instructor, after my sisters and me. If he was part of another group of seven...

"We're in trouble," I said.

"No shit. If they have anything close to our training, it's six against two and a half."

"I heard that," Fleming called to us.

"I was counting Chandler as half, sis, since she's only got half a brain."

I ignored the jab. "Plus they have a chopper and who knows what weapons, and all we've got is a few shotguns and half a magazine left for the Skorpion."

We watched the security monitor for a few more seconds, but Tristan and Isolde weren't moving, weren't talking.

"Is that all they said?"

"All I could say for sure. Helicopter is still circling. They're planning to strike back, front, and lighthouse on Scarlett's signal."

Nice of them to tell us. "At least we have a little time to prepare. I assume you can shoot."

"Better than you."

I wasn't so sure about that, but I didn't want to waste time arguing. "Take the Skorpion and go to the lighthouse. It'll give you a 360 view of the island."

She glanced back at the screen, and I saw something cross her face.

"Or do you have other plans?" I asked.

"Of course not." Hammett trotted off the way I'd come. "I live to follow your dumbass orders."

I peered at the duo on the monitor, then out into the fog, wondering why she'd hesitated and what she might have seen and decided not to share.

# Hammett

*"Sometimes lying is not a wise course of action," The Instructor said. "But that doesn't mean you have to reveal one hundred percent of the truth."*

Use the time to prepare? Hammett was born prepared. And she damn well didn't intend to use the time to sit around and wait for a group of tragic lovers to wipe them out. Especially if they'd been trained by The Instructor. Offense was more her style. With Chandler's eyes on the front door and monitor and Fleming watching the back of the house, Hammett should be able to slip out with neither being the wiser.

She rounded the corner into a utility room and spotted a door. Opening it, she entered a cylindrical space that reached fifty feet up: the lighthouse. Steel grate stairs corkscrewed to a landing at least forty feet up, and behind the spiral staircase hunched the girl, her cute dog sitting beside her. Arms wrapped around her legs, Julie sniffled softly.

"So this is where you went." Hammett was talking to the dog, but the girl answered.

"Don't come near me." She wiped her face with her fingertips. "I mean it. Stay away."

Hammett didn't move. "Afraid I'm going to try to hug you or something? Don't worry, I'm not the type."

"I'm sorry. I just…"

"Whatever." Hammett craned her neck to peer up into the lighthouse tower. "Is there an exterior door back here?"

"There are only two. The front door and the one in the kitchen."

And Hammett couldn't slip through either of those with her sisters Davy Crockett and Jim Bowie waiting around for Pancho Villa to storm the fortress.

"You can see everything from the lighthouse," Julie offered.

"I need something on this level."

"There's a big window to the side of the utility room."

"Thanks," Hammett said. That might do nicely. "Be sure to keep Kirk in here no matter what you hear. It's the most protected place in the house."

"Uh…thanks, I guess."

Hammett smirked. "I could give a shit about you, little girl. But that's a pretty cool dog."

Hammett shut the door behind her, cloistering dog and girl inside. She found the window right where Julie said it would be. It had a large frame, plenty big enough to crawl through, and the corner of the house shielded it from view of the kitchen. The only downside was it looked as if it might be painted shut.

She gave it a wiggle, then a thump with the heel of her hand, and miraculously it slid open. Hammett eased through and closed it, leaving a small crack to fit her fingers into on the way back in. Holding the Skorpion at the ready, she moved out into the fog.

Hammett's little reconnaissance mission shouldn't take long. She'd be back well before nightfall. And by then, she intended to have compromised at least one or two of those tragic lovers and to be a bit more informed about The Instructor's plans.

By all rights, Chandler should thank her, but Hammett wasn't going to hold her breath. Her sister was putting personal feelings before the mission. Mistakes like that cost lives. She needed some sense beaten into her. Or a bullet to the head.

The terrain on the island was rough, low brush spotted with outcroppings of granite. In partnership with the fog, it provided decent cover. The trick would be finding the enemy, since they were sure to be taking advantage of the environment, too.

After fifteen minutes of duck and cover, Hammett had nearly resigned herself to taking on the two at the engine house and letting Chandler watch, when she detected a scent that shouldn't be there.

Cologne. Polo by Ralph Lauren.

She followed the scent, walking softly on the balls of her feet, listening for a cough, a shift, the clearing of a throat.

There it was. A sniffle.

Hammett followed the sound to a ridge of stone near the cliff's edge. A man hunkered low behind some stunted goldenrod. He was dressed in jeans and a flak jacket, a well-worn cowboy hat jammed on his head.

*Of course he wears Polo. Must be attracted to the horse in the logo.*

His location gave him a clear shot at the kitchen window. Even from Hammett's current position, she could see the edge of the table Fleming had turned on its side.

He sniffled again. Probably from cologne fumes, as he'd apparently dumped the whole bottle on himself. A couple days' beard growth stubbled his chin, and his teeth were movie-star white. Hammett knew the type. Redneck metrosexual. Tough rawhide exterior, but when you applied pressure in the right places, he could be made to crumble.

And Hammett knew all the right places.

She made a wide circle, using the distance buffer and crash of waves to hide her movement. She had over an hour left before sunset. No hurry. Best to take her time and keep the element of surprise on her side. Rush things and she might end up having to kill instead of capture, and then she'd be as clueless about The Instructor's plans as she was now.

Unaware of her approach, the target reached for the radio on his belt and touched a button. Then he shouldered his assault rifle.

Under the barrel and forward of the magazine, Hammett recognized the distinctive shape of an AG-C/Enhanced Grenade Launching Module.

She'd gotten it all wrong. The enemy wasn't waiting until dark to strike. They'd played her, and played her well. They were striking now, probably from multiple directions, and Hammett was in no position to stop them.

# Chandler

*"There might be times when your past will come back to haunt you," said The Instructor. "Shoot first."*

I watched the monitor, then the fog, then the monitor, my mind racing. I had played every possible scenario of this siege through my mind, and every way it added up, our chances were poor. It would be one thing if we had a side we didn't have to protect, or we had more weapons, or if it was just the three of us and Julie wasn't in the mix. But the six operatives that we knew of were likely better armed and better rested, and didn't have an innocent to protect.

I'd faced greater odds in the past few days and been incredibly lucky in the outcome. But there came a time when luck ran out.

I sure hoped this wasn't my time.

The operative we'd identified as Isolde reached for the radio on her belt, but instead of bringing it to her mouth to speak, she merely pressed a button, then the hulk accompanying her turned directly to the camera, raised his gun, and static overtook the monitor.

Shit, shit, shit. We'd been discovered.

They weren't waiting until dark. Either it had been a deliberate ruse, a staged radio conversation to throw us off, or Hammett had lied.

They were coming for us now.

I'd just completed the thought when the living room window shattered, followed by the hiss of a gas grenade.

Tear gas is horrible, and in an enclosed space, it's hard to overcome. As soon as the smoke started, my eyes began to burn. I squinted and pulled the neck of my sweater up over my mouth and nose, trying to buy time. We had to get out of here.

"Fleming! Fall back to the lighthouse!"

Shotgun blasts came in response.

"Fall back!" I yelled again.

The sound of shattering glass came from the kitchen. More tear gas. Damn. How had they gotten to the back of the house unseen?

My sister swore, curses dissolving into coughs and sputters.

I peered out the window, struggling to see, something, anything. Movement stirred in the brush. I fired off a few shells, no idea if I came close to hitting anything. At this distance the shot sprayed so wide, it didn't do much good.

"Fleming?"

Gunfire erupted from the kitchen, then more shattering glass from the windows next to me.

The explosions hit fast. *Bang, bang, bang,* blinding me and ringing through my head. I dropped my shotgun and stumbled forward, one hand clawing the wall in an effort to keep my balance. A high-pitched whine filled my head, muffling all other sound.

Flashbangs, or stun grenades, are nonlethal explosives used by military and law enforcement to disorient, when subjects are to be captured. They rendered me blind, dizzy, temporarily overloading my optic nerve and doing a number on the fluid in my inner ear. I clung to the wall, struggling to stay on my feet and regain my bearings.

The door gave way to a boot. Two figures rushed in, both wearing gas masks. One was a strapping black female, long hair plaited into cornrows. The other was male, lighter skinned, only one eye visible through his face shield.

Not the two caught on the security camera, but a different pair who had worked their way closer to the house while I was focused on the monitor.

I fell to one knee. My balance was still off, and I was in no shape for a fight, but I needed to strike now. In a matter of seconds I would be dead. I had to reach my shotgun.

The woman raised a .45, which looked tiny in her gigantic hands.

"She's mine," the male yelled, loud enough that I could hear over the high-pitched ring. "Go."

She hesitated.

My whole head felt swollen, my throat closing up, my nose running profusely. I couldn't stand, and no matter how much I blinked, I couldn't clear the purple ghosts the stun grenades had imprinted on my vision.

Figuring she was going to plug me no matter what her part-ner said, I threw my body from the wall and crabwalked back-ward, praying I'd run into my gun before her bullet ran into me.

"Now, Earnshaw," the man repeated.

She moved past, toward the hall, just as my hand hit the sawed-off barrel of my gun. Heat seared my palm, but I grabbed it anyway. Fumbling at first, I managed to find the trigger and wrapped my hand around the stock.

Too late.

Through the burning slits of my eyes, I could see the male operative loom over me.

When he'd first burst in, I'd still been half-blinded by the flashbang, and I hadn't noticed the patch covering one eye. I could see him more clearly now.

Clearly enough to realize I knew him.

Part of my training involved learning to memorize faces so I could recall them in detail months or years later. It was an auto-matic response, one I no longer had to think about. But even so, I wouldn't have needed any of the training to recognize and remember this man. Tear gas or not.

"You son of a bitch," I said between coughs.

I whipped the shotgun around from behind and pumped a round into the chamber.

He was on me before I could pull the trigger, wrestling the weapon from my grasp, planting a knee into the side of my head.

The blow reverberated through my skull, adding to my gas-induced misery, but I managed to keep my senses. I grabbed his leg with one hand, attempting a heel strike to his crotch with the other.

He caught my hand before impact, and bent it back at the wrist. Then he brought a pistol to my head.

Just that easily, he'd bested me. Again.

"I've missed you, *querida*."

Ears still ringing, I couldn't really hear his inflection, but I didn't have to. I could see the amusement in his eye.

I'd known him as Heath, never realizing it was a codename, obviously short for Heathcliff. The last piece of the puzzle I'd failed to put together until now.

"He sent you here to kill me?" I asked.

"He?"

I gave him the hardest stare I could, considering I could barely keep my eyes open and he had a gun to my temple. No matter how many tight situations I'd faced and survived, a gun barrel to the head always made an impression.

Despite the gas mask hiding his lips, I could tell he smiled. "I'm not here for you at all. Although this is a pleasant diversion."

If not me, why was he here? Hammett? Fleming? With the ringing in my ears, pain jangling my skull, and every mucous membrane on fire, my brain was as compromised as my balance.

"Why?" was all I managed to force out.

"Why am I here?"

I nodded.

"I only divulge my plans during pillow talk. No, wait…that's you, not me."

God, I hated this cocky son of a bitch.

"How's the eye?" I asked.

"Good enough to see you're as pretty as ever. So sad, though."

"Tear gas will do that to a girl."

He smirked.

That should have been a clue for me, back when I first met him. Never trust a man who smirks.

"I should kill you," he said. "Or at least bring you in."

"Why don't you, then?" The longer I kept him talking, the better my chances of getting out of this.

"You aren't the objective. And I have a soft spot for the pretty ones."

"Even the ones who stab you in the eye?"

"I probably had it coming. Serves me right for letting my guard down around you."

"So who are you here for? Hammett? Fleming?"

Gunfire erupted in the kitchen. But before I could figure out what to do about it, Heath hit me again, this time with the butt of his gun, and I could do nothing but slump to the floor.

# Fleming

*"No matter how prepared you are, you'll eventually be surprised," The Instructor said. "Your life depends on how quickly you can recover."*

*Breeched!*

The past few days had worn on Fleming enough that controlling panic had become second nature. When the tear gas came in through the window and the firing began, Fleming spat on her shirt collar, pulled it up over her nose and mouth, and rolled out the back exit, overlooking the ledge. Through the haze of fog and gas, she made out a guy in a cowboy hat, hunkering down behind some rocks. She fired twice, keeping him pinned down, hearing the report of Hammett's Skorpion somewhere to the west.

The tear gas meant this mission was a smash and grab, not a hit.

Fleming would not be grabbed. Not again.

If it came down to that, she'd rather eat her gun than go back to the secret prison. The only way they'd take her off this island was in a body bag.

Fleming fired again, counting her shells, making sure she kept two left.

One for her.

And one for Julie.

# Julie

Julie covered her ears.

*Oh my God! Oh my God!*

The house was exploding, and she didn't know what to do. Chandler said stay there. So did her sister. But they couldn't have known there would be bombs.

Kirk pressed against Julie and licked her hand, warm and wet. She ran her palm over his head. He was worried about her, she knew. He wanted to protect her. But not even Kirk could protect her from bombs. No more than Chandler could.

And what about Chandler and her sisters? All Julie could hear were explosions and gunfire. Were they in trouble? Were they even alive?

How could she sit here cowering while Chandler was dying?

But what could Julie possibly do to help?

Julie had held a gun once. She'd shot someone. And she'd never wanted to touch one of the things again.

She wished she had one now.

She wished she could do more to help Chandler and her sisters. More than hiding. More than holding back her tears. More than keeping herself from getting hurt.

Julie couldn't hear Kirk's growl, but she could feel it. A tiny vibration ran through his body. The fur stood up along his spine.

The door to the utility room rattled.

Oh God, someone was here.

Julie scooted her butt along the floor, farther under the stairs. Her pulse was so loud her entire head throbbed with it. She grasped Kirk's collar, her hand shaking.

He let out a flood of barks, low and brutal and meaner than she'd ever heard from him.

The door flew open.

For a second, no one came. Then a rifle barrel stabbed into Julie's line of sight, followed by the biggest woman she'd ever seen.

At least Julie thought it was a woman. A mask covered the face, and long, black braids cascaded over broad shoulders, but her hips flared out and her waist was narrow. She was dressed in a military uniform, boxy and bulletproof and ending in combat boots. She moved like Chandler did, fast and efficient. And when she centered her aim on Kirk, Julie forgot to breathe.

She released his collar.

Kirk sprang at the woman, moving so fast he looked like a brown blur.

An explosion shook the air.

Julie clamped her hands over her ears, the blast echoing through the lighthouse. The gun. The woman had fired the gun.

Kirk kept going, clamping onto the woman's leg.

She struck him with the butt of her rifle and then stared straight at Julie.

Julie's ears rang, and although she saw Kirk barking and the woman yelling, she couldn't hear a thing. She saw the woman coming, but she couldn't make her body move. She couldn't think. She had nowhere to go.

The woman grabbed her by the arm, by the hair.

Julie held onto the stair rail, pain searing her scalp. She stomped the woman's feet, kicked her shins, but it made no difference. The woman bellowed something and gave a yank, and the iron tore from Julie's hands.

Kirk latched on to the woman's leg again, shaking and ripping, and she struck him, sending him smashing onto the floor.

"No!" Julie screamed.

The woman dragged her to the hall window. Julie hit and clawed, but none of it mattered, none of it made any difference.

They had come back. They were taking her. All her worst fears were again coming true.

*Oh God, Chandler. Where are you?*

# Hammett

*"Often during an operation, sacrifices have to be made,"*
*said The Instructor. "Be willing to look past personal*
*attachments and selfish needs and see the bigger picture.*
*Prior to going in, know what's expendable and what is*
*not, so that in the heat of the moment, the tough deci-*
*sions are already made."*

As soon as she heard the shooting start, Hammett raised
the Skorpion and fired on the cowboy. But he'd chosen his
position well, and had hunkered down a millisecond before
she pulled the trigger. Lead pinged off rock and threw dust
in the air, but the best she could hope for was to keep him
pinned down. The moment he realized she wasn't able to end
him from her spot down slope, he fired the grenade into the
kitchen.

Glass shattered, echoing the chaos Hammett could hear
unfolding from the other side of the keeper's place. A slow smoke
wafted from the broken panes.

Tear gas.

*Interesting. They aren't here to kill us.*

Contrary to Chandler's obvious suspicion, Hammett hadn't
alerted The Instructor to their whereabouts. Much as Hammett
wanted to kill Chandler and Fleming, she wanted that son of a
bitch dead first.

But if this second Hydra team had come to take them alive,
it could be to Hammett's advantage. Allowing herself to get captured would give her access to The Instructor.

Something to consider, depending on how this little battle
played out.

Fleming got off a few shotgun blasts, and the cowboy returned to lead instead of tear gas. Between Hammett and Fleming, they had one man trapped in a protected location, which left at least four or five other operatives free to gun for Chandler.

Explosions rocked the other side of the house.

Shit. Hammett hardly ever screwed up, but there was a chance that—this once—she'd made a mistake by leaving her post.

The frantic bark of a dog erupted from the lighthouse.

Hammett spun around. Keeping low, she raced back toward the sound. Even with the tear gas, Fleming had the cowboy on his heels. She didn't need help. Kirk did.

Hammett spotted the two from the engine house outside the window she'd exited. The big guy was stretching his arms through the open frame, as if accepting a delivery.

The chick with the slashes spotted Hammett before she could get a round off, laying down a spray of cover fire.

Hammett dove to the ground, the lichen-covered granite peppered with lead.

The hulk pulled something through the window, and as Hammett blinked the dust from her eyes, she could see the package was Julie, the girl squirming and screaming.

A woman came next, almost too large to get through the window. She was built a lot like the bodybuilder Tristan, and Hammett might have mistaken her for a female athlete on some 1980s Eastern European Olympic team if not for the cornrow braids and dark skin. The right leg of her BDUs was torn, her calf bloody. She limped alongside Izzy and contributed to the lead flying Hammett's way.

The barking intensified, and Kirk's face bobbed into view. The fur around his mouth was dark, his teeth red. Biting back. Defending his mistress.

The first time Hammett saw that dog, she knew he was special.

Kirk surged again, nearly making it through the window, scrambling to get a hold on the sill.

Tristan muscling Julie away, Izzy stepped out from behind him, gun raised, and—

*NO!*

Izzy's rifle cracked.

Kirk's body jolted back from the window, then he slid from Hammett's view.

For a few seconds, Hammett couldn't move. Another climbed through the open sash, a man this time, but Hammett wasn't focused on him.

She stared at the Goth bitch who'd shot Kirk, a hum rising in her ears. Then she scrambled to her feet and started running.

The group moved away from the window, but still the barrage of bullets kept coming. Hammett circled the outcropping, using the rock as a shield, working her way closer. Forget capturing and interrogating. She wanted to kill someone.

Preferably every last one of them.

Tristan rounded the lighthouse, carrying Julie in one beefy arm. Isolde went with him, helping the woman Kirk had bitten. The final operative waited, pinning Hammett down with suppressing fire, keeping her behind the rock and giving the others a head start. By the time he retreated, she knew they were probably gone, but she pursued anyway.

Hammett reached the engine house to find the tram car at the bottom of the hill, the three and the cowboy she'd seen earlier already loading Julie into a sweet boat obviously built for speed. The last man was already halfway down the walkway.

Hammett squeezed off a few rounds, but her hands were shaking, her dash to catch up with them taking its toll, and she missed.

She never missed.

The last man reached the dock and jumped into Chandler's boat; Hammett turned and raced back to the lighthouse. She passed the front door, circled to the open window. Blood smeared the white sill, and a soft whimper came from inside.

Hammett climbed in. She felt calm, steeling her emotions as surely as she was able to block physical pain.

Blood darkened Kirk's fur, covering his neck and shoulder. He was panting, ears back. But when he saw Hammett, his tail attempted a halfhearted wag.

Hammett thought back to Max, her dog when she was a kid. All the times she cried into his neck. All the times she held him while sleeping. He was only a pug, unable to defend her as Kirk had defended Julie. But he'd allowed Hammett to retain a tiny part of her humanity. Proof that some things were worth caring for. Some things needed to be protected.

When Max died, Hammett never got another dog. Her lifestyle would have been unfair to any poor pooch. The travel. The constantly changing addresses. Plus owning a dog would have slowed her down in an emergency situation.

But Hammett still had dogs in her life, even though she didn't actually own any pets. Her one charitable contribution in an otherwise violently selfish life was a sizable annual donation to a no-kill dog shelter.

It was a side of her no one ever knew about. A secret she'd go to the grave keeping.

"Don't worry, boy. I'm here."

Hammett stripped off her sweater, ripping the sleeve, tying it gently around Kirk's mouth so he didn't snap at her while in pain, then pressing the rest of it against his wound to stanch the bleeding.

Kirk couldn't die because of her miscalculation.

She wouldn't let him.

# Chandler

*"This job is filled with risk, and you have to be ready to face that fact," The Instructor said. "Don't care about any person, any secret, any value so much that you can't accept its loss, because there's nothing as weak as decisions made from a position of fear."*

I couldn't be sure how much time had passed before I woke up, but the lingering tear gas made me guess it hadn't been long. Throbbing cheek pressed to the hardwood, I listened to gunfire exploding around me, picking out the Mossberg. Fleming was still OK. I could hear her shooting between fits of coughing coming from the back porch. But there wasn't any other gunfire.

So where was Hammett? And now that Heath and the woman with him had ventured deeper into the house, was Julie still OK?

My eyes burned, my throat thick, head spinning. Forcing myself up on my elbows, then my hands and knees, I struggled to think. I was caught unprepared and thoroughly beaten. I shouldn't be alive, and why Heath hadn't put a bullet in my brain when he'd had the opportunity was beyond me. But whatever the reason, I had another chance, and I was going to take it.

I started crawling for the lighthouse. For the past few years, I tried never to think of Heath, although I'd dreamed about him from time to time. Sometimes we'd be making love, sometimes I was killing him, but mostly I'd hear him laughing at me, and I'd wake feeling angry.

I grabbed hold of that anger, used it to push me to my feet and propel me down the hall.

Heath had taken my shotgun. I had no other weapon except for a folding knife, and no real idea what I would do if I ran into him or the hulking woman who'd stormed in with him. Might as well attack a T. rex with a nail file.

The door leading from the utility room to the lighthouse was open. My shotgun lay on an old workbench, and I picked it up, checked for shells. Full.

Why had he left it for me?

My pulse raced, and I felt shaky with adrenaline overload and the lingering effects of the gas. Falling back on my training, I moved to edge of the door and listened for a second. Only the *pop* of Fleming's gunfire outside reaching me. I entered, weapon leading the way.

The cylindrical space was dark, shadows gathering behind the spiral stairs, but I didn't need light to see that Julie was no longer in the spot I'd left her.

My pulse ratcheted up a notch. I peered up into the tower, but I could see nothing beyond the weak light outside reflecting off the lens in bull's-eye swirls.

"Hammett?"

No answer. No movement.

The shooting outside thinned, then stopped.

I moved back into the utility room, shotgun in front of me, and continued to the hall. There were dozens of possibilities. Julie could be hiding, in the bathroom, in her bedroom. The lighthouse could have been compromised, and Hammett had taken her somewhere safe.

I paused before moving into the hall. I felt a dank breeze whisper across my skin, fresh air diluting lingering tear gas fumes. I heard the shuffle of movement around the corner. Stepping into the hall, I brought my shotgun around, aiming at the sound.

Hammett crouched on the floor, the Skorpion in her hands pointed straight at me.

"It's me."

She lowered her gun, and I did the same.

Then I noticed Kirk lying on the floor, blood wet on his fur, her sweater wrapped around his muzzle and chest.

"He's still alive," Hammett said. She was pressing against Kirk's wound.

"Julie? Where's Julie?" I peered out the open window. Blood smeared the sill.

"They got Julie."

My mind shuddered. It couldn't be. I didn't believe her. "How?"

"They got past you, that's how."

She was right. I'd been overwhelmed. I'd hardly put up a fight.

Somehow I had the presence of mind to stop, to listen. I heard nothing, no beat of helicopter blades, no gunfire, nothing. "They took her to the boat?"

"They were headed in that direction."

"You didn't follow?"

Hammett looked up at me, eyes hard. "You should have let me go out there, take them out before this whole thing started. Instead, they called the shots and left us playing catch up."

She might have been right, and if it had been just the three of us, I would have agreed with her. But I'd had Julie to think of, Julie to protect, and now...

I started back down the hall and into the living room, moving fast.

"Chandler?" Fleming called. Her voice sounded as if it had been worked over with sandpaper.

"They took Julie," I said over my shoulder as I slammed out the door.

I raced along the path, my head clearing in the outside air. I'd promised Julie she'd be OK, that I would protect her, keep her safe.

I'd failed.

I passed the engine house and noted the camera, or what was left of it, dangling from a cord underneath the eave. Reaching the top of the rails leading to the dock, I heard the buzz of one boat motor and then another cutting through the fog.

I couldn't see much from this distance, but I could make out enough to know the dock was vacant. My boat and their boat were gone.

I ran back to the lighthouse as fast as I could move. The exertion working out some of my frustration, sharpening my mind. I found my sisters in the living room, clustered next to Kirk.

I went straight for Hammett. "Why did you tell me you saw Isolde say they were moving at nightfall?"

"Because she said it. She must have known we were watching."

It was an easy answer, but one that fit with my observations on the security monitor. The sudden way Tristan spun to face the camera, shooting it as if he'd known it was there all along. But I wasn't willing to believe her. Not yet.

"Why did they take Julie?" I brought up my shotgun, not pointing it at her, but keeping it ready all the same.

Her hand rested on the handgun in her back waistband. "I don't know."

"How did they get to her?"

"Why would I know any of this? I don't even know why they would want that girl. What value is she to them?"

"Didn't you see them coming from the lighthouse?"

"You move that barrel one more inch, Chandler, and you'll be dead before you can ask your next question."

"Put the guns down," Fleming said. "Both of you."

I lowered my weapon slowly and handed it to Fleming because I didn't trust myself with it.

Hammett stared at me for a good long time, then tucked hers away. As soon as I saw her hands, I went at her with a heel strike to the solar plexus.

She partially blocked the blow, but I could hear the air rush from her lungs. Then in one move, she countered with an elbow to the side of my face, which glanced off the cheekbone already bruised by Heath.

A shotgun exploded, the sound shaking the house and ringing through my ears. I spun around to see Fleming holding the weapon, barrel pointed at the ceiling.

"We have to get out of here," she said, eyes boring into me. "And you need to stop fucking around."

Hammett shot me a venomous look and knelt to pick up Kirk and hold him close, as if shielding him from the crazy lady.

As if she was one to cast judgment.

Hammett turned her focus to Fleming. "What are we supposed to do? Swim?"

"There's another boat," I said. I could barely hear my own voice. If I survived this with my hearing intact, it would be a miracle.

If I survived at all.

"Then let's go."

Grabbing the bags we'd just hauled up the slope, we headed back down. Hammett shouldered the first-aid case and the duffel, leaving her arms free for Kirk. Fleming heaped the rest on her lap. By the time we'd reached the engine house, I could feel the distant sound of helicopter blades beating the air.

I raced to the pulley controls inside the engine house, fired up the diesel engine, and set the lever to full speed. The tram car seemed to take forever to inch up the track.

Unlike trams designed to carry passengers, this one was strictly for cargo, and I wasn't sure how safe it was, especially for Fleming. But as the helicopter sound became louder, I was increasingly sure if we didn't get to the dock and soon, safety standards wouldn't matter.

Finally it reached the top.

"Get in!" I yelled.

Fleming paused, as if wondering how she was supposed to wheel herself aboard, but after setting Kirk down, Hammett took one of Fleming's wheels, I took the other, and we heaved her into the cart.

While Hammett climbed in with Kirk, I raced back into the engine house and set the controls to lower us back down the incline. Then I caught up with the tram car and jumped on with my sisters.

"Aw, shit," Hammett said, staring behind us, her expression grim. "Apocalypse, now."

The explosions started on the far end of the island. The sound reached me first, then the smell, then the heat.

Napalm B was a thickening agent mixed with fuel and used in incendiary bombs. It smelled like a gasoline fire. Burning at 800 to 1,200 degrees Celsius, napalm killed not just from fire and heat, but from the carbon monoxide it produced. That alone could kill people the fire never reached.

A tidal wave of fire washed across the island, spreading toward us.

The tram's engine wouldn't get us to sea level fast enough. My sisters must have realized the same thing at the same time, because as one we fired on the cable, the pulley, and the hoist mechanism.

We broke free of the machine, a runaway train. I threw my body over Fleming. Hammett did the same with Kirk. Gravity and momentum took over, quickly doubling the speed of our descent, but not before a seventy-mile-an-hour firestorm swept over us.

I'd never crawled inside of an oven, but I could guess it felt similar. Superheated air blew over my back and head, searing through my clothing. Over the smell of gas and fire and smoke, I caught a whiff of my burning hair. The pain was instant, sort of a cross between severe sunburn and lashes from a whip. I peeked through my hand, unsure if I was on fire or not, and saw Hammett clutching Kirk, the flames around her blowing out as the cart accelerated.

Before I could cheer the good fortune that we hadn't burned alive, we reached the bottom of the tram track, and I remembered there weren't any brakes.

We hit a bump, my head banging into Fleming's chair, then we were racing across the dock and skidding over the edge and hurtling through the air—

—into the northern Atlantic.

The cold, salty water hit me in the face, a welcome relief at first, and then the tram car splashed to a stop but I kept going, still clutching Fleming, and we skipped across the waves like stones until we slowed enough to sink.

I opened my mouth. A big mistake while underwater. Brine rushed over my tongue, and I fought not to scream or gasp or swallow.

Fleming thrashed, and I released her. I didn't like water, and though part of me knew Fleming was a better swimmer than I was, the true reason I let go of her was to save myself.

The ocean filled me with more raw panic than the napalm and tram ride combined.

I flailed, trying to figure out which way was up, peeking my eyes open in the stinging seawater and seeing a glimmer of light. I kicked, arms clawing at the water, blowing out my cheeks to spit out the salt. Something grabbed me, and I realized it was Fleming, moving me up toward the light. I broke the surface, gasping for air, amazed to still be alive. And Fleming broke the surface to my left.

Treading water, we watched flames lick up the side of the lighthouse, clear even through the fog, the whole island ablaze. The sparse vegetation wouldn't fuel a fire long, and rock didn't burn, but napalm did until it exhausted itself, and the effect was spectacular. Orange reflected off the waves, making them look more like lava than water.

I didn't see the helicopter anywhere. The ocean, and the pounding in my ears due to my rapid heartbeat, made it difficult to hear.

"You OK?" Fleming asked, bobbing on the waves beside me.

I did a body inventory, letting my senses report any pain or lack of sensation, but didn't notice any new damage. I could hardly believe it. "Yeah. You?"

"No."

"What's wrong?" I studied her face in the flickering light of the inferno, fearing the worst.

"I don't think I'll be able to walk again."

I spat out more salt. "Funny."

We swam to the wooden tram car, which floated like a raft ten meters from the pier. Hammett, Kirk, and Fleming's wheelchair were still on board, though her chair was on its side.

"Now isn't the time for a swim break, ladies," Hammett called to us.

"I hate her," I said.

"Break one of her fingers," Fleming said between strokes. "You'll feel better."

Fleming put her back to the tram car, stroking the water with wide sweeps of her arms. I took the other corner, pushing with my hands and scissor-kicking, moving it toward the dock. The waves were with us, and it didn't take long before we were back on the pier and headed toward the boathouse. Although Julie never left the island, I'd thought it necessary for her to have a means of escape in case of an emergency. So I'd gotten her an old aluminum ten-footer with an 8hp Mercury outboard motor. It was a tight squeeze with Fleming's chair, but we all managed to fit. It took a few pulls and some finessing the choke before I turned it over. Then I took control of the motor, and got us the hell out of there.

The boat rolled and swayed and heaved on the waves, much too light for even limited ocean travel, and I had to wonder if it was any more seaworthy than the tram car we'd left behind. I should have gotten Julie something bigger.

I'd add that to my growing list of *should haves*.

"This boat sucks ass." Hammett cradled Kirk in her arms. She'd given the dog a sedative from the first-aid kit tucked in the storage compartment built into Fleming's wheelchair, and his head lolled to the side. I couldn't tell if he was alive or dead.

"We'll be fine," Fleming said, but judging from the look she shot me, she wasn't so sure.

Neither was I.

At least our cold, nausea-inducing boat trip had given me a chance to clear my head and get my emotions under wrap. Although my promise to keep Julie safe weighed at the back of my mind, the attack on the island had forced me to push my feelings about the situation into a box and slam the lid. And that's where I intended to keep them.

Getting back to the SUV so we could figure out how to save Julie was the important thing now. I'd deal with how I'd failed her later.

# Julie

Julie was shaking. Not just from fear, but from cold. She sat sandwiched between the braided woman who'd found her in the lighthouse and the brute who'd carried her to the boat. Her hands were cuffed in front of her, and she was unable to move.

Julie had experienced nightmares like this, plenty of them over the years, but she'd always jolted awake, dripping with sweat and shaking but safe in her bed, Kirk looking on with concern and wagging his tail.

This time, there would be no waking. And no Kirk...

She wanted to cry, but was afraid of what would happen if she did.

Explosions popped like fireworks in the distance. Out over the waves, the night sky glowed murky, thick and orange.

Chandler never would have let them take her. Now as the sky glowed and the smell of smoke hung in the dank air, Julie had to face the fact that Chandler and her sisters were probably dead.

Another sob worked its way up her throat, wracking her body, choking her. Chandler had been Julie's source of hope and strength since she'd come to the island. Now Kirk was gone, Chandler was gone, and Julie had nothing.

Tears squeezed from already swollen eyes, and she quickly wiped them on her sleeve, hoping she'd have a chance to burn the jacket later.

The boat glided along the shoreline. Lights twinkled up ahead, indicating some sort of civilization. Not a town, but maybe a marina or resort.

The man steering the boat glanced into the back of the craft, the brim of his Stetson casting his features in shadow.

"Earnshaw, darlin', you might want to get yourself cleaned up. You can get real nasty infections from dog bites."

The braided woman glanced down at her leg, as if she'd just noticed the blood soaking her torn pants leg. "Got a first-aid kit?"

A man even larger than Earnshaw rose from the seat in front of the boat, tossed a first-aid kit into the back, and Earnshaw caught it in one hand.

"Damn dog," said the big woman under her breath.

Julie's throat tightened.

"Your fault, Izzy. What took you so long to shoot the thing?"

Izzy held a straight razor in one hand, and was staring at her bare, bony forearm. From her wrist to her biceps were dozens of black lines. Her other arm had similar tattoos. The girl had to be close to Julie's age, but she had the gaunt face and hollow eyes of an anorexic.

She caught Julie staring.

"Every line is for someone I wasted," Izzy said in a low monotone. "I make a slash, then fill it in with ink."

Julie couldn't pull her eyes away.

"The short lines," Izzy said, pointing to one that was half the length of the others, "those are the kids."

The cowboy guffawed. "Izzy, you are one scary girl."

Izzy ignored him, instead leaning closer to Julie. "How long should the line be for a dog?" she asked. "Or should I even bother?"

Julie clamped her lips shut, trying to keep another sob from working free. Kirk had been taking care of her, defending her. The sweetest dog in the world, he'd only attacked because he'd known these people were there to hurt her, and he'd done his best to fight back. She didn't have to close her eyes to see Kirk jerk back from that windowsill when the bullet hit. She'd never forget his whimper as he'd fallen from her sight.

That this horrible woman would curse him and talk about his death like it was nothing made her want to scream. It made her want to hurt these people as much as they'd hurt her.

But she couldn't. She just couldn't.

Julie turned her head away, squeezing her eyes shut.

"We know who you are," Izzy said. "You really thought you could hide out on that island forever? Look at me."

Julie felt a hand on her face, her eyelid being pried open. She gave in, opening her eyes, then watched in horror as Izzy stuck out her tongue and ran the razor across the tip, drawing dark blood.

"We're killers," Izzy said, her lips glistening red. "Death is in our blood. But we've got nothing on you."

"Enough talking," Earnshaw said.

She struck out with a fist, so fast Julie barely saw it coming.

The blow slammed through Julie's head, and the glow of the burning island, the cold of the night, the pain of losing everything that mattered faded to nothing.

# Fleming

*"Know your enemy as you know yourself," The Instructor said. "The better you know each, the likelier you are to win."*

Fleming was concerned about Chandler. She didn't seem to be herself, and was making too many mistakes.

They'd made it to the coast and back up the Kennebec River to the place Chandler had hidden the SUV, and now they were on the highway, headed for Portland. But even Chandler's driving seemed to be a touch erratic, and Fleming hoped it was just pain and exhaustion, and not something more serious, like giving up. If they wanted to get out of this situation, hope was paramount. Once hope was gone, resolve followed. Without resolve, you might as well just shoot yourself in the head, save The Instructor the trouble.

But that could be back-burnered for the time being. The important thing right now was to get online and figure some things out. In Wisconsin, Fleming had been using a borrowed laptop, and had returned it to Lund after cleaning her tracks. During the ride to Maine, when Chandler had been sleeping, they'd stopped on the road to get a laptop computer and a 3G plan after wiring Tequila his money.

So as Chandler drove and Hammett tended to Kirk, Fleming connected to the Internet with a fake IP address and hacked into Hydra's database to hunt for clues as to what the hell just happened. She was careful not to mess with anything, using a back door she'd installed previously in a rootkit, which was all but invisible.

She'd spent time searching through the site, and had copied the source code so she was familiar with the navigation tree. Page by page, Fleming searched the JavaScript for the Hydra team member names. She knew her own codename, as well as Chandler's and Hammett's, were encrypted using a hashing algorithm generated by photons—a method Fleming herself had invented, and was thus far unbreakable by anyone but her.

Ironically, it was the method used on the Hydra database. And The Instructor apparently hadn't had time to change it since Fleming had gone rogue only a few days ago.

She had to remote access her own computer to get the tools needed, and then cut and pasted the numerical code for the name "Isolde" into her program's search box.

Fleming got a hit, and pasted the results into Notepad and cleaned it up, removing all the computer language.

Hydra Deux Abbreviated Dossiers

Codename: Rochester—Deceased.

Codename: Earnshaw—Stats: African American. Blk hair, brn eyes. Two hundred twenty pounds. Six feet one inch. Specialties: Hand-to-hand combat, wrestling, judo, grappling. Bench press 500 pounds. Stamina. Loyalty. Weaknesses: Undercover ops. Seduction. Long-range weapons. Steroid abuse.

Codename: Scarlett—Stats: Caucasian. Blnd hair, gray eyes. One hundred twenty-five pounds. Five feet seven inches. Specialties: Undercover ops. Pilot. Vehicle and machinery expert. Interrogation. Speaks English, French, German, Russian, Mandarin, Portuguese, Spanish. Computer hacking. Sniping. Edged weapons. Fourth dan black belt in karate. Weaknesses: Argumentative. Narcissistic personality disorder. Seduction. Strength and stamina. Grappling.

Codename: Isolde—Stats: Caucasian. Brn hair, brn eyes. Ninety pounds. Five feet six inches. Striped tattoos on arms. Specialties: Edged weapons. Interrogation. Poison. Long- and short-range firearms. Pilot. Weaknesses: Borderline personality disorder. Self-mutilation. Sadistic personality disorder. Strength and stamina.

Codename: Rhett—Stats: Caucasian. Blnd hair, blue eyes. One hundred eighty pounds. Five feet ten inches. Specialties: Undercover ops. Seduction. Explosives. Demolition. Short-range weapons. Vehicle and machinery expert. Hand-to-hand combat, tae kwon do, krav maga. Weaknesses: Attention deficit disorder. Lacks motivation.

Codename: Heathcliff—Stats: Mexican American. Blk hair, brn eyes. One hundred seventy pounds. Five feet nine inches. Specialties: Long- and short-range weapons. Hand-to-hand combat, capoeira. Undercover ops. Seduction. Pilot. Computer hacking. Speaks English, Spanish, French, Portuguese, Farsi, Arabic, Italian. Weaknesses: Women. Obedience. Missing one eye.

Codename: Tristan—Stats: Japanese American. Blk hair, brn eyes. Two hundred sixty pounds. Six feet one inch. Specialties: Hand-to-hand combat, judo, sumo, grappling. Bench press 540 pounds. Driving. Speaks English, Japanese, French, Mandarin,

Cantonese, Korean, Arabic. Weaknesses: Undercover ops. Steroid abuse. Temper.

She shared aloud the pertinent bits with her sisters. A short silence followed.

"Hydra Deux," Hammett eventually said. "Are they supposed to supplement us? Or replace us?"

Fleming frowned. "Considering how long training takes, this group has been around for a while."

"Several years," Chandler said, looking at Fleming. "I met Heath before. Previous mission. A sanction in Vegas."

Fleming remembered. "The eye."

Chandler nodded.

Hammett looked from one to the other. "You took out his eye?"

"With a shish kebab skewer," Fleming said. Chandler had held her own in that mission, although in the end, it had to be counted as one of her less successful. She'd leave it up to Chandler to tell the rest or not, whatever she chose.

"He had skills on par with mine, but I didn't know he was Hydra."

Apparently she'd chosen not.

"I wonder how many of these assholes The Instructor trained," Hammett said. "Present company excepted."

Fleming scanned the dossiers again. "We were lucky to get out of there alive."

"How far to the vet, Chandler?" Hammett asked. Kirk's head was in her lap.

"Ten minutes."

Fleming took the time to perform a similar computer search for her own name, and came up with another group of abbreviated dossiers for the first Hydra group.

Codename: Ludlam—Deceased.

Codename: LeCarre—Deceased.

Codename: Clancy—Deceased.

Codename: Forsythe—Deceased.

Codename: Fleming—Stats: Caucasian. Brn hair, brn eyes. One hundred and twenty pounds. Five feet six inches. Specialties: Computers. Programming. Math. Eidetic memory. Pilot. Vehicle and machinery expert. Undercover ops. Seduction. Leadership. Long- and short-range weapons. Edged weapons. Hand-to-hand combat, judo, karate, tae kwon do, capoeira, krav maga. Speaks fifteen languages. Weaknesses: Since accident, no longer suitable for field work. Demoted to research and development, running operations, intel.

Fleming winced at the depiction of what she once was, and the realization of what she'd been reduced to. Rather than dwell on it, she kept reading.

Codename: Hammett—Stats: Caucasian. Brn hair, brn eyes. One hundred and twenty pounds. Five feet six inches. Specialties: Undercover ops. Seduction. Interrogation. Eidetic memory. Pilot. Vehicle and machinery expert. Long- and short-range weapons. Edged weapons. Hand-to-hand combat, judo, karate, tae kwon do, capoeira, krav maga, kendo, jujitsu. Speaks twelve languages. Weaknesses: Antisocial personality disorder.

That sounded like Hammett. *Antisocial personality disorder* was just another way of saying *psychotic*. No surprises there.

Codename: Chandler—Stats: Caucasian. Brn hair, brn eyes. One hundred and twenty pounds. Five feet six inches. Specialties: Undercover ops. Seduction. Interrogation. Eidetic memory. Pilot. Vehicle and machinery expert. Long- and short-range weapons. Edged weapons. Hand-to-hand combat, judo, karate, tae kwon do, capoeira, krav maga, kendo, jujitsu. Speaks ten languages. Weaknesses: Self-doubt. May crack under pressure. Panic control.

Chandler's abbreviated dossier was almost the same as Hammett's, except Hammett was nuts, and Chandler, apparently, was unreliable.

Fleming thought back to the many times she'd worked as Chandler's handler. She'd been efficient in every op, always resourceful and committed. And yet…

Chandler sometimes took too long to make a decision. That arose from doubt. And there were a few ops where she acted erratic, made mistakes, like the one where she'd encountered Heathcliff.

Could Chandler have cracked on a mission and hid it from Fleming?

It was possible. She was a good actress. Maybe she'd been covering her fears all along.

Fleming turned off the computer. She glanced back and forth from Hammett to Chandler, wondering which one was the weaker link. Who was more unreliable.

Then Fleming wondered, if the situation arose, who would be harder to kill.

Hammett would be tough to outsmart and overpower. So would Chandler. But in Chandler's case, Fleming had real feelings for her. They'd had a bond since Chandler had known her as Jacob. But in the last week, they'd gotten as close as two sisters could be.

Yet Fleming could see Chandler's recent, erratic behavior. And with Julie taken, the threat was to more than just the three of them. The threat had become global.

*Could I kill Chandler if I needed to?*

Fleming didn't know how to answer that. Worse, she didn't know if she wanted to answer it.

For now, all she could do was wait and watch.

# Chandler

*"The windmill needs the wind, not vice versa," said The
Instructor. "Be the wind."*

Our first stop was a twenty-four-hour urgent care pet clinic
in Portland. I wasn't sure how to take Hammett's concern for
Julie's dog. The woman killed people without a thought, and yet
she willingly plunked down a big chunk of our limited cash to
make sure Julie's dog got the best of care, and another chunk to
make sure the vet didn't report the gunshot wound to the police.

"Why do you care?" I asked her.

"Why do you care that I care?"

"We have other things we need to be doing."

Actually, we really didn't. Fleming was on the computer, figuring some things out, and that left me and Hammett to twiddle
our thumbs until Fleming told us what to do.

Hammett shrugged. "I like Kirk."

"There are millions of dogs in London," I said. "If you forgot,
that's the city you almost obliterated."

"You still stuck on that?" Hammett rolled her eyes. "Let it go,
already."

"Let a nuclear attack go?"

"*Attempted* nuclear attack. It didn't happen."

"But you still launched a nuke at all those dogs."

Hammett crossed her legs. "I never met those dogs. But I
have met Kirk."

"So it's OK if a few million dogs die as long as you don't
know them, but not OK if one dog you do know dies?"

"I don't think either situation is OK. In the case of London,
the dogs were collateral damage. But don't get all morally

superior. If you had a choice, London gets destroyed, or Fleming dies, what would you choose?"

I hesitated. I wanted to pick saving London, but part of me knew Hammett was right. I'd be more inclined to save someone I loved than a bunch of people I didn't know. That was precisely the choice I'd made when I'd chosen to save Lund, Fleming, Tequila, and myself rather than the president.

I elected not to pursue the conversation, instead thumbing through old magazines and trying to get comfortable in the cheap plastic waiting room seat.

It took an hour, and the vet finally returned to say the dog was out of surgery and stable. Hammett wanted to see him, and the vet allowed it. When she returned, Hammett's expression was so intense it radiated heat.

"I'm going to gut the bitch that did this."

I was glad I wasn't the bitch who did it.

Next we stopped at a twenty-four-hour drugstore in Portland and picked up three boxes of hair color, a highlighting kit, a comb and a pair of scissors, plastic wrap, clip-in blond hair extensions, and a variety of makeup. My clothing was torn, burned, and crusty with salt. But since my choices were limited in a drugstore, that would have to wait until the next day.

We made another stop to fill the SUV with gas. Then we rented a room in a run-down motel, using the driver's license Hammett had stolen in Wisconsin.

The place smelled like mildew and sweaty feet and was not worth the hundred-and-fifty-dollar "fall color" special they were running, especially since most tree leaves were just starting to change. But they took cash, didn't ask questions, and at that point, for a few hours of rest and a chance to regroup, I would have paid much more.

I started with a shower, rinsing the salt from my sore body and the smell of gasoline from my heat-damaged hair. Heath had left a nasty bruise on the side of my head, reddish purple stretching from my hairline to under my cheekbone. Minor compared with the other damage my body had sustained over the past few days. In fact, I'd accumulated so many injuries it was sometimes hard to see where one wound left off and another began.

I did some stretches while the water beat down on me. The biggest hurdle to overcome when trying to function while in pain was stiffness. As much as stretching hurt, it helped me retain my full range of movement, which was essential when fighting for your life.

By the time I dressed my wounds, wrapped myself in a towel, and emerged feeling somewhat human again, the room had been transformed into a beauty salon. Also wearing a towel, Fleming sat on one of the beds, her head swathed in tan goo and covered in plastic wrap. Wisps of hair scattered around her on the orange-and-pink floral spread. Holding the scissors and comb like a pro, she snipped away at a towel-clad Hammett, cutting her hair with reckless abandon.

Even though my jealousy seemed even pettier after losing Julie and nearly dying on the island, the sensation of being left out of the Sister Club tweaked me as it had on the road trip to Maine.

Fleming glanced at her watch and then at me. "Can you take over here?" she asked.

Even more awkward than being shut out was the prospect of fixing Hammett's hair. "You're doing a great job."

"I have to rinse out my color or my hair is going to fall out," she smiled. "You were in the shower a long time."

I had been, partly because the warm water had felt good and partly because I'd wanted to put off dealing with Hammett as long as possible. "OK."

Fleming handed me the scissors and comb and then lifted herself into her chair. As she wheeled away she said, "Might as well tell her now."

I wanted to pretend I didn't know what Fleming was referring to, but it would be no use. If Hammett was going to help us get Julie back and stop The Instructor, she needed to know exactly what we faced.

But I had a question I wanted answered first. "How'd they get to Julie?"

Hammett sighed like I was the stupidest person on the planet.

"How'd they do it, Hammett?" I repeated. Then I thought of another approach. "How did they get to Kirk?"

Her expression went blank. A tell. When I didn't want someone to know what I was thinking, I did the same thing.

"How did Kirk get shot while you were there?"

Hammett pressed her lips into a pale line. "Staying put was a mistake."

I could guess where this was going. "You went out to find them instead of keeping watch from the lighthouse."

"You can't play defense with people like this. You sit back and wait for them to strike, and you might as well flop onto your back and offer up your belly."

Even though she hadn't followed my orders, Hammett was right. And I should have been able to see their plan. It was what I would have done, after all—deceive the enemy, use their own defenses against them, take them by surprise—but instead of keeping a clear mind, I'd been afraid. I'd hunkered down, seen what I wanted to see. And then when the strike came, I'd underestimated it, and we'd been quickly overwhelmed.

"You know I'm right."

I managed a grudging nod.

"So why did you do it?" she asked.

"We had to protect Julie. I couldn't afford to risk her being hurt."

"Shit, Chandler. You risked all of us for Julie? Why would you do something so stupid? What makes this girl so important to you?"

I had a lot of reasons for caring about Julie, but Hammett needed to know only one. "Have you ever heard of a place called Plum Island?"

She frowned, a crease digging between eyebrows identical to mine. "Animal Disease Center, right?"

"That's not all they do there."

"Human disease?"

"Take that a step further."

The shift was subtle, a twitch of her lips, a slight dilation of her pupils. I could see her mind fitting pieces together. It was disturbingly close to looking in a mirror.

"Biological weapons."

"Yes," I answered.

"What does that have to do with Julie?"

I forced myself to go Zen, to keep my emotions in check. It was something that normally came easy for me, but it had gotten exponentially harder these last few days.

"Several years ago, Julie visited a free health clinic in New York. The next thing she knew, she awoke in a lab on Plum Island."

"Human experimentation?" Hammett asked.

I nodded. "They injected her with a virus, an experimental strain."

"Exactly what virus are we talking about, Chandler?"

"Ebola."

I'd rarely seen Hammett surprised, but at that horrifying word, her eyes flared.

Then she shook her head. "But Julie's still alive."

Hammett was catching on. Most people didn't survive Ebola. The virus attacked the human body on a cellular level, liquefying tissue, turning internal organs into a bloody virus soup. Normal strains killed in days, and there was no cure. The strain I was talking about only took hours.

I'd seen it up close and personal.

It had been devastating.

"Julie has a unique combination of antibodies," I explained. "That's why they picked her. She's immune to Ebola."

"So now she's a carrier."

"Yes."

"The Typhoid Mary of Ebola," Hammett said. "Holy shit."

"Yeah."

"So we weren't the target. She was. And you let The Instructor take her. You unbelievable dumbass."

I sat in the spot Fleming vacated. A heavy ache centered in my chest, and I worried if I thought about Julie too much, I might even start to cry. I needed to focus not on what had happened to her, or even what was happening now, but on getting her back, making her safe once again.

"And you keep blaming me for them showing up," Hammett continued. "You're the one who led them there. That's why they went in with tear gas. To take her alive. They were probably surprised to see us."

I didn't respond. Comb in one hand, scissors in the other, I started to snip. Cosmetology school hadn't been part of our training, but I'd taken courses in my free time. Maybe Hammett and Fleming had, too. In our line of work, it never hurt to know how to change your appearance.

"Don't you think you should have told me this earlier, Fearless Leader?"

"I didn't trust you. I still don't."

"And because you didn't, you let The Instructor snatch a biological weapon from under our nose."

I wanted to say that Julie wasn't a weapon. She was a person. But, yet again, Hammett was right. If I'd emphasized Julie's importance earlier, Hammett would have stayed close.

I had thought they were after us, and I'd been wrong. And now I'd endangered not only Julie, but the entire world.

"I blew it," I said softly.

"No shit. You are the Queen of All Fuckups."

I compartmentalized my feelings, shoving them away, and snipped away in silence, trying to lose myself in the mundane task.

"Careful there, dumbass. If the world is ending because of you, I at least want my hair to look good."

I didn't reply.

After giving Hammett an uneven, punkish cut, I slathered on the platinum-blonde dye, getting ready for the pink and purple highlights we'd apply later. We were both silent as I worked, and I was grateful Hammett didn't prod for further information about Julie.

Since my hair was now a blond pixie, I was going to go very dark, and once Hammett's color was on, she applied mine. Fleming was shooting for a specific look, and when she emerged from the shower with light-blond hair that matched the clip-in extensions we'd purchased, it seemed like we might be on our way.

"You two have your chat?" Fleming asked.

"Yes," Hammett answered. "There's one thing that makes no sense."

"What's that?" she asked.

I expected another insult. But instead, Hammett said, "The Instructor's detachment, they were wearing gas masks, but not any kind of hazmat gear. A unit with that much training isn't easily expendable, not even for The Instructor. Why would he risk them getting sick?"

I thought for a second, then winced at the obvious. "Maybe they've been inoculated."

"There's no immunization for Ebola."

"There is for this strain."

Fleming twisted in her chair to stare at me.

I nodded in answer to her unasked question.

Hammett looked from me to Fleming and back again. "What did I just miss?"

"There was a vaccine," Fleming said. "It was developed by a medical researcher named Pembrooke."

"So this Pembrooke is working for The Instructor?"

"He's dead," I said. "Years ago."

"You killed him?" Hammett asked.

"A man named Jonathan Kirk did."

Hammett narrowed her eyes on me, as if sensing there was a much bigger story, and I was relieved she didn't ask for more details, because I wasn't about to give them. Some things were too personal to share, especially with Hammett.

"So where's this vaccine he developed?"

"My blood."

"Wait a minute here," Hammett said. She moved away from me and sat on the second bed. "You were infected with Ebola?"

I gave a nod.

"Damn," Hammett said. "Does it affect the brain, causing overwhelming stupidity?"

"Stop acting like a bratty kid," Fleming told Hammett. She rolled her chair toward me. "When did they take your blood?"

"It must have been after you fished me out of Lake Michigan, I woke in the hospital, handcuffed to the bed, an IV pumping sedatives into me. At the time, I assumed the needle marks were from the IV or something they'd given me."

"So The Instructor knew about Julie even then," Fleming pointed out.

So that settled it. Hammett couldn't have been the one to betray our location. The tracking chip that I hadn't known was in me had led The Instructor to Julie some time ago, either the night I'd taken her to the island or another visit after that. In addition, Julie had indeed been the target of the raid, and I had to wonder how long The Instructor had been planning whatever he was putting into motion now.

Hammett folded her arms over her chest. "Well, I'm not going anywhere until I get that vaccine."

"Does the first-aid kit have an FBTK?" I asked Fleming.

She nodded.

Fleming reached into the compartment of her chair and rummaged for the field blood transfusion kit. After cleaning off my arm with an alcohol pad, Fleming unwrapped the needle.

"And I thought we were going to paint each other's toenails next," Hammett said, baring her forearm and grinning. "This is a lot more fun."

# Heath

*"You've had the best training the world can offer," said The Instructor. "What you do with that training is your choice."*

His codename was Heathcliff, and he set his carry-on on the conveyor belt, his shoes in a bin, and stepped through the metal detector. The TSA agent was hot, a petite blonde with pink cheeks and a mouth in the shape of a bow. Just the type of woman he wouldn't mind having search him for weapons. Tonight, she passed over him without a flicker of interest and turned her attention to an older woman behind him who looked like she came straight out of a clean-cut family sitcom, a real terror threat.

Just as well.

After seeing Chandler again, this little wisp of bland would only disappoint him.

Mmm, Chandler.

He had hated hitting her, but at least he hadn't been forced to take her life. And even though Scarlett had torched the island after their departure, his money said Chandler wouldn't succumb to a bit of napalm and fire.

Chandler was *la encarnación del fuego* herself...the embodiment of fire.

Heath adjusted his eye patch. If she was someone else, he would have killed her for taking his eye. *La venganza* would be in his blood.

But with Chandler, the only thing in his blood was lust.

Besides, she might be useful.

He collected his shoes and bag and made his way out of security. The airport of Portland, Maine, was small, and he was lucky to only have one stop at Dulles on his way to his ultimate destination. Maybe while he was in the DC area, he should stop in and say hi to The Instructor.

He smiled, amusing himself. Of course, he had no way of knowing where The Instructor currently lived. No one did. Even his name was hidden.

Unless it happened to be *El Diablo*.

There were many devils in this life, and The Instructor was certainly one.

Heath was lucky the plan called for him to split from the others once they had the girl. He was grateful not to have to see The Instructor right now. That man could read micro-emotions like no one he'd ever known. The Instructor would question Heath about seeing Chandler again, just to judge his reaction. The old man might even sense that Heath wasn't being fully forthcoming.

Heath had to be careful. The time was near. Soon the game would play out—though to Heath, this was never a game. But whatever it was called, he would win.

All he needed was a little help.

# Years Ago...

Her codename was Fleming, and she'd just killed a man.

She used a corner of the sheet to wipe down the syringe and fitted it into the ambassador's shaky hand, his thumb firmly on the plunger. His lips were already blue, his breath coming shallow and with difficulty. It wouldn't take long now. The second dose she'd given him was more than enough to shut his system down.

Permanently.

She pulled back the sheet and removed the condom from his limp body. The sex had been surprisingly good this time. It was a shame the bastard used his diplomatic connections to pad his own pockets. Selling explosives to a terrorist group targeting a school filled with children made it hard to feel bad for him. She'd been with him two weeks now, gathering intel, determining exactly who he'd sold to, where his lethal merchandise had gone. And tonight she had delivered the coup de grâce. Killing was never pleasant, but justice for a man like this held a certain amount of satisfaction.

Even if it was a shame to kill a man who was so talented in bed.

She climbed out onto the plush rug and moved around the room. From the moment she'd entered the five-star hotel, she'd made a mental note of each item she'd touched. Now she wiped each clean: the bedside lamp, the doorknob leading into the powder room, the mirrored coffee table in the sitting area, the glossy end caps of the butter-soft leather sofa.

She moved around the suite naked, leaving her dress on the floor of the bedroom. If the bodyguards outside entered for any reason, embarrassment at seeing the boss's woman naked would send them back into the hall, giving her a chance to escape before they demanded to see the ambassador.

Once she'd erased all signs of her presence in the suite, she flushed the condom and returned to the bedroom. The ambassador was no longer breathing, his skin already starting to cool. She left the bag of heroin on the nightstand, tourniquet limp around the man's arm, the syringe resting on the sheets where it had dropped from his hand. If she was lucky, the bodyguards wouldn't disturb him until morning, allowing him to party it up the rest of the night.

Fleming dressed in her black bra and panties and pulled on her dress, a slinky black sheath, then gathered her strappy Jimmy Choos. She retrieved her evening bag from the chaise where she'd tossed it and moved to the bank of windows looking over the sparkling lights of Milan.

The bag was extraordinary, sparkly silver and much more useful than it looked. Fleming emptied the cash and lipstick from the bag, sticking both in her cleavage, then she unfastened the silver ornaments on either side of the purse. The strap was made of a thick wire that was woven throughout the body. Fleming unwound it, transforming the handbag into thirty meters of wire, then she removed the locking mechanism on two of the adjacent windows and slid them both open.

The night was warm, a light breeze carrying scents of roses from the balcony garden across the alley and exhaust from the street.

Picking up the wire she'd unwound, Fleming dropped one end out one window and the second out the other, the wire straddling the short stretch of wall in between. She retrieved the ornaments—actually a set of hand clamps to prevent the wire from ripping into her palms—and placed them on the wire. She wound the wire between her legs, over her specially designed panties, over her hip and across her chest, around her back and out her shoulder, positioning one clamp on the incoming section of wire and one where it fed out. She lowered herself out of the window, back first, her shoes dangling from her fingers, her bare feet against the building's exterior.

Fleming realized many people had a fear of heights, and she was glad she wasn't among them. Ever since she was a girl, she loved climbing trees. Her father had taken her rock climbing for the first time when she was only eight, and later that summer, she was grounded for practicing rappelling off the roof of her apartment building.

Even though she was only five stories up, looking down on the city made her feel powerful and free, almost as if she could spread her arms and fly. While killing was a necessary part of her job, this type of thing was the portion she actually enjoyed. Testing herself physically. Performing feats few had mastered. Tonight's descent from the building was tame compared with the things she could do, but it was satisfying nonetheless, and she smiled as she lowered herself silently down the building toward the alley below.

One story.

One and a half stories.

With more than three stories left to go, she felt a tremor in the wire.

Something was wrong. Something was—

She looked up the moment she heard the faint *ping*, felt the wire give way, as if its support had been an illusion.

Then gravity took her.

Weightless.

Falling.

Both aware and in complete disbelief. Accepting it and denying it. No time to consider anything other than her trained reaction.

Fleming had practiced falling while at Hydra, and her body knew what to do. Ankles together. Absorb impact with the legs. Protect the head and spine. Relax.

But even as she folded herself into the proper position, she knew she was too high up.

The ground came suddenly, unexpected even as it was obvious.

A shock unlike any she'd ever felt.

Unimaginable force.

Then the pain swallowed her whole.

Through her feet, up her legs, jolting through her spine. She felt her knees bend, trying to diffuse the sudden jolt like a spring bending, bending…

She crumpled to the cobblestone, toppling forward into a shoulder roll, arms wrapped around her head.

Unbearable agony.

Pain screamed through her legs and up her spine. She couldn't think. Couldn't see. Couldn't move.

How long she lay there, Fleming couldn't tell. Each minute was an hour. She thought she might have screamed but couldn't be sure. She couldn't be sure of anything, only her suffering. Sweat broke out over her skin. Chills claimed her body, hot and cold.

She tried to clear her mind. To focus on survival, even though what she wanted more than anything was to pass out. Squinting in the darkness, she stared down at her legs, but what she saw didn't make sense. They were bent in so many wrong directions it didn't seem real. As if they had no bones left at all.

She heaved, vomited, and tore her eyes away from the abomination she had become.

On the street, a car whipped by, its windows open, techno dance music pouring into the night.

The street. If she could get out of this damn alley, reach the street, she could get help.

The Instructor's words poured through her mind. *"You're a ghost. You don't exist. If you are compromised, you're on your own."*

If she caught the attention of a passerby, or the police, she would be taken to a hospital. From there, it wouldn't take long for them to question why she'd been rappelling down the side of a hotel in the middle of Milan. And when they found the ambassador, she'd be imprisoned, questioned. Ultimately denied by the country she loved.

Bad as the pain was now, things could always get worse.

Fleming stretched her hands out in front of her, gripping the cobblestone's edges with her fingertips then pulling, dragging her body across the rough stone, her legs trailing behind her like dead earthworms on fishhooks. Fleming felt like she was going to be sick again, and for a moment she clung to the ground as if it was vertical and she was in danger of slipping off. Her heart pounded in her ears. Her breath came fast and hard, a gasp in, then a forceful blow through her mouth, trying to push out the pain.

But there was no relief.

Fleming closed her eyes, picturing herself lying there on the ground, as if she were standing over her own body.

*I'm hallucinating.*

*It's the pain,* she answered herself.

*I just want to pass out.*

*You can't pass out.*

*It hurts so bad.*

*If you pass out, you'll die.*

*Maybe I want to die. I'll never walk again.*

*There's more to life than walking.*

*Walking. Running. Dancing. Fucking. Never again. Any of it.*

*Don't quit now. You're stronger than this.*

She stretched her hands out again, the wire tangling around her. Dragging herself a few more feet, she felt a whimper building in her chest.

Reach. Pull.

Darkness narrowed, only a circle of light from the streetlight overhead.

*I'm not strong enough.*

*Yes, you are.*

Reach. Pull.

A high-pitched scream warbled in the air. Not from her. Something else. A siren.

*I can't make it.*

*Yes, you can.*

Reach. Pull.

She smelled sweat and garbage and roses and blood.

*I want to die.*

*You've got the rest of your life to die.*

Reach. Pull.

Lights flashed around her, red and urgent. The darkness narrowed and the dizziness engulfed her. Her head bobbed, then dropped to the ground.

Fleming reached her limit.

She couldn't pull. She couldn't help herself.

*I'm done.*

*I tried.*

*Yes, you did.*

*Can I pass out now?*

*Yes?*

*Can I die now?*

And then she was being lifted, men's hands on her, and Fleming saw the ambulance and realized she wasn't going to die, no matter how much she wanted to...

# Fleming

*"Acting is one of the most useful weapons in your arsenal," The Instructor said. "While violence can produce results, a little acting will get the job done and leave no one the wiser...until it's too late for them to stop you."*

Chandler and Hammett dropped Fleming off at a car dealership in Waltham, Massachusetts. It was the nearest dealer boasting a used Honda Odyssey minivan equipped with hand controls and a chair lift. While Fleming could capably drive unmodified vehicles, she needed a lift van for her part of the plan. Hand controls would also allow her to keep one hand on her gun, something not without its advantages.

The problem was that a custom van, even a used one, cost a lot of money. More than they'd gotten from the crack house. So Fleming had to improvise.

She had her computer and a few other essentials in the duffel bag they'd gotten in Wisconsin, hanging on the back of her chair. She wore her leg braces, and her crutches were tucked into the chair alongside her.

As she watched her sisters drive away, Fleming felt a knot of uncertainty tighten in her stomach. A lot had to go right for them to get out of this mess, not the least of which was those two not killing each other before they reached Chicago.

But she had her own concerns. Even though Fleming faced a much shorter drive than Chandler and Hammett—only seven and a half hours compared to their sixteen and a half—she had a lot to do and not much time to do it. Fleming needed to get this vehicle as quickly and cleanly as possible.

Finklestad's Automotive Sales was approaching closing time, and as she wheeled her chair across the brilliantly lit parking lot and to the showroom door, she could hear a vacuum running inside. Completing the awkward task of opening the door and maneuvering the chair inside, she was struck at how vacant the place was. No salesmen were on the floor. No sound but the cleaning crew.

"Hello? Can someone sell me a car?"

Like magic, a skinny man in a baggy suit raced from one of the back offices. When he saw her, he stopped and a droopy-eyed look of pure pity rounded his eyes.

"Hello there," he said. "What do we have here? What can I do for you tonight, young lady? Do you need some help?"

Fleming was used to people talking to her as if she was hard of hearing or had the mind of a six-month-old child, their eyes flicking nervously back and forth between the top of her head and the wheelchair. But being accustomed to it didn't mean she didn't get a strong urge to slap those people every time.

She took a deep breath of Zen. "I'm interested in a minivan with hand controls."

"Of course you are," he said, his voice dripping with condescension. "I'm Eric."

"Eric Finklestad?"

"No, Mr. Finklestad spends most of his time at his Boston location. He has eight dealerships around here."

"Good to know." At least she didn't have to feel guilty for targeting a small, struggling business.

Eric the salesman thrust out his hand, his face twitching as if he'd had too much caffeine. "And you are?"

Fleming shook. His palm was clammy and his grip disinterested at best. "Tammy Schaefer," Fleming said, providing the name of the SUV's owner. "I saw you had the van in your online listings."

"May I get you something to drink? Coffee? Soda?"

"I'd like to test-drive the van."

He nodded, but didn't move. "Are we waiting for your caretaker?"

"My caretaker? Do I look like a funeral home? I'm thinking you mean my caregiver."

"Yes. Your caregiver. You need a license to test-drive."

"The only caregiver I have is my seeing-eye dog. He makes sure I don't walk into traffic. He has a license, but I don't think he's allowed to drive."

"I...uh..."

"I have a driver's license and a certificate of insurance." Fleming pulled the woman's wallet out of the duffel bag and removed both. The photo resembled her more since she'd dyed her hair, but it wasn't close to passing the scrutiny of the average bouncer at a college bar. "The picture isn't very good."

He took them and to her relief only gave the photo a cursory glance.

But he also didn't move to get the van. "So we're not waiting? Maybe for a parent or husband?"

If he asked again, Fleming was committed to choking him—possibly to death—and finding some way to locate the van keys herself.

"It's only me," she said, pouring on the syrup. "The accident killed my husband and parents, and left me without the use of my legs. A worthless cripple, barely able to take care of herself. Thank goodness the insurance check made me rich, because I'd never be able to function without it."

His eyes lit up at the word *rich*. "You poor, poor dear."

"Can we please hurry with the test-drive? I'd hate for you to be in the car while I soiled my diaper, and I'm due to at any moment because I also lost my rectum in the accident."

"That's...that's terrible."

"It's not all bad. Thanks to the good Lord's mercy, I still have control over my bladder. Mostly. Though when I pee, it's more than half blood."

"I'll pop in and get the keys, and we'll be on our way. Are you sure...that...?"

"That I can drive? Yes. You know how when people go blind they develop a better sense of hearing? Well, my upper body has grown twice as strong since I lost use of my legs. See?"

Once again Fleming offered her hand, and when Eric took it she squeezed hard, grinding his knuckles together. Eric yelped, and tried to pull his hand back.

"I'm not hurting you, am I?" she asked, knowing she was.

"I...um...yes, you're very strong."

"Then go get the keys and let's test-drive this bitch."

She released him, and he went off with the license and insurance in a half walk, half jog. A moment later he emerged from a back hallway jangling a key in his hand.

"Here we go. I made a copy of your ID and insurance." He handed them back to her. "Now let's find you a set of wheels. Er, other wheels. A spare set."

"You're too kind."

Eric fetched the van at lightning speed, bringing it to a stop in front of her. After demonstrating the lift installed inside the rear side door by loading her and her chair into the vehicle, he climbed into the passenger seat. As soon as Fleming lifted herself from chair to seat with her arms, he handed her the keys.

Even before she started the van, she knew it was perfect. The steering wheel had an accelerator ring that stuck out around the horn. Pressing it was like hitting the gas pedal. The hand brake was to the right of the wheel, under the turn signal. Chalking up her anger to hanging around Hammett too much, Fleming gave Eric a genuine smile this time and pulled out onto the street.

"So, this van is loaded. Leather interior. Heated seats. CD player. Auto locks and windows. Steering wheel tilt. Anti-theft devices."

"Really?" Fleming asked. "What kind of monster would steal a wheelchair van?"

"You wouldn't believe the depths some people go to."

"I bet."

Fleming drove around the city, testing the van's controls and drivability, looking for a good spot to take her next step. The area was quite developed, houses, businesses, and schools flanking every street.

"I want to see how it handles on highways."

Eric checked his cell phone. "Uh, look at the time, will you? It's getting kind of late."

"I really want to buy this van tonight. Is the late hour a problem?"

"Um…"

"My rectum is holding out OK. I have the rubber prosthesis holding everything in, like a cork."

"That's…um…nice. But we're closing very soon."

"I'm prepared to pay cash."

"OK, no problem. A few more minutes won't hurt."

Fleming kept driving. Spotting a sign, she took an off-ramp near Compton.

"Walden Pond! I've always wanted to see Walden Pond."

Fleming took one turn, then another. But even the roads around Walden Pond were more populated with houses and highways than she liked, a fact that seemed utterly wrong. Finally she found a stretch of nothing but dark forest.

"Would you mind if we stopped? Just one second?"

Eric glanced at his cell phone again, starting to look a little desperate. "Why?"

"I'll be quick," she said, pulling off the road. "I want to say that I walked in Thoreau's woods." Fleming quoted her favorite Walden line. "'However mean your life is, meet it and live it; do not shun it and call it hard names.'"

"You've got to be kidding me."

"I know. Thoreau was kind of weird. But he had some smart ideas."

Eric let out a very unsalesmanlike grunt. Fleming half-expected him to point out her inability to actually walk in the woods, but either the late hour or the promise of a cash sale inspired the man to hold his tongue.

"Can you help me? I just want to rest one foot on the ground for a moment."

"Fine. But then can we go back and write up the sale?"

She nodded. "After I'm done here, you can do anything you like."

He dutifully climbed out, and as he was circling the van, Fleming reached into the back where her chair rested on the lift, the duffel still draped on the handle.

When he opened the door and offered his hand to assist her, she almost felt bad about greeting him with the business side of a shotgun.

"Hands up. Back away from the van."

Eric stared, his mouth open. "What the—"

"Just do it, Eric."

His face radiated more petulance than fear. "But you're hand-icapped! Handicapped people don't steal!"

"I'm in an affirmative action program. It gives criminal opportunities to the disabled. Throw me your cell phone."

He didn't move.

Fleming pumped the weapon, the sound making Eric jump back a foot. She'd removed the loaded shell earlier because nothing got people's attention quite like the *cha-chink* of a shotgun shuck.

"Sweet Jesus!"

"Down on your knees." Fleming had an idea. "No, wait. First take off your pants and underwear. Then get down on your knees."

Eric turned even whiter. "Please don't shoot me in the rec-tum. I don't want a rubber cork prosthesis."

"I'm not going to do that. I just need something to wear after you change my diaper."

"Oh...no...oh God..."

"That's nothing. Next I'm going to take your legs. There's a doctor downstate who will transplant them onto mine. Yours aren't too hairy, are they?"

"My legs! You can't!"

Wow, this guy was stupid.

"I'm just doing this to delay you, Eric. Keep you from knock-ing on the doors of one of the houses we passed and begging for help. Now take 'em off."

Eric pulled off his slacks, and then his boxers, standing naked, his shirttails hanging limp against white skin while one hand attempted to retain his pride.

"Now dance for me," Fleming said.

"What?"

"Dance to make me feel like a whole woman."

Eric moved his feet, shaking his bony hips in some offbeat, white-boy rhythm. When Fleming felt she'd sufficiently humiliated him, she blew him a kiss, set down the gun, shifted the van into gear, and got the hell out of there, leaving Eric slack-jawed in her rearview mirror. She probably should have killed him. It would be safer. But as idiotic as the man was, she had no taste for ending him.

Finding an area remote enough to strand Eric had forced her to drive farther than she'd planned. It took even longer to wind her way back to Waltham and the interstate, dumping Eric's pants and cell phone on the way, less the cash from his wallet. Eventually the scenery started looking familiar. She found her way to I-90 West, then I-85, and made her way south, watching for police the whole way.

# Chandler

*"You're only as good as the company you keep," The Instructor said. "But sometimes you need to be bad."*

We'd driven the stolen SUV in uneasy silence for almost two hundred miles before Hammett finally spoke.

"So, what's your number?"

"My number?"

She put her bare feet up on the dashboard and wiggled her toes. Her nails were painted red. "When I was a teenager, your number was the number of guys you slept with. After Hydra, it was the number of guys you killed."

Nice.

"I don't want to talk to you, Hammett."

"About your numbers?"

"About anything."

"Because you know my number is higher on both counts."

The previous silence hadn't been pleasant, my head swarming with negative thoughts, but this conversation didn't seem like an improvement.

"I'm sure yours are higher, Hammett. And I don't want to hear—"

"One hundred and sixty, and two hundred and eleven."

"I told you I—" I did a double take. "What?"

"One hundred and sixty," Hammett repeated. "And two hundred and eleven."

I had no idea how to respond to that. Both numbers were so high I had trouble believing them. But Hammett seemed nonchalant, and neither her voice nor her body language indicated she was lying.

"Do you want to know which are sex and which are deaths?" she asked.

"No. I want to go back to us not talking."

"Fine."

We rolled over the Ohio border, as evidenced by the sign welcoming us, and I checked the gas gauge. Still a quarter tank left. Behind me the sun was setting, bright enough to make me flip the dimmer switch on the rearview mirror. I could still smell the gas station tuna sandwiches we'd eaten hours ago, their plastic wrap balled up in the cup holder. I cracked the window, letting in some fresh air and some noise from the wind.

"The one-sixty were hits," Hammett said.

"What? Jesus."

"I know. I can't believe I slept with more than two hundred people."

"I meant the hits, Hammett."

"It's weird you're focusing on the deaths, and not the sex partners."

"That number is astonishing, too. Can you even remember all the guys?"

"They weren't all guys." She smirked, then winked. "And yes, I remember every one. Every death, too. Except those weren't all one-on-one. Well, technically, neither was all the sex. But the deaths, more than half were from bombing an embassy. Also, a lot were on vacation."

"You kill people on vacation?"

"No. I'm talking about the sex again. After a hit I like to take a few weeks off, unwind. I find that I'm really horny after an op. I go through partners like Kleenex. Are you like that?"

I was, except for the multiple-partners thing. But I didn't feel a need to share that with her. Hammett continued, not needing any prodding.

"Before I killed my shrink, he said my hypersexuality could be due to the abuse when I was a kid." Hammett wiggled her toes and began picking at a nail. "But I think that's crazy. Sexual abuse doesn't make you more sexual. It makes you hate sex. It took me a while to get over that."

What was going unsaid hung in the air like the cigarette odor after a poker party. I didn't want to talk about her past abuse. I didn't want to talk to her, period. But when someone opens up to you like that, what are you supposed to do? Ignore it? Pretend it wasn't said, and all is right and rosy in the world?

She could have been lying to get my sympathy. It would be pretty low, but Hammett was pretty low in general.

Yet, there was an undeniable ring of truth about it. I remembered my childhood. It had been grim. Add sexual abuse to the mix, there was no telling how I would have turned out.

Or maybe I knew that answer and didn't want to think about it.

"I know we hate each other," Hammett said. "But since we're working together, it can't hurt to know how we tick."

"If you're even telling the truth."

"Fair enough. But we both know I am."

Ten more miles passed in silence.

"Was it your stepfather?" I finally asked.

She nodded. "Started on my twelfth birthday. Went on for two years."

"Then you got away from him?"

"Then I killed him. Funny. He was my first sex, and my first murder."

"Hammett, that...that's not sex. That's molestation."

"I know. I'm a victim, Chandler, not an idiot. But like it or not, he was my first. On both counts. Want to hear something really fucked up? It was so bad, I disassociated myself from it. Pretended I had an older sister named Rebecca, and she was the one being abused. And me, Betsy, I watched what was happening, but it didn't hurt me because it wasn't me."

I didn't know what to say. While I knew Hammett was a psychopath, I couldn't help but feel sorry for Betsy.

"That which does not kill you makes you bitter. Stronger, too, I guess. But I would have preferred getting that strength some other way, like in the gym, or playing an organized sport. You don't list *rape* on your college application as a character builder."

"Are you..." I wasn't sure how to put it.

"Over it? Sometimes I think so. Other times, not. I've done worse to people. A lot worse. You were never...?"

"No."

I hadn't had a happy childhood. With the foster homes after my parents' deaths, the bastard who had eventually adopted me, and my sadistic boyfriend Cory taking me along on his killing spree when I was fourteen, I'd had a few hurdles to jump in my young life. But I'd never experienced what Hammett had. Or more accurately, what Betsy had.

"But you were raped," Hammett said. "By The Instructor."

I thought back to training, his offer to me, and a bad taste hovered at the back of my mouth. "I...It wasn't rape. It was consensual."

"He didn't come into your room and force himself on you?"

"No. He told me a sex drive was healthy and normal, and I could use him if I needed it."

Hammett snorted. "And you took him up on it."

"Yeah."

"I didn't. I laughed in his face and called him a pervert. I was right, I guess. A few weeks later, he came at me when I was sleeping."

"That's…Jesus…"

Hammett shrugged. "Wasn't the worst part of Hydra training. Not by a long shot. In fact, crazy as it sounds, it got me over my fear of sex."

That was a lot to process. I let her words sink in, nothing but the hum of tires on pavement filling the space between us.

"Shocked?" Hammett said. I could feel her watching me out of the corner of her eye.

I was, although I probably shouldn't have been. But that wasn't the reason for my silence.

"I don't understand."

"Understand? What is there to understand?"

I glanced from the highway for a moment and focused on her. "How could you work for him afterward?"

Hammett looked at me, her expression puzzled. "You know what Hydra was all about, right? What The Instructor did?"

I brought my eyes back to the road.

"He made us fearless, Chandler. We are badass motherfuckers."

I shook my head, although even as I was doing it, I recognized it was pointless to deny what she was saying. Although I'd never felt fearless. Not exactly.

"We're weapons. We use our bodies to kill people. Sometimes, in order to create the opportunity to kill them, we have to sleep with them. You've slept with targets."

I had. And I didn't want to discuss it. I didn't want to think about it at all.

"Don't tell me you're weird about this," Hammett said. "You can't say murder is OK but rape is despicable."

"It is despicable."

"They're both despicable. You've drawn some pretty creative ethical lines in the sand. You can murder some people, but not others. You can torture people, but only if you don't enjoy it. You should never rape, but you can slit a man's throat while he's inside you. You have to see the disconnect there. It's beyond hypocritical. It's self-deceptive."

My instinct was to ignore her, to figuratively plug my ears with my fingers and sing la-la-la-la. She didn't know anything about me or my life. Hers had been different. Very different. She'd been through things as a child and with The Instructor—life-altering things—that I hadn't.

We weren't the same at all.

But I couldn't leave it at that. Because as much as I wanted to tell myself that I couldn't even begin to imagine where she was coming from, the truth was, like nearly any woman, I could identify with it.

"Hammett…what was done to you…as a kid…"

"I worked it out."

"That was as wrong as wrong can be."

"I said I worked it out. The Instructor, he knew about my past. My last hit with Hydra was a child molester. If there was an award for suffering before death, that guy won it. The things I did to him…I had to stop twice and puke."

I noticed the tears spiking Hammett's eyelashes, even though her voice stayed steady. She turned away and looked out the window.

"When he finally died, I got his hard drive off his computer. List of all his pedophile buddies. So I looked them all up, one at a time. Made sure when they got to hell, it was with their dicks stuffed in their mouths."

She drew herself up in her seat and stared straight ahead, her lips pressed into something between hard resolve and a smile. "I guess you could say I went rogue."

The Instructor had told me a little about this a few days ago, the first time I'd seen him since training. In light of recent events, my biggest surprise was that his story that day had any truth to it at all. I'd assumed every word was a lie.

"And you recruited your sisters—"

"*Our* sisters. The Instructor sent them after me." Her expression morphed into a full smile. "I won them over, which forced The Instructor to see things my way."

"And he brought you in as an independent contractor."

"On the London thing. Yes."

"He manipulated you," I said, waiting to see how she would respond when the psychoanalysis spotlight was turned on her.

"Hmm?"

"The Instructor. He knew that pedophile hit would be personal. Knew it would send you over the edge."

Hammett laughed, abrupt like a bark. "Never thought about that before. I suppose it's possible. Why not? That son of a bitch knew everything about me. Better than I knew myself."

"He used you."

"Yeah. Sure seems like it now. When he started his little side project, he arranged for me to break with Hydra so I'd be there to run it for him. Makes sense."

"His little side project was to discredit the president. And when that didn't work, to kill him and get the VP in power. Does he own the VP?"

"From what I've surmised, yes." She shook her head, chuckling. "The man is a piece of shit, but you gotta admire his style."

"So how did you go from killing child molesters to nuking London?"

"The money was good."

"Seriously? Genocide is OK if you're paid enough?"

"Your hypocrisy is showing again, Chandler. You get paid for killing one person, and that's fine. But getting paid more to kill a lot of people violates some code? That's bullshit. Either you kill for money, or you don't. Either life is sacred, or it isn't. Everything else is shades of gray."

We drove the next ten miles without talking. Much as I didn't want to understand Hammett, or her insane motivation, I felt like I was starting to. That was bad, because understanding led to empathy, which would get in the way when it came time to kill her. She'd had some tragedy in her life. But she'd also tried to kill millions. People like Hammett shouldn't be allowed free rein. Even if she had been manipulated.

"So what's your number?" Hammett asked. "Are you even in double digits?"

"Let's not talk anymore."

"Well, shit, let's do something. We got another five hours in the car. If we can't pretend to be human beings, then at least put on the radio."

I put on the radio. Hammett fussed with the dial for a few miles, unable to listen to an entire song straight through. And much as I didn't want to, I found myself totaling up numbers in my head. I wasn't in danger of breaking either of her records, and at my pace I wouldn't ever break them unless I lived for another hundred years. But I was easily in double digits in both categories. And unlike my sister, my sanctions far outnumbered the men I'd slept with.

I wondered if that was a good thing or a bad thing.

Hammett switched off the radio, seemingly unable to decide upon a station. We drove another thirty miles, then pulled off the highway and stopped at a gas station. I kept my head down, mindful of pump cameras, and Hammett paid cash and returned with two black coffees and some questionable-looking fruit.

"I like apples, figured you must, too."

I did, but instead of acknowledging it, I said, "We aren't the same, Hammett."

"I know. You're boring, and a grump ass, and an idiot, and a hypocrite, and I'm more fun and have bigger tits."

"If by *fun* you mean *psychotic*, I agree." I pulled back onto the interstate.

"You say I'm psychotic. But I don't hallucinate, I'm not catatonic, and I don't have delusions or thought disorders."

"You fired a nuclear missile at England. I'd say that qualifies as a thought disorder."

"You just can't get over that. I was following orders, doing a job. And it was a political move, not personal. The dead would have been collateral damage."

"I think that satisfies the *delusion* requirement as well."

Hammett bit into an apple. "Point is, I didn't nuke anyone. It isn't fair to blame me for something I didn't finish."

I bridled at that. "Of course it's fair! The very fact that you'd even think such a thing is proof that you have a severe mental disorder."

"According to your boyfriend, you're just as bad as I am." Hammett lowered her voice to imitate Lund. "*You ended a man's life, and felt nothing at all.* That sounds pretty psychotic to me. Pot, meet kettle."

I grabbed the other apple from her lap, realized I didn't want Hammett picking out my food for me, then set it back down.

"What?" she said. "I'm going to poison you while you're driving at seventy-five miles an hour? I think that satisfies your *delusion* requirement."

She was right, and I took the apple again, polishing it on my shirt. "We're done talking."

"You've said that already."

"I mean it this time."

"You didn't mean it when you said it before?"

I realized that was a ploy to keep me talking, so I didn't respond. We ate our fruit in silence. Mine had a large bruise on one side, and I wondered if Hammett gave it to me on purpose. Then I wondered if she was correct, and I was acting delusional.

Did delusional people know they were delusional?

Hammett opened her window and tossed out the core. When she closed it again, she said, "I want to be the one who kills him."

"The Instructor?"

"Yeah."

Now that I could completely understand. "He's all yours on one condition."

"Name it."

"No talking for the rest of the trip."

Hammett was blessedly silent until we reached Illinois.

# Julie

*Beep...beep...beep...*

The familiar sound of a heart monitor woke her.

Julie didn't have to open her eyes to know she was in a hospital bed. She could feel the flimsy gown, smell the clash of scents, a touch of hospital mixed with a large dose of warehouse. Her mouth was dry and her head still rang from Earnshaw's fist.

She remembered being awake when they'd taken her from the boat and loaded her into a van. The inside of the van looked more like an ambulance, with medical equipment and a stretcher in the back. But her memories felt like they belonged to someone else. Slippery and hard to grab hold of.

Julie forced her eyes open and saw concrete walls. Her wrists and ankles bound to the bed frame. She was tired, so tired she couldn't keep her eyelids open, and she knew it was from sedatives dripping from the IV tube snaking into the back of her hand.

Plum Island. Julie knew she was back. Yet somehow it wasn't the same. Maybe it wasn't Plum Island, since Chandler had destroyed the lab there. But wherever she was, she wasn't the same girl. This time, she knew what was going on. She knew what the people who took her wanted.

And most of all, she knew she was powerless to stop them.

# Fleming

*"Plans backfire,"* The Instructor *said. "Learn to improvise."*

In New Jersey, Fleming switched license plates off a minivan parked outside of a strip club. Skirting Philadelphia, she began to feel fatigued, and increasingly vulnerable. She stopped at a gas station to top off the tank, made use of the ladies' room, and bought some fruit and energy drinks to get her through the long journey she had to go. Then it was back on the road.

Normally, Fleming enjoyed being alone. Solitude allowed for contemplation, self-reflection. Her life with Hydra had been stretches of inactivity punctuated by life-or-death situations. The downtime allowed her to recharge for the periods of intensity.

But these last few days had been all about intensity, and Fleming couldn't shut her mind off. Though exhausted, her brain was working overtime, trying to plan six steps ahead so nothing went wrong. That wasn't easy. Each move required anticipation of counter-moves, and that led to hundreds of variations, the vast majority of which ended with Fleming and her sisters dead or imprisoned.

She couldn't handle being locked up again. But the more she dwelled on the plan, the more convoluted and impossible it became. Maybe it would be smarter to run away and hide on some island, or in some third-world country. Plastic surgery, laying low, staying off the grid.

But she knew that wouldn't work. Every time she heard a noise at night, she would imagine it to be special-ops assassins. Every man flirting with her in a bar would be a spy. Every time a phone rang, it was to detonate a bomb under her chair.

Fleming was paranoid for a reason. She knew what it was like to be hunted by the government, because she used to be the one hunting people. And no one could disappear forever, unless the government wanted them to.

The only way to live a long, happy life was to clean up this gigantic mess, no matter how impossible it seemed. Or else she might as well just pull over and eat her shotgun right now.

Fleming reached the outskirts of Baltimore just as the sun was starting to rise. By that time she would have killed a dozen people for a single espresso, but she forced herself to drive past at least six Starbucks and head straight to the address they'd found for the robotics technician, Bradley Milton.

The neighborhood was quiet, upscale condominium communities, fenced gardens, ample green space. People jogged and walked dogs and biked, and Fleming even saw a Rollerblader, surprised the fad was still around. She turned into the complex parking lot, no attendant or gate, and had just located his unit in the maze of buildings when she saw the man himself, travel mug in hand, heading for his car.

He was lean with some muscle tone, and taller than she'd surmised from the photo she'd called up on the Internet. Medium-brown hair and brown eyes, he sported black-rimmed glasses and a rumpled look that screamed nerd cliché. Fleming was willing to bet he was wearing a pocket protector under his jacket.

She'd hoped to be set up to intercept him before he left for work this morning. Seeing that he was already climbing into his dark blue Volvo, she was obviously too late. Planning a kidnapping was a sensitive thing. Pulling it off all by her lonesome without getting hurt, injuring Milton, or pulling the police into the situation would take an artist. A *con* artist.

She'd done it before, most recently to poor Eric, and she could do it again. But she couldn't do it on the fly. Not with her original plan. She would have to figure out another approach.

Fleming circled the parking lot and pulled back out to the street. She'd done some digging on the lab where he worked before she'd left for Baltimore, and the prospect of grabbing him there wasn't good. Cameras covering the parking lot and twenty-four-hour security at the entrance would make it difficult to get near him and almost impossible to get away clean. Once he reached his lab, she'd be out of luck until he made the return trip home.

Unless she could interrupt his morning commute.

Fleming turned into a side street and pivoted into a quick U-turn. What she was about to attempt was risky. Maybe downright crazy.

She pulled up to the stop sign and halted, then lowered her window an inch, the dawn twitter of birds mixing with the low groan of the minivan's engine, and something else.

An approaching vehicle and the hum of tires.

Heart thrumming in her chest despite her efforts to control its pace, she waited for a glimpse of Milton's car starting its arc around the curve in the boulevard.

He drove past, and she pulled out, falling in behind him.

Causing a fender bender was tricky. If she hit the gas too hard, if his vehicle was moving too fast, if her timing wasn't right, she wouldn't be solving a problem, she'd be creating a bigger one.

After so many years in the Midwest, driving on the narrower streets here in the East, with tighter turns and no shoulder to speak of, felt strange. Add to that the new car and controls she wasn't familiar with, and she was hesitant to try anything while they were moving. Too risky. She needed a stop sign or a light.

Light after light turned green in front of Bradley Milton's car, as if the man was blessed. Fleming was beginning to think she was out of opportunities, when the last light at the base of a hill near the laboratory turned yellow. Then red.

Milton's brake lights flared.

"That's it, sweetie. Slow down. Nice and safe."

Fleming slowed as well, not wanting to cause her scientist whiplash, but while he came to a halt, she kept her van rolling. She had just begun to brace herself for the impact, when she noticed a car to the right at the intersection.

A car sporting black-and-white paint and a light bar on the roof.

She hit the brake, her van jolting to a stop as the police car made its way across the intersection, and Fleming kissed her last chance at grabbing Milton this morning good-bye.

# Scarlett

*"After Hydra Deux training, you'll be assigned a partner," The Instructor said. "I've handpicked this person, to complement your own skill set, and to compensate for your weaknesses. On your own, you're formidable. Together, you'll be unstoppable."*

Scarlett glanced at Rhett sitting next to her, noting his strong chin peppered with a day's worth of stubble, deep-set blue eyes, ruffled blond hair, brown T-shirt hiding the body of an underwear model, and well-worn black Stetson hat, and she wanted to shoot the son of a bitch. She hated his Southern drawl, hated how he grinned and flirted all the time, hated his whole Duke Boys demeanor. He was a competent operative, and could be relied on to watch her back, but whenever he opened his mouth she felt like knocking all of his teeth out.

Unfortunately, no one else on her team was any better. Tristan was a muscle head who had the personality of the side of beef he resembled. And Heathcliff was a cyclopic lothario with a seriously overinflated opinion of his abilities. Scarlett wouldn't have wanted either one as a partner. In fact, she couldn't think of any man in the world she wanted to be teamed up with. The only use for anyone with a Y chromosome was as breeding stock, and only if they weren't allowed to talk or move.

Lest Scarlett consider herself a castrating lesbian bitch, she didn't like the women on her team any better. Isolde was an anorexic little S&M emo freak who needed a bullet in the head, and Earnshaw was a disgusting, steroid-chomping beast who was a worse mouth breather than any of the men.

But then, what could one hope for in a group of professional assassins?

"You got that look again," Rhett said, the words slipping out lazily as he tucked a toothpick into the corner of his mouth. "The one where it looks like you're sniffing manure."

"Fancy that."

"Frown lines in the corners of your mouth. And that little crease between your eyebrows. Shame for a sweet filly like you to get all wrinkly."

"Unlike you. Your face is so craggy and sunbaked I could cut it off and make a handbag."

"What's the problem? On your period?"

She batted her eyelashes and gave him a fake smile. "Yes, Rhett. I'm menstruating. That's why I'm unable to find you charming. It has nothing to do with you being a sexist, revolting prick."

Scarlett turned her attention back to the computer. She was going state by state, accessing DMV records, looking for new vehicle purchases. Most specifically, vans customized to be wheelchair accessible. It was a long shot, and the shittiest detail to pull. Heath and Earnshaw were on their way to Mexico. Tristan and Izzy to Canada. Their missions were interesting. Scarlett's sucked the farts out of a dead crack whore. But since the lighthouse, she and Rhett had been holed up in this shitty, two-and-a-half-star motel, first logging time on airport security cameras in Maine, New Hampshire, and Vermont, using facial recognition software to search for Chandler and her sisters, and now stuck with this tedious vehicle search.

A damn shame. Both Mexico City and Toronto were a lot more exciting than being stuck here.

"You know, I thought I won the lottery when I got partnered with you," Rhett said. Her insult hadn't fazed him one iota. "Poor ol' Heath got stuck with a former Olympic wrassler, and Tristan got that skinny Goth girl who cuts on herself, but I landed a full-blooded, good-looking lady with curves in all the right places. I thought we could have ourselves some fun while working together. After all, you got the same needs I do."

"True. But I also have standards."

Rhett grunted, his version of laughing. "Why do you hate men so much, Scarlett?"

"I don't hate men, Rhett. But I don't like you. Luckily, I don't have to like you to work with you."

"Who do you like?"

"Ashley. I love Ashley."

"A girl? That's hot."

"Idiot." Truth was she really didn't like anyone, including herself much of the time. But this wasn't the appropriate time for arguing, or for psychoanalysis. There were still twelve states left to search, and it wasn't going any faster with John Wayne staring over her shoulder.

"Why don't you use the other laptop, do a stolen vehicle search?" Scarlett said, mostly to get Rhett away from her.

"You know, darlin', if you let me, I could make you feel real good."

That prompted a grunt from Scarlett. "No doubt. Put your big .45 in your mouth and pull the trigger, and I'll have multiple orgasms."

Rhett's eyes narrowed. "Lady, you're just plum mean sometimes. You know Izzy and Tristan are getting it on. I think the big guy loves her. And I heard even Earnshaw and Heath had a little one-on-one time."

"That's disgusting."

"No, baby. It's natural. We got a big ol' bed in the other room, and could work out all our frustrations there. Who knows? You might even wind up liking it."

Scarlett turned to him again. She relaxed her face and lowered her eyelids, making her voice husky with a hint of Southern belle. "You know what I'd really like, Rhett?"

"Name it."

"For you to fucking do a fucking stolen vehicle search."

He frowned. "Plum meaner than a snake in a hot skillet. You sure you weren't born with one of them African killer beehives up your bottom?"

She patted his cheek, hard. "You'll never get close enough to check."

Rhett stood up and stretched his hands over his head—probably to show Scarlett his six-pack abs when his shirt lifted up—then plodded in his stupid-ass cowboy boots to the other side of the desk, where another laptop awaited.

He was blessedly silent for fifteen minutes, then let out a hoot. An honest-to-Christ hoot.

"I found our little disabled buddy. Believe it or not, she stole a van in Massachusetts. Even made the news."

Rhett swiveled around his laptop, showing her an article from the *Waltham News Tribune.* A woman matching Fleming's description had taken a handicapped-accessible van for a test-drive and turned a shotgun on the salesman.

She should have killed him.

"Eric Brockney," Scarlett read the man's name. "How about we pay him a visit?"

"You pack, I'll drive."

"I'll drive. And you can pack your own shit, I'll pack mine."

Scarlett smiled. It might not be a big lead, but it got her out of this damn motel.

The smile faded when she considered a five-hour car drive with Rhett. Maybe she should let him drive, and she could try to get some sleep. But sleep would be impossible, because when Rhett drove, he hummed country and western songs, the same three over and over again.

Christ, she hated him.

"I'll make you a deal," Scarlett said. "I'll do my best to be nicer to you. And I'll even let you drive. But you aren't allowed to hum."

"Hum?"

"You hum songs while you're driving, and it makes me nuts."

Rhett rubbed his chin, then stuck out his hand. "Deal."

He held out his end of the deal for eight minutes before he started to hum. Scarlett poked him, raising an eyebrow. Rhett stopped, then started again eleven minutes later. She hit him in the arm. He lasted eighteen minutes, then the humming kicked in, and she made him pull over and let her drive, swearing to never make another deal with the asshole ever again.

# Fleming

*"When carrying out an assignment, there is no room for personal feelings," said The Instructor. "Sometimes good people get hurt. Sometimes evil people are rewarded. None of that is for you to decide. Just keep your eye on the objective, do your job, and let the universe dictate justice and karma."*

After all the training Fleming had, some might assume she would have developed patience over the years. Unfortunately, it had never been her strong suit. She was an excellent marksman, but the job of sniper, with its long hours of waiting, had never appealed to her. Surveillance had never been a favorite either. She much preferred action. Taking a situation into her own hands. Doing something.

The injury to her legs was the ultimate irony. But though the accident had changed everything about her life, it had never taught her patience. She'd simply transferred her need to be active to the technological end of the job. Inventing, directing Chandler's missions, gathering cyber intelligence. After the accident, she hadn't been able to take a physical role in her work, but she'd found a way to do something all the same.

At the moment, Fleming was convinced that tracking the movements of a nerdy, work-obsessed scientist had to be the most boring assignment of her career.

She checked her watch. It had taken her hours to set up. Unable to trust any of the official safe houses in the city, Fleming had rented a storefront in a nearby suburb. First month, plus deposit, for fifteen hundred cash to a harried realtor who wasn't even sure which set of keys opened it up.

Situated in a strip mall in a portion of the city struggling with economic recession, the store had been vacant for nearly a year. Half of the other spaces in the mall were vacant as well, front windows soaped, not much foot traffic to speak of, cheap rent and perfect for her needs. She'd bought a tiny refrigerator, an electric frying pan, air mattresses, and sleeping bags. She'd stocked the place with all the food and supplies they'd need, including another computer with a Wi-Fi package. A local Radio Shack sold her a several protoboards of various sizes; a multimeter; a pinhole camera; a mini microphone; earbuds; crystal oscillators; a soldering iron and accessories; and assorted wires, capacitors, resistors, transistors, diodes, coils, integrated circuits, and batteries. Finally, a trip to a hardware superstore got her fifteen meters of steel cable, wire clamps, and some heavy-duty padlocks. Last on her list was a handful of really nice fountain pens, wide Montblancs.

Since late afternoon, she'd been ready and waiting in a park she'd noticed this morning while following Bradley Milton to work. Perched on the crest of a hill overlooking the lab, the park gave her the perfect vantage point. So there she'd been ever since, strapping on her leg braces so she'd be ready, then sketching a schematic on graph paper for the device she and Bradley would build. Fleming was terrific with electronics, both the design and the construction. She designed and etched her own circuit boards. But she wasn't an expert in robotics, particularly of the miniature variety.

So she doodled, and waited, and punched components into her protoboard to get an idea of the circuit needed, and waited, and searched the Internet for schematics and supplies, and waited, and ate a 7-Eleven tuna on wheat, and waited.

The sun dipped in the sky. Employees left for the day; only Milton's car and one other remained in the lot. The cleaning crew arrived. Milton had left for work at dawn and was still there at nearly ten o'clock at night.

This guy really needed to get a life.

As if she was one to judge. Fleming sighed, looking at the pages of schematics she'd drawn, and the patchwork circuit she'd created on the protoboard. After her accident, fieldwork had been impossible. The Instructor urged her to explore the tech end of spycraft, and with some extra training Fleming discovered she was a prodigy at electronics and computers. Her transceiver designs were cutting-edge, her encryption codes extremely sophisticated, and she was able to pour all of the frustration and pain her legs caused her into intellectual pursuits, which, if she hadn't been working for Uncle Sam, could have given her patents that made her extremely wealthy.

Funny, that. What turned out to be the biggest tragedy in Fleming's life also gave birth to her biggest gift.

Given a week, Fleming could have taught herself robotics and built the device herself. But there was a ticking clock. Once The Instructor released the video of the president's death, Fleming wouldn't be able to show her face anywhere in the world. They had to get intel immediately, and that meant getting help. Even if the help was unwilling.

Another half hour passed before there was movement below. Light streamed from a door in the lab, and a tall, thin man stepped into the parking lot.

*Finally.*

Fleming started the van and maneuvered her way back to the street. Having followed the scientist to work in the morning, Fleming knew his route, and her vantage point in the park brought her to the condo well before him. All the parking spaces were filled, so she pulled the van alongside a row of bushes near the mailboxes, in clear view of unit 140, and the sole empty parking space bearing that number.

Hitting the controls on the dash, she opened the driver's rear sliding door and brought the lift carrying her chair down to pavement level. She then lifted the paper bag from the backseat and opened her door and the van's sliding door behind her. By the time Milton's Volvo turned into the lot and pulled into his parking space, she was ready.

Positioning a crutch on the pavement, she lurched forward, tearing the paper bag and letting its contents spill across the asphalt. Four apples, five cans of pineapple, and a cantaloupe rolled toward a startled Bradley Milton. The cantaloupe came to a rest against his shoe. Two of the cans disappeared under his car.

"Oh no!" Fleming floundered from the van struggling to balance on one crutch. She was painfully aware she looked pathetic, wobbling around on the crutch, which is why she never used them, preferring her chair. At least the stark reminder of never really walking again worked to her advantage this time. She didn't have to do much acting. And after all that had happened in the past few days, she easily summoned tears to complete the picture.

Bradley Milton stared at her as if mortified, his hands hanging limp at his sides. "Can I help?"

"I'm so embarrassed."

"Don't be. It's not a big deal. It'll just take me a second." The gangly scientist got down on hands and knees to fish cans out from under his car. His cute little butt in the air, Fleming couldn't help thinking about things other than the mission. Of course she'd keep this strictly professional, but there was nothing wrong with a little fantasizing now and then.

"I'm sorry for causing all this trouble."

He scrambled to his feet, a can in each hand. "No trouble." Looking her straight in the eye, he gave her a smile that seemed refreshingly genuine.

Fleming found herself smiling back. "I'm just so clumsy sometimes."

He glanced at her leg braces, then back up at her face. "Um, that's not true. I mean, I'm sure that's not..."

If she wasn't being tricked by the parking lot lighting, she could swear his cheeks were a touch pink. "It's OK. I'm used to it. Something like dropping groceries is a mishap for most people. For me, it's a disaster." She added a little laugh, designed to put him at ease, but when it came out of her mouth it sounded more flirty than anything.

So sue her. Under that nerdy scientist look, he was downright cute.

Judging from the way he held her eyes, he thought the same about her. "I'm Bradley."

"Thanks, Bradley. I'm Ian."

He canted his eyes down and to the side in the most adorable way. "Nice to meet you, Ian. That's a lovely name. Like the James Bond writer, Ian Fleming."

"He's one of my favorites," Fleming said.

"Mine too. Spy novels are a guilty pleasure of mine."

Fleming had pulled off abductions before. Hell, she'd once been an assassin with skills comparable to Chandler's. But the people she'd kidnapped and killed had been a nasty part of a nasty game. None had been civilians, and the guileless nature of Bradley's introduction, as if he really was just meeting a woman in a parking lot, threw her a little.

Or if she was honest with herself, maybe it was her own reaction that had her a touch flustered. "It's nice to meet you, too, Bradley."

"I've never seen you around here before. Did you recently buy one of the units?"

Fleming was hoping she wouldn't have to answer that question, at least not until he was closer to the van. "Yes. This building." She pointed to the one next to Bradley's.

"Welcome to the complex. I like it here, but I'm not around much. I tend to be a workaholic. What do you do?"

She hadn't pegged him as nosy. But he didn't seem suspicious, just interested. "I'm opening a shop nearby. Computer and electronics repair."

"Really? I design robotics."

"Well, maybe you'll need one repaired someday and come to my shop." She gave him a full-wattage smile.

Bradley held up the cans. "I can carry these in for you. Which unit are you in?"

Fleming had no keys to the building, and she wasn't about to expose her lie. "That's not necessary."

"It's no trouble."

The guy was either an excellent actor, or he was sincerely trying to help. Since acting was not usually part of the science nerd repertoire, she was leaning toward pegging him as simply a nice guy. If she didn't put an end to this conversation soon, she ran the risk of starting to feel guilty for what she was about to put him through.

"I've worked really hard to not think of myself as a burden after the accident. Please, if you'll just set the cans in my lap, I'll take care of the rest."

Milton gave her a sheepish look. "I didn't mean—"

"I know you didn't. Just...I'm sorry."

He held up a can as if to cut off the apology. "Don't worry about it. I understand."

Damn, Fleming thought. He really was a nice guy.

She forced her spine to stiffen. She had to keep her mission front and center in her mind. The fact that Bradley Milton was cute and nice didn't change the reason she was here. And what she had to do.

He finished tracking down the last of her groceries, and when he handed her the cantaloupe, Fleming made sure she touched his fingers when she took it.

"Thank you, Bradley. Just when I thought there were no good men left."

"No trouble. It was really nice to meet you, Ian. I...uh..."

Fleming smiled again. She could tell he was trying to ask her for her number, or maybe to his place for some coffee.

"Do you have a girlfriend, Bradley? Usually I'm not so bold, but I really think you're cute."

"Really? Thanks. All I have is Sasha. She's a fox."

"So it's a friends with benefits thing?"

"What? No! I mean, she's really a fox. A domesticated silver fox."

"I've heard of those. Bred in Russia. They act like dogs."

"Sort of somewhere between dogs and cats. Sasha is very lovable. I feel bad I work such long hours, but she likes to watch TV while I'm gone. Nature shows mostly, although she likes Jon Stewart for some reason."

"She's a liberal?"

Bradley laughed. "Possibly. Would you like to meet her?"

"Some other time, perhaps? It's really late now. But…Can I get your phone number?"

"Uh, sure."

He fumbled for his wallet, and took out a bent business card that must have been in there for months, maybe years.

"I'll call you tomorrow, Bradley. Maybe we can catch a late dinner."

"I'd like that, Ian. Nice to meet you."

He offered his hand, and Fleming took it, holding for longer than necessary. Then he went off to his building, and she pretended to go to hers.

When Bradley was out of sight, Fleming went back to his car and slashed two of his tires.

# Chandler

*"Fear is natural, but it can also be deceptive," said The Instructor. "Make sure the threats you see are real, because if you're focused on the wrong one, the one you don't see could kill you."*

Thanks to a blown tire in the middle of nowhere Pennsylvania and a nap that went overtime in a rest area off the Ohio tollway, it was nighttime by the time we reached Chicago. Our business postponed until office hours tomorrow, Hammett and I headed for the bland camouflage of the suburbs. After a couple of amazing burgers at a place called The Assembly, we drove halfway around the world to find a liquor store so Hammett could pick up a bottle of bourbon. Then we checked into a hotel near the restaurant.

We'd barely stepped in the door, when Hammett said, "Let's go out, get laid."

I stripped down to my underwear and sat down on one of the double beds. Each bed sported two pillows, and I was glad to see it. The perfect evening for me involved jamming one of those pillows over my head and muffling out the sound of her constant jabber.

"Come on. It would be fun. Who knows how long we'll have before The Instructor releases the video and we're made into instant hermits. In the meantime, we should go out, blow off steam. We could pick up a couple of hotties, and if they don't give us at least three orgasms each, we'll gut them like the pigs they are."

I might have found the comment funny, *if* I knew for sure that she was joking. "You really think that's a good idea?"

"It might keep me alive. Being with you all this time is boring me to death."

"Drink your booze and let me sleep." Of course, I didn't intend to sleep.

She snapped on the TV and leaned back with her bottle of Blanton's. Much as I didn't like her, she had good taste.

I shimmied between the sheets. The bed wasn't fancy, but it felt good. Even though we'd gotten some rest in the SUV, I was still fighting exhaustion, and I wondered how Hammett could even joke about going out.

If she was joking.

Still, lying down was nice, and I rolled to my side, my back to Hammett, and slipped my shotgun under my pillow. As tired as I was, I didn't trust my psycho sister, and I wasn't going to nod off, giving her the opportunity to break my neck in my sleep.

I listened to Hammett flip through the vast array of channels at least five times. Finally she set down her bottle on the bedside table and switched off the light and television.

I stared into the darkness, wondering how Fleming was doing in Baltimore, listening to Hammett's breathing slow and fall into a steady rhythm. I ran my fingertips over the reassuring shape of my shotgun. Either she was faking it, or she'd drifted off. I wasn't going to take a chance on which.

If she moved, I would know it.

And I would take her out.

# Years Ago...

Her codename was Chandler, and when she was ten years old, she spent a hot summer afternoon picking out her parents' caskets. They were lovely caskets, polished hardwood, cream velvet inside, and costing much more than a pair of matching boxes destined to be buried in the ground should. She clutched her caseworker's hand, a gentle older woman named Elise who smelled like cinnamon and Aqua Net, and tried not to notice how still the air was in the funeral parlor, how cold, like the inside of a refrigerator, like the chill of icy water, like the depths of a tomb.

Two days later, she was in that same funeral parlor, and even though Elise had made sure she was wearing a sweater over her dark blue dress, she still felt chilled to the bone. She wondered if she would be warm if she curled up in the box beside her mother's body. She wondered if the stern-looking funeral director would yell at her if she tried.

After the funeral, a group of ladies from a church she never attended served lunch. Ham sandwiches, potato salad, brownies with thick chocolate frosting. There weren't many people at the funeral, the neighbors, some folks who said they were from her parents' work, some others who seemed friendly and talked to her in soft voices. Most stayed for lunch, and from the look of it, most found the food plenty good.

To Chandler, it tasted like sawdust, and she wished more than anything that she could carry the brownie outside and eat by herself.

The lunch seemed to drone on forever, and Chandler occupied herself watching the handful of kids play some sort of secret game while casting sad glances her way. They invited her to join in, but she refused, shaking her head. Then Elise took her hand again and loaded her into her shabby car and dropped her off at a house with a tree fort in the backyard and introduced her to the Blasniks, her new foster family, whose house was perfect and homey and friendly, and the parents and kids looked at her with sympathy in their eyes.

The little girl ran away from the Blasniks, and the Johnsons after that. Some of the families were nice. Some weren't. It didn't matter either way. She didn't belong with any of them.

But before she could escape from the Ryans, Elise visited her again, this time to take her to the man who'd adopted her. The man who would be her new daddy.

Driving through a neighborhood of houses, one bigger than the next, Chandler sat belted in the backseat, looking at the Christmas lights and pretending to listen to Elise's assurances that she would like her new home, and that even though her new daddy didn't have a wife nor other children, he would love her and take care of her as if she were his own.

"Here it is!" Elise said in a false-cheery voice as she pulled the car into a short, sloped driveway.

The house was huge, with double garage doors facing the road like the imposing gate of a castle. The rest of the house looked fortress-like as well; big, solid, and built of red brick, it was devoid of twinkle lights or evergreen garlands or a menorah. Peering up at it, Chandler felt a shiver climb up her spine.

Elise turned off the engine and twisted to face Chandler. Her eyebrows pulled together at the top, her forehead wrinkling with lines of concern. "You have to stay at this house. Promise me, OK? Because if you don't, I'm afraid I'm not going to be able to find another family who will take you."

Chandler dropped her gaze to her hands. She didn't want to stay here or anywhere else. She wanted to go back home. She wanted her parents to be alive again, loving her, taking care of her.

"Promise me, sweetheart."

Chandler moved her head in something Elise might interpret as a nod.

"Good girl," Elise said, then climbed out of the car and waited until Chandler did the same.

The air was cold and smelled of fresh snow. Chandler's feet felt heavy, but she forced them to move, following Elise up the walk to the front door. Elise pressed the doorbell, and chimes rang through the house, low and imposing and echoing like church bells. A moment passed and the door swung wide.

A man filled the space. Tall and with square shoulders, he stared at her, his eyes hard under bushy brows. Hair short and face clean-shaven, he looked as if he was accustomed to wearing a uniform. Something with gold braids on the shoulders.

"You're late," he said to Elise. "This is the girl?"

"Yes."

"Fine."

He stepped to the side, leaving space in the doorway, and Elise pushed Chandler into the marble foyer.

The house was huge and castle-like on the inside, too. Decorated in stark white, grays, and black, it felt cold as snow. One arched doorway led into a formal white living room, another a kitchen, another an office furnished in dark wood and leather. Nowhere did she see any decorations for Christmas, or anything that could be considered a room where a child would be allowed.

The man started to close the door before Elise had a chance to step inside. "Leave us, please. I need to have a talk with the girl, set some rules."

"Very well." Without another glance in Chandler's direction, Elise pivoted and walked down the steps.

Tears welled in Chandler's eyes. She'd never thought of Elise as a comforting woman, she'd never liked her much at all, but she'd been the only recurring person in Chandler's life since the accident. Seeing her walk away, being forced to stay in this hard place, was more than Chandler could take.

The man closed the door, blocking Elise from Chandler's sight, then he turned back to face her. "Are you crying?"

Chandler swiped at her eyes with the back of one hand.

"You sniveling little bitch. You're crying, aren't you?"

Chandler didn't know what to say. He could see her tears. It seemed stupid to deny them. So she just stood there, looking up at the man, wishing she was someplace else.

He drew his hand back and slapped her.

Her head snapped to the side. Stumbling back, she hit the wall, blobs of light spinning in front of her eyes, heat and pain blooming over her cheek.

"There will be no more of your sniveling. Got that?"

Chandler tried to nod, but her head hurt so badly, she couldn't manage more than a tiny bob.

"You're in my house now, and you will live by my rules. And your first rule is no crying."

Tears still streamed from Chandler's eyes, and try as she might, she couldn't stem the flow. She hoped he wouldn't notice. She hoped he wouldn't hit her again.

"You will call me Father."

Chandler shook her head. This man wasn't her father. Her father was dead, buried in the cemetery alongside her mom.

She thought of Cinderella. It was a childish story, one for little kids far younger than fifth grade, but Cinderella's stepmother was cruel, just like this man. "Stepfather."

"You think you can talk back to me?" He drew back and slapped her again.

She bounced off the wall. Lights whirled around her head once again, and a metallic taste filled her mouth.

"I'm your father. I'm all you have."

"Stepfather."

He hit her again.

This time she slumped to the floor. Cupping her hands over her face, she let the tears flow as hard as they wanted and waited for the next slap.

"You ungrateful little shit. Your first parents coddled you too much. I heard they died because you were homesick. Is that true?"

She wanted to say no, to yell out that it was a lie, but the words stuck in her throat. If she had stayed at camp, if she had been a good girl, if she hadn't called home, begging for Mom and Dad to pick her up, they wouldn't have been on the road that day. They would be alive.

And she could be with them instead of here.

"You're responsible, and you know it. Pitiful. You can't even look me in the eye."

Sobs shook her body. She took her hands away from her face, her palms wet with tears and smeared with blood.

"You're not going to get any coddling here. You're going to get what you deserve. And you're going to be grateful for every scrap."

He was right. About all of it. And right then, she would gladly have him hit her and kick her and beat her until she died. If she was dead, she'd no longer have to face what had happened.

The tragedy she'd caused.

The emptiness she could never fill.

The reality she could never change.

# The White House

President J. Phillip Ratzenberger waited patiently for the Secret Service to do their bug sweep, then closed the door and picked up the phone. Before he dialed the number, he noticed the damn cat hiding under the desk.

"Shoo, Chaz." He poked the cat with the foot of his toe, and it hissed and bounded off. Ratzenberger considered calling in his men to have it removed, and decided to wait until after the call. He punched in the digits, and waited for The Instructor to answer.

"Yes, Mr. President?"

"I asked you to keep me updated."

"I have been. The target is secure. Our teams are proceeding with the amplification of the virus, which should be completed on schedule."

"What of Hydra?"

"Hydra Deux has been able to locate one of the sisters. She should be in custody shortly."

"She'll lead you to the other two?"

"Not likely. She's tough, and has proven adept at staying quiet."

Ratzenberger frowned, then scratched the inside of his left nostril. "What is the threat level of the other two sisters?"

"I would assess it as high."

"Is the story in place?"

"Yes. Awaiting your approval."

Ratzenberger watched as Chaz leaped onto the Resolute desk. He swept the feline off, pushing it back onto the floor.

"Release the video," he told The Instructor. "I want them out of the game."

"Yes, Mr. President. I can imagine your predecessor's cabinet is kissing up to you so they aren't replaced."

Ratzenberger smiled. "Indeed they are. Funny how quickly some people can adjust their attitudes once you become the leader of the free world."

"I want to be Secretary of Defense."

The president laughed. "Well, I'll certainly put you on the short list."

"You misunderstand me, Mr. President. That wasn't a request."

Ratzenberger's grin became a scowl. "Is that a threat? Who are you to give me orders?"

"It isn't an order, or a threat. We're just two powerful men, helping each other. You're in office right now because of me. You're able to carry out your plan to vastly improve the United States because of me."

"You've been well paid for your work."

"I expect to be well paid as Secretary of Defense."

"We'll discuss this later."

"Have you ever seen what the Ebola virus does to a body? It liquefies your insides. Your cells turn to mush. Blood leaks out your pores. As fast as the doctors can pump blood into you, it flows right back out. And my people are able to transmit Ebola through the air. Like through that air conditioner blowing down on you right now."

Ratzenberger shot a nervous glance at the air vent on the far wall.

"Let me tell you," The Instructor continued, "if I had to choose, a cell phone blowing up is a much nicer way to go. But I know you and I are friends, so we'd never do anything to harm one another."

The president cleared his throat. "I...I have some things to put in order. I'll make the announcement next week."

"Thank you, Mr. President. It will give us some time to get to know each other on a personal level. I expect, once Operation MD2 gets into full swing, you will enjoy unprecedented popularity not only among this nation but worldwide," The Instructor said. "Which will be perfect, come next election, when you pick me as your running mate."

# Fleming

*"If you want to make someone do what you want, you have two choices," The Instructor said. "You can reward them. Or you can punish them."*

The drugstore alarm clock woke Fleming up at 5:00 a.m. She stretched on the air mattress, surprised by how sore she was, and forced herself out of the sleeping bag and onto the floor for some yoga. After twenty minutes she was bendy and sweaty and needed a shower, but the store she'd rented had just a sink and a toilet.

If all went well, she'd get one soon. Instead, she toweled off, washed her face and brushed her teeth, then did what she could with her hair and minimal makeup.

Dressing in a new outfit—a short skirt and red leggings with black Chuck Taylors, and a bulky sweater that bared one shoulder—she judged herself sufficiently cute enough to go abduct Bradley.

By a quarter to six, she was back in his parking lot, behind the wheel, waiting for him to come out to go to work. He appeared at six, like yesterday, but when he saw his Volvo he stopped before getting in. That was Fleming's cue to start up her van and back out. When she pulled up to him, she rolled down the window.

"Good morning, Bradley. What happened?"

"Huh? Oh, hey, Ian. Two flat tires."

"Did you run something over?"

"I don't know. They seemed fine last night."

"Do you have spares?" Helpful Fleming, master of the obvious.

"I have one in the trunk, but not two."

"Need a lift to the tire shop? There's a twenty-four-hour Walmart nearby."

"Um…would you mind?"

"No problem. You saved me last night, I'm happy to return the favor. Climb in."

Said the spider to the fly.

When Bradley hopped into the passenger seat, he offered a shy grin. "Thanks, Ian. This is really cool of you."

Fleming gave him another full-wattage smile, but he didn't notice because he was looking at her legs and seemed to be liking what he saw. She tried to remember the last time a man had looked at her legs with something other than pity. With her braces off and colored leggings on, Fleming guessed they looked relatively normal.

"Do you work out?" she asked, pulling out of the parking lot.

"I try to. There's a gym at my work. Management felt too much desk time turned employees into vegetables, so…oh God." Bradley turned white. "I'm sorry. I didn't mean anything by the vegetable comment. I mean, not that you're a vegetable or anything…"

He made a face and put his hand over his eyes.

This guy was really too cute. "You know the worst part about eating vegetables?"

"What?" he asked, peeking through his fingers.

"Taking off the diaper."

Bradley made a choking noise, then began to laugh. "That's... That's the most tasteless joke I've ever heard."

"I bet the vegetable wasn't tasteless, though."

He laughed even harder. "Wow, you're...that's horrible."

"I'm not a vegetable, Bradley. And I don't wear a diaper. I have feeling in my legs. Since the fall, they just don't work like they should. But don't feel you have to walk on tiptoes around me, just because I can't."

"I'm just...It's been a while since I've talked to an attractive woman. A looong while. I'm one of the top people in my field, but a pretty face makes me act like an idiot."

"You think I'm pretty?" Fleming knew she was pushing it, but this was more fun than it should have been.

"You're very pretty, Ian. Are you, um, seeing anybody?"

Fleming thought about Tequila, and her stable of other studs she could call on the fly whenever the need arose. But she played it coy. "No one that doesn't need batteries."

"What do...Oh, I get it." He laughed. "Wow, you really speak your mind, don't you?"

"Does that bother you?"

"No. I think it's great."

So far, so good. Now to reel him in.

"Look, the reason I asked if you work out is because I have this piece of equipment at my shop, and it weighs about a hundred pounds, and I'm having trouble getting it on the table. I thought, maybe, if you wouldn't mind..."

"Where's your shop?"

"On the way to Walmart."

"Happy to help. Least I can do."

Fleming drove to her shop, parked, and spent a minute climbing into her wheelchair and using the lift to get out the side door.

"Not very efficient," Bradley said. "Why didn't they design it so you could drive while in your wheelchair? With an electric ramp straight out the back, instead of a side lift. Be a lot faster."

"That's a great idea," Fleming said, meaning it.

"Wouldn't take long to convert. Wouldn't be expensive, either. Need some sort of restraint system, in case of accidents. A wheel lock. Could probably do it for under two hundred bucks."

Spoken like a true engineer. Solving problems that aren't even his.

"This is my store, here. I can't thank you enough for this."

And Fleming meant it. If Bradley did what she needed him to do, he'd be saving her and her sisters' lives.

She wheeled up to the front door, checked to make sure no one in the parking lot was watching, and then let Bradley inside. Fleming switched on the overhead fluorescent lights.

"Did you just move in?" Bradley asked.

"Yesterday. Inventory and all my supplies coming in this week."

"Where's the heavy object that needs lifting?"

"In the back."

Fleming stuck close to his heels, reaching under her chair and pulling out the shotgun.

"Over there. You see the length of wire with the open padlock on it? Loop it around your ankle and secure the lock."

"What?" He turned around to look at her, a goofy grin on his face.

His grin disappeared when he noticed the gun.

"Is that thing loaded?"

Fleming flipped the safety and pumped the shotgun, ejecting one shell and loading the next.

Bradley rushed to comply, encircling his ankle and fastening the padlock with shaking hands.

"Now listen closely. I'm not a computer repair person. I'm a spy. I design integrated circuits and computer programs. But I have limited experience with robotics, especially miniature. I need you to build something for me. If you do, you'll go free, with a very large cash reward."

"Is this a joke?"

"No, Bradley. It's not."

"You're a spy?"

"Yes."

"You're the one who slashed my tires."

Fleming nodded.

"Are you undercover? Is the wheelchair fake?"

"No. My legs really don't work. But this gun does. Take out your cell phone."

He did. His expression had more surprise than fear. Fleming would have to fix that. She needed him afraid in order to make him compliant.

The textbook thing to do was to hurt him. Break his nose. Shoot his knee. Something to convince him he had no choice but to follow her every instruction.

But, shit, he was a really nice guy. Maybe instead of causing him pain, she could just threaten him. And there was one threat all men responded to.

Fleming held the shotgun in one hand, and rolled toward him, backing Bradley up to the desk.

"Sit."

He did, so they were eye to eye. With her free hand she locked her wheels, and then took a tactical folder out of the armrest. His eyes got wide when she flicked the knife blade open with her thumb.

"Call in sick to work."

"My boss doesn't get in until later."

"Leave a message. You have a stomach virus. Won't be in today."

As he dialed, Fleming set down the shotgun and reached between his legs, one hand grasping him through his trousers, the other bringing up the knife.

"Any nonsense and I cut it off. Got it?"

"Oh God."

But Fleming didn't think his prayer was fear-induced. Barely a few seconds after she grabbed him, Bradley was fully aroused.

"Seriously?" she said. "I've got a knife on you. How is that sexy?"

"It's not. Jeez, Ian…I…it's been…it's been a long time since I've been with a woman. I'm sorry. I just…"

"How long?" Fleming asked.

"What do you mean? How long is my—"

Fleming already knew that because she could feel it for herself. "How long since you've been with a woman?"

"Years," he said, face downcast.

"You haven't had sex in years?"

"Yeah. Look, this is really embarrassing."

Fleming didn't find it embarrassing at all. She found it pretty damn amusing. And a little exciting.

"How many years, Bradley?"

"I'd rather not talk about it."

"Tell me."

"Um…twenty-eight."

"Twenty-eight years?"

"I'm…I'm a virgin."

Fleming laughed. "Really?"

His eyes narrowed. "Not for lack of trying. I just…College was really busy. Now I'm working all the time, my office is nothing but men, there isn't any place to meet women."

Fleming squeezed him harder, and also pulled a little, causing him to gasp. She couldn't believe it. She had been with lots of men, but never a virgin. And she'd never felt someone get so hard, so fast.

She considered her options. There was the stick and the carrot. Which would be more effective in this case?

"Have you ever fooled around?" she asked.

"Yeah. But nothing…um…nothing to conclusion."

"Never had a blow job?" she asked.

"No." His voice was barely a croak.

"Are you lying to me?"

"I'm not. I haven't."

"Call work. Say you're sick."

He finished dialing and said in one quick breath, "Mr.-Manning-it's-Bradley-I-can't-make-it-in-today-stomach-flu-sorry-bye."

Then he hung up, staring at Fleming expectantly, like a puppy waiting for its reward.

"Here's what I need," she said, taking his phone and tucking it into her wheelchair. Then Fleming told him, in great detail, what she wanted him to build.

"Wow," he said when she'd finished. "Tall order."

During her lengthy explanation, his erection hadn't waned.

"Can you build something like that?"

"There are challenges. But yes."

"Can you build it within a few days?"

"I don't know. Maybe, with the right equipment."

"I can get all the equipment you need. But I need it within seventy-two hours. If you can do it, I'll give you twenty thousand dollars, cash. And…" Fleming gave him a sly smile. "I'll sleep with you."

Bradley's eyes got wide. "Are you serious?"

"Does James Bond get laid in every book?"

"Yeah, of course."

"Same thing, but reverse roles."

"You're not going to believe this, but I've had fantasies of this happening. Except the spy was Angelina Jolie."

"Angelina is frigid compared to me. Are you up to this?"

"Yes."

"Would you like to kiss me?"

"Oh my God. Yes."

Fleming tucked away the knife, realizing she didn't need it anymore. When she leaned in and touched her lips to his, he kissed like a high school boy, eager and inexperienced and seemingly in awe of his good luck.

The next few days would be easier, and more fun, than Fleming could have hoped. Popping his cherry sure beat torturing the poor guy.

# Julie

The door opened with a slight squeak, and soft-soled shoes padded across tile.

Julie kept her eyes closed, peering through the fringe of her lashes, careful not to move, not to change the rhythm of her breathing.

She didn't recognize her visitor, an older woman with dull blond hair and a mole on her chin the size of a ladybug. If Julie had seen her before, she didn't remember. But then, in all these hours of sedation, she didn't remember much.

The woman wore scrubs and a white lab coat. She scurried around Julie's bed, efficiently checking the monitors and IV, and singing a tune under her breath that Julie had heard before. It took a few moments before she could name it.

The theme to *The Brady Bunch*.

The woman fiddled with Julie's arm, and a ripping sound rose over the story of a lovely lady and the incessant beeping of the heart monitor. For a few seconds, Julie couldn't place the sound. Then the woman turned Julie's arm up, palm to the sky, and Julie realized the Velcro cuff fastening her wrist to the bed was gone.

Her arm was free.

If she were Chandler, she'd know what to do. But she was only Julie, so she simply lay there, pretending to be unconscious, too frightened to move.

The woman switched to wordless humming as she rolled a stool to Julie's bedside and wound a rubber tourniquet around her upper arm. She tore open a sterile packet and withdrew something and brought it to Julie's arm.

The scent of alcohol snapped at Julie's senses, then pain pricked the inside of her elbow. The woman filled one vial. Pulling the tube free, she left the needle in place and hooked up another vial. And another.

Drawing blood as if milking a cow.

Tears stung Julie's eyes, threatening to squeeze through her lowered lids.

After the woman drew her last vial, she refastened the Velcro and padded out of the room.

As soon as she heard the door close, Julie drew a shuddering breath and let the tears come. They coursed down the sides of her face, flowing around her ears and puddling inside.

Chandler wasn't here.

Chandler couldn't save her.

Julie would have to save herself this time.

No, not herself. That wasn't right. That wasn't possible. Saving herself would only mean more people in white coats would find her, shut her in labs, harvest her poisoned blood.

This clarity brought resolve. She had to prevent them from succeeding. No matter the cost.

Julie couldn't save herself.

But maybe she could save the world.


# Scarlett

*"There are two types of interrogations: those where the subject is required to live, and those where the subject dies,"* The Instructor said. *"Both can be messy. Plan ahead."*

Much as it bugged her, Scarlett let Rhett do the talking. Though his good ol' boy charm didn't work on her, weaker-minded people (which was almost everyone else) tended to find Rhett instantly likable. When you liked someone, you wanted him to like you back, and tried harder. For all of her considerable skills, Scarlett was terrible at flirting. The course on seduction at Hydra Deux was the only course she hadn't excelled at. She was so bad that when The Instructor had slept with her, he advised her to avoid sex in the field, or with targets.

Scarlett didn't take it personally. She wasn't frigid. But she found sex to be perfunctory, rather than sensual. Performing in front of a partner made her self-conscious, too aware to enjoy herself. That reluctance tended to spill over with her personal interactions with people. So being partnered with Rhett did make some sense, because he had charisma to spare. Within two minutes of finding Eric Brockney at Finklestad's Automotive Sales in Waltham, Rhett had become his new best friend, and they were trading jokes like they'd been buddies for years. Neither man even seemed to notice she was there.

Scarlett didn't mind. Her specialty would come later.

She climbed into the backseat as Rhett test-drove a newer-model Mustang GT, spinning tires and screeching around corners as Eric droned on and on about suspension and horsepower and torque.

"So, partner, we asked for you specifically because you're famous," Rhett said. "We read 'bout you in the paper."

"Best thing that ever happened to me," Eric said. "I've sold four cars today, just because of the publicity."

"Wasn't it scary?"

"Naw. Girl was crippled. I bet the gun wasn't even loaded. I felt sorry for her, more than anything."

Rhett dropped a gear, slowing the Mustang down. "Me and the old lady back there would love to hear about it, if you don't mind."

Scarlett ignored the *old lady* comment and forced herself to be patient while Eric told a rambling and obviously embellished tale of how he'd been abducted and carjacked. Scarlett knew a great deal about Fleming, and Eric's account didn't sound at all truthful. If Rhett bought the bogus story, he didn't let on, but Scarlett noticed that while asking questions Rhett had managed to drive into a mostly secluded industrial park. The majority of the buildings and parking lots looked empty, closed for the night. A very good location for what was to come next.

"I've decided I'm going to take the car," Rhett said when Eric had finished bragging about his heroics.

"That's great! This has been my best day ever!"

That's when Scarlett put the barrel of her Glock 26 against Eric's temple.

"He's stealing the car, dumbass. And now you're going to tell us what really happened, without all the bullshit."

With some prodding, Eric gave a truer account of his encounter, and Scarlett had to smile at the part where Fleming made him take off his pants and dance for her. That woman had lost a great deal, but she still had a sense of humor. Good for her.

"Do the police have any idea where she went?"

"They know exactly where she went. She's in Baltimore."

Rhett and Scarlett exchanged a glance.

"How do you know that?" Rhett asked.

"The van had an anti-theft system installed. It can be tracked by GPS. The Massachusetts police are trying to coordinate with Baltimore PD to return it, but there's paperwork involved in recovering a vehicle that crossed state lines."

"Does this car have that GP thingy?" Rhett said, his down-home crap annoying Scarlett all over again.

"No. I swear it doesn't."

Scarlett took down the name of the anti-theft company. Then she told Eric to get out of the car.

"Pants and underwear off. You know the drill."

Eric reluctantly followed orders, looking sufficiently humiliated. "Do we really have to do this?"

"Yes. Now dance for me," Scarlett demanded.

He hopped from foot to foot, shaking his arms to some unknown beat, but Scarlett didn't find it especially amusing. In fact, it was rather sad. So sad that she shot Eric four times in the stomach, and once in the neck to silence his screams.

"I kinda liked his dancing," Rhett said.

"I like his bleeding better. How long to Baltimore?"

"We need to go to the other car, grab our stuff, wipe it down. Maybe eight hours."

Scarlett made a face. "We're switching cars?"

"Baby, didn't you hear the salesman? Three hundred horse-power. I love this ride."

"Can you manage to drive without humming?"

"Hell yes."

Rhett managed to keep his promise for almost an hour, then lapsed into humming again. Rather than point it out and start an argument, Scarlett closed her eyes and imagined making Rhett dance naked for her while she shot him. It wasn't sexual in the least, but it did give her something to focus on until she fell asleep and didn't have to hear him anymore.

# Chandler

*"Make friends with your enemies," The Instructor said,*
*"and make sure your friends don't become enemies."*

I awoke to a bright light glaring from the window and the hiss of the motel shower.

For a second, I didn't know where I was, then it came back to me. Arriving in Chicago late. Checking into the hotel in the suburbs. Resolving to stay awake, my gun tucked under my pillow to ensure...

I jolted into a sitting position and tossed my pillow to the side. No shotgun.

She'd taken it from me. She'd—

"Looking for this?"

Hammett stood buck naked in the bathroom doorway, a towel wrapping her hair and my shotgun dangling from her finger.

"You stole my gun?"

"I didn't want you shooting yourself in the head while snoring."

I sprang out of bed and crossed the room, then snatched the weapon from her hand. "I don't snore."

"Sure you don't. There must be a backfiring motorcycle under the bed. You know, sleep apnea can often be the sign of a more serious disorder. Like congestive heart failure."

"My heart is fine."

"Even after Lund dumped you?"

I considered shooting her, then set the gun down. Wouldn't be fair to the maid to have to clean up the mess.

"Hurry up in the shower. It's already getting late, and I want breakfast before we meet these little friends of yours."

I squeezed past her and shut the bathroom door behind me.

So much for my being on guard. I'd slept all night, didn't even remember dreaming. I was lucky I wasn't dead.

Although I wasn't sure I felt that lucky anymore.

The shower felt good, but I made it quick. After watching Hammett eat enough food to feed a normal woman for a week, I forced myself to down a couple of eggs from the hotel breakfast buffet, and then we headed downtown to Chicago's north side.

I parked next to a well-maintained park and walked with Hammett to our destination a block east. It was a nice neighborhood, lots of boutiques and overpriced cafés, and an overabundance of women who had small dogs in their handbags. Who started that trend, and why?

"Chihuahua, six o'clock," Hammett said. "In a Gucci purse. I want one."

"Kirk is too big to fit in that bag."

"The purse is nice. But I'm talking about the dog."

"Why?" I asked.

"He's adorable. Look at him."

I did. The dog looked like someone had squeezed a rat in a French press until its eyes bulged out.

"Adorable," I said.

"I'm killing that woman and taking her dog."

"No, you're not."

Hammett began to cross the street, toward the Chihuahua. I grabbed her arm and was immediately forced to counter a judo throw, my fists wrapped in her shirt, one leg between hers, struggling for balance as she held my shoulders.

"This isn't the time," I said.

"For the dog? Or for me to break your neck and leave you dead in the street?"

"Either. You've got some serious anger-management issues."

"Fuck you, Goody Two-shoes. I'll end you here and now."

"Case in point. Can we get through just one hour without you threatening to kill me? Can you handle that?"

Her face didn't change expression, but she released me. "Fine. Later then."

I blew out a breath. "You are such an asshole."

"Takes one to know one."

"And you act like an eight-year-old."

"I'm rubber, you're glue. That bounces off me and sticks to you."

I quit before she began whining "I know you are but what am I."

We crossed the street after the Gucci woman safely passed, and walked up to the security door I'd visited a few days ago. One the wall next to it was a brass placard: MCGLADE INVESTIGATIONS. I remembered what Jack Daniels had warned me the last time I was here, and decided it was worth repeating.

"If he says something rude, you have to promise not to kill him."

"I don't kill people because they're rude, Chandler. I'm not a fucking psycho."

Actually she was a fucking psycho and killed people for no reason at all, but I let that go. "Promise me."

Hammett blew out a breath and rolled her eyes. "I promise, Mom."

I pressed the buzzer, and Harry's voice came through the speaker: a high-pitched, poor attempt to imitate a woman. He sounded like Mickey Mouse on meth.

"McGlade Investigations, may I help you?"

"Harry, it's Chandler."

"I'm not Harry. I'm Mr. McGlade's secretary. Do you have an appointment? He's very busy."

"If you don't let me in, I'm keeping all the equipment you lent me."

"I see we just had a cancellation, and a slot in Mr. McGlade's schedule opened up. You may come in."

The door buzzed. I led Hammett up to the second floor, and we walked up to a door that had a large magnifying-glass logo on it.

"Is this guy for real?" Hammett asked.

"It gets better. Don't kill him."

We entered and found McGlade behind the very large desk in his lobby. He was in his late forties, scruffy and dirty looking despite the expensive suit, and had a sort of voyeuristic stare, like you were in a porn movie he was watching. While I couldn't say I actually liked the man, he had helped me out and I owed him, both favors and money.

The favors were what bothered me.

He dramatically rubbed his eyes, then blinked in an exaggerated manner. "Did I die and go to Doublemint heaven?"

"This is Hammett," I said.

"Weren't you in a wheelchair before?"

"That's Fleming," I said.

"Fleming is crippled," Hammett said. "I have full use of my appendages."

"So I see. Can you raise up one leg and lick the back of your calf?"

Hammett simply stared at him.

"What if I gave you five bucks?" he asked.

"We need your help," I said, eyeing my sister and gauging her homicidal impulse level.

"Last I recall, you owed me a date."

"That will have to wait."

"I'm not a man who likes to wait. And I can't help but notice you aren't carrying a large duffel bag full of the equipment I loaned you."

I hid my wince. "I can pay for that. And we're going to need more equipment."

"That stuff was worth over twenty grand."

I dug some cash out of my bag and dropped it on the desk. "That should cover it. With interest. We need guns."

"The price just went up. After all, I could have my license revoked if I sold weapons to the woman who killed the president."

Shit. The Instructor must have released the video. Before I could answer, Hammett had done a handspring over the desk and had straddled herself across McGlade's lap, a knife at his throat.

"I promised my sister I wouldn't kill you," she said. "But I could cut your ears off."

Harry's eyes went wide. "I...am...I...am..."

"Spit it out."

"...so turned on right now."

Hammett wiggled, changing position, then laughed. "Yeah, you are. Not bad for an older guy."

"Your grumpy sister owes me a date, but I think I like you more."

Hammett threw her hair back and grinned. "Everyone does. She's a pain in the ass."

"So maybe we can go out later? Before the authorities catch you and execute you?"

"Why put off until later what we can do right now?"

Hammett hiked up her dress, her other hand working McGlade's zipper. "Is your fly Velcro?" she said, grinning.

"Yeah. I also had some Velcro underwear, but they got ripped off."

I decided this was something I didn't need to see, and wandered off down the hallway, into an office. Unfortunately, I could still hear them.

"Wait, let me..." Harry said.

"Hey! Wrong entrance, buddy!"

"Sorry...oh...oh, there it is...oh God!"

"That's it. Like that. Good."

"That's…that's…how can you do that?"

"*Unngh.* Practice. Now reach up and grab nipples."

"Oh, that feels incredible!"

"*My* nipples, jackass. Not your own."

"I can…let me…"

"What the *fuck* is that?"

"It's my hand. Fake hand. Lost my limb."

"It's…it's vibrating! Holy shit!"

"I've got a higher speed. Wait."

"*OH MY GOD!*"

"You can keep the knife at my throat. It's OK."

"*Unngh…unngh!* Oh, Harry!"

"Call me Spartacus!"

I found a TV and switched on CNN. Sure enough, there was me on a cell phone, punching in the code that killed the president. As if things weren't already bad enough.

Hammett began to moan. So did McGlade. I turned up the volume but still heard them. After the longest minute of my life, Harry finally yelled, "*Fire in the hole!*" so loud that people heard it in Indiana. Hammett cried out a few seconds later, though it sounded more like whimpering. I wondered if I'd ever whimpered during sex, but couldn't imagine it, especially with Harry McGlade.

I walked back to them, not sure what to expect. Maybe the same shame and embarrassment I was feeling. Instead, Hammett was smoothing out her dress, and McGlade was halfway through a can of Red Bull. When he finished, he crushed it in his robotic hand like it was a paper cup.

"So, guns, is it?" he asked, all business. "I may be able to help you. What do you need, and when?"

Hammett looked like her regular homicidal self again, except for a red flush on her neck and cheeks, and hair that looked like she'd spent an hour sailing during a monsoon.

I pulled the weapons list from my bag. There was a buzzing sound, and I realized his fake hand was still vibrating.

"Right away," I said. "As you know, we're in a bit of trouble."

"A damn shame. If it were up to me, you'd get a medal. The president was a dick. And the new guy is even worse. You should take him out, too."

"I've got a list as well," Hammett said.

"You do?" I asked. I hadn't known she'd made one, too.

Hammett gave it to Harry, who raised an eyebrow as he read it. "Damn. You are a wicked little thing, aren't you? What are you going to do with that?"

He pointed at the paper. Hammett looked at me, then leaned over and whispered in his ear.

"I was married once," McGlade said. "You remind me of her. She's currently in a prison for the criminally insane."

"She sounds fun," Hammett said.

"I'll need to make a few calls. But I think I can get all this by the end of the day. Except for that special thing you want. That'll take some time."

"How much?" Hammett asked.

"For you, my little Tootsie Roll, I'll loan it all to you if you promise to return it. For Chandler, who doesn't know how to return stuff, we're looking at another fifteen K."

I didn't have that much left, and wondered if we'd have to knock over another crack house.

"She's good for it," Hammett said.

"Still, I'd prefer payment up front."

"Maybe I'll trade you something for it," Hammett said, swiveling his chair around to face her.

"I'm not sixteen anymore. I need a little more refractory time. Are you into spanking?"

"Giving or receiving?"

"Both."

Hammett rolled her hips and offered a fake pout. "Well, I have been a *very* naughty girl."

McGlade reached into his desk drawer and pulled out—of all things—a Ping-Pong paddle.

"I'll be in the car," I said, heading for the door. By the time I made it to the stairs, I could hear the steady *thwack! thwack!*

accompanied by high-pitched yelps that could have been either Harry or Hammett. When I'd warned my sister not to kill him, I hadn't thought it would be via fucking him to death. If that was her intention, I hoped we'd get our weapons first.

I waited on a bench in the park, my thoughts drifting from the pair of deviants I'd left to Lund. I didn't want to think about him. Not only because I had feelings for the guy and he'd crushed me, but because of what he represented.

Normalcy.

I'd never had a normal life. Perhaps because my destiny had been decided for me, and I'd never had the opportunity to choose anything normal. But if I got out of this alive...

I spent ten minutes people-watching. Spotted the obligatory young couple with the baby stroller. Two people my age, walking hand in hand. An old man and an old woman shuffled over, sat down, and gave each other a chaste public kiss.

"How long have you two been married?" I asked.

"Thirty-six years," said the man.

"Forty-one," said the woman.

I smiled. "Which one is it?"

"Both." The man grinned and winked. "Our spouses are back at the retirement home. We're out for a little afternoon delight."

Hmm. OK. Maybe normalcy was overrated.

The elderly couple left, off to commit geriatric infidelity, and Hammett eventually came out of McGlade's building. She looked more relaxed than I'd ever seen her.

"That guy's a real piece of work," she said.

"Did you kill him?"

"No. He gave me his number. Like, for what? I'm supposed to call him next time I'm free?"

"Maybe it's love."

"He'll have our stuff by tomorrow. Did you know he married a serial killer?"

"I only met Harry a few days ago."

"I only met him a few minutes ago. He's a real piece of work. Where to next?"

"We need to talk to someone else. You can't kill her, either."

"Who?"

"Cop. Her name is Jack Daniels."

"Seriously?"

"Yeah."

"What do we need her for?"

I told her. Hammett frowned. "Think she'll go for it?"

"All we can do is ask."

"If she says no, do we slap her around?"

I'd tussled with Jack before, and the woman was formidable. I would have enjoyed watching Hammett get punched a few times.

"No. If she won't play ball, we think of something else."

Which was a tall order. If Jack didn't help us, we were likely dead.

# Heath

*"There are many ways to get what you want," said The Instructor. "Killing is only one of them. But if it's the best option, don't hesitate to take it."*

Despite the business he was in, Heath didn't enjoy killing people. Sure, there were a few dispatches that were rewarding—corrupt politicians and business leaders who profited off the backs of others were some of his favorites—but while the other members of Hydra Deux seemed to enjoy killing anyone for any reason, Heath liked it best when justice was dealt and innocents spared.

Unfortunately, when innocents refused to cooperate, sometimes there was no other way.

"You ever think about taking some time off?" Heath asked Manuel Diaz in fluid Spanish. It was the language of his youth. Many of his thoughts were still in Spanish, but every time he spoke it for any length of time, he felt a heaviness press down on his chest and a void open up in his belly.

He downed a few gulps of Modelo Especial.

Manuel took a swig of his beer as well, then shook his head. He'd just spent the better part of an hour explaining to Heath how grateful he was to find work, especially something as well paid and glamorous as groundskeeper at the Plaza de Toros México, the largest bullfighting arena in the world. He probably thought Heath hadn't been listening.

Of course, Heath had heard every word.

In fact, Heath knew all about Manuel's financial problems before he'd arranged to "accidentally" run into him at his neighborhood watering hole. He knew that Manuel had a wife named Juana, who worked at a stand in their neighborhood food market selling chilies. Of his five children, three were girls, ages fourteen, twelve, and six. The oldest was pregnant and unmarried. His two sons were nine and four.

A half hour and two beers later, Heath had laid the groundwork with Manuel, describing his experience as an *aficionado practico*, or amateur bullfighter, until a steer had taken his eye and he'd had to retire from the sport. Now it was time to make his pitch. And Manuel himself would choose whether he made some extra money for his family or left them without a provider.

*Plata o plomo?*

"I would love to have a taste of that world, be an *arenero*, however I can, just for the exhibition. I could fill in for you."

Manuel gave his head an almost imperceptible shake and stared into his beer.

"Just for a few days? I will pay you."

"And then you will take the job for good, and my family will starve. I'll have to go north again."

Before returning home by choice, not deportation, Manuel had spent three years in Houston, tending a rich family's horse stable and sending money back to his family. This guy was salt of the earth, as they would say in the States. A good man. A hard worker.

Heath would regret taking him out, leaving his family destitute. "I will pay double."

Manuel paused for a moment, considering, but then shook his head again. "Double wages for a few days will not feed my family like a regular job will."

Heath had a roll of cash on him. He also had a Sig Sauer SP2022. Either way, he needed the man's job for the next few days, and he would resolve this tonight, either here in the bar or later in the street.

Last chance, *cabrón*.

"Five hundred American dollars, and you introduce me as your cousin, filling in while you attend your mother's funeral."

Manuel choked on his Modelo Especial. "Five hundred?"

"For a few days off and an introduction."

"Why?"

"I have lost my eye, but not my passion for the fight."

"It's hard work."

"Believe me, I don't expect it to be easy." But if this played out the way he intended, he *did* expect it would be worth it. To him, to Manuel's family, and to all the people of Mexico. "Do we have a deal?"

Manuel nodded. "Come to work with me tomorrow morning. If my employer says it's OK, then it is a deal."

Heath smiled and raised his bottle. "It will be OK. Don't worry. I'll convince him."

# Fleming

*"Spying makes for strange bedfellows," The Instructor said. "Sometimes literally."*

After a long, detailed discussion, Bradley gave Fleming a list of supplies he needed, which could all be purchased at a nearby electronics shop. Fleming had already pirated a computer-aided drafting program online using a torrent site, and she left Bradley alone to get started while she went out, making sure the Internet was off.

"Can you stop at my place, bring me some clean clothes, deodorant and toothbrush and such?" he asked, eyes on the computer monitor. "My keys are on the table, next to my wallet."

Fleming considered the situation. Bradley didn't seem like a guy who'd been kidnapped and coerced. He seemed like this was business as usual. And he didn't even complain or resist when she cut off their impromptu make-out session. Honestly, he was less like any man she'd ever met and more like a puppy.

"Sure," Fleming said. "Anything else?"

"If I'm going to be here a few days, can you also bring Sasha?"

"Your fox?"

"She'll get lonely. If that happens, she starts chewing on my stuff. Her leash and food are in the kitchen pantry."

Fleming hesitated, not convinced this was a good idea.

"If Sasha's safe, I can concentrate fully on this design," Bradley said. "I could go with you to get her if it's too much trouble."

"I'd rather you stay here and work. I'll get her."

"Thanks, Ian. Is that your real name?"

"No." Fleming wasn't sure why she admitted it.

"What is it?"

"I don't use my real name anymore."

"So what should I call you?"

"Ian is fine."

Fleming's real name wasn't Fleming. In fact, the only person still alive who knew her real name was The Instructor. Her many male admirers all knew Fleming under different names. Which Fleming preferred because it made them easy to sort out. If someone called asking for Jenny, or Aria, or Francesca, Fleming immediately knew who it was.

"OK, I guess I'll stick with Ian."

"Do you prefer Bradley or Brad?"

"Bradley."

"You're probably aware your name is Milton Bradley backward."

"I may have heard that once or twice. Or eighty thousand times."

"Did your parents like board games?"

"I didn't have parents," he said. "I was raised by two brothers named Parker."

She caught the joke and smiled. "Cute."

Bradley smiled back. "My parents did like board games, actually. I grew up in the suburbs, had a white picket fence around my house, and a dog named Spot. For real. How hokey is that?"

"Sounds nice," Fleming said, meaning it.

"It was. Idyllic. I was destined to grow up to be a nerd, but I can't complain about anything. I've had a nice, uneventful life, up until right now." He lowered his voice. "You're the most exciting thing that has ever happened to me, Ian. Can I ask you a question?"

"As long as it doesn't violate national security."

"Are you kidding?"

She shrugged. "Kind of."

"Have you had a lot of boyfriends?"

"Yes."

"What did they call you?"

"I've used a lot of names over the years."

"Am I the first to call you Ian?"

"Yes."

"Did you pick it because you knew I liked Ian Fleming?"

"No. I didn't know that."

"But you must have known something about me. That's why you picked me, right?"

"Google search. Your name came up. I know a lot about electronics, but not much robotics. I could have taught myself, but we need this right away. Kidnapping you was the quicker solution."

"Who is *we*?"

"Can't tell you."

"I know what we're building. What are you going to use it for?"

"Can't tell you."

"Can you tell me when I can kiss you again?"

Fleming blushed a little, an odd reaction for her. "Maybe when I get back with your fox. There's some food in the fridge, in back. Coffee, too. If you try to yell for help, or get attention by breaking the windows or setting a fire…" Fleming thought about saying she'd kill Sasha as a threat. Instead she said, "Then no kissing later."

Bradley's eyes got wide. "I'll…I'll be very good. No problem."

Fleming kept her smile hidden. If only all men were that easy.

She pocketed his keys, told him she'd be back soon, and then wheeled out to the van and drove to her first stop, a semiconductor manufacturer. After some earlier back-and-forth discussion, Fleming and Bradley decided upon the microchip they'd use for the project, and Fleming bought one for cash. Next stop was a specialty electronics store, where Fleming bought everything she needed to etch her circuit board design. Then it was off to Bradley's place.

When she'd been a field agent, one of Fleming's specialties had been breaking and entering. She had a burglar's touch: the ability to enter and assess strange places, move about undetected, and stay calm and coolheaded when things went wrong.

While going into Bradley's condo wasn't actually burglary, it felt similar. Prowling through a strange domicile, adjusting to the layout while looking for something, grappling with the sense that she shouldn't be there. The sense of anticipation was a lot like walking through a haunted house attraction on Halloween, maneuvering carefully through the unknown, expecting something to pop out at any moment.

In this case, what popped out was a silver fox. And it popped right onto Fleming's wheelchair, staring up at her with the cutest little face she'd ever seen. Blue eyes, pointy ears, a mottled black-and-white coat, and a ridiculously bushy tail that swished back and forth.

"You must be Sasha." She patted the vixen on the head, surprised by how soft her fur was. No wonder people paid so much for coats. It was nothing less than glorious. Fleming might have to rethink her policy on wearing animal hides.

"Then again, it probably looks better on you than it would on me."

The vixen immediately curled up onto Fleming's lap. No watchdog, this one. The only protection Sasha offered against home invaders was possibly snuggling them to death.

Fleming rolled into the kitchen, getting a feel for the space. For a bachelor, Bradley kept a surprisingly tidy house. No dishes in the sink. No dirty clothing strewn about. Stove top wiped down, garbage taken out.

She was only there for a few items, but curiosity got the better of her and Fleming began to snoop around a bit. His DVD collection was primarily action, science fiction, and Japanese anime. Books were sci-fi, thrillers, and some horror. Lots of magazines, mostly robotics and electronics, organized on the shelf chronologically.

Nothing interesting in the fridge, except for a potentially life-threatening amount of energy drinks, so many that Fleming wondered if he had stock in Red Bull.

As she gathered clothing in his bedroom, she found the obligatory spank magazines in his dresser, *Playboy* and *Penthouse Letters* and a few specialty publications that seemed centered around blow jobs and eating pussy. Good information for later.

His clothes were unremarkable, average to above average labels, folded neatly and hung up in an organized way that made picking out an outfit convenient. There were some well-worn running shoes, a few pairs of dress loafers. Fleming didn't find any photo albums, and there was a box of papers she didn't bother rifling through.

She figured Bradley might have more hints to his personality on his computer, but Fleming had no desire to search it. If anything, she had a desire to get back to the store to see Bradley. The idea of corrupting a virgin was occupying more of Fleming's mind than she would have liked to admit, and even though she decided to wait until their project was complete, those magazines had given her some delightfully wicked ideas.

Sasha slept in Fleming's lap like a cat, a big bundle of black and white and gray fur. Fleming hooked a backpack filled with what she'd taken on the back of her wheelchair, and then put a leash on Sasha in case she woke up and tried to bolt. But she didn't. The fox remained sleeping even as Fleming rotated her collar one hundred and eighty degrees.

"I thought you guys were supposed to be crafty and alert."

Sasha yawned.

While Fleming didn't have the soft spot for animals that Hammett apparently had, she found the fox to be ridiculously charming.

Her cell phone rang. Chandler. Fleming picked up.

"The video was released."

"Shit. Good thing I grabbed my guy before he saw that. You meet with the PI?"

"Yeah."

"Get what we needed?"

"Tomorrow. Waiting for our other friend now. Keep out of sight."

"You too."

Fleming frowned, stroking the fox. She'd logged off the Internet before leaving Bradley, and he didn't have a radio or television, so for the moment it should be OK. If he saw that video, sex might not be enough to persuade him to help.

Fleming wheeled herself to the door, locking it behind her. She tried to keep her mind on her next move, but instead found herself thinking about Bradley in a way that was anything but professional.

A virgin. A real live virgin.

Fleming was still sore from the strenuous sex she'd had with Tequila, but she felt ready to go again. When it came to men, she liked all types. The macho, athletic types who liked to show off with marathon lovemaking sessions were fun. But so were the sensitive guys who fell all over themselves trying to please her. Guys who gave massages and foot rubs and went down on a girl for hours.

She loaded the van, setting Sasha in the passenger seat. The fox curled up, tucking her head under her tail so it resembled one of those Russian fur hats. Pulling out of the condo parking lot, Fleming remembered Bradley's kiss, and all the potential it hinted at.

Breaking him in was going to be fun.

She was considering what to do with him first when her subconscious poked her. Suddenly razor focused, Fleming turned right at the next light and eyed the rearview mirror.

The black Mustang that had been behind her for the last five minutes turned as well.

Fleming was being followed.

# Chandler

*"People close to you will get hurt," The Instructor said. "Don't make friends."*

Lieutenant Jacqueline Daniels was wearing a gray pantsuit, black pumps, and a black duster jacket than hung to her knees and concealed her shoulder holster. She was in her forties, but moved like someone younger. Fought like it, too. I knew that from experience.

I'd only met Jack a few days ago, but she'd already helped me out several times. Now I needed her once more.

She approached at a quick clip, walking across the courtyard of Daley Plaza, pigeons clearing a path for her. I was standing next to the Picasso on the south side of the Daley Center, pretending to take a picture of it with my cell phone. Hammett was across the street, on Dearborn, looking for tails.

"Were you followed?" I asked when she stood next to me.

"Nice to see you, too. And no, I wasn't."

"You're sure?"

"I've been doing this longer that you have, Chandler."

"Sorry. Things have gotten…well, I'd say worse, but they've been pretty bad for as long as I've known you."

"Did you rescue your sister?"

I nodded.

"Good." Jack gave me a once-over. "I like the new hairstyle, but you look like you're ready to keel over."

"I feel like it, too. Thanks for coming. And for not bringing the entire Chicago PD along to arrest me."

Especially since the only weapon I had on me was the folding knife. Tough to conceal a shotgun in your pants pocket.

"Yeah. You're quite the celebrity. Did you do it?"

I met her stare and put every bit of my acting skill into the lie. "No. It's a frame."

Jack didn't say anything. I endured her gaze, only showing her what I wanted her to see. She was a homicide cop, and a damn good one, which meant her bullshit detector was the best of the best. But I had the best of the best training, and my lying skills were solid.

"If I thought you did it, I'd arrest you."

"You'd try to arrest me, you mean."

"Convince me you're not a presidential assassin."

"The man behind this is the one who trained me. He's working with the VP."

"The vice president killed him?"

I nodded.

"Can you prove it?"

"No. At least, not yet. But I'm going to try to get proof."

"How?"

"I need you to plant a recording device for me."

"Where?"

"The White House."

Jack laughed, then caught herself when she saw my expression hadn't changed. "You're not kidding."

"This isn't about saving my ass, Jack. I just came from Maine, where a young woman was kidnapped by my former boss. She's a carrier for the Ebola virus. They're going to use her to make biological weapons."

Jack put her hands on her hips. "Even if I believed you, which I'm not sure I do, this is all way out of my league. It sounds like an over-the-top spy novel."

"Says the woman who recently drove a truck full of explosives into a sewage treatment plant."

I'd read up on Jack before this meeting. That was one of many well-known acts of bravery she'd committed in order to save lives.

"How do you expect me to bug the White House?"

"White House tours are by appointment only. You need to contact your congressman. You're a hero cop, the toast of Chicago. I'm sure you can pull some strings."

"You expect me to take you with?"

"No. Too dangerous. You can't be seen with me."

"I don't think they'll let me tour the Oval Office."

"The bug will be robotic. Just drop it inside and we'll get it where it needs to go."

Jack folded her arms across her chest. A bad sign.

"I understand if you can't do it," I said. "If you get caught, it's treason. If they find out you're helping me, they'll kill you. Or worse. But if you help, you'll be saving untold lives. Possibly preventing the biggest epidemic since the Spanish flu killed 50 million people ninety years ago."

I had no way of knowing what The Instructor was going to do with the Ebola, but I was already lying to Jack, so there was no reason not to lay it on thick.

"The president was just killed," she said. "They might not be letting anyone take tours."

"Maybe not. But you're my only shot."

More silence. I could have tried pushing harder, giving Jack more information so she could understand better. But I was already putting this woman in great danger. The less she knew the better off she'd be.

"You're either lying to me about something or holding something back," Jack said.

"What does your gut tell you to do?"

"My gut tells me I should bring you in. We can protect you, inform the media, expose all of this."

"We need proof first. And I wouldn't last a day in custody. They'd get to me."

"They're that powerful?"

"They killed the president, Jack. These people have power on a scale that's unimaginable."

I could practically hear the gears turning in her head.

"You've seen evil, Jack. You know what people are capable of. My former boss, he's just as bad as some of the serial killers you've caught. Except he has the power to commit genocide on a scale that's unheard of."

I cast a quick glance over Jack's shoulder, looking for Hammett. She was gone.

That's when I saw the flashing red and blue lights. Police cars, three of them, barreling down Dearborn and coming this way.

# The White House

Ratzenberger removed several tissues from the box on the Resolute desk and mopped at the thick makeup on his face. He'd been president for only seventy-two hours and was already sick of press conferences.

Hopefully they'd catch and kill that operative bitch soon. But then, there was a story about to break that would eclipse even a presidential assassination.

Ratzenberger wadded up the tissues, threw them at the garbage can, and missed. A microsecond later, Chaz pounced out from under the desk and sprang onto the Kleenex.

He pressed the button for the Secret Service. A moment later, one of his men appeared. New guy, couldn't remember his name.

"I'm the president of the goddamn free world. Why can't I keep a damn cat out of my office?"

"I'll remove him, Mr. President." The agent scooped up Chaz, then closed the door behind him.

Ratzenberger had actually looked into having the cat eliminated. But the feline had its own blog, for crissakes, and if it suddenly disappeared, he'd probably have to hold another damned press conference.

He took more tissue, wiping off the lipstick that his makeup artists insisted wasn't lipstick but rather a *color enhancer*, and the phone rang.

"What?" he asked, irritated.

"Amplification is complete, Mr. President. The packages are en route."

"Hmm? Oh, yes. Excellent."

Silence. This guy made Ratzenberger nervous. Having him in his cabinet would make him even more nervous. But the old saying was worth remembering. Keep your friends close, and your enemies closer. Ratzenberger just wasn't sure yet which The Instructor was.

"Was there something else?"

"We're closing in on the crippled one."

"Good. I want this finished."

"And my cabinet position?"

"When MD2 is in full swing, you'll get your appointment."

"Soon, sir, you'll be known as the greatest president since Thomas Jefferson."

Ratzenberger beamed at the compliment. He regarded the Louisiana Purchase as the single greatest act ever achieved by a government official. Greater even than the Declaration and the Constitution. Out of all forms of wealth in the world, land was the most valuable. Anyone who ever played the game Monopoly—or the game Risk, for that matter—knew that the winner was the one with the most property.

"And when will you arrive with my vaccine?" the president asked.

"We've got an entire facility dedicated to making it. With our new technique, we can make three hundred thousand doses in a day."

"But when is *my* dose coming?"

"You'll get yours. Very soon."

The Instructor hung up, and it took Ratzenberger several seconds before he realized those final words might very well have been a threat.

# Fleming

*"Anyone can drive," The Instructor said. "Only the best of the best can drive well."*

Fleming used to be an excellent driver.

Since the accident, she made do, but was in no danger of winning any trophies. The hand controls on the van made it easier, but the van itself was no match for a Mustang, and she wasn't feeling at one with the vehicle like she used to when she had use of her legs.

Losing her tail wouldn't be easy. But that wasn't the only thing that plagued Fleming's thoughts. Her most pressing issue was: *how did they find me?*

The Hydra sisters each had tracking chips installed. Fleming had a healing wound on her abdomen where hers had been removed. But without the chip, how could they have found her?

She stopped at the next red light, hands on her shotgun, eyeing the rearview. They were three cars back, playing it casual.

Could they have traced her computer activity somehow? Maybe when she was hacking the Hydra database?

Possible. But Fleming was sure she hadn't been tailed from the motel. She was also sure she hadn't been tailed from the shop when she left Bradley. They'd picked her up after she'd left his condo. They had no reason to tie her to Bradley. It was almost as if…

"The van. They're tracking the van."

She recalled something that annoying salesman, Eric, had told her. The van had anti-theft devices.

Shit. It probably had a tracker on it. Either GPS or an RF transmitter. Her abduction of Eric had probably made the news, and they interrogated him. She knew she was taking a risk when she decided to spare his life.

Fleming blew out a big breath. OK, if the problem was the van, she had two options. Ditch the vehicle, or find out where the tracking device was and disable it.

Neither would be easy. Especially since, in a stupid effort to look as normal as possible around Bradley, she'd left her leg braces back at the shop. Which meant if she left the van it had to be in the wheelchair. With Sasha, no less.

Fleming scanned her head for information about this town, procured while searching for computer shops. She recalled the address of a department store, assumed it would be attached to a mall, and headed in that direction.

The Mustang seemed in no hurry to catch up, staying several car lengths behind. They probably wanted her alive, which gave Fleming a small advantage, because she would happily kill them once given the chance.

When she reached the mall, Fleming circled around half of it, then dialed information again and asked for a taxi service.

"I'm disabled, confined to a wheelchair. Do you have a van that can accommodate me? One with a chair lift?"

No, they didn't. Fleming tried again, with the company's competitor, and arranged for them to meet her at Macy's lower north entrance in ten minutes. Then she parked in a handicapped spot, got into her wheelchair, and placed Sasha and her shotgun in her lap, covered by Bradley's stuff.

A quick check of the Mustang told her it was several rows over. Fleming used the chair lift, which was interminably slow. After she reached ground and locked the vehicle, she forced herself to stay at a normal speed while heading into the mall. There had been two people in the Mustang. Protocol would dictate one stayed in the vehicle and watched the van, and the other follow her.

Once inside, she immediately looked for the security hall-way, and found a door marked "No Admittance" to the right. She headed for it.

Locked.

With picks, it would have been open in ten seconds, tops. But Fleming didn't have lock picks on her, and didn't have time to improvise a set. So she rolled farther into the mall, contemplating her next move. She passed a candy shop, a shoe store, and came to an open area surrounding a staircase going down.

Sasha poked her head out of the pile on Fleming's lap, taking in the sights. Fleming ached to look over her shoulder, to see how close her pursuer was, but instead beelined for the staircase.

She hesitated at the top. Thirty steps at least, and falling was something Fleming feared more than almost anything. Since the wire snapped in Milan and she shattered both her legs, Fleming had been petrified of heights. But even a fall of just a few feet could cause debilitating pain when you had dozens of pins and screws in your legs.

But if she was lucky, whoever was chasing her wouldn't think she'd take the stairs, and outthinking the enemy was her only chance.

She leaned back and gave her handrails a swift tug, balancing on two wheels. It was a trick she knew well, but this wheelchair had been modified and was heavier than what she normally used. Plus the stuff on her lap, including a squirming Sasha, played hell with her balance.

Maybe pulling the shotgun and fighting her way out was smarter. Or ducking into one of the shops and hiding. Or...

"Ah, hell."

Fleming teetered at the top of the stairs—

—then pushed herself over.

The first step was jarring, but she kept her hands tight on the rails, keeping steady, resisting gravity and momentum.

Another step.

Another.

She focused on balance, on feeling, ignoring the siren in her head telling her this was insane, a siren reinforced by her eyesight, staring down at the thirty-degree drop into pain, surgery, and possibly death.

Sasha whined, sort of a chirping sound, obviously agitated by this turn of events. Fleming ignored her, ignored the stares of the crowd, ignored everything but the fluid in her inner ear, telling her how to position her hands and body.

Five...six...seven...eight...

She pictured her body skewered on a rod that was perfectly vertical. If the rod moved forward too much, she pushed forward to catch up. Too far back, and she leaned forward to compensate.

Thirteen...fourteen...fifteen...

Only a few more stairs. Almost there.

Then Sasha stood, trying to crawl up Fleming's neck, and the wheelchair began to tip forward. Fleming felt a jolt of panic, unable to compensate for the shift in weight, picturing herself pitching down the last few steps, her legs snapping like kindling, the failure and agony and—

"Whoa, there! I gotcha."

A male voice, and firm hands on the push handles behind her, stopping Fleming's tumble, easing her down the final five stairs to a gentle landing.

"You OK there, darlin'?"

Fleming looked up, saw a handsome man in a Stetson staring down at her. Stubbly chin. Blue eyes.

"Yeah. Thanks."

"Now what made you go and take the stairs like that?"

"I don't like waiting for elevators."

"No kiddin'. Whatcha got there? Some cute little animal. Cat?"

"What? This?"

Fleming lifted her hands, bringing up the shotgun just as the man dove to the side. She fired as he rolled behind the staircase. Then she tore ass across the mall as people screamed and fled, picking up speed, Sasha trying to dig into her lap as if it was an underground den.

She rounded a corner, unsure if Stetson was behind her, unsure of how she'd guessed he was Rhett from Hydra Deux other than a hunch. He had both eyes, so he wasn't Heath, and he wasn't a bodybuilding Asian, so he couldn't be Tristan. Something about how quickly and easily he moved when he saved her made Fleming peg him as an operative. The way he ducked before she brought up her shotgun confirmed it.

Now she had to get away, and the odds weren't favorable to her. Especially since he was probably contacting his partner—Scarlett, no doubt—to join in the chase.

Fleming rounded a corner, heading for Macy's, wishing among the many modifications to her chair she'd thought to include a rearview mirror.

*Modifications to my chair...*

Catching a glimpse of herself in a storefront display window as she rolled past, Fleming saw Rhett was right on her ass, reaching for the wheelchair handle.

She slapped her handrail, opening it up, pulling the braided length of fishing wire—

—releasing a quart of two-stroke motor oil in her wake.

An oldie but a goodie, and Fleming heard the slap of Rhett eating the tile, followed by his cursing because she'd modified a classic by adding a few dozen treble hooks from a tackle box to the oil. When you fell, you reached out with your hands to break your fall, and palms and fishhooks didn't play well together.

Rolling past another glass storefront, Fleming saw Rhett was no longer behind her. She turned another corner, coasting into Macy's, burning her palms on her handrails to slow herself down. Then it was a quick but careful trek through the store, keeping to the sides and staying hidden behind displays, until she found the north entrance and her taxi waiting for her.

The lift took forever, and the driver bristled when he noticed Sasha.

"No pets, lady."

"It's OK. I'm handicapped. She's my seeing-eye dog," she said.

"That don't look like no dog."

"Haven't you heard of a foxhound?"

"Oh. I guess it's all right then."

During the ride, Fleming worked to get her heart rate and breathing under control. She considered the probability of Hydra Deux knowing where her workshop was, and decided it was low. If they knew where she was holing up, they wouldn't have made a grab for her in a public mall.

He dropped her off at a fast-food place three blocks from the shop she'd rented, and Fleming rolled the rest of the way back, looking over her shoulder every few seconds.

When she made it into her parking lot, Fleming used a palm strike to knock a side mirror off a Toyota, with plans to attach it to her chair. When she was sure she hadn't been followed, Fleming waited, watching for the Mustang or any other suspicious vehicle to show up. None did. After a half hour of surveillance, Fleming entered her store and locked the door behind her, hoping to see Bradley hard at work on their project.

But the very last thing she expected was for him to be gone, the padlock open, and the loop on the steel cable empty.

# Years Ago...

Her codename was Isolde, and she'd grown up on a dirt farm in rural South Carolina.

From an early age, she had certain proclivities that smarter parents would have recognized as warning signs. They knew enough to not let her tend the chickens, because baby chicks seemed to go missing after she fed them. They knew enough to not let her tend the pigs, because one day Pa caught her poking one with a sharp stick. So her chores were mostly weeding the garden, and helping Ma sew and cook and clean, which she hated even more.

On the eve of her tenth birthday, she visited a local creek with some of her schoolmates—she considered them schoolmates and not friends because she didn't really get along with people. Her schoolmates didn't like her, because even at ten she was painfully thin, and she hardly ever talked except to say mean things.

But on this day, Tommy Lee Forble had firecrackers, and one of her favorite things to do was to catch carp by hand and stuff their mouths with explosives. She could remember one time where the fish lived for a whole ten minutes with most of its head missing.

She'd spotted a nice catfish, mouth big enough to hold a whole pack of firecrackers, swimming near the shore, and took off her shoes to wade in after it. Three steps into the cool water, something sharp pierced her foot. When she bent down to look, she saw she'd stepped on a waterlogged board with a rusty nail stuck into it. The nail came right up through the top of her foot, blood bubbling up out of the wound like a red volcano.

She didn't cry out. Though she registered the sensation of pain, it felt more curious than agonizing. She lifted her foot slightly, then brought it down again, hard, letting the sensation ripple through her.

By the fifth or sixth time doing this, one of her schoolmates noticed and began to scream.

Her parents rushed her to the big hospital in Rock Hill, where a kind-faced doctor poked a huge needle into her arm that hurt worse than the nail did.

She didn't even blink.

# Isolde

*"If you're having too much fun, reel it in," The Instructor said. "There's nothing wrong with enjoying your work. But remember it is work, not playtime."*

Neither Izzy nor Tristan commented on the awe-inspiring majesty of Niagara Falls as they crossed the Rainbow Bridge into Canada. Tristan only talked when spoken to, and Izzy lacked whatever part of the brain made human beings respond to beauty.

She didn't understand art, music was white noise to her, and she'd never been able to read an entire novel.

Her anorexia wasn't due to body image problems. Izzy didn't like food. The tastes and textures revolted her, and she hated the smacking sounds people made while eating, herself included. She survived on protein drinks and regular intravenous supplements. The protein crap was disgusting, and half of it she threw up. But the IV...

Izzy liked needles. She liked being poked, and sliced, and burned, and scraped. She liked sex with Tristan because he hurt her. The term for it was *algolagnia*. Izzy was physically wired to gain pleasure from pain, either her own or the pain of others. It was a true neuropathological disorder, though Izzy didn't consider it detrimental at all. She wasn't bogged down by all the weakness inherent in human emotion. She didn't love anyone, or need anyone. A happy day for her was torturing and killing a target, and then relaxing by tearing off one of her fingernails and sticking her finger in a lemon.

They reached customs on the Canadian side, and Tristan produced the forged paperwork and IDs. The customs agent asked them to open the rear of the truck, and Izzy hopped out and complied, pulling up the cargo door with a well-known soda pop logo on it, keeping a straight face as the dude aimed his flashlight at the crates of cola cans.

"Want one?" Izzy asked.

"Hot cola? No thanks."

He checked the invoice and customs forms, and then the pinhead actually did a rough count of boxes to see if they matched.

They matched. But the ones in the middle contained weaponized Ebola.

"The taste you'll die for," Izzy said, quoting the slogan.

"No kidding. I'll stick with organic. This stuff will kill you."

"Wise choice."

He stamped her papers, and Izzy pulled down the door and secured the latch. Then Tristan pulled into Canada, heading toward Toronto.

"Easy peasy," she told Tristan. "Not even that dumb cow Earnshaw can fuck it up."

He didn't reply.

Izzy fished her Swiss Army knife out of her front pocket, and spent a moment contemplating its many tools. She picked the saw, and stuck it up her nose.

The mucus membranes inside the nostrils were particularly sensitive, and she'd long since plucked all of her nose hairs out, one by one. So instead she lightly scraped her septum, the pain bringing tears, and then blood.

It was delicious agony.

"Punch me," she told Tristan, sticking out her tongue so the blood didn't drip on the truck, leaving DNA.

"When we get there."

"Come on."

He didn't hit her, but Tristan did put his hand on her thigh, pinching with his bodybuilder hands until Izzy screamed.

She licked her upper lip, closed her eyes, and let ecstasy take her.

# Chandler

*"There is action and there is reaction," The Instructor said. "If you're reacting, it's often too late."*

The cop cars screaming toward us and Hammett gone from her post, my only option was to run. Jack's betrayal meant my slender hopes at surviving this ordeal had been dashed. Fleming and I were dead, or worse.

I bolted, vaguely hearing Jack yell after me as I sprinted across the plaza, scattering pigeons to the four winds. I expected more police. Hell, I expected the entire US military. But as I ran, I didn't encounter any resistance at all.

I bolted down Clark, turning west on Randolph, passing city hall. The Chicago River was three blocks ahead. If things went sour, we were to rendezvous at the SUV, parked on Canal Street. I glanced overhead, looking for helicopters, seeing none. The streets were full of pedestrians, but in a busy city like Chicago, no one paid any attention to a woman sprinting.

I found my rhythm, letting my limbs and breath settle into a steady tempo, and my phone buzzed on my hip. I cut down an alley, slowing down enough to pick up.

"Where the hell did you go?"

Hammett.

"Cops," I said.

"They were going somewhere else, Chandler. It's a big city. Crime happens. They weren't there for you."

I slowed my pace down to a jog.

"What about Abbey Road?" I asked. Prior to the meeting, we agreed mentioning Beatles albums would be a signal if one of us had been compromised. It was possible Hammett was under duress, being forced to flush me out.

"You're an idiot. You took off for no reason."

Shit. I stopped in the alley. "So where were you?"

"Across the street. Where I said I'd be."

"I didn't see you."

"Of course you didn't see me. I was staying out of sight. That's what you do during surveillance."

Double shit.

"Your cop friend took off. Want me to tail her?"

"Negative. Let her go."

"I thought we needed her."

"We do. I'll call her again."

"How about I just grab her, make her do what we want?"

"That won't work on her."

"It works on anyone."

"Just listen to me, Hammett."

She snorted. "Yessir, fearless leader. You've been doing such a great job so far."

Hammett hung up. I aimed myself toward Canal Street, trying to slow my breathing.

But I couldn't.

I stopped in the middle of the sidewalk, my chest heaving, my heart hammering, and I couldn't regain control over my body.

I closed my eyes, breathing through my nose, trying to picture my heart rate slowing down. Trying to make my blood into ice water. Relaxing my muscles. Clearing my head. Focusing on my diaphragm. Going through all the rituals as I'd been taught. All the things that The Instructor had forced me to learn, so I could be superhuman.

But that was the problem. I wasn't superhuman.

*I was less than human.*

My shitty stepfather was right: I was a pitiful, whiny bitch. I had no friends. No husband. No children. No life. I finally found out I had sisters—something I'd wanted my entire life—and I'd already killed four of them and was on my way to killing the other two via my own gross incompetence.

A sob welled up in my chest, then burst out so loud it actually startled me. I squatted down next to a Dumpster, hugging my knees, almost every part of me bruised or cut or burned or shot, but that pain was nothing compared to how much I realized I hated myself.

I hated myself more than I hated my stepfather. More than he hated me. More than I hated my psychotic ex-boyfriend Cory, or Hammett when she was waterboarding me, or The Instructor, who was the soulless son of a bitch who had taken whatever humanity I had left and snuffed it out.

I was no better than an animal. No, I was worse than any animal. They had reasons to kill. I was just following orders like some brainwashed Nazi.

I was the worst of the worst. An assassin. A scumbag. A cancer on society. I hadn't amounted to anything, just like my stepdad had predicted. I was a despicable killer, no better than Hammett, except she could keep herself together while I fell apart.

No wonder Lund dumped me.

The tears came, and I cried like I hadn't cried since I was a kid. The only pride I had, the only thing that kept me waking up every morning, was my job. And now I couldn't even do that. The world's greatest operative was having a pity party in a stinking Chicago alley. The best thing for everyone would be if I walked out into traffic, let a bus finish me off. There was nothing left of me anyway. I honestly couldn't remember what I was even fighting for. To clear my name? For what?

Lund was right. I was a monster. Thinking I could escape this life, become a normal person, was a stupid fantasy. I'd never end up happy. I'd end up dying alone, and it was a fate I deserved because I was such a—

"Chandler?"

I looked up, saw Hammett standing over me.

"What happened? Are you hurt?"

"Go away," I managed to say between sniffles.

"What the hell is wrong with you? Are you crying?"

"I'm done."

"Done with what?"

"Fuck off, Betsy! I said I'm done!"

I stood up, not bothering to wipe the tears off my face, and began walking toward Randolph.

"Chandler, the car is this way."

Hammett caught up to me, grabbed my arm. I twisted away.

"What's happening here?"

I kept walking. Hammett got in front of me, drawing her .357 and pointing it at my forehead.

"Get your shit together, sis. We don't have time for your little breakdown right now."

We stared at each other, her annoyed, me broken.

"Do it," I said.

She pulled back the hammer.

I closed my eyes, trying to come up with some comforting final thought, and failing at something even that simple.

Then my head was reeling back, and I felt a harsh sting on my cheek. I stared up at Hammett, who had put the gun away and used her open palm on me instead.

"Enough, Chandler. We're going."

"I'm not going any—"

She slapped me again, so hard I saw stars.

"This isn't the time or the place," Hammett said. "Follow me back to the goddamn vehicle."

I didn't move.

Hammett shook her head. "Seriously? After all the shit we've been through these past few days? You decide now is the time to give up?"

She slapped me three more times, until I fell to my knees. My ears were ringing, and my cheek was on fire.

"Why didn't you do this earlier? Would have saved me a whole lot of trouble."

Another slap. I felt ready to pass out.

"I don't give pep talks," Hammett said. "And I know threats aren't going to work. Fleming and I are better off without your sorry ass. So I'm just going to slap the shit out of you until I get bored, then finish the goddamn mission myself."

Hammett hit me once more, and I tasted blood.

She grinned, shaking her head. "I think you're actually enjoying yourself. What is this? Penance for you? Let's step it up a notch."

The next blow was a kick, dead center in my chest, sprawling me out onto my back.

"You're a crummy leader," Hammett said. "And you fight like a girl."

She kicked me again, a football punt between my legs. I brought my knees to my chest, moaning.

"Why are you covering up? This is what you want, isn't it, sis? What you deserve?"

Hammett kicked again, and my body reacted without me even thinking about it. I caught her foot, twisted, and brought her down to the pavement with me.

We locked eyes, and I felt something flare inside, bubbling up through the self-pity.

Anger.

Hammett went for a strike to the nose, and I blocked it with my palm and elbow, then snapped her in the chin.

She rolled away, and then we were both on our feet, circling each other.

"Maybe there's hope for you yet," Hammett said, her tongue snaking out and licking the blood from the corner of her mouth.

She launched herself at me, a muay Thai flying kick, and again instinct took over and I brought up my forearms to absorb the blow, then pivoted my hips, caught her arm, and judo threw her to the ground, still holding her left wrist.

The rest of her fingers formed a fist, but her splinted, broken pinkie jutted out. Without thinking I grabbed it and yanked back.

Hammett howled, and I realized Fleming was right. Breaking Hammett's finger did make me feel better.

I let her go and stepped away, palms up.

Hammett looked up at me, her teeth clenched. "Done feeling sorry for yourself?"

I nodded. I wasn't sure how long it would last, but at the moment, I was spent, and besides the physical pain Hammett had dealt me, I didn't feel much of anything. It was a relief.

"Then can you please snap my goddamn finger back in place?"

I reached for her, wary of another attack, but Hammett kept still as a statue. When I put her finger back in place, she grunted. I pulled her to her feet.

"Nice throw," she said.

"Thanks. And thanks for..."

"Don't mention it. I'm still going to kill you eventually."

We walked back to the SUV, and I called Jack's office.

"Sorry. I'm a little jumpy."

"Apparently."

"So..."

"I'll do it. I just called Senator Crouch. He's making it happen. I can be in DC by tonight. But there's a problem. You can't take tours alone. I have to bring someone with."

"Do you have anyone?"

"Not on this short notice."

I knew someone, but Jack wouldn't like it.

"Give me your cell number," I said. She did. "I'll call you tomorrow. And Jack?"

"Yeah?"

"Thanks."

"We heroes have to stick together."

She hung up.

I didn't feel like a hero. I felt like a fraud. A fraud, a liar, a cheat, and every bit the reprehensible killer.

"No one ever called me a hero," Hammett said. Apparently she'd been able to overhear Jack's words. "Even when I was killing for Uncle Sam."

"Me neither."

"A hero is a protector. A savior. Only person I ever tried to save is myself. But you? You saved London. How did that feel?"

"That was Fleming, not me. I tried to save Julie, but you know how that turned out."

"You'll get another chance. I've got a feeling there will be more lives on the line than just hers. Maybe we'll both know what it's like to be the good guy for once."

I highly doubted it.

# Julie

The door's squeak woke Julie from what seemed like an endless doze.

She had no idea how much time had passed. It could have been an hour, or it could have been five. But she was ready. At least, she hoped she was.

The same woman, dull blond hair, mole that resembled a bug, padded across the floor to Julie's bed. She checked the monitors first: heart, blood pressure, God knew what else. Julie noticed then that she had a catheter inserted, and the idea of it made her squirm, so she tried not to think about it too much.

Nurse Brady Bunch moved on to the IV.

Once Julie made her move, they would know the sedative wasn't enough to keep her under. Julie would only have one shot at this. She had to make it count.

When she heard the Velcro tear free, she was ready.

She opened her eyes and levered herself up in bed. Grabbing the Velcro binding her right wrist, she ripped it and wrestled her other arm free.

The nurse, or whatever she was, was twisted around, gathering her syringe from a rolling tray. Gasping, she spun around and stared at Julie. "But you—"

Julie didn't hesitate. Channeling her inner Chandler, she swung her fist around and into the side of the woman's head.

The nurse fell, smashing into the tray and then the floor. Vials and needles clattered across tile. The blow shuddered through Julie's elbow, and for a moment her forearm and hand felt numb.

"Stop!"

Julie was shaking, tears streaming from her eyes. She grasped the tube feeding her drugs and ripped the tape holding the needle, then the needle itself. Blood beaded on the back of her hand, but she didn't care. The monitor pads came next, leaving the machine screaming the flat tone that meant someone had just died.

The nurse scrambled to her feet, a purple bruise already coloring her jaw. "I'm calling security!"

"Tell them to bring their guns."

She stared at Julie as though believing she'd lost her mind.

Julie almost wished she had. Unfortunately, this was the sanest thing she'd ever done. She might have done it long ago, if not for Chandler, if not for Kirk. She couldn't abandon either of them.

Now both of them were gone.

The nurse slammed out of the room, and Julie turned her attention to getting out of bed. The catheter was more difficult to remove. But when she was finally untethered, she grasped the bar at the side of the hospital bed trying to release it.

It didn't move.

Neither did the other side. Her mind was still muddled and sluggish, and for the life of her, she couldn't remember how to lower the sidebars, if she ever knew at all.

But Julie wasn't going to let that stop her. She scooched to the end of the bed and slid out onto the floor, the tile cold under her bare feet. She was in good shape, but she hadn't moved in a while, and her inactivity combined with the sedatives made her head feel light and her limbs heavy.

Using the bed rail to steady herself, she made for the upended tray. Crouching down, she felt under the tray with her hand. The tray itself was simple, and all the edges smooth, its few pieces attached with rivets. She moved down the single leg to the wheels, feeling the joints where the wheel portion attached.

There.

The rumble of voices came from the hall outside.

Her fingers trembled, but she managed to get ahold of one of the screws holding the contraption together. It wasn't much. But there was nothing better in the room. She wasn't strong enough to take the rails off the bed. She doubted the machines would provide a sharp edge.

She loosened the screw, twisting as fast as she could until it came off in her hand. The tip was pointy, and while not sharp, it might be sharp enough.

Taking a deep breath, she dragged the point across the inside of her left wrist.

The door flew open. A man in a white space suit burst through, his features obscured behind the glare of his Plexiglas mask, followed by the woman Julie had clocked in the head.

"See?" Nurse Brady screamed. "She's awake, and…What are you doing?"

Blood streaked across the pale skin of Julie's wrist, but it wasn't coming fast enough. Bleeding to death would take forever at this rate, and that was time she didn't have. She needed to end things now.

She raised the screw to her throat.

"Put that down, Julie," the guard said. He was young man, maybe a few years older than Julie. He spread his gloved hands and approached slowly, his face kind. The nurse approached from the other side.

Julie raised her hand. "My blood will kill you."

"I'm immune, you stupid little bitch," said the woman. "Do you really think I'd take your blood without protection?"

Of course. Immune, like Chandler had been.

At the thought of Chandler, Julie's throat closed, tears blurring her vision. She grabbed the wheel frame from the table and hurled it at the nurse.

The guard stepped closer.

"Shoot me!" Julie begged.

"I don't have a gun," he said.

"I'll rip your suit open."

"I'm not trying to hurt you, Julie. I'm trying to protect you. My name is Derek Fossen. And I'm a—"

"What's going on here?" A gruff male voice came from the doorway.

Fossen stepped aside, and an older man stepped into the room. He was dressed in a black shirt, pants, and sports jacket, and his silver hair sparkled in the overhead light. Julie had never seen the man before, but everything about him said he was in charge.

"Put that down, Julie," he said.

She looked at the man, at Fossen, at the nurse—

—then she drove the screw into her neck. The sharp point cut, pain piercing her skin, hot blood sticky in her fingers. But it wasn't enough.

"You're going to have to kill me."

"I'm not going to let that happen."

A sob bubbled up, lodging in her throat.

"You also know you can't kill yourself with that screw."

"The hell I can't." Clenching her teeth together, she stabbed again.

"Julie," the old man said. "Stop right now."

She stabbed herself again and again, a scream erupting from her throat.

Fossen grabbed her wrist, pushing her down onto the bed, pinning her there, saying, "Stop, please stop it," over and over.

Julie screamed and thrashed, trying to get free and finish the job.

"Julie, that's enough," the old man said. "Stop this right now, or I kill Chandler."

"Chandler?"

She stopped fighting, and shivers spread over Julie's skin. Maybe there was hope. Maybe it wasn't all over.

"Chandler is alive?"

# Fleming

*"If used properly, sex can be the most powerful weapon in your arsenal," The Instructor said. "If used improperly, it can destroy you."*

Fleming stared, slack-jawed, at the open padlock. She couldn't believe it.

Bradley had escaped.

She didn't understand how she could have read him so wrong. Fleming had been sure that he liked her and wanted to help, that the promise of sex was enough to keep him rooted and working diligently. Could he have been lying? Playing her somehow? Had he gone to get the authorities? Or maybe he hadn't done this alone. Maybe that cowboy had gotten here first, and now Bradley was—

"Oh, hi, Ian."

Fleming's head snapped to the rear of the store, and she saw Bradley standing there, grinning. What the hell?

"Hey, you got Sasha! Come here, girl!"

The vixen jumped out of Fleming's lap and bounded into Bradley's arms.

"I hope she wasn't any trouble."

"You took off the padlock," she said, incredulous.

"Yeah. It kept bumping against my ankle. I can put it back on if you want me to."

Fleming rolled closer. "How?"

"I'm a robotics engineer, Ian. Machines are my thing. I can pick a lock with a paper clip."

"So why didn't you..."

"Leave? And miss the chance to kiss you again?"

He smiled shyly, and Fleming felt a blush creep up her face and her pulse begin a foxtrot.

Bradley stroked Sasha, who was yipping in a way that sounded a lot like giggling. "I made a lot of progress on the project. I need your circuit board, but the servo for the wheel works great."

"Come here," she said, her voice husky.

He set down the fox and came over, eyebrows furrowing. "Is everything OK? If I did something wrong, I..."

She felt as if she'd tumbled out of a Jerry Bruckheimer action movie and somehow wound up in a John Hughes film. A boy had stuck around to help her, at great risk to himself, simply because he wanted another kiss. Did it get any better than that?

"Kiss me," Fleming said.

Bradley bent down, tentative. Fleming grabbed his collar and pulled him roughly to her, pressing her lips to his. He tasted like black coffee, and moaned slightly when their tongues met. She moved her hands to his chest, feeling his corded muscles through his shirt, and he cradled the back of her head, running his long fingers through her hair, stroking her scalp. Fleming took his other hand, placed it on her side.

"Bra," she said.

He skimmed his hand around to her back and fumbled with the clasp, taking too long.

"Rip it."

And then there was a quick tug and her bra clasp released, her breasts free. Fleming moved the fabric to the side and directed his hands to her nipples. His touch made them stiffen, and she shivered, reaching for his belt and his fly.

"Oh God, Ian…"

She unzipped his jeans and he sprang free, and when Fleming wrapped her hand around him, she found he was shivering.

"Stand up straight," she told him.

Bradley leaned away from her wheelchair, eyes wide, and she took him into her mouth. The gasp it elicited made her smile.

She ran her tongue over him, firm, strong licks from his base to his head, cupping his balls with one hand. She took him full into her throat, then pulled back and teased him, running the tip of her tongue around his ridge, eliciting loud groans that resonated as both pleasure and relief. Holding him between her lips, she glanced up and smiled. He had the most adorable look on his face: a cross between ecstasy and disbelief. She flicked and kissed and teased some more.

His breathing became rapid, his eyes glazed. Deciding that she wanted him to finish in her mouth, she moved back down, scooping up his length with her tongue. Still working his balls, she began to rapidly stroke with her other hand, alternating between pumping and twisting her fist around his width, all the while continuing to draw him deep into her throat.

It didn't take long for his hips to spasm, and for him to lose control and cry out, and she kept sucking until he was done.

"Ian…that was…it was…"

She stared up at him, drinking in his expression while he continued to stroke her hair.

"Just the beginning. Take me to the mattress."

Bradley blinked, then scooped her up out of the chair, his strong arms wrapping around her and carrying her as if she weighed nothing. He placed her down on the air mattress as if she were a fragile, delicate thing.

The way he touched her…the way he looked at her…

"My shirt," she told him, wanting to be completely naked, his eyes all over her, that little smile of wonder warming every inch of her skin.

With trembling hands, he removed the already loose shirt and bra, staring at her naked breasts with an expression of wonder and lust. Without prompting, he bent down to take a nipple in his mouth, and Fleming sighed as he captured it lightly in his teeth and licked. He gave its partner equal attention, and didn't have to be told to remove her skirt and leggings.

When they were off, Fleming had that moment of dread when a new lover saw her ruined, scarred legs for the first time. But she needn't have worried with Bradley, because his eyes locked onto her pussy as if it was the only thing in the world that existed. His hands moved down, caressing her, so softly it was almost maddening.

"Harder."

He began to rub, sending a shock of pleasure rippling up Fleming's spine, and then he was working his fingers in and out of her, churning them at the same time, and she forgot all about how inexperienced he was and gave herself over to him, arching her hips and moaning.

Maybe he'd picked it up from all the porn he indulged in, but somehow once Bradley had warmed up, he seemed to know exactly what he was doing. When to be firmer. When to be softer. He read every shift of her body, hanging on each movement, each moan, each clue she gave him, completely focused on her words.

Fleming felt the pressure building, and building, and she bit her lower lip and closed her eyes and groaned deep in her chest and then, all at once, his magical fingers were gone.

Her eyes flipped open, and she wondered what was wrong. Had he finally seen her legs and gotten turned off? Had her passion scared him somehow? Was it plain old virgin insecurity?

She was about to ask, to help him if she could, when he suddenly pinned her to the mattress, his arms around her legs, his tongue and lips devouring her.

Bradley needed no help. No direction. He was as good as the best she'd ever had, knowing when to lick, when to pull away, coaxing the moans, and eventually the screams, out of her, bringing her to a mind-blowing climax that went on and on, leaving Fleming feeling like she'd been deflated.

But even though she stopped her gyrations, he didn't stop his oral assault, somehow knowing she was sensitive after her orgasm, using his fingers again, forcing her arousal, coaxing her to meet his passion once more before again pressing his mouth to her and making her come once more.

And he still didn't stop.

She tried to pull away, to convey he'd done enough, but he started with his fingers again, playing her like a virtuoso on a familiar violin. Fleming felt herself lifted, and then she was on her shoulders, her legs up around his neck, and for a third time his mouth took her.

Fleming reached blindly for him, and found him wickedly aroused, and as he devoured her she managed to find her voice and say, "Fuck me...Bradley...please..."

He lowered her to the bed, his cheeks glistening, eyes wide, and she guided him into her and he began to pump like a jackrabbit, a starving man given a sandwich, and though Fleming normally preferred the slower approach, his intensity and need overwhelmed her, and she began to climax almost immediately, her arms around his neck as his hands found her nipples, and soon his cries were matching hers, and thirty seconds later, Bradley Milton was no longer a virgin.

They lay there, entwined, sweating and gasping for breath, Fleming luxuriating at his weight on top of her, his stubble against her cheek, the smell of his sweat. Then he began to tremble and she thought, "Oh God, is he crying?"

"That was AWESOME!" he said, and he stared at her with a huge smile on his face, and she realized he'd been giggling, giddy with happiness. She joined him, a polite laugh that quickly became infectious, and he rolled next to her, both of them staring at the ceiling, guffawing until Fleming's diaphragm began to hurt.

When they got ahold of themselves again, Bradley gave her the sweetest kiss on the cheek and said, "Thank you, Ian."

"Fleming," she said. "Call me Fleming. That's what those who are close to me call me."

"Fleming. I like it."

"You sure you never did this before?"

"No. But I've been practicing a lot on my own. Was I OK?"

Fleming giggled, then trailed a finger over the hair on his chest. "You were great."

"So were you. God, you're so beautiful."

The warmth that was in his eyes infused his voice, and Fleming soaked it in.

"You're amazing, Bradley."

"Me? You're the amazing one. I still can't believe I got so lucky."

Less than an hour ago, Fleming had been running for her life. Twenty minutes ago, her head had been filled with dire scenarios and paralyzing self-doubt. But Bradley's simple act of kindness, of trust, of wide-eyed delight, somehow had restored Fleming's faith in humanity, and in herself, in a way that made her feel young and fresh and naive.

She wanted to stay cuddled up just like this. Unfortunately, that wasn't possible.

"We need to get some work done," she said. "But I'm famished. Why don't we get something to eat first, then—"

"I know just what I want to eat."

And then his head was between her legs again.

Fleming thought about protesting, but instead she just shook her head and let the sensations envelop her. At least for a little while longer.

Virgins. Who could have known?

# Hammett

*"There is never room for doubt," The Instructor said.
"Save the introspection for after the mission, or the mission will end with your death."*

Hammett glanced over at Chandler in the driver's seat and frowned. Her sister basically had a nervous breakdown in that alley, sobbing and refusing to defend herself, and that was unacceptable. Hammett had seriously considered killing her, and leaving the body where it could be easily discovered. That would take the immediate heat off Hammett, but the problem of The Instructor still remained. As long as that asshole was still alive, Hammett would always be hunted. Maybe not as a presidential assassin, but as a loose end that needed to be snipped.

So crybaby Chandler had gotten a stay of execution.

Once they nailed The Instructor, however, all bets were off. Chandler, and Fleming, would have to be taken out.

Strangely, Hammett had lost much of her desire to do so. Forty-eight hours ago, her sisters were the enemy. Now that they were on the same side, Hammett was warming to them both.

Not that it would matter when the time came. Over the years, Hammett had killed plenty of people she'd liked.

"You could try the disassociation route."

Chandler stopped at a red light and said, "Hmm?"

"You know. Pretend the pain is happening to someone else, not you. Worked for me for years."

"I'm not you."

Hammett winced as she wiggled her broken pinkie. "OK, now this hurts. Watch."

Chandler glanced at her while Hammett closed her eyes and concentrated on her finger, transferring the pain somewhere else rather than feeling it herself. She'd long ago given up her imaginary sister, Rebecca, but still retained the ability to separate herself from the signals that were happening in her body.

After a few seconds of focusing, Hammett jammed her broken finger into the dashboard.

There was a cracking sound, bones grinding together, but Hammett kept her face neutral and didn't make a sound. She felt the pain, but in a detached way.

"You're out of your goddamn mind," Chandler said.

Hammett opened her eyes, still maintaining her concentration. "Life is shit, Chandler. But if we can reduce how we react to the shitty stuff, it's bearable."

She grasped her pinkie and shoved it back into place.

"That's never going to heal."

"We both have lots of wounds that will never heal, Chandler. So we either learn to live with them or fall apart."

The light turned green. Chandler hit the gas. They were both silent for a few blocks. Hammett eased herself back into the moment, the pain returning, but she was able to detach herself just enough to keep it manageable. That was the trick. If you turn off sensation, you turn off reaction. Fine if someone is hurting you. But not so good in a fight, because you're so focused on yourself you aren't fighting back.

"So how do you do it?" Chandler finally asked.

Hammett allowed herself a small grin. "Pain, pleasure, all sensations—even thoughts—are chemical and electrical. They take pathways through your body. These pathways can be very short, like a neurotransmitter in your brain hopping from synapse to synapse, or longer, like your nervous system announcing you have a broken finger. If you concentrate, you can imagine the route of the pain and derail it somewhere else. Like forcing a car on a highway to take a detour so it doesn't reach its intended destination."

"Sounds like new age bullshit."

"Pull over someplace. I'll show you."

"We're meeting Harry."

"Not for another hour. Find a spot."

Chandler turned onto Michigan Avenue, heading south down the Magnificent Mile. She took a ramp down to Grant Park North underground parking, pulled the automated ticket from the machine, and when the gate rose they spent five minutes weaving through the thousands of parked cars before finding an open spot. They exited the vehicle, keeping their heads down so their faces weren't caught on the security cameras, and located stairs to take them up into Millennium Park, Chicago's newest civic center and tourist attraction.

They walked past the McCormick Ice Rink, which wasn't yet open, and up to AT&T Plaza, a large concrete surface that was packed with people, all snapping pictures of a gigantic stainless steel sculpture called the Cloud Gate, nicknamed the Bean by locals because of its shape.

Hammett shook her head, marveling at the waste of taxpayer dollars. A half-billion bucks for some trees and grass, an outdoor theater, and a kitschy hunk of art that reminded her of a bedpan. How many dogs could have been rescued for that amount of money? The mind reeled.

Chandler led them through the crowds, down a path, and into a garden where acres of shrubs and flowers and grasses seemed out of place against a backdrop of skyscrapers. They found a secluded spot, and Chandler put her hands on her hips, waiting.

"Close your eyes and give me your finger," Hammett told her.

"I don't want you breaking it."

"I'm not going to," she said, taking out her buck knife. "I'm just going to stick a blade under your fingernail."

"Like hell."

"I said I can teach you to disassociate pain. But I can't teach you to stop being a pussy."

Chandler pursed her lips, then extended her hand.

"Now close your eyes and concentrate on your index finger."

Hammett gripped Chandler's knuckle and placed the tip of the blade under the nail. Chandler reflexively tried to pull her hand back.

"You want to learn this or not?"

"I'm asking myself the same thing."

"Just relax."

"Relax. Sure. It's like being on vacation. All that's missing is a beach."

Hammett sighed, annoyed. "Do your breathing exercise. The kind where you're doing body inventory. Except stop the inventory when you focus on your index finger."

Chandler remained still. Hammett noted her breathing had slowed.

"Are you focusing on your finger?"

"Mmm-hmm."

"Stay loose. Don't flinch. The pain will be sharp, but I'm not causing any serious damage. Now hold very, very still."

Hammett pressed the blade up under Chandler's fingernail. Chandler didn't flinch, but her breathing rate increased.

"OK, you feel the pain. Now concentrate on it. Focus on it completely."

Hammett gave Chandler thirty seconds to follow instructions. Her breathing was still faster than normal.

"You sense the pain in your fingernail. It hurts. But for it to hurt, your nerves have to report the damage to your brain. That means the pain travels up your arm, to your spine, to your brain. Or, more specifically, nociceptors are firing in your finger, sending signals to the dorsal horn in your spine, which tells the thalamus in your brain that you are hurt. Imagine the path these signals are taking. It happens fast, but not instantaneously. You can control your heart rate and breathing. With practice, you can control this as well."

Hammett let Chandler absorb that. In the meantime, her own senses were subconsciously analyzing their surroundings, scanning for threats. Hammett smelled at least six kinds of flowers, mixed in with car exhaust and fertilizer. She heard vehicles going past on Monroe and Columbus, the honk of a bus. A faint easterly breeze coming from Lake Michigan tickled Hammett's ears. There were six people around her other than Chandler: two men walking ahead, a family of four to the north, none out of the ordinary.

"Slow it down," Hammett said. "Imagine the signal traveling up your arm like a wave. You can't stop the wave. But you're not going to try. Instead, you're going to deflect it somewhere else. Instead of the wave going to your spine, it's going to go up to your arm, then out your elbow. Picture your elbow shooting out the wave of pain. It doesn't get to your head. It just runs through your body without you feeling it."

Hammett counted to ten, then gave the knife a tiny jiggle, blood dribbling down the blade. Chandler stayed stock-still. Hammett pushed it in another millimeter. Chandler didn't flinch.

Hammett was impressed. Granted, the tiny prick of a knife was a lot easier to block than a broken finger, or being tortured or raped, but it was a good start.

"OK, now imagine the wave again. But this time, it isn't going out your elbow. This time you're letting it go to your brain. You're allowing yourself to hurt. Feel the difference between detouring the wave, and allowing it to get through."

Hammett heard Chandler's breathing speed up.

"You can't stop a river. The water has to go somewhere. But you can deflect it. Now let the pain go further, up your arm, but allow it to exit your shoulder before it reaches your spine."

She felt Chandler relax again. Her sister really did have terrific control over her body.

"Open your eyes."

Chandler stared at her, but Hammett could sense her concentration was elsewhere.

"Nice job. You can do this with emotional pain as well. It's harder, because a thought travels a shorter distance, so it takes more focus to deflect. Also, there's a big drawback to doing this."

Moving slowly, almost leisurely, Hammett raised her palm and slapped Chandler across the face. Chandler reeled back and blinked, obviously surprised.

"Normally you would have instinctively blocked my blow, but you were too focused on your finger. This technique diffuses pain, but leaves you open to attack."

"Good to know," Chandler said.

Hammett folded the buck knife and stuck it in her pocket. "Keep practicing and you can learn to balance pain aversion with awareness of external stimuli."

Chandler nodded. Then, while examining her bleeding fingernail, she said something Hammett couldn't have expected. "Thanks."

Hammett stared at Chandler's face, searching for signs of insincerity. She found none, and had to exercise great self-control not to smile.

Chandler was beginning to trust her. That would make killing her later much simpler.

"Want to grab some food? If I'm going to ball Harry again, I need some energy."

"I don't see how you can sleep with that guy."

"He's not so bad. And that fake hand of his is pretty cool."

"But he's such a pig."

"Any port in a storm, sis. We're on the run. That means we take whatever we can get, whenever it comes along. Because it might be the last time."

"If my time is up, I don't want my last time to be with a creep."

"So you're content with your last being Mr. Morality, who dumped your sorry ass? Is that what the breakdown was all about?"

Chandler didn't answer.

"Say what you will about Harry, he's not going to judge you. That's what girls like us need. Someone who doesn't live in a glass house."

Chandler frowned.

"Admit it. I'm right."

Her sister tilted her head to the side, just a little, giving in. "For someone so obviously psychotic, you have your moments."

"Let's go eat before we hug and start getting mushy."

Hammett led the way. Partly because she was hungry. Partly because she was worried, if the syrup got any thicker, that she and Chandler would actually hug.

And that it might feel good.

# Scarlett

*"Losing the element of surprise is unfortunate, but not terminal," The Instructor said. "But once the enemy is aware of you, increase the pressure."*

Scarlett wiped away some iodine and traces of motor oil, then dug the scalpel in deeper. The fishhooks in Rhett's palm were deep, barbed, and a bitch to remove. Rhett had spared her any whining while she worked, but Scarlett had no sympathy for him. Thanks to his screwup, Fleming knew they were onto her. She'd also abandoned her vehicle, which would make her a lot harder to find.

When the last hook came free, Scarlett set about cleaning his wounds once more. Rhett was numbed with a local anesthetic, but he still winced when she dumped isopropyl alcohol on the oozing slashes. Then she unwrapped a gut suture and began to sew him up.

"You have a touch like an angel," Rhett purred.

"Shh. Concentrating."

"Just sayin'. Someone who treats a man that tender can't hide her true feelings."

"Is that right?"

"Certainly is. Some would say what you're doing right now is an intimate act. Even more intimate than making love."

Scarlett looked up from her stitching and put on a smile. "I'm thinking about performing an intimate act with your mouth right now."

Rhett winked. "Do tell."

In half a heartbeat, Scarlett held the suture up under Rhett's nose. "How about me sewing your lips together? Because if you keep hitting on me, that's what I'm going to do the next time you fall asleep."

"Easy there, darlin'. Just being friendly."

"We work together, Rhett. We aren't friends. Remember that."

"I surely will."

Scarlett went back to sewing, and Rhett was quiet for the remainder of the procedure. When she finished, Scarlett taped over the stitches, then leaned back and cracked her neck.

"I was thinking," Rhett said, "that the only way she could have gotten out of that mall was carjacking or calling a cab."

"You call the police, see if anything was reported. I'll take the cabs."

"Yes, ma'am."

There was only one taxi service in town with a shuttle equipped for wheelchairs. Scarlett spoke to the dispatcher and pretended to be Fleming, claiming she lost an earring in the backseat.

"Can you have the driver look? Also, can you ask him which side of the street he dropped me off on? I can't remember, and I need to tell my boyfriend to check the sidewalks."

Within a minute, Scarlett had the fast-food restaurant where the cab had taken Fleming.

"Also, I called a cab a bit later," Scarlett lied. "I might have left it in that cab as well."

"I don't know who you called, but we only have one record of a wheelchair pickup today."

Scarlett hung up. "I'm driving this time," she said.

Rhett held up his injured hand. "Fair enough. What's the plan?"

"She's in a wheelchair. She can't be too far from where they dropped her off. We take a look, ask around, see what turns up. How hard can it be to find a cripple?"

# Julie

"Do you want to see Chandler again, Julie?" the older man asked.

There was only one way she could answer that question, and even if it would have been smarter to lie, at that moment, Julie couldn't manage it. "Yes."

"Then stop trying to hurt yourself."

Julie's whole body trembled. Again tears flooded her eyes, but this time she managed to push them back.

*No crying. That's what Chandler would say.*

"Let her go, Fossen."

The guard in the space suit released her wrists and got up off the bed.

"Drop the screw, Julie," the man said. His voice was still commanding, but now there was a note of understanding softening his eyes.

"Chandler...Where is she?"

"We'll talk about Chandler, but not until I know you're safe. Drop the screw."

Julie ran her fingertips over the ridges, sticky with her blood. When it came to killing herself, she'd proven pretty inept. Her attempt to stop what these people were doing was an epic fail, and even now, she knew if they chose to rush her, she couldn't do anything to stop them.

"Why are you being nice to me?"

The man's pale lips twitched at the corners. "You're a smart girl, Julie. And I have to apologize for not treating you better all along. The fact is, we need each other. If I can make you understand what is happening here, earn your cooperation, then everything will be better. For both of us."

"And Chandler?" Julie asked.

"Especially for Chandler."

"OK." Taking a deep breath, she let the screw fall from her fingers.

The guard circled the bed and guided her to stand in front of the man in charge.

"Show Miss James to room 7. Make sure she can't escape this time."

"But Chandler, where is—"

"I'll explain everything. Now, you need to go with Fossen and wait for me. I won't be long."

Julie nodded. She didn't trust this silver-haired man, no matter how nicely he treated her. But if there was a chance she could help Chandler, she would play his game. At least for now.

"Thank you...sir."

"I'm called The Instructor."

An odd name, but Julie dutifully repeated it.

The Instructor looked away from her and nodded to the guard. "And Fossen? Get her a bandage for her throat and wrists. There will be some in the room."

Fossen nodded and then guided her into the hall.

In the heat of trying to kill herself, Julie hadn't thought about the fact that she was half-naked, only a flimsy hospital gown between her and total exposure. Now self-consciousness nibbled at the corners of her mind, and the waxed tile in the hallway felt cold on her bare feet.

Still, she felt stronger than she had since she'd been taken from the lighthouse.

When she'd seen the island burst into flame, she'd assumed Chandler and her sisters were dead. She'd believed she was all alone, and everything was up to her. Now that Chandler was alive, everything had changed.

Now there was hope.

Derek Fossen steered her into a room and flicked on the light once they were inside. She'd expected this room to be like the first one, cold tile and austerity, but she couldn't have been more wrong. The floor was covered with plush carpet, and the wall was painted in a warm beige and adorned with artwork even Julie recognized as expensive. A nice sofa and chairs dominated the room, and a wood desk angled out from the corner.

She glanced up at her escort. "Are you sure this is the right place?"

"Yes." He crossed to the desk and pulled some items from one of the drawers. Then he motioned to the desktop. "Sit here, please."

Julie did as he asked. Her gown rode up a little, and the desktop felt cold on her thighs and bottom, and when the man leaned over her, she felt more self-conscious than ever.

With gentle fingers, Fossen swept Julie's hair to the side. Then, using a series of alcohol pads, he cleaned the blood off her neck and wrist, his touch light even through the gloves.

When the pad brushed the cuts on her throat, Julie cringed.

"Sorry," he said.

"It's OK."

He continued, even gentler this time, and Julie tried not to react, even when the pain brought tears to her eyes. Soon he'd cleaned her wounds and finished by taping gauze squares over the cuts.

"Is that better?" he asked.

"Yes. Thanks. Are you a doctor?"

"Yes."

She'd assumed he was a guard. She expected security in a place like this, but she'd always thought of doctors as healers. "You're in a biohazard suit. You obviously know what they're doing with me."

Fossen nodded.

"So how can you help them? Didn't you take an oath to do no harm?"

"It's complicated."

"They're going to use me to kill people."

Fossen peered down at her, and even through the face shield she thought she read pity in his eyes. Then his face hardened again, bland and unreadable.

"There are a few magazines on the side table, if you want something to read."

He motioned to a stack. Then, giving her a final nod, he left the room and closed the door behind him, a lock clicking into place.

Julie perched on the edge of the sofa, pulling her flimsy gown over her legs as best she could, and prayed she was ready for whatever came next.

# Fleming

*"You don't win a battle playing defense," The Instructor said. "When attacked, attack back."*

Fleming lay on the air mattress, wonderfully sore, while Bradley made sandwiches using their meager rations. He brought back two, and Fleming realized this was the second time in three days that a lover had fixed her some food. But Bradley wasn't like Tequila, who'd fed her, and probably bedded her, almost as a professional courtesy. This young man hadn't seen and done the things Fleming had. He still had an innocence about him, a naïveté Fleming found both refreshing and sad. Soon enough, life would kick the stuffing out of him, like it did with everyone eventually.

The sandwich was bologna, cheese, mayo, and tomato slices on sourdough bread. Bradley sat on the mattress next to her as they ate, running his fingers over her hips. They eventually trailed down to her legs, running across the deep trenches of scar tissue.

"Does it still hurt?" he asked.

"Only when I'm awake."

"How did it happen?"

Fleming lost her good mood and reached down to push his hand away. "That's a bit personal, Bradley."

"More personal than what we just did?"

"In a way, yes."

"I want to know everything about you."

"That's not going to happen."

"Because you're a spy?"

"Yes. And more than that. I'm a private person."

"Have you ever told one of your boyfriends what happened to your legs?"

"Not in detail."

"Tell me."

"No."

He reached for her legs again, and Fleming grabbed his finger and twisted it back, pinning his face to the mattress.

"No means no."

"I like you a lot, Fleming."

"I like you, too, Bradley."

"All of you. Including your legs."

Fleming wasn't sure how to reply to that. She released him, and once again he placed his hand on one of her scars.

"Does rubbing hurt?"

"Bradley…"

He began to stroke her ruined leg, slowly, softly. Fleming tried to remember the last time a man had touched her there, and she realized no one had since the accident. There had always been an unspoken agreement to keep hands off. The men she'd been with had either found her legs to be as disgusting as Fleming did, or they'd been too polite, or too focused on other parts of her body.

"Are they always bruised like this?" he asked, still rubbing.

"No. It's been a rough few days."

"Am I hurting you?"

He wasn't. Not physically. But this was somehow more intimate than the sex they'd just shared.

"We need to finish eating and get some work done."

"Let me give you a massage first."

"No. I need to etch the circuit board."

She tried to sit up, but he put a gentle hand on her chest.

"You're my first," he said. "I'm just one of many to you. I want to do something no one else has. Let me rub your legs."

Jesus. He was like a puppy dog with his eager determination.

"Fine," she said, sighing. Then she closed her eyes and waited for it to end.

Bradley started at her toes. Her feet looked perfectly normal, not like the mottled lunch meat between her ankles and hips. Bradley rubbed her soles, her heels, stroking between each toe, and Fleming realized how much she missed foot massages. All too soon he moved up to her calves, his fingers probing the divots and bumps in her flesh, not hard enough to hurt very much, but making Fleming aware of every pin, every screw.

"I can feel metal," he said, almost excited by the discovery. "Do you set off metal detectors?"

Fleming frowned. "Yes."

"Cool."

"No, Bradley. It isn't cool. You know what's cool? Being able to walk."

"If I can accept who you are, why can't you?"

Fleming didn't know how to answer that. Bradley continued to knead and prod and rub his way up her legs, violating every crevice.

"Are you ticklish?" he asked.

"I used to be."

And then the insensitive son of a bitch dug his fingers into Fleming's inner thighs and tried to tickle her.

Fleming was so surprised he'd try something so obviously stupid that it overrode her natural instinct, which was to punch him in the head. By the time she recovered from the shock and was making a fist, a noise burst out of her mouth that was both unexpected and foreign.

Laughter.

*He's actually tickling me!*

Fleming opened her hand and tried to push him away, overcome by giggles, her whole body shaking in those wonderful/

terrible involuntary spasms that she hadn't felt in what seemed like a lifetime. Fleming had hated her legs so much, she could hardly believe they were the cause of her amusement.

After a few seconds, Bradley moved his hands higher, to her belly, and then abruptly stopped.

"Whoa. Are those stitches?"

Fleming, still in the throes of laughter, looked down at the incision in her stomach where the tracker chip had been removed.

The tracker chip...

"Bradley, get me my computer."

He must have sensed her seriousness, because he immediately obeyed. Fleming once again used the back door to access the Hydra database. All of the Hydra sisters had been given a GPS tracking chip during training without their knowledge, attached to their duodenums. It had allowed The Instructor to keep track of his operatives.

Now Fleming wanted to know if he'd done the same for Hydra Deux.

After searching through code for five minutes, she brought up a page that seemed promising. Sure enough, superimposed on a map of North America, seven blips registered. One was in Texas. One in Mexico City. Two in Toronto. One in Baraboo. And two in DC, roughly twenty miles away.

Fleming picked up her cell phone and shared the news with Chandler.

"So, what do you think?" Chandler asked after Fleming's explanation.

"I think you and Hammett need to check out Toronto, and either Texas or Mexico."

"We're going to see Harry now to get weapons. He's going with Jack to DC to tour the White House."

"Does the cop know that?"

"Not yet. I'll keep you posted."

"Same here. You doing OK with Hammett?"

"We're managing. How's your end of things?"

Fleming stole a glance at Bradley and felt herself flush. "We're managing, too."

"You slept with him."

"What?"

"I hear it in your voice."

"Anything for the cause. I'll call when I have something to report."

Fleming hung up. She hadn't lied to Chandler. Sleeping with Bradley had been a means to an end, a way to make him comply. An enjoyable way, but business nonetheless.

She looked at him again, sitting at the desk computer, eating his sandwich, and shivered when she remembered his hands on her legs.

*Easy, tiger. He's just a tool to use. Nothing more.*

But staring at Bradley, Fleming wondered if she was lying to herself.


# Chandler


*"Fight until you have nothing left in you," The Instructor said. "Then keep fighting."*


"The Jericho 941 in .45 ACP, traditional double action, three extra clips with ten rounds each. An excellent weapon."

McGlade held the gun in his good hand and used his robotic one to work the slide, chambering a round. Then he handed it to me across his desk.

"Magazines," I corrected.

"Huh?"

"You called them clips. They're magazines."

"Like *Penthouse*?" Harry held up one of the mags and squinted at it. "I don't see any beaver."

"You'll see the beaver later," Hammett said, winking.

Jesus. Why didn't I just stay quiet? I snatched the magazine from Harry's hand and gathered the others from the desktop.

"And for the pretty one, a Mateba Model 6 Unica, also known as an autorevolver. Chambered for .44 Magnum. I've never used one before, but it just oozes sex, doesn't it?"

"Fuck yeah," Hammett said, taking the weapon from McGlade. It looked like the bastard child of a revolver and a semiautomatic pistol, futuristic in a Robocop kind of way. As far as I knew, it was the only mass-produced semiauto revolver. Normally, a revolver was cocked by pulling back the hammer, or pulling the trigger. The Mateba cocked itself after each round was fired, using its own recoil to rotate the cylinder.

I had gun envy.

"For Chandler, a Paragon Seal automatic knife, drop point, almost nine inches long with an anodized aluminum handle. Perfect for slicing, stabbing, or bashing the enemy in the back of the head. And for Hammett, an Emerson karambit."

McGlade flicked his thumb, opening up a short, hooked blade that looked like an eagle talon. The handle had a hole in the bottom that a finger went into, a thumb or a pinkie, depending on which direction it was held.

Now I had knife envy, too.

"Capable of skinning an entire buffalo or carving holes through oak trees. Have you used one before?"

She took the weapon from him, and a quick blur later she had the blade to his throat.

"I trained in the Philippines," Hammett said. "And I'm planning on gutting people, not skinning buffalo."

"And once again, I am inappropriately aroused."

Hammett pocketed the knife, and Harry cleared his throat and stuck a hand in his front pocket to make adjustments.

"Moving right along, two vests, Safeguard Stealth body armor, Level III-A ballistics, Level 2 for edged blades and spikes. Both in slimming black. Might I say it's a shame to cover up those fine boobs?"

"You may."

"You have fine boobs."

I already had boob envy, so I didn't mind the comment.

"Thank you," Hammett said. "Did you get my things?"

"Absolutely. Specialty shotgun rounds, twelve-gauge. We have dragon's breath, piranha, fléchette, and armor-piercing. I've never heard of piranha shells before. What's in them?"

"Razor-sharp steel tacks," Hammett said.

McGlade leaned in close to her. "You are the sexiest woman to ever walk the planet."

"Did you find armor-piercing rounds for the Mateba?" Hammett cooed.

"Those are illegal. And yes, I got a box for you."

"What's that?" Hammett asked, pointing at a pair of hand-held devices that looked like Star Trek phasers.

"Chandler asked for those. Digital thermometers. Point and pull the trigger, and it registers the surface temperature." Harry picked it up and pointed it at Hammett. "And baby, you are hot."

"Ebola dies at sixty degrees Celsius if held at that temp for at least thirty minutes," I said. "There are also other ways of killing it. UV and gamma radiation, bleach, detergents, lipid solvents."

"How about shooting it?" Harry asked.

I stared at him, wondering if he was joking. With Harry, you never knew where smart-ass ended and stupidity began.

"I was joking," Harry said. "And right now you're thinking I'm an idiot."

"Does it bother you?"

"Depends. Do idiots make you horny?"

"Can you move this process along, please?"

He aimed the temp gun at me. "Ouch. Cold like a dead fish. Are you sure your sister has a pulse?" he asked Hammett.

"Unfortunately," she answered.

"What else did you get?" I pressed, not wanting to be part of their comedy routine.

"All the crap you wanted. Paracord, compasses, GPS locators, radar detectors, first-aid kits, gas masks, Surefire Guardian 900 lumens flashlights, field glasses, night-vision monoculars with headsets, lock picks, cockneeds..."

"What's a cockneed?" Hammett asked.

McGlade snaked his arm around her. "Mine needs you, baby. Right now."

"How about that special thing I asked for?"

"I'm working on it. But I wouldn't mind an advance on what you owe me."

They kissed, and for the second time that day I felt awkward and had to walk away from the groping and gyrating. This time I didn't venture farther into McGlade's office, which I'd learned from experience didn't dampen the noise. Instead I mumbled that I'd be waiting by the SUV, thanked Harry, stuffed my back-pack full, and left his office.

As I loaded the vehicle, I tried not to think about how every-one was getting laid but me, and fought the desire to call Lund. I knew he wouldn't take me back, but I just wanted to hear his voice, which made me feel even worse about myself. Codename: Chandler, Lovesick Idiot.

Maybe Hammett was right. I needed a bad boy, and Lund was a good boy. But my track record with bad boys had been shitty. Was there such a thing as a bad boy who deep inside was a good boy? And why was I thinking about any of this while running for my life?

Oh, yeah—because everyone was having sex and I wasn't.

Funny how that worked. An hour ago, I'd been ready to eat my gun. Now I just wanted to get laid.

I suppose all the training and conditioning in the world couldn't stop a girl from ignoring her base needs.

I killed time by pinching my injured fingernail and practic-ing the techniques Hammett had taught me. I wasn't quite buy-ing her explanation of pain management. When I imagined the pain exiting my body, I still felt it in a detached sort of way. But it didn't bother me as much. Which, I supposed, was a pretty cool trick to know. Though I wasn't going to have surgery without anesthesia anytime soon.

After twenty minutes, Hammett came out carrying her back-pack of supplies, a notable spring in her step. She went to the backseat, but instead of putting her stuff in, she took stuff out.

"Harry's letting me borrow his 'Vette," she said by way of explanation.

"Isn't that dangerous? What if you lead The Instructor to him?"

"He's got eight sets of phony plates and registrations in his trunk. He's kind of like a perverted, bionic Sam Spade. I dig him."

"So, what's this secret thing Harry is getting for you? You've asked for it twice."

"It's a surprise."

I had a feeling I wouldn't like what Hammett considered a surprise. "Did you want Toronto or Texas and Mexico?"

"Toronto, definitely. *Je parle très bien français. No hablo a español muy bien.*"

Her Spanish sounded perfect to me. But I was just fine with heading south. A long drive in the hot sun would help me clear my head. Besides, if I had to guess, I'd say as a Latino, Heath was the Hydra Deux operative The Instructor would most likely send to Texas or Mexico. Taking out my frustration on that son of a bitch might be just what I needed to get my feet back under me.

Hammett finished grabbing her gear, and dug into the bit of money we had left over from the drug house robbery.

"If I'm going to get into Canada, I need some extra supplies. Can you make it to Texas on five hundred?"

I did a quick gas calculation in my head. "Yeah."

Hammett shoved the rest of our cash into her bag and gave me a share of the special shells Harry had procured for her. Then we stood on the sidewalk and silently stared at each other. It was almost as awkward as watching her make out with Harry.

"Well," she said.

"Well."

"Good luck."

"You too."

I wasn't about to hug her. I wasn't even going to offer to shake hands. But the fact that she wasn't making an effort either left me feeling oddly empty.

She nodded slightly, then turned and walked off, and as she crossed the street I wondered if I would ever see her again, and if that would be a good thing or not.

For a dangerously unhinged psychopath, the bitch was growing on me.

# Julie

Julie had begun to doze off when the knob rattled, the door swung wide, and The Instructor walked into the room. He closed it behind him and walked to the desk, acting as if Julie wasn't even there.

"You said you'd tell me where Chandler is."

Julie's voice sounded small, like a weak child begging for a favor. She hated that, but she was never good at hiding her feelings.

He picked up a desk phone. "Hold all my calls." Hanging up, he crossed to where Julie was sitting.

"Please, could you—"

His hand shot out so fast Julie didn't see it coming. Hand flat, he slapped her right cheek hard enough to throw her against the sofa's arm.

"You don't have the right to ask me anything."

Julie's head jangled and the taste of blood bloomed in her mouth. She struggled to sit upright.

He swung again, sending her bouncing off the cushions and sliding to the floor.

"Stop it!"

He loomed over her, and at first Julie thought he was about to kick her in the face. She rolled into a protective ball, not knowing what else to do, praying he would stop.

No kick came.

Her head throbbed, her mouth tangy with blood. She looked up at him through tears and a curtain of hair.

He said nothing, just stared at her.

Julie willed her head to clear, only to realize her fall had left her hospital gown bunched up to her waist.

She pulled it over her hips, trying to cover herself.

"Get up," The Instructor said.

Julie scrambled to her knees.

"Sit," he said, pointing to the sofa.

She did as he said. Julie was crying openly now, and she let the tears come, not able to stem them.

"I'm sorry I had to do that, but you need to understand that what happened today can't happen again. No attacking the nurses. No hurting yourself. Do you understand?"

Julie's face felt hot, her cheekbone throbbing with each beat of her pulse.

"Answer."

"Yes," she said.

"You're too important to our country, Julie. You're too important to me."

"Please tell me what happened to Chandler." To her shame, she flinched a little, expecting him to take another swing.

Instead, he sat on the cushion beside her.

"Such a pretty thing," The Instructor said. He reached out, stroking the bruise on her cheek.

Julie shuddered. She wanted to move away from him, but there was nowhere to go.

"You're very valuable to us, Julie. We spent years looking for someone with your specific genetic markers. Years, and a small fortune. You're going to go down in history as a true patriot. A hero. Your blood is going to help our nation grow stronger than it has ever been. The true, dominant world power."

"By killing people?"

"To make an omelet," The Instructor said, "you have to kill a few unborn chickens."

"I...I hate the thought of people dying because of me."

"All wars have casualties. All growth is painful. I'm full of platitudes. Often thought of writing them all down someday, maybe publishing an inspirational tome. I think this e-book thing is going to be a boon for readers."

He moved his hand to Julie's shoulder, rubbing her like a creepy uncle.

"You're immunized," Julie said.

"Indeed."

"Why isn't Dr. Fossen? Don't you have enough?"

"We used a synthetic viral protein to make the vaccine. It's quite ingenious, really, and we have a lot of it. But, like you, Dr. Fossen requires a bit of extra persuasion to do the right thing. So I'm withholding it from him until he's finished with his project."

"What's his project?"

"You are, my dear. He's amplified enough of the virus to infect two large urban centers. But that's just phase one of the plan. We need more—a lot more—for phase two."

"Phase two?"

"You don't have to worry about that. Neither does Dr. Fossen."

Julie knew that meant she probably should worry about it, but right then she was so overloaded with worries and information she couldn't understand that she was at a loss to do anything at all.

She pulled in a deep breath.

"You like Derek Fossen, don't you?" asked The Instructor.

She couldn't lie. He was the first person in this place who seemed human. "I guess so."

"How long has it been since you've had a man, Julie?"

Julie didn't answer.

"Must have been a long time. You've been at that lighthouse, living like a hermit, for years. Don't you miss the companionship? The intimacy?"

Julie did. More than anything. But she wasn't going to reveal that to this creep.

The Instructor dropped his hand, grazing her nipple through the thin fabric. "I understand the needs a healthy young woman has. Say the word, we can be together."

Julie recoiled.

"You don't hide your feelings very well, do you?" he said.

"I'm...I'm sorry."

"Would it help if I told you being nice to me could make a difference, at least where Chandler is concerned?"

"A difference?" Julie wasn't stupid. She knew exactly what he meant. Since he'd been staring at her when she was naked from the waist down, she'd even half expected a proposition like this. But she needed to buy some time, give herself a chance to think.

"A difference to whether Chandler lives or dies. How much pain she suffers."

"And if I have sex with you, you won't hurt her?"

"It would help me be more...charitable."

Julie owed Chandler everything. The years living in the lighthouse had been lonely and long, but she had been able to live them. She'd taken long walks with Kirk, enjoyed countless books; she'd even started writing stories herself. Chandler made that possible. Without her, Julie would have been stuck in a lab all that time...or dead.

Maybe that would have been for the best, after all. If she had died back in New York, this man wouldn't have her blood now. He wouldn't be able to use it to kill people.

Julie looked down at her hands, shaking and useless. She couldn't change the past; she could only do what was in her power right now.

The only person who had a real chance of stopping this man was Chandler.

Julie looked back at the man and forced a smile to her lips, but even though she'd intended to say yes, the words wouldn't come.

"I'm sorry. I can't."

"I can't say I'm not disappointed."

Julie had meant the words for Chandler, not The Instructor, but she didn't correct him. She just hoped he wouldn't hit her again.

The Instructor laid a hand high on her thigh, his palm hot through the thin fabric. "I know you've been through a lot today, but I want you to really think about my offer. You're easy to read, Julie; I can see you're considering it."

She forced a nod.

"Good girl." He skimmed his fingers up and down the outside of her leg, inching below the gown's hem with each movement upward. "In the meantime, I'll send Dr. Fossen to take your vitals and bring you some food."

"Thank you."

"Just let Fossen know when you'd like to see me."

She forced a nod.

The Instructor stood and walked to the door, stopping before opening it. "I really hope you'll take me up on my offer. I can make serving your country a much more pleasant experience, and if everything goes well, I'm the only one who can arrange for you to see Chandler."

# Isolde

*"Practice is always useful," said The Instructor. "But nothing beats the real thing."*

Huddled over a folding table in the fairground tent, Izzy frowned at the laptop, wondering how the most technologically advanced country in the world, with arguably the most state-of-the-art military, produced a clunky flight simulator with controls so poor they were only outclassed by the shit graphics. Honestly, there were so many jaggies it looked like a spastic third-grader animated it with construction-paper cutouts. Izzy had no idea where The Instructor found this program, but Xbox had nothing to fear. Even the sounds were remedial, beeps and buzzes that were so annoying she seriously considered throwing the computer across the room, then hunting down the idiot who did the programming and torturing him to death by making him play his own damn game.

She glanced at Tristan, who was unloading the truck. Hauling cases of soda seemed a lot more fun than what she was doing. But Izzy forced herself to continue. She was an efficient pilot, even better than Scarlett on some aircraft, but she'd never flown one of these before and needed the practice.

Turning back to the computer, Izzy restarted the program and went through the laborious preflight check, then took off in a light drizzle with a 7-mph northwesterly wind. It was almost as exciting as watching grass grow, and Izzy believed a grass-growing computer simulation would have been more fun as well.

The tent door opened, and a dude with a clipboard came in. "Hey! Why are you unloading? This isn't one of the refreshment tents. Put those cans back on the truck, eh."

Tristan rolled his shoulders, meeting Izzy's stare, but she shook her head.

"I got this."

Strolling over to him, a spring in her step, Izzy said to the walking dead man, "But we have the *frabojamitz* permit for it."

His eyes crinkled at the made-up word, and by then she was on him with her straight razor, slashing his larynx, slicing his vocal cords so nothing came out but a wet wheeze. Her next cut was across his eyebrows, the blood flowing fast and blinding him. He flailed out his arms and Izzy did a dodge, turning a pirouette in her Doc Martens, the razor biting into his biceps, then a follow-up digging into his back, deep enough to catch on his spine. She severed it, and his useless legs lost their ability to hold him up.

Tristan went to watch the door, and Izzy straddled the dying man, humming to herself, removing bits of his face as he choked and bled out. When he finally died, Izzy's leggings were soaked with blood, and she was in much better spirits. She made a nice, deep slash in her forearm, then rubbed black ink into it, luxuriating in the sting.

"Messy," Tristan said, a rare instance of speaking without being addressed first.

"The grass will soak up the blood."

Tristan lumbered to them, then dragged the man over to the truck and jerked him up into the back. Hopping up next to him, he pulled the body through the maze of soda cases and hid it in back next to the other body they were keeping on ice.

Izzy stripped off her clothes, then used some bottled water to get the blood off. Tristan watched her, that hungry look in his eyes. Unlike many anorexics, Izzy had no delusional self-image issues. She didn't look in the mirror and see someone fat. She saw someone who looked like they'd lived for a year in a concentration camp, nothing but androgynous, emaciated muscle and saggy skin, and the chest of a twelve-year-old boy.

"Enjoying the show?" Izzy teased.

Tristan grunted, then unzipped his fly.

The sex was rough, painful, just like Izzy liked it. But, as usual, it was over too soon, which meant Izzy had to go back to the damn flight simulator.

Damn The Instructor. Damn him to hell.

She returned to the computer, saw her aircraft had crashed, and had to start over.

Still, it would be worth it. If the calculations were correct, they'd kill a half-million people tomorrow. They'd die horribly, bleeding and crying in excruciating agony, infecting anyone they came near.

The thought brought a rare smile to Izzy's face. She rebooted the simulator and got back to practicing.

# Fleming

*"Killing is like riding a bicycle,"* said *The Instructor.*
*"Once you learn how, it's easy to do it again."*

After working with Bradley on the breadboard creating the circuit for the robot, Fleming copied it to a PCB computer-aided design program and printed it out on a sheet of Mylar. Then Fleming turned out all the lights, except for a red screen on her laptop, and peeled off the protective backing from a photosensitive board, and placed it and the board design in a photo frame. Then she exposed it under a fluorescent light for ten minutes, and mixed some positive-type printed circuit board developer with water in a dish. After the exposure was complete, Fleming put the PCB in the solution, agitating it like one would a photograph in a darkroom. When her design appeared on the board, she rinsed it off and prepared to etch.

"Would you be offended if I said you're adorable when you work?" Bradley asked.

"No. Why?"

"Because you're extremely competent, and I don't want to belittle you by commenting on your appearance."

Fleming laughed. He was definitely the cuter of them, in too many ways to count.

The etching solution—ferric chloride and water—chemically milled the PBC by removing the unwanted copper. That took about fifteen minutes, and then Fleming cleaned the finished board with nail polish remover, and began to drill holes and solder on components.

They worked for more than an hour, hunched over the table, fusing Bradley's robotics with Fleming's surveillance bug. Despite their calculations, the finished board, complete with microphone, speaker, wheel and motor, transceiver, antenna, battery, and fisheye camera, didn't fit into the desired housing.

"Let me have the Dremel tool," Bradley said.

As he worked, Fleming kept an eye on her laptop, watching the enemy blips close to within a mile of her location. She did a weapons check. Fifteen shells for the shotgun. Eight bullets in the Skorpion. Two rounds in the armrests of her modified wheelchair. Assorted stabbing and slicing weapons. She added oil to the compartment in her chair to replace what she'd dumped in the mall, then dissolved Styrofoam packing pieces from her various purchases in a jar full of gasoline for later use.

"How does this look?"

Bradley held up the bug. It looked just as Fleming hoped it would: like an ordinary Montblanc pen.

"Great. Does it work?"

Bradley grinned. "My part does. I dunno about your end. Your soldering was…interesting."

"Interesting?" She raised an eyebrow.

"I cleaned it up best I could, but even my skills have limits." He winked at her, and Fleming laughed.

"You know I can kill you six different ways with one hand."

"I'm guessing *solder me to death* isn't one of them."

"Did you finish the external transceiver?"

"First thing I did. It's bulky."

It had to be. The bug had its own transceiver, but had a range of only a hundred meters. For Fleming to control it and receive its data, it had to communicate with another transceiver that had a longer range, one outside the White House perimeter.

"Did you upload the remote control program?"

Fleming nodded. "But I haven't linked to the TracFone yet."

"We can test it without that. Just use your Wi-Fi to try it out."

Fleming accessed her network, found the new device, and typed in the code. Then she started the remote program Bradley had given her. A window opened, and a digital circle appeared on the screen. In it were four arrows, laid out like compass points.

Bradley set the pen on the floor. "I used gaming controls. They're—"

Fleming knew gaming controls. She'd played enough Doom and Quake while recuperating. She pressed the *W* key and the pen moved forward, quicker than she'd expected. It went in a straight line, about as fast as a cockroach could scurry. She pressed *D*, which should have made it go right, but the pen just stopped.

"Only one wheel," Bradley said, "so to turn—"

There wasn't an axle in the pen, so the left and right buttons wouldn't work. So Fleming pressed *S* and the pen began to move backward. As it did, the tail end dragged on the floor and turned the pen to the left.

So it was like parallel parking a car. Forward is straight, backing up changed the direction. Smart and simple.

"Can I adjust speed?"

"Go into options. There's a limiter."

"Will it go over carpeting?"

"If it isn't too thick. I've got these same wheels and servos on a little RC car I made. It'll go up grades of up to thirty degrees, work on dirt, even through small puddles."

"Battery life?"

"Depends. I don't know what your microphone and camera draws, but you should be able to run the servo an hour, maybe more."

Fleming couldn't check the camera yet, because that required a Wi-Fi setup. But she was pleased with Bradley's work.

"It's excellent, Bradley. And much quicker than I expected."

"I'm a motivated employee. So I was thinking maybe we could…" He smiled shyly.

Fleming was surprised. "Again?"

"It's been hours."

"Are you popping Viagra behind my back?"

"I don't need Viagra. Just looking at you is enough to—"

"Hold that thought." Fleming raised up her hand, halting him. Her attention had been snared by her computer. The GPS tracker.

Rhett and Scarlett were within a thousand meters of the shop.

"I need you to stay here, lights out. Don't come out no matter what."

Bradley looked perplexed, then fear widened his eyes and he nodded.

"Don't make any noise. I'll be back soon."

She wheeled toward the door as Bradley hit the lights. Before she left, she heard him whisper to her in the dark.

"Fleming?"

"Yeah?"

"Be careful."

"I will. Remember what I told you."

"Please come back. I think I'm falling in love with you."

Normally, Fleming would have found his naïveté cute but dismissible. Puppy love was an obvious side effect to getting laid for the first time. But he said it with a tremor in his voice, obviously frightened, and it made Fleming consider that this could be the last time they'd ever see each other.

# Scarlett

*"The life of an operative is ninety-five percent boredom and five percent terror," The Instructor said. "Eventually you'll long for the boredom part."*

"You're humming again."

"Was I?"

Rhett smiled at her, all innocent and flirty. Chances were, the moron was unaware of it. But he also might have been doing it intentionally, just to annoy her. Ultimately it didn't matter. If he kept it up, Scarlett was going to cut off his balls and shove them down his throat to shut him up.

She stopped at a red light. They'd been looking for Fleming for hours, an ever-spiraling radius from where the cab had dropped her off. They were about two kilometers from center, driving through this business section of town, knocking on doors and flashing Fleming's picture at everyone they met. So far not a single person out of dozens recognized her. Which showed just how uninformed the nation was, because Fleming's face matched the agent who'd killed the president.

Then again, the picture they had of her wasn't very good, eyewitness ID was notoriously faulty, and the wheelchair was the deal-breaker. Still, it made Scarlett wish that people paid even a little bit more attention to what was going on around them. Instead, the world was populated by zombies completely unaware of their surroundings, self-absorbed to the point of single-mindedness.

The light changed, and they eased up to a strip mall, most of the stores vacant. Scarlett pulled into the parking lot and killed the

Mustang's headlights. Habit made her senses report. She smelled Rhett's aftershave, the Armor All the dealership had used on the car's interior, and through the slit in the window, a cold breeze carrying car exhaust. Besides the low grumble of the engine, she heard the double *cluck* of a Canada goose, and spotted a gaggle of six, waddling along like they owned the place.

There were five cars in the lot, and Scarlett circled slowly, minding the geese so they didn't get uppity and announce her presence. The only two shops that appeared open were a sandwich place and a currency exchange. The rest had soaped or newspaper-covered windows, signs on doors begging for renters. She parked, killing the engine, setting the handbrake. Scarlett didn't see any lights on. And yet, if she were a lone operative looking for a place to hunker down, this shopping center was perfect. So if Fleming were here, where would she—

Scarlett saw movement outside just as Rhett grabbed her hair and tugged her to the side.

A thundering *boom!* and the front windshield spiderwebbed, spraying Scarlett with tiny rectangles of safety glass. Instinctively she went for the 9mm in the middle armrest and began to fire just as Rhett did, shooting through the broken window without seeing where they were aiming.

Trapped in a car during a gunfight was begging for sudden death, so Scarlett groped for the handle and then spilled onto the pavement, tucking and rolling behind the open door, knowing her odds weren't good depending on Fleming's position, but Rhett was doing the same so there was a fifty percent chance that—

*Boom!*

The moment Scarlett heard the blast she felt the burning slap and tug in her leg. Buckshot, and a lot of it. Then the pain came, white hot and blinding, and Scarlett emptied her clip into an arc around her and tried to push herself away with her good leg. "Rhett!"

He answered with more gunshots, and then he was dragging her by an armpit to the rear of the car as the shotgun roared a third time, disintegrating the driver's side window.

Adrenaline surging, Scarlett squinted at her leg in the darkness. It looked as if someone had dumped a plate of mostaccioli Bolognese on her pants from the knee down. Seeing it made the pain worse. She ripped the seam out of her sleeve, pulled it off her arm, and tied it around her thigh as Rhett reloaded.

"Cover your left," Rhett said, then took off right, jogging in a crouch. He'd circle around, try to catch the cripple from behind. Assuming Fleming was the one who'd fired. There was a chance, albeit small, that her sisters were with her. Scarlett didn't think so. If they were together, Fleming wouldn't have been the one doing errands and wouldn't have stolen the van on her own.

Scarlett wished she'd spoken up, told Rhett not to follow Fleming into the mall. Then they could have followed her back to her hideaway with the element of surprise still intact. Then they could have known for sure if Fleming was alone. Then they could have—

"Fleming!"

A male voice, definitely not Rhett.

Scarlett followed the sound and spotted a tall young man wearing glasses, running into the parking lot. His hands were empty, and in the glow of one of the overhead parking lights, he seemed panicked. Not a pro.

Scarlett pointed her nine at the man. An easy shot at this distance, even with her injury. And shooting someone always felt good, which would help dull the pain she was in.

She squeezed the trigger.

# Fleming

*"Don't get close to people,"* The Instructor said. *"It never ends well."*

In hindsight, Fleming should have attacked from the side.

But when the Mustang rolled up and killed the engine, Fleming had just enough time to get in front of it and fire. She'd chosen a heads-on approach because there were two people in the car. Unfortunately, the shot didn't kill them, and they reacted immediately.

Fleming managed to wound the woman, Scarlett, but was then forced to wheel away before Rhett could get after her. As he assisted his partner, Fleming surged into the parking lot, weapon in lap. She assumed Rhett would try to flank her, because Fleming had the same training. So she decided to make a wider circle and wait for him to come.

Then Bradley—dear, adorable, brilliant, incredibly stupid Bradley—decided to come out and scream her name even though he'd sworn to stay put.

Puppy love was going to get him killed.

Fleming knew she had to stick to her plan, and that realization gnawed at her like a live rat sewn into her stomach. If she showed herself, she'd die. That meant Chandler would die, too, and who knew how many others to Ebola.

Thousands? Millions?

She coasted behind one of the few parked cars in the lot and held her breath, listening for approaching footsteps.

Instead, she heard gunfire. Small caliber. Single shot. Final.

Fleming felt as if her heart stopped. For a moment she was unaware of her environment. For all her training, it seemed to disappear around her, Fleming's senses drowned out by sorrow and rage. Then—

"Fleming!"

Bradley's voice. Choked and scared.

*But still alive!*

Fleming's momentary relief was replaced by the sick sensation of knowing what would happen next.

She heard Scarlett barking orders, and then Rhett replying.

"Fleming!" Scarlett called out. "I just shot your boy's ear off. If you care about him, you'll show yourself."

Fleming stayed put. The mission was to rescue Julie, kill The Instructor, stop whatever plan the president had, and clear their names. The mission didn't include giving up her position and surrendering to the enemy to save a boy toy.

"Suit yourself. We'll be in touch. Don't stray too far from a mailbox, because we'll be sending you pieces of him every hour."

Fleming felt like puking.

A minute passed. Then the Mustang raged to life and squealed tires, tearing off down the lot, away from her. When it was gone, she wheeled back toward her shop, and saw the small, silver object on the sidewalk.

A cell phone. Resting on a spatter of Bradley's blood.

She snatched it up, then locked herself inside the store, lights out. The Baltimore PD showed up a few minutes later, spent a half hour searching the parking lot, then began a door-to-door check. While they did their job, Fleming did hers, removing the battery from the cell phone Scarlett had left, then building a makeshift RF detector on her breadboard while holding a penlight in her mouth.

After the cops left, Fleming packed up the gear she needed, then called a cab. It took her back to the mall, and her van. She circled the vehicle with the detector held in front of her, watching the LED blink then go solid when she held it over the left rear wheel well. Fleming used a hammer and tire jack to break the body, and then destroy the anti-theft device.

Invisible again, she got into the van and started it up.

Fleming was trained to focus on the mission and to bury her feelings. She couldn't let personal attachments get in the way. Over the years, several of the men she'd slept with had died, some by her hand. This wasn't the time to think about Bradley. He'd served his purpose, and was no longer needed.

She got onto 295 South, heading for DC.

Fleming only stopped once during the hour-long drive, at a fast-food place where she ordered a hamburger with extra napkins.

The hamburger went to Sasha, curled up in the passenger seat.

Fleming needed the napkins because it was hard to see with tears blurring her vision.

# Scarlett

*"I've taught you to kill," The Instructor said. "But you also have to learn how to heal."*

Rhett found one of those shitty, rent-by-the-hour motels on the outskirts of Baltimore, the kind that was all one floor and you parked in front of your room. The drive had been agonizing. As soon as they'd gotten away from Fleming, he'd kicked the shattered front windshield out. She'd sat in the backseat, keeping a gun to Bradley's head, gritting her teeth as the cold air rushed in and slapped at her bleeding leg. They made it without attracting any police attention, and Rhett brought the kid in first, taking an interminable amount of time to secure him before coming to get her.

As expected, the accommodations were sparse. Queen-size bed with a mattress almost as thin as the blanket. A TV at least fifteen years out of date. A cheap particleboard dresser and puke-green drapes that never should have survived the 1970s. The bathroom smelled like bleach. The carpet smelled like a dog's ass.

Rhett carried her in, placed her gently on the bed, and frowned.

"Gotta ditch the car. Gave the kid a shot to put him out."

"Give me a shot."

"Can't. You need to stay alert while I'm gone. Nothing stronger than aspirin."

"I hate you," Scarlett said, and had never spoken truer words.

"Save the hate for later, when I'm digging the shot out of your leg."

Rhett loaded a full magazine into her 9mm, placed it next to the bed, checked to make sure the hideous drapes were completely closed, and then left her there.

Scarlett wadded the corner of a filthy pillow into her mouth and bit down on it, bleeding and crying until he returned. She used every trick she'd been taught to relax her body and manage the pain, but it was impossible. So instead she fantasized about killing Rhett. Growing weary of those scenarios, she turned her imaginary wrath on Bradley. He'd tell them everything he knew about Fleming. And even if he did so willingly, Scarlett was going to make him suffer, if only for guilt by association. She had some serious skills when it came to causing pain.

Against her better judgment, she examined her leg. Scarlett tried to be detached, cynical, and she counted fifteen buckshot wounds before turning her head to the side and vomiting onto the floor.

Rhett couldn't have been gone for more than an hour, but she felt every second of it. When he finally showed up, he had a dopey smile on his face.

"Sorry for the wait, Scarlett. Damnedest thing happened. Was pulling into an all-night supermarket to ditch the 'Stang, and the prettiest little thing parks right next to me, sees the damage and the blood, starts asking me questions, all concerned about my welfare. Some people are just good-natured, you know? Every once in a while I lose faith in human nature, but a simple act of kindness restores it. Anyway, that's what took so long. Snapped her neck, dumped her in the woods. Her car is a black Honda, parked behind our room."

"Put me out," she said through clenched teeth.

"As you wish, ma'am."

He smiled, tipped his Stetson, then prepared the syringe. Rhett wasn't the best battlefield medic, and there would no doubt be plastic surgery in Scarlett's future from the shitty job he did, but he'd get the lead out and patch her up. She may not have liked him, but she trusted him.

Well, mostly.

"And my clothes stay on," she warned. "You try anything while I'm out…"

"Why, Miss Scarlett, I am offended you'd even suggest such a thing. Besides, that pretty young Honda lady has already obliged me in that area."

"You're disgusting."

"Who? Me? Man has needs, and I had to kill her anyway for her car. Who knows? Maybe I made her last few minutes on earth a bit better."

Scarlett highly doubted it, but she kept quiet. "Just fix my goddamn leg and keep your dick in your pants."

"Yes, ma'am. I'm just hoping I don't have to amputate. Ain't got a bone saw, so I'd have to shoot through your femur."

He smiled and then jammed the needle into her arm.

# Chandler

*"Information is always useful," said The Instructor. "But make sure it's correct."*

Relieved to get on the road and away from Hammett, I cruised down I-55 to St. Louis, where I followed I-44 to Tulsa. Once I cleared the Ozarks, the land became a combination of monotonously flat and gently rolling hills. The lack of topographical variety and light traffic made driving easy, and for the first time since my life had fallen apart, I felt some sense of control.

Outside of Tulsa, I stopped at a truck stop for fuel, a bathroom break, and one of those stale fruit pies found in vending machines, intending to drive a couple of more hours before I let myself take a nap in the SUV. Not the most comfortable of situations, but with my face all over the television, I had to avoid being seen. Even a McDonald's drive-through posed a risk.

I took solace in the fact that Hammett was dealing with the same issues. The thought of her sleeping in her car, eating stale fruit pies, was enough to make me smile.

Climbing back behind the wheel with my snack, I pulled out my phone to check in with Fleming. It was late, and I thought she might be sleeping. I was surprised when she answered, sounding a little breathless.

"Keeping the help sexually satisfied?"

"How far are you?"

"Tulsa." Unlike me, Fleming was perfectly comfortable talking about sex. Hell, both my sisters had slept with more men than I'd probably said hello to. I was the only awkward one in the bunch. That Fleming had brushed off my question had me wondering.

"So did you have a spat, or..."

"I'm working, Chandler. Getting ready for Jack to arrive."

"Fine. Sorry." I wasn't sure what it was, but she was upset. "You sound like Minnie Naughton."

"Minnie isn't the problem." In other words, according to our simple code, she hadn't been compromised.

"So what is it?"

"I'm handling my shit, Chandler. What do you need?"

Jesus. Something was definitely up. But there was nothing I could do about it.

"I'm checking in, like we agreed. Where am I headed?"

I could hear the clicking of a laptop keyboard. "Both operatives are in Mexico. Looks like the second one is also heading to Mexico City."

"Mexico City it is."

"Cross at Laredo. The drug cartels have been sending a lot through that checkpoint, keeping border control busy. Their resources are wearing thin."

"Laredo. Got it."

"Chandler?"

"Yeah?"

I was figuring she'd spill what was on her mind, but instead she surprised me.

"You're a good operative. No...a great one. Really."

Heat stole into my cheeks. I don't know why I expected my psycho sister to keep my breakdown quiet. If it had been her dissolving into tears, I would have reported it to Fleming immediately. But still, I felt embarrassed and a little betrayed. Stupid.

"You've talked to Hammett?"

"No, why?"

So her comment wasn't based on something Hammett said? I frowned into the phone. In the years Fleming had been my handler, she'd never given me a pep talk.

"What makes you think I need the pat on the head?" I asked.

Seconds plodded by before she spoke. "Remember when I read you the short dossiers for Hydra Deux?"

"Yes."

"There are dossiers for us, too."

I'd talked to Fleming a lot on the phone over the years, and I was pretty good at reading her, even back when I'd known her as Jacob and her voice had been electronically disguised. Judging from my sister's tone now, I wasn't going to like what she had to say.

"And something in mine made you think I needed encouragement?"

A pause. "Yes."

"What did it say, Fleming?"

Another long pause. "Under weaknesses, it listed self-doubt. 'May crack under pressure. Panic control.'"

My throat felt tight. I wasn't sure what I was supposed to think about that, what I was supposed to feel. It was like having my stepfather inside my head all over again, pointing out my shortcomings, listing my flaws.

My stepfather, The Instructor, what was the damn difference?

"Are you OK?"

"I can't say the assessment is wrong, Fleming."

"Can you handle this? Be honest with me."

"A day ago, I would have had to say no. But I've got it now."

"You're sure? A lot hangs in the balance."

"And that's why I won't fuck it up."

"OK. You never have before, Chandler. Remember that. You've always found a way before."

"As soon as you hear anything, let me know."

Walking back to the SUV, I ended the call, then ripped off the pie's wrapper and took a bite, although I don't remember tasting it. Then I got back on the highway and focused on the reassurances I'd given Fleming.

And tried to believe them myself.

# Hammett

*"There are many ways to die,"* The Instructor said. *"Drowning is one of the worst."*

After a quick stop at the airport and a nine-hour drive east, Hammett parked across the street from a gas station in West Seneca, New York, and waited for the right sort of woman to drive up. She had to be alone, in a nice car, dressed well. It was a little after midnight, and didn't take long for Hammett's criteria to be met. As the woman pumped gas, Hammett crossed the street in the evening chill, approached her with a friendly smile, then put the .357 in her face.

"Purse," she demanded.

The terrified woman handed it over.

"Coat."

The trench coat came next.

"Now Macarena."

"What?"

"The dance. Really popular in the nineties." Hammett began to hum the song, and the shivering woman went through the motions.

"Look at the camera," Hammett said, pointing her finger to the camera above the pump that she had her back to. "And smile. This will end up on YouTube eventually."

Incredibly, the woman nodded, and her dancing improved significantly. Hammett watched for a few seconds, amused, then jogged back to her car when the woman was facing the other way as the dance required.

Not as satisfying as killing her, but oddly amusing.

She drove north into the heart of Buffalo, found another gas station, and used the restroom. As expected, the stolen purse was filled with high-end makeup, and Hammett went to work.

When she was finished, the result was somewhere between movie starlet and Vegas showgirl. The coat was long and covered her clothes. She gave her reflection a flirtatious wink, smiled, and then went back to the 'Vette to find a nice hotel.

While Hammett's face was now infamous, the video playing on every TV channel showed Chandler without makeup. Anyone who has ever seen before and after pictures of celebrity make-overs knew how different a woman looked when her face was done up. The presidential assassin looked like a militant lesbian who'd just run a marathon through hell. Presently, with her multicolored hair, Hammett looked like a famous rock star. Hiding in plain sight was the best way to go unnoticed.

She drove up to Niagara Falls, valet-parked the Corvette at a boutique hotel called the Jiacomo, and asked for a Jacuzzi suite. The lobby was immaculate. Marble floors and lots of earth tones and patterns in an art deco–meets–Mayan revival style: more now than now. Dramatic stems of Heliconia Mayan Gold branched from decorative clay vases. And the rich smell of complimentary espresso and chocolate chip cookies wafted through the air.

When the clerk wanted to see an ID, Hammett leaned forward and whispered, "Look, you may not know who I am, but I'm famous, and if the press finds out I'm here, it'll get ugly. How about I leave the deposit in cash and you sign me in under Jane Smith?"

He nodded like he understood what was happening and agreed. Funny part was, Hammett hadn't been lying to him. He gave her the key and some fresh-baked cookies, and she took the elevator to her floor.

The room was very nice: spacious, quality furnishings, lots of earth tones and patterns in a style similar to the lobby, a fireplace, and a big, comfy bed. Hammett used the phone book to find a pizza place that was still open. She ordered a small thin crust with the works and a salad, and watched CNN while nibbling on chocolate chips until the deliveryman arrived. When he did, she found perverse satisfaction in the fact that while she paid for her order the TV was showing Chandler killing the president.

She drew a bath and ate while soaking. Chandler was probably at a rest area somewhere, sleeping in her car, eating vending machine food, and the image tickled Hammett. Tough chick, but no style at all. And very close to the breaking point.

Hammett considered Chandler's behavior in the alley. You didn't need a doctorate in psychology to see the woman was hurting. But was it just stress and exhaustion? Or something deeper?

And more important, why did Hammett care?

She finished her salad and half the pie, and then toweled off and slipped into bed, naked except for some newly applied bandages.

Hammett was able to disassociate herself from her multiple aches and pains, and sleep came almost immediately.

Four hours later the nightmare woke her up.

It was the same every night, so regular that Hammett could set her watch by it. As usual, she jackknifed out of bed, dripping in sweat, a scream close to breaching her lips, her mind's eye still envisioning Father's face.

A moment later the memory was gone, and Hammett was back in charge of her body's reactions, slowing her breathing and heart rate. She got out of bed because further sleep would be impossible, changed the dressings on her various injuries, and then did forty minutes of sit-ups. This caused several of her wounds to bleed, and she showered, changed bandages once more, and then flipped through the phone book while she put on her makeup.

Hammett had breakfast in the hotel's opulent dining room— eggs and bacon, granola and yogurt—and while eating recalled another boutique hotel she'd stayed in, years ago in Spain, where she had a seafood paella that ranked among the best meals of her life. Maybe, when this was over, she'd go back. Take some time off.

That is, if she lived that long.

After breakfast, Hammett drove up Robert Moses Parkway, next to the Niagara River, scouting for the best place to enter Canada. She had no ID, let alone a passport, so the only way to get to Toronto would be as an illegal alien. About eight kilometers up, past the Lewiston-Queenston Bridge, Hammett found a narrow bend of river. She parked and walked into the tree line with her binoculars.

The river cut a steep trench into the rocks on both the US and the Canadian sides, but the grade was navigable. Hammett could hear and smell the rushing water, and the closer look revealed it was too fast a current to swim unassisted, even though it wasn't more than a hundred and fifty meters from shore to shore. Indeed, it was fast enough to qualify as rapids. The chill in the air, and the time of year, meant the water was probably cold as well. A wet suit wouldn't hurt.

She stood there with her binoculars, scanning the area. It took her twenty minutes before she spotted the first patrol, on the Canadian side. Two guys on three-wheelers. Their uniforms gave them away. While not dressed like Mounties, they did look like cops, brown jackets with gold patches on the shoulders reading CBPA: Canadian Border Protection Agency. Surprisingly, they were armed.

But so was Hammett, and she had more than just a pistol.

She waited another fifteen minutes, and saw a boat motor past. US Border Security, the Citizen's Academy. Hammett smiled. This should be a piece of cake.

After her reconnaissance, Hammett returned to the 'Vette and headed south to Buffalo, to the watersports store she'd looked up. The young guy behind the counter was obviously a displaced Californian, bleached-blond hair, remnants of a tan, a Malibu T-shirt. His nametag read DAVY.

"Can I help you, dude?"

"A Sea-Doo scooter."

"Awesome. Gonna do some diving in Erie?"

"Gonna swim the Niagara River into Canada."

"Awesome. But those are some gnarly rapids, bro. You'll need some major horses."

He demonstrated one of the higher-end models, capable of four miles an hour. It was black, and shaped like a small torpedo with handles, which is essentially what it was. But rather than carry a bomb, it carried a person, much faster than they could swim underwater.

"How long does it last on a full charge?"

"Ninety minutes, bro. Needs to be charged for four hours first."

Hammett hit the trigger button, and the propeller whirred.

"Power light is down to one LED," Davy said, pointing at the indicator. "Needs a charge."

Hammett only needed it for a few minutes, tops. "How long will this charge last?"

Davy shrugged. "Dunno. But you don't want to lug it around when it's out of juice. Big pain in the butthole. It's neutrally buoyant, but not fine to swim with, know what I mean?"

"I'll take it. I also need a wet suit and a mask."

"Groovy gravy. How about fins?"

Hammett didn't think swim fins would help her much in a strong current. The same went for a snorkel. She wanted to swim under the surface, and could hold her breath with the best of them. Full scuba gear would only make her heavier and slow her down.

Davy found a wet suit for her, holding it up. "Red is totally your color, dude."

"I want black."

"Black is totally your color, dude. You're gonna look bitchin' in this."

"I look bitchin' in everything."

"Hells yeah, bro. You got some major muscle tone. Pilates?"

"Hand-to-hand combat," Hammett said.

"Bitchin'."

"Can you charge the scooter on AC?"

"Wha?"

"AC power? You know, AC/DC?"

"Totally. Saw them in '03 with Rush and the Stones in Toronto. SARS-a-palooza. Half a million people there, bro. Tomorrow is supposed to be even huger. Canadafest, Downsville Park. I got tix. Lineup is killer. Slave to the metal."

He began to headbang, lifting up his fist with his index finger and pinkie sticking out in the universal symbol of *stoned loser*.

"Hey, Ozzy." Hammett gave him a tap on the arm. "I want to know if I can charge the Sea-Doo using my car's cigarette outlet. Also known as AC power."

"Wha? Nah, bro. Wall plug only. But there are inverters."

"Do you sell them?"

"Nah. But you need any energy drinks? Buy two cans of Insanity Blitzkrieg, get the third free. My fave flavor is Inferno."

Hammett decided if she had to listen to Davy for much longer, chances were high she'd wind up killing him. So she paid and got out of there without trying on the wet suit. Checking the time, Hammett saw she still had a few hours before checkout at the Jiacomo, so that would have to be where she charged the Sea-Doo.

Cruising west on Robert Moses Parkway, Hammett noticed she had a tail. White sedan, light bar on the roof. Buffalo police. Hammett knew the speed limit, knew she was fine. The cop was on a fishing expedition. But if he was running her plates, and McGlade's came up fake or stolen...

The cop's lights went on, and the siren wailed. Hammett frowned, then reached under the seat and tucked the .357 between her thighs. She pulled over to the side of the road, considering her options. Killing a police officer wouldn't be wise. But she couldn't let herself get arrested, or even delayed. Depending on the cop and depending on why he was pulling her over, perhaps she could charm her way out of this, or bribe him. But if he insisted on license and registration—which she didn't have—her options were limited to fleeing. Whether she shot him first or not would be a judgment call.

She watched his approach in the rearview mirror, the stereotypical cop swagger. He was older, forties, beer gut, expression unreadable behind his mirrored sunglasses. Hand on his holster.

Hammett rolled down her window.

"License and registration."

"May I ask why you pulled me over, Officer?"

"Your taillight is out."

Goddammit, McGlade.

"Really? I didn't know. This isn't my car, but thanks for telling me. It's dangerous driving without a taillight."

"License and registration."

"I saw an auto parts store a few miles back. I can take care of this right away. I really don't want to be wasting your time on little old me. My brother is a policeman, in Chicago. I think you guys have the hardest job in the world."

She gave him her best smile, and casually dropped her hand to her lap.

"I need your license and registration, ma'am."

Shit, he wasn't going to budge. So…kill him or not?

Hammett noticed his hand, saw the wedding band. That didn't matter. She'd killed family men before. But she imagined the story on the local news, hero cop killed during a routine traffic stop, grieving widow pleading for justice.

No, there was a better, cleaner way. A Corvette could smoke a police car, and Hammett was a damn good driver. She winked, blew him a kiss, and floored the accelerator. The 'Vette squealed, the rear end fishtailing on the fat rear tires. Hammett cut left, skipping over the patch of grass between the two opposite lanes, tearing two trenches into the earth and then whipping around into eastbound traffic. Past 190 was Cayuga Island, a large residential area. Side streets, driveways, backyards, plenty of places to hide. She hit 80 mph, and the car still had plenty to give. All she needed to do was get a mile head start and—

It all happened in a millisecond. The small shape in her lane—brown, four legs, dog! Slamming on the brakes and turning hard. Missing the animal by a hair but heading right for the embankment. Screeching and pinning the gas again, pulling into the skid, missing the concrete but headed for more grass. The rear end catching a tree, spinning wildly, airbags popping in Hammett's face. The car tilting on its side. Coming to an abrupt, hard stop, headfirst into the bag as water flooded in through her open window.

The river.

She was in the Niagara River.

And the strong current pulled at the car, taking it toward the second-largest waterfall in the world.

# Fleming

*"The mission comes first," The Instructor said. "You're a weapon. Weapons don't form attachments. You can't afford to make this personal."*

Fleming didn't sleep. She kept glancing at the cell phone on the van's dashboard, the phone Scarlett had left her. It was off. It had to be off. Turning it on meant listening to messages of Bradley screaming and begging.

The most difficult part was that she knew where they were. Fleming could track Scarlett's and Rhett's chips. But what could she do in a wheelchair with limited weapons? She'd barely been able to save herself. Saving Bradley was beyond her capabilities. Especially when there were more pressing things to do, such as stop an Ebola outbreak that could destroy humanity.

So she pored over her transceiver, got everything working perfectly by morning, and called her contacts and set to meet them at a café on Pennsylvania Avenue. Then she put on too much eye makeup and lipstick—as good a disguise as she could muster when her face was so famous—and started the van.

She got there early, like a good spy should, and found legal parking on the street. She fed and watered Sasha, then began the laborious process of exiting the van in her wheelchair.

When Fleming got to the restaurant, she went through the motions of checking for surveillance and memorizing exits, a practiced action made more difficult because the escape route had to be handicapped accessible. The place smelled of cinnamon. Faint easy listening blandness played through speakers set high on the walls, barely discernible over the clatter of dishes and conversation. Sick to her stomach for a variety of reasons, she ordered a coffee and some wheat toast, then waited for her help to arrive.

Lt. Jack Daniels showed up first. Fleming had never met her, but knew who the woman was when she walked in. Average height, brunette, athletic, dressed in a designer pantsuit, she might have been just another urban professional on the way to the law firm or the board meeting. Except for the eyes. Daniels had eyes like a cop, sweeping the restaurant with laser precision, assessing and dismissing threats. When she spotted Fleming, she walked over without a smile or a nod.

"Nice outfit," Fleming said, meaning it. The suit was gray, flattering, and allowed full movement, which meant Jack could run or fight or shoot if needed. The only impractical thing the cop wore was black pumps. Fleming hadn't worn heels since the accident.

"The tour starts in half an hour. Who's coming with me? It has to be two people."

"I've got a disguise. I'm going to dress up as an elderly Chinese man."

Jack's expression stayed blank.

"He'll be here shortly," Fleming said.

Jack sat down, remaining silent. Fleming didn't bother with small talk or thanks. Jack may not have been a spy, but she was a pro, and they both knew their part. The waitress came by, gave them coffee. Jack didn't order any food.

"The toast is pretty good," Fleming said. It came out lame, but it was damn good toast, even if her stomach didn't appreciate it.

Jack frowned. "I'm about to commit an act tantamount to treason. I'm not very hungry."

Fleming didn't know Jack, and Jack barely knew Chandler. Yet, here the woman was, helping out. Doing the right thing. Fleming tried to wrap her head around that.

She'd done the right thing, many times, but it was usually a spur-of-the-moment decision, or the result of an order. Fleming didn't have the freedom to choose between right and wrong. And, admittedly, she wasn't sure it was an option she wanted to have. Completing a mission didn't leave room for guilt. An operative lived in the moment, didn't question her own actions lest she get killed.

Fleming wondered if she would hop on a plane to meet a complete stranger because another stranger asked her for help against some convoluted plot to murder innocent people. Probably not.

Jack, however, followed a different set of rules. Which meant Chandler was able to manipulate her into doing something that no Hydra agent would ever do. Did that make Jack gullible? Or braver than Fleming would ever be?

Fleming leaned in closer. The diner was full, the din of rattling dishes and conversation more than enough to mask her voice, but why risk being overheard? "You're right. You're taking a huge risk, and while I'm sure you're used to that, this is on a whole different level. So why are you doing it?"

"Good damn question."

"Got an answer?"

"A good one? Not really."

"It isn't treason, Jack. The guy is crooked. He killed his predecessor. Betraying a politician isn't betraying your country."

"I'll tell that to the firing squad."

"You're saving lives. You know what almost happened to London. This could be worse."

"You don't need the hard sell, Fleming. I got that already. That's why I'm here."

Fleming studied the older woman. She seemed annoyed but determined. "You know why I think you're here?"

"Do tell."

"I think it's because you're one of the good guys."

Jack shook her head. "You're the hero. You're the one who saved London."

Fleming thought about Bradley, probably getting his knees broken at that very moment. "I'm not a hero. I'm a tool. A weapon, used to get certain things done. Some of those things are good. Some aren't."

Jack stared at Fleming, hard as she'd ever been stared at. "Bullshit. We always have a choice. You're choosing the path you take, same as me. Sometimes those choices aren't easy. But they're yours. A gun can't decide for itself when it fires. But you can."

"It's different in the military."

"It isn't that different. You're still a human being."

Sometimes Fleming wondered about that. This mission had several aspects to it. They were saving themselves. They were getting revenge. But they were also saving innocent people. Beneath all the selfishness, Fleming, Chandler, and even Hammett were helping the world.

But would they be doing it if they had no selfish reasons? If they were ordered to, yes. But volunteering for it? Fleming didn't know.

She eyed Jack. She was sure of one thing. "What we're doing here, it's for the greater good."

Jack sipped some coffee. "That's a nice answer. The problem is there's no universal indicator of greater good. Is it simple numbers? Two lives are always worth more than one. Right? What if the one is someone you love? Personal bias always comes into play, Fleming. We aren't computers, able to calculate what the best choice is. We're human beings. We make mistakes. We're selfish, with our own agendas. And we're very good at justifying everything we do."

"Right now we're both here to save a lot of people."

"Sure. But to what lengths should one go in order to save those people? Is killing OK then? I'm a cop, not an assassin."

"Haven't you killed people?"

"You're not one for small talk, are you?"

"We don't have time for small talk. We're both pros, we're both trying to make things right. If you'd prefer to discuss sports, how are the Cubs doing?"

"Season is over. Look, I've killed, but only when it was me or him. Otherwise I arrest the bad guys, let the courts worry about justice."

Fleming drank the coffee, found it sour. "So you wouldn't kill someone to save others?"

"I wouldn't follow orders to kill someone because I was told it would save others. But then, I'm not the one who just saved millions of Londoners."

Fleming hadn't been following orders then. She'd acted on her own initiative. But she was curious where Jack was going with this.

"We need the military to protect our country," Fleming said. "Sometimes we act before we're acted upon. That's why soldiers need to follow orders."

"In theory, yes. But in practice? How much of what our military does has to do with the agendas of men in suits? Those who seek power and money? When did this shield meant to protect us become a private security force to control oil prices, stock prices, and who gets elected?"

"It's always been that way. Power corrupts. But it's still for the greater good. You can't argue ideology in the face of reality."

"That's precisely when ideology needs to be argued. It's OK to throw out our Constitution and the Bill of Rights in order to serve the greater good? That's the whole point of Homeland Security, isn't it? Personal safety at the expense of personal freedoms. Who cares if our government kills our enemies without a trial or even evidence, as long as we're protected? Who cares if we kill our own citizens? We trust those in power to do what's right for the country, when they're acting in their own self-interest just like anyone else."

Fleming wondered if Jack would feel the same way if she'd been trained under The Instructor.

"There are bad people in the world, Jack."

"I know that better than anybody, Fleming. But without laws, without due process, it gets grayer and grayer who the bad people are. How much of the gray do you accept for the few times it is truly black and white? How many innocent people have to suffer just so we can nail a few bad guys?"

"So if you were trying to save the lives of thousands, maybe millions, but someone you cared about was suffering as a result, what would you do?"

"I don't put myself in a position where I ever have to choose something like that."

"But if you were forced to. Save a busload of strangers or your fiancée."

"I don't sleep with a busload of strangers."

"So you'd save your boyfriend?"

"I didn't say that. But I'll tell you something. I've lived my whole adult life trying to do the right thing in order to help others. Maybe I'd be happier if I tried to do something for myself every once in a while. And frankly, if someone I loved died and I could have prevented it, I don't know how I'd go on."

Again Fleming pictured Bradley. His face. His eyes. His voice. It was her fault he was in this mess. But instead of helping him, she was here, trying to serve the greater good.

Just like she'd been serving the greater good every time she killed some enemy of the state.

Fleming didn't know Bradley that well. But she didn't know the people she'd assassinated either. Just following orders hadn't worked out so well at the Nuremberg trials.

"Oh, Christ," Jack said, frowning at the entrance. "Seriously?"

Fleming didn't have to look to understand her reaction. "We didn't have much of a choice at the last minute."

"And you didn't tell me because you knew I wouldn't help."

Harry McGlade grinned wide as a zebra's ass, waving at the women. He was shouldering a duffel bag, and wore a suit that looked as if it had been slept in. He made his way through the crowd toward them.

"It was Chandler's call," Fleming said. "If it matters, we both had to promise to go out with him."

"Take plenty of penicillin afterward," Jack said. "And it wouldn't hurt to boil yourselves."

Harry took a seat. "Hiya, Jackie. That's quite the severe suit you have on. Don't you have any clothes that show off your boobs?"

"Don't you have any that aren't wrinkled? We're going to the White House, McGlade. You could have shaved."

"I did. Just not my face." He turned to Fleming, offering his hand. "Hello again, my little à la carte hors d'oeuvre."

Fleming took it, reluctantly. "Hello, McGlade."

"I love the eye makeup. And the red lipstick is killer. I'll pay you ten bucks, right now, to watch you eat a banana."

"Does being blunt like that ever actually work?"

"It worked on your sister." He winked. "Twice."

Fleming took her hand back. "You slept with Chandler?"

McGlade made a face. "Chandler? No, she's too moody and self-absorbed. The other one, with the bigger fun bags. The psycho."

Fleming's eyes widened. "Hammett?"

"Yeah. She held a knife to my throat the whole time. Hot."

Jack shrugged. "McGlade has a thing for psychos."

"And Hammett didn't kill you?"

"Well, I am a little dehydrated. And I have some chafing." He kicked the duffel bag under the table, toward Fleming. "Early Christmas present, from me and your sisters. Lots of fun shotgun rounds, a pistol, some clips—er, magazines—for the Skorpion."

"You brought that on a plane?" Jack said. Fleming was thinking the same thing.

"Checked baggage. It's cool as long as you declare it."

"I can't bring him on the tour," Jack leaned away from McGlade. "We'll get caught."

Harry shook his head. "No way. I'm too crafty for words."

"You're too stupid for words."

"I'm a private eye, Jackie. I'm all about being sly and discreet. That's how I'm able to take so many pics of cheating wives and husbands. I practically invented subterfuge."

"You can't even spell subterfuge."

"It starts with an S. Or is that one of those silent C words? The silent C always screws me up."

"Actually," Fleming said, "if he just acts like himself, any surveillance will focus on him. Then you can drop the bug where I need you to."

McGlade nodded. "Textbook *Mission Impossible* stuff. I'm the distraction, the decoy, and while I draw the attention, you do the deed that betrays your country and lets you go down in history as Ms. Benedict Arnold. Frankly, I'm disgusted with your behavior."

"What if he draws so much attention we get caught?" Jack asked.

"Then I don't know you," Harry said. "Every man for himself."

Jack's shoulders slumped. "I think I'd have better odds if I just asked random people in the diner if they'd like to visit the White House with me."

Fleming checked the clock above the glass counter filled with pies. "No time."

"Jackie, partner, c'mon. Have I ever let you down?"

"Repeatedly."

"This will be fun. We get a nice tour. We save the world. I get to have a four-way with triplets." Harry shot Fleming a pointed glance. "That's still on the menu, isn't it, Wheels?"

Jack's frown deepened. "You had to bribe him with sex?"

Fleming's turn to frown. "For some reason, appealing to his good nature didn't sway him."

"My good nature is in my pants." Harry beamed. "I call him Snatchmo."

No one reacted.

"Get it? He wants mo' snatch."

Jack stood up. "I'm asking random strangers."

Fleming told Harry to cool it, and asked Jack to please sit back down. Then she explained exactly what she needed them to do.

"Piece of cake," Harry said.

Jack eyed him, obviously dubious. "Are you serious?"

"Absolutely." He yelled at the waitress, "Carrot cake! And hurry up, we're visiting the White House!"

Fleming checked the time again. She thought about Bradley. Then she thought about billions of people, crashing and bleeding out because of Ebola.

"Not that one," McGlade called. "The bigger slice next to it!"

Jack gave Fleming a forlorn look. Fleming returned it.

The next hour was going to be intense.

# Scarlett

*"Your ability to function may become compromised,"*
*The Instructor said. "You must be able to continue at a*
*diminished capacity. Or else, find another career."*

Scarlett woke up to pain.

Her leg felt like it had been trapped in a meat grinder with the gears still turning. Every movement, every breath, brought a wave of tear-bursting agony.

She looked around the motel room, seeing Rhett was gone. Where was that asshole? Didn't he know she needed morphine? Scarlett was about to call out to him when she heard the voices in the bathroom.

"So you don't know Fleming's plan?" Rhett.

"I told you. She kidnapped me. I don't know anything about her or her plan." The hostage. Crying.

"Why did she kidnap you?"

"Because I'm really good at miniature robotics. But I don't know what she wanted."

"You didn't build anything?"

"No."

"So why weren't you tied up?"

"I...I escaped."

"You escaped, ran outside, and then called her name?"

Silence. Then a scream.

"That's nothing, hoss. I can make you hurt a lot worse than that. And that little lady in the other room, she's a lot better at this stuff than I am. She actually likes it. And I bet when she wakes up with her leg all shot to shit, she's gonna be angrier than a rattlesnake on a honky-tonk dance floor during the 'Boot Scootin' Boogie.'"

Scarlett cringed at the metaphor, but Rhett was right. She was pissed off and eager to take it out on another human being. Sometimes the only way to feel better was to make someone else feel worse.

Bradley screamed again, longer this time.

Setting her jaw, Scarlett heaved herself into a sitting position. The pain was dizzying. She swung her bad leg over the side, tears running down her cheeks, concentrating on what she was going to do to the boy. In her kit, she had a blowtorch. When out in the field, and when the survival of the person being interrogated wasn't important, Scarlett found that nothing gave you more bang for the buck than good old fire. It looked and sounded scary, hurt worse than anything, and kept hurting. Unlike other forms of interrogation, with fire, people didn't talk in order to stop the torture. They talked if promised a quick death.

Thinking about the boy, his fingers burned off, begging for death, was enough to get her to stand up.

It was awful, and she screamed, long and loud. Rhett came out of the bathroom, wiping his hands off on a white towel stained pink.

"Good morning, darlin'. You're looking chipper."

"Drugs."

"Yes, ma'am." Rhett prepared a few syringes. "One to numb, one to take the edge off. I should change those bandages, too."

"Get my blowtorch," Scarlett said through clenched teeth.

"Yes, ma'am. Hear that, son? Miss Scarlett here is getting her blowtorch. We're gonna have ourselves a squealer barbecue."

There was a pounding on the door. Rhett's pistol appeared instantly in his hand.

"This is the owner! I hear screaming in there."

"Sorry 'bout that, hoss. We'll keep it down."

"You'll be gone in five minutes. I want you out. The police are on their way."

Scarlett turned to Rhett and said, "Kill that asshole."

Rhett shook his head. "That's the pain talking. If the police are coming, we have to clear out of here."

"We can kill them, too."

"Scarlett, sweetheart, you know that's not in our best interests. Let's get junior packed up and take him to the lab. We'll have privacy, and more tools to work with. It's only a six-hour drive. I'll get us there in four."

Even one hour in a car sounded about as much fun to Scarlett as brushing her teeth with a belt sander, but the drugs were already starting to kick in, taking the edge off of her temper.

"Fine. But I'm not dealing with him moaning and crying."

"The car has a nice big trunk," Rhett said. Then he smiled and winked. "Plenty of room for you."

"You're hilarious."

"Can't help it. Southern charm is in my genes."

Scarlett knew that Rhett was actually born in Ohio, but she chose not to go there because it always ended with him getting angry. And when Rhett was angry, he hummed his three country tunes louder than normal.

"I'll alert the lab, tell them to expect us," Scarlett said. "Have we heard from Fleming?"

"Nothing yet. Called a few times, letting the young lad cry into the phone. She isn't picking up."

"What a heartless bitch," Scarlett said.

"All spies aren't as sweet as you, darlin'."

Rhett prepared another syringe to knock out Bradley for the trip.

"Not too strong," she cautioned. "I want him to be awake and aware when I begin working on him later."

Rhett smiled. "See what I mean? Sweeter than blackstrap molasses. I'm surprised you don't have honeybees buzzing around you."

Scarlett ignored him, instead thinking about her blowtorch.

She could practically taste the screams.

# Heath

*"Playing with fire might be exciting," said The Instructor. "But some fires are hotter than others, and they don't just burn. They incinerate."*

"It's about time. I called you an hour ago. I have a surprise for you."

Heath closed the door of the shitty apartment and paused before turning toward the voice. If he was lucky, Earnshaw had a gun on him and was planning to put a bullet in his back.

Too bad he wasn't feeling all that lucky.

"On three, OK?" Her voice lilted in a way that made him cringe. "OK?"

He grunted.

"*Uno, dos, tres.*"

He didn't move.

"Turn around."

Steeling himself for what was bound to be a bad scene, he forced his feet to do a one-eighty.

Earnshaw stood in all her huge, muscle-bound glory, naked except for a wisp of a pink lace thong and a pink lace bra about to explode with her pecs.

*Aye dios mio.*

When Heath had agreed to be part of Hydra Deux, he'd envisioned his partner would be female. With Earnshaw, this was in question. There were times he suspected she was more man than he was.

Sadly, this might be one of them.

Of course, that hadn't stopped him from taking a taste a few weeks ago. Who could blame him? He had an open mind when it came to women. He'd resisted bedding Earnshaw for years, then horniness and boredom and downright drunkenness had worn him down. Sleeping with her had been a big mistake.

"I bought them for you. What do you think?" Earnshaw did a pirouette that looked more bodybuilder than ballerina. The fact that her voice was almost as low as his didn't help matters.

He'd gotten her call while cleaning the *patio de caballos* at the Plaza Mexico. Shoveling horseshit had been hard work, as Manuel had warned, but it was nothing compared with servicing Earnshaw, something he never intended to do again.

"*Muy bonita,*" he lied.

Earnshaw gave him her version of a come-hither look, a strange combination of blushing ingénue and raging bull. "You really think so?"

One of these days, Heath really had to learn to keep his zipper closed. After this, he probably needed to give up women for good. Unless he could find the right woman. And he had just the woman in mind. Chandler.

Of course, she probably wanted him dead about now.

Heath smiled.

"I'm so glad you like it."

Earnshaw started toward him, snapping him back to reality.

"Of course I like it. But there's no time."

"No time?" Smile turned to pout.

Over the course of their partnership, Earnshaw had told him many things about herself, much more than he'd shared with her. Most of her stories had centered around her years as a female wrestler, stories of travel and sweat and endless training.

The fascinating part was that while she was a phenomenal wrestler, she'd always secretly dreamed of going to Hollywood and acting in the movies. She was clearly delusional and one of the worst actors he'd ever seen, every expression falling somewhere between intestinal discomfort and tears. Heath figured she'd lucked out that The Instructor had found her when her Olympic dreams shattered, and she'd never had the chance to make that trip to Hollywood. She only would have been disappointed. Better to have the opportunity to express her true talent.

Killing people.

The Instructor had given him explicit instructions that she avoid playing roles in the field. But that didn't keep her from trying out her lack of acting chops in an effort to manipulate him.

As long as she didn't use her muscles to force him to do what she wanted, he would probably be OK. But since her biceps were bigger than his, the risk remained ever present.

"I have to get back to the plaza. The Ebola—where is it?"

"See the soda truck parked out front?"

He had. "The canister is inside?"

"Packed behind the soda."

"Good. I'll drive it to the plaza."

"Not without me. I deliver the virus, you do the rest."

"Let me guess, The Instructor said you're to keep an eye on it, and me, at all times?"

She pursed her lips.

"You'd think he didn't trust me."

"He doesn't."

"Did he say why?"

"Didn't ask."

"Do you trust me?"

Earnshaw stepped toward him, grasped his hands, and placed his palms smack on her gigantic lace-covered breasts, then she took his face in both hands, as if afraid he'd pull away, and gave him a long kiss on the mouth. "I trust you as long as you stay close. Real close."

He should tell her he didn't want her and be done with it. She could take it. She'd have to. But the truth was he didn't want to hurt her feelings. He didn't even like Earnshaw, but he got the idea she hadn't had many men in her life. He didn't want to be the one to make her cry.

Or worse, have her break his neck in his sleep.

So he closed his eyes and resigned himself to take one for the team. As her hands drifted down his body, he tried to imagine it was someone attractive. An actress. A supermodel.

For some odd reason, Chandler popped into his head.

"See?" Earnshaw said, grasping him. "I knew you liked me."

And then she was pushing him to the bed, climbing atop, clamping her big thighs around him in a move that felt less like making love and more like being pinned for the three count. He kept thinking about Chandler. Kept focusing on her face, her body, and blocking out the deep-throated groans and manlike hands pawing his chest.

Then she kissed him, which completely destroyed the fantasy because Chandler didn't have razor stubble on her face.

Still, he managed to seal the deal, and hopefully endear Earnshaw to him long enough to betray her when the time came.

And the time was coming soon.


# Years Ago…


His codename was Heathcliff, but back when his sweet *madre* was alive, he was known as Armando.

That was still his name after they put her in the ground, dead from tuberculosis. But Armando knew it wasn't the disease that took her. The disease was only the result. The cause was poverty, no health care, years of toil picking garbage at *el dompe* in Tijuana.

The day she died, he sold everything except a cooking knife, his birth certificate, and the clothes on his back and used the money to bury her properly. Then armed with the knife and his American birth certificate, he abandoned Tijuana and walked across the border into a land of wealth and excess.

He was born in America and lived there as a young child, but now at the ripe old age of fifteen, he didn't remember much. Not that it mattered. He had come for only one purpose, and it had little to do with making a better life.

He'd come to live up to the meaning behind his name. Soldier. Warrior. He'd come to fight the battle his mother couldn't.

He'd come to kill his father.

That was Armando's American Dream.

Armando stole four hundred and thirty-nine dollars at knifepoint from a convenience store in Chula Vista, then using his new wealth, bought a bus ticket, a cheap revolver from a gangbanger in an alley, and a bottle of Mountain Dew.

After switching to another bus in San Diego, he finally stepped off into the dry heat of Phoenix. Armando didn't know where his father lived, but the man wasn't hard to find. Armando was smart and crafty, and his father was a prominent man with no reason to hide, and by nightfall the son found himself scaling a stucco wall and landing in a courtyard complete with an azure swimming pool surrounded by palms and climbing vines. Grapefruit and orange perfumed the air, the trees heavy with spring flowers.

*Dios mio.*

Keeping to the shadows, Armando crept along the wall. Light shimmered from the pool. Soft music tickled the air from speakers hidden here and there among the plantings. The place was magical, like some kind of fantasy oasis, a world far removed from what he knew.

*El Diablo* lived in paradise while conscripting Armando's mother to garbage hell.

The house rose high above the trees, dramatic stucco arches and clay tile roof. It seemed even bigger than the San Diego bus station, spotlights shining from beneath, and for a moment, Armando wondered how he would ever find a single man in a space so large.

He supposed he'd better start looking.

The windows and doors were closed, but after testing one of the sliding doors off the patio, he discovered closed didn't mean locked. Armando slid the glass open and stepped into the house.

The air inside was cold and smelled of some kind of flower Armando did not know. He walked softly across terrazzo floors, passing a kitchen gleaming with stainless steel appliances and so many cabinets he couldn't imagine what could possibly fill them all. A sitting area flanked the kitchen, leather furniture and book-shelves laden with more books than he knew existed. A dining room boasted a long table surrounded by twelve chairs. Other rooms sprouted off like endless limbs of a tree.

"Hold it."

He turned to face the voice, reaching into the back of his jeans where he'd stashed his revolver.

A man stood at the dining room's arched entrance. Pale skin and blue eyes, he stood erect, powerful, and in his hand, he held a gun, pointed at Armando.

"Hands up where I can see them. I will shoot you."

Armando hesitated. This was his father. The shape of his jaw, the line of his nose, so like Armando's. And for a moment, he had the urge to run his fingertips over his own face, just to compare.

"Robert?" The man looked behind Armando.

And then Armando heard the steps.

Rough hands closed around his wrist and bent it behind his back. Another hand took his revolver and then skimmed down his body and found the knife he'd tied to his calf with string.

It was over, all his plans, all his intentions. Ended because he'd been so busy gaping at the way the rich live, he hadn't been ready to strike.

Now it was too late.

But although Armando had failed, he held his head high, staring into the man's face with hatred, defiance to the end.

"What's your name, boy?" *El Diablo* said, a slight smile on his face. "*¿Cómo te llamas?*"

"Armando."

"Why did you sneak in here? Hmm? To steal? Well, look around. You don't get this kind of home by stealing, boy. Stealing only lands your ass in prison."

"I not come to steal." Armando's English was no good, but his father must have been able to figure out the words, because he answered.

"Then why did you come, boy? To beg? To get a handout? I should have known."

"No."

"You here illegally?"

"I was born here."

"Anchor baby, eh? Well, you need to get your ass to work and learn some English, make something of yourself, son."

Armando looked into the man's eyes to see if he had recognized him. But there was nothing there. No recognition. And Armando had to conclude that he had used the word *son* as an expression, nothing more. "My *madre*, she worked for you. Maria Elena Castellano."

"Don't remember her."

"She clean house."

"I've had lots of maids."

"She deported."

"I have important friends. I can't have illegals working for me. I don't have time for this. Robert? Call the police. I got this." He nodded to the pistol in his hand.

Armando's arms were suddenly free, and he stumbled forward. He no longer had his revolver or his knife, but he would kill his father with his bare hands if he had to. Even if he died trying, his sacrifice would be in honor of his mother.

But he needed to say something first.

Armando had practiced the words in English all the way on the bus, but now his throat was so dry he had trouble pushing them from his lips. "I came because you are my father. I came to kill you."

The man's pale skin grew a little paler. Then his lips pulled back from his perfect teeth and his chest began to rumble with laughter.

He frowned, as if something was finally clicking in his memory. "What was your mother's name again?"

"Maria Castellano."

"Pretty? Mexican?" He laughed again. "Nope. Don't remember. But I'll bet you have a birth certificate that has my name on it."

"*Si.*"

"Some women will resort to out-and-out lies to get their babies born on this side of the border."

Armando eyed the gun and wondered how close he could get before a bullet took him down.

Footsteps sounded on terrazzo, and the bodyguard walked back into the room holding out a mobile phone like the ones Armando had seen some of the missionaries use.

"You want me to call the police, sir?"

"No. I have a better idea." He took the phone and punched in a number. "If you really are my son—and I'm not saying you are—you gotta make something of yourself, understand?"

Armando's English wasn't so good, and he was pretty sure he misunderstood. "Make me into something?"

"A soldier. A weapon. You got some anger in you. That can be put to good use."

Armando wasn't about to give up on seeing this man die, but this was a twist he had never imagined, and he wanted to know more. "How?"

"If you were born here, you should serve your country. Become a soldier." The man's index finger hovered over one of the buttons. "It's either that or the police, and I can guarantee your path in life will be much different if I call them."

Armando paused, listening to a grand clock chime through the house. Then finally he gave a nod.

His name meant soldier, warrior, and that is what Armando would become. And the next time he faced his father, he wouldn't have his weapon taken. The next time, he'd be prepared.

The next time, Armando would have his revenge.

# Hammett

*"There is no fear more primal than drowning," The Instructor said. "That's why waterboarding is so effective."*

As the Corvette filled with water, Hammett's first coherent thought was of Julie's dog, Kirk. If Hammett died, the mission would fail, which meant the dog would likely be euthanized.

The thought of it snapped her car crash–scrambled brain back into reality.

Hammett remembered the cop pulling her over. Taking off. Swerving to avoid a dog. Skidding out of control. Hitting the grass, then a tree.

And now—

Now she was fucked.

She pulled the .357 from under her thigh and fired upward, deflating the airbag pressed against her face. Her window was still open from her exchange with the police officer, the Niagara River pouring into the vehicle like it was being pumped. Hammett smelled the burnt odor of the airbag exploding outward and the gunpowder from her shot, and then her nostrils were filled with water and she craned up her neck and took a last choke-filled breath before the 'Vette sank.

Hammett went Zen, forcing calm in the hysterical face of certain death, making her heart rate slow down so she didn't burn the oxygen in her lungs while using her adrenaline boost to focus on her immediate needs.

First, grab the Sea-Doo.

Second, the weapons duffel bag in the trunk.

It was too late (and damn near impossible) to put a wet suit on while in the water, so she shoved it aside in her search for the scuba scooter.

The water was cold enough to cloak her entire body in instant gooseflesh, and though Hammett had amazing lung and diaphragm control, anything below sixty degrees Fahrenheit meant taking her best time holding her breath and cutting it in half. She reached around, slow and methodical in her search for the neutrally buoyant Sea-Doo, her vision not helping in the murky water, the car swirling and tilting to disorient her even more than the accident did, aware that the undertow and currents were taking her ever so closer to—

The falls.

Holy shit, she was headed for the falls.

When researching the best place to cross, Hammett right-fully picked a spot downriver from the falls. She didn't want to risk even the slightest chance of free-falling fifty-one meters over their edge. Hammett knew the history. Five thousand dead since they'd started keeping records in the mid-1800s. Forty people killed every year. Survivors? A few dozen. Surviving without injuries? Unless you were in a well-constructed barrel and got obscenely lucky, surviving unscathed was impossible. You had a better chance of living through a lightning storm while strapped to a fifty-foot metal rod.

The car upended, Hammett now hanging upside down by her seat belt. In a way it was fortuitous, because the Sea-Doo bumped her in the head and she was able to grab its handle. But now she'd completely lost her sense of direction, and the murk had become so dark Hammett couldn't tell where the surface was.

Figuring she had forty-five seconds of air left, tops, Hammett released her seat belt and kicked off against the steering wheel, her feet tangling in the deflated airbag. She dropped the .357 and tugged the keys from the ignition, stuck them in her teeth, then looped the seat belt through the Sea-Doo handle and refastened it. Then Hammett shimmied out the window, fighting to keep from getting hung up, muscling her way through until she was free of the car.

But she wasn't free of the current.

The undertow shook her in its angry fist, pulling and shoving and slapping her in so many directions that she felt like a feather in a tornado. Hammett clutched the doorframe with both hands, knowing she had to get into the trunk. That's where the weapons were, and without them, Hammett's mission was as dead as if she'd drowned in the river.

She kicked, but it was impossible to swim against the current, so she had to make do with going hand over hand across the 'Vette's undercarriage, grabbing the frame, the exhaust—which had already cooled in the frigid water—struts, the rear tire, and finally the trunk. Hammett worked by feel, locating the lock, sticking in the key, opening the trunk, wrapping a strap from the duffel bag around her shoulder.

With less than twenty seconds of air left, Hammett made her way back to the driver's side door. The car began to pitch forward, nose first, and she blew out some carbon dioxide to make herself less buoyant and made it to the open window. She reached inside for the Sea-Doo, gripped the seat belt, and hit the release button.

Nothing happened.

She tried again, yanking on it, but the water or the cold made the button stick.

Hammett had no idea how far she'd drifted, but she could hear the falls, a white noise rumble in the water growing steadily louder. Without the Sea-Doo, she wouldn't make it to either shore.

She hooked her foot onto the steering wheel to stay with the twirling car, then used both hands to unzip the duffel bag, snaking a hand in to find her karambit knife. She didn't find it, but her fingers did brush against the flashlight. She clicked it on, and the interior of the bag was flooded with light.

Her oxygen reserves near depletion, Hammett found the knife, stuck the light in her teeth, zipped up the bag, and quickly cut the Sea-Doo free. The edges of her vision had begun to darken, her brain fogging like she'd just woken up. Soon she'd have to suck in a breath, and Hammett knew she'd rather pass out first, even if it meant dying. As part of Hydra training, all of the sisters had been waterboarded. Drowning was awful, and she didn't want to relive the experience.

Hammett felt like she was moving through glue, her limbs sluggish, her thoughts fuzzy, but she managed to pull the scooter through the window and hit the thrust.

It buzzed to life, rocketing her away from the car. Hammett fought to hold on, somehow managed to get her other hand onto the handle, and then she was racing toward the surface.

She bobbed out, cutting the throttle and taking a huge gulp of cool air mere milliseconds before true panic set in.

Then Hammett looked around, and true panic set in.

The current was so fast she'd drifted several kilometers and was already parallel with Goat Island—the landmass that separated the US and Canadian falls.

Goat Island was about a thousand feet to the north. Canada was two thousand feet south. And the famous horseshoe falls, three thousand feet away and coming fast.

Hammett had to make a quick decision. The cop must have seen her car go into the river, and now the authorities were alerted. Going back to the US side was the safer bet, but crossing by river later would be out of the question, because too many people would be on the lookout for her.

That meant getting to the Canada side before going over the falls. A lot riskier, but the Sea-Doo held its own against the powerful current.

The falls were loud enough to interfere with her thoughts, but not so loud that Hammett wasn't hit with the obvious.

*I'd have to be a fucking idiot to try for the Canada side.*

She gunned the Sea-Doo, heading north to the banks of Goat Island. The Sea-Doo cut through the undertow, pulling her toward the Three Sisters Islands—small landmasses south of Goat Island. The water turned white, dropping her a meter or so, but nothing short of a nuclear blast was going to make Hammett let go of that scooter. Though she covered a lot of distance quickly, the rushing water took her past Three Sisters, to a smaller speck of land called Brother Island, and Hammett was sighting the rocky shoreline to see where she'd dock when the Sea-Doo whined to a stop.

Dead battery.

Hammett tried to get it started again, fooling with it for several long seconds, and then she ditched it and swam for her life.

She was strong.

The current was stronger. And it was taking her right to the falls.

Hammett realized, with a very high certainty, that she had perhaps thirty seconds left to live.

Even if she avoided the talus—the craggy rocks at the bottom of the falls—a drop from that height could be fatal even if she hit nothing but water. Broken bones. Ruptured organs. Concussion. Unconsciousness would kill her just as easily as splattering against the scree.

The sound now was deafening, thunderous, the water jetting her forward like the world's deadliest flume ride. Hammett went under, got smacked around, then surfaced again and saw a tiny scrub of land, filled with trees and bushes, situated just before the water fell off the horizon. If she could reach it, she could hold on until rescued. It would mean arrest, but she'd rather face an army of cops than certain death.

She had one chance. It was a small chance, but she clung to it with fervent hope.

The land came up fast—

—Hammett reached for a rock—

—bounced off—

—and then she was plummeting over the brink.

# Fleming

*"One mistake can ruin an op," The Instructor said. "Don't work with those who make mistakes."*

Fleming rolled up to the corner of Jackson and Pennsylvania, into Lafayette Square, near the big, black statue of Rochambeau. He was on a high stone pedestal, dressed in his best French general's uniform, pointing into the distance. At what, Fleming didn't care, but the certainty the statue conveyed, the conviction in its pose, was the complete opposite of how Fleming was feeling.

Like Rochambeau, Fleming had a goal. But rather than feeling brave and confident, Fleming was on the verge of vomiting her oatmeal.

She directed her wheelchair toward an ornate lamppost across the street from a row of brownstones, terraced ivy-covered row houses that spoke of history and money. She unfolded a large map, letting it obscure her movements as she quickly used a screw hose clamp to attach a black box to the post. The radio transceiver booster, with a Wi-Fi dongle on it. It took only thirty seconds, and when she was done it looked like part of the post, some sort of meter or industrial equipment that some city construction workers put on for whatever reason. Hiding in plain sight.

Then Fleming took out her laptop and scanned for Wi-Fi hot zones in the area. She found several strong signals—probably from the nearby homes—and quickly broke the encryption and piggybacked on a wireless connection. Then she put in an earbud and rolled back to Rochambeau, listening to Harry's voice.

"So the senator gave you AIDS?"

Another man's voice. "No, Mr. McGlade. I'm Senator Crouch's *aide*."

"It's not some sex thing?"

"I assist the senator."

"Assist him…sexually?"

"Forgive Harry," Jack said. "He was dropped on his head as a boy. Repeatedly. On purpose."

"Not true. I'm just naturally plucky."

Fleming checked the video feed, saw nothing but black even though the camera was active. Jack must have the pen in her pocket. That probably also accounted for the slightly muffled sound quality.

"This is the presidential library," the aide said.

"Can we check out books?" McGlade asked.

"No. It's for the president's personal use."

A snort. "What a waste. I've seen him in front of a tele-prompter. Reading is not one of his top skills."

"Excuse us a moment," Jack said. Then, in a low whisper, "Stop it. Right now."

"Stop what? My pluckiness? I'm too full of pluck."

"You're full of something. Just stop being you for ten minutes. OK?"

"Role-play? That's hot. How about I'm the cable guy, and you're the horny housewife willing to do anything for free HBO."

"I just threw up in my mouth."

"That happened to me on a one-night stand. The chick threw up in my mouth. It was disgusting. I could barely finish."

Fleming began to head back to her van, the laptop almost fully closed. It was cool out, plenty of people walking around, some locals, some sightseers. No one looked out of place or seemed to take an interest in her. Fleming didn't see anyone else in wheelchairs, but she rarely did.

She tried not to think about Bradley.

"Well, that sure is a lot of books. So, when do we get to see the West Wing?" Harry asked.

"I'm not sure we're allowed. I believe the president is in the Oval Office right now."

"Cool! Do you mind if we bug him in the Oval Office? I really want to bug him."

*Jesus, Harry.* Fleming closed her eyes, wondering how Chandler could have picked this guy.

"Let me check with the Secret Service. Pardon me a moment."

Jack whispered, "Harry, when we're done here, I never want to see you again."

"You're just saying that. Deep down, you know you like me."

"I don't go that deep."

"After all we've been through, partner? You're mean."

"And you're an asshole."

"And you look fat in that outfit."

"And you can't get laid without paying for it."

"Not true. Your mom didn't charge me."

"That's because your dick is so small she couldn't find it."

Fleming shook her head. They sounded like bickering siblings. Except for the mom comment. She crossed the street with the light, tuning in to her surroundings, looking for anything out of the ordinary, and came up to her parked vehicle. Then began the painstaking process of using the chair lift to get into the van. It was made less laborious by Sasha bounding out and hopping into her lap.

Fleming shifted her computer, then petted the fox, who yipped in appreciation. Then it jumped off her lap and bounded into the street.

"No! Sasha!"

She watched, feeling helpless, as the vixen stepped into oncoming traffic, sniffing the air. Fleming set her computer aside and leaned forward in her chair—to do what? Throw herself into the street to save an animal?

But Fleming didn't need to, because Sasha turned at the sound of her name and pranced back toward the van. She stared up at Fleming, as if expecting an order.

"Get back in here," Fleming said.

The fox squatted, peed, then leaped safely inside.

Fleming blew out a big sigh of relief. If anything happened to that fox, Bradley would...

Bradley. Who was now being tortured, while Fleming ignored him.

She was ready to dive into traffic to save an animal, but unwilling to help a man she really liked? What kind of person did that make her?

Fleming looked at the cell phone Scarlett had left her, resting on the dashboard, still off, when her earbud came to life.

"This way. We'll take the West Wing colonnade."

"Colonnade?" McGlade said. "Is that like lemonade, made out of colons?"

"It's an outdoor walkway, Harry, lined with columns." The weariness was obvious in Jack's voice.

"I see. Think they named it that because of all these columns?"

Fleming closed the side door of the van, stared at the phone once again, then set up her laptop. Still a black screen on the video feed.

"Look at all those flowers," McGlade said, no doubt eyeing the famous White House Rose Garden. "Our tax dollars at work. Is there a bathroom nearby?"

"There are several in the West Wing."

"When the president pinches a loaf, does he call it an *executive action*?"

"I don't know."

"Can we see the button? The one near his bed that he uses to launch a nuclear attack? I promise I won't press it."

"What? I don't think there is such a button."

"Did you ever ask?"

"No, I haven't."

"Ever ask him about Area 51? The aliens?"

"No."

"I heard they're mating with attractive earth women. Don't worry, Jack. You're safe."

"And you're an ass."

"I also heard the government has Satan locked up in a secret compound in New Mexico. Any truth to that?"

"Look, I'm just an aide to Senator Crouch."

"Does the senator ever touch you in the bathing suit area?"

"Is he for real?" the aide asked.

Jack sighed. "Unfortunately. You might try ignoring him, but it hasn't worked for me so far."

"Because I'm persistent," Harry said.

"I'm guessing," said Jack, "that in a previous life I was Attila the Hun, and this is some sort of karmic payback."

"I heard the government cloned Attila the Hun," Harry said. "Any truth to that?"

Strangely enough, Fleming had heard that one as well. Hopefully McGlade wouldn't ask about seven identical sisters who worked for a secret government agency.

"Who's this guy?" McGlade asked.

"Marine sentry."

"He just stands there, staring straight ahead?"

"That's what sentries do."

"Can't we go back to the library, get the poor guy a book?"

"That's a great idea, Harry. Give the guy guarding the president a distraction."

"It's not like guards helped the last guy. Boom!"

"You really have no sense of decency, do you, Harry? He was the president of our country."

"I voted Libertarian. Let's stop invading foreign nations, legalize drugs and prostitution, and limit the federal government to running the post office."

"And the military? You know, the armed forces that protect our country?"

"Disband it. Then give every citizen a Mac-10 and require them to carry it at all times."

"That's insane."

"Really? Think of how polite everyone would be if, at any moment, any person could shoot anyone else. I think we'd all get real Zen real quick. Especially with legal weed and ten-dollar BJs."

The video feed came to life, and Fleming stared at a room with an elongated table. Jack had the pen out at waist height; the fish-eye lens on the top made everything wildly distorted, but Fleming could see this was the Cabinet Room.

"This is the Cabinet Room," the aide said. He was a weaselly little guy who looked like Peter Lorre.

Harry made a face. "I don't see any cabinets."

"It's called the Cabinet Room because—"

"Yes, fascinating, so where's that shitter? The brown turtle is poking out his head. He's touching cloth here." He grabbed his rear end, possibly for emphasis.

"Are we going to be able to see the Oval Office?" Jack asked.

"I'm sorry, but no. The washroom is this way. Please follow me."

The aide turned, leading the way. Harry gave Jack an obvious nod, and Jack set down the pen next to the wall. Fleming watched them follow the aide out of the Cabinet Room. Then she brought up a pdf floor plan of the West Wing, and the remote control program.

Here we go…

Fleming pressed the *W* on the keyboard.

Nothing happened.

Fleming felt her breath catch. Had she missed something? Could the White House have some RF shield? Was there—

The camera moved forward.

Lag. It took a few seconds from the control to go through the Internet, to the transceiver on the lamppost, to the pen. Not a long delay, but she should have expected it.

Dividing her attention between the floor plan and the camera, Fleming inched her way out of the Cabinet Room, checked the hall for people, and then beelined toward the Oval Office. When she reached the corner, she pressed *S* to back up, doing half of a three-point turn. As expected, a Secret Service agent was stationed outside the Oval Office.

Fleming took the pen behind a marble pedestal with a bust of some important dead guy on top; she couldn't make out whom from this angle. Now she had to wait until someone opened the door and gave her a chance to get inside. A huge risk, but she had no other options. And if she did manage to make it, then Fleming had to hope the pen wasn't immediately discovered. It couldn't be traced back to her, and Jack was smart enough not to leave fingerprints, but that bug was the only chance they had of figuring out Ratzenberger's plan, and Julie's location.

She heard faint voices in her earbud.

"I can't believe you clogged the White House toilet." Jack Daniels talking.

"What's the big deal?" Harry. "They probably have a full-time plumber on staff. I bet they have two, considering how much this administration is full of shit."

"I'm never going anywhere with you again."

Fleming watched them walk past, the aide looking embarrassed.

"You say that. But within a few weeks, you'll call me to get your ass out of some trouble. That's how it always works. Some crazy-ass killer will have you up against the wall, and then it'll be, 'Please come save me, Harry.'"

"I'd rather jump naked into a thornbush than ever ask you for help."

"Kinky. Can I watch?"

Their bickering continued until they were out of the microphone's range. They'd done their part. The rest was up to her.

Less than five minutes passed before fortune smiled; a chef walked by, pushing the president's breakfast. Fleming gunned the servo and got the pen under the wheeled cart, moving with it all the way into the Oval Office. The agent checked the food, knocked, and announced its arrival. Once inside, Fleming made a beeline for the nearest dresser, to the left of the desk where the president sat, and backed the pen up against the wall while the chef presented eggs Benedict, grits, orange juice, wheat toast.

The president ate in silence while going over some papers, stopping often to pick his nose. Class act.

Then, appearing so suddenly Fleming actually flinched away from her computer, a big, furry face filled the screen, wide yellow eyes staring.

Oh, shit. A cat.

A paw shot out, whip-quick, batting the pen to the side. The camera turned upside down, rendering the wheel and servo useless.

Another swipe and the pen was pulled forward in the cat's claw.

Fleming hit the *W* key, hoping for a miracle. The pen somehow righted itself and shot forward, coming out from under the dresser. The cat pounced in front of it and struck a stalking pose, down on its front paws, eyes gleaming and tail swishing.

Fleming backed up, the pen turning, and headed for the drapes behind the desk.

The cat batted the pen once more, sending it rolling to the wall.

"Goddammit, Chaz! Someone get this cat out of here!"

Fleming once again tried the servo, but it didn't move. The cat had broken the motor, and the pen was lying right there on the floor, in plain sight.

A moment later there was a knock, and a smartly dressed woman came in, making kissy sounds and reaching for the cat. She scooped it up under her arm and began to walk away.

Then she stopped. Turned around.

Looked directly into the pen.

"Just leave it," Fleming said. "Please."

But the secretary didn't leave it. She bent over, grabbed the pen—

—and placed it on the president's desk.

Fleming now had a fish-eye close-up of the POTUS as he continued to shove eggs into his mouth. He didn't seem to notice the pen at all.

Close call. Damn close.

Sasha rubbed against Fleming's legs, demanding to be stroked. Fleming blew out a stiff breath and dropped her hand to pet the vixen's luxurious mane. It made her think of Bradley, which made her look at Scarlett's cell phone.

*Don't turn it on*, she told herself. *Stick with the mission.*

A long minute passed.

Then another.

Fleming reached for the phone.

"It'll be Bradley in pain," she said aloud. "I don't need to hear that, because there's nothing I can do."

She put the phone back down, stared at her laptop, and waited.

# Hammett

*"Everybody dies," The Instructor said. "Life is all about putting that off for as long as possible."*

Hammett figured her odds at surviving were damn near nil. Good thing she was the kind of girl who liked a challenge.

As she went over the brink of Niagara Falls in a funeral shroud of freezing water, Hammett drew her arms into her chest, holding her sides. She crossed her ankles, clenching her buttocks hard as she could, blowing out air as she fell, expecting to splatter against the rocks, or at the very least break her legs and ribs and spine as she hit the water's surface.

The free fall lasted longer than she expected. Perhaps it was the adrenaline slowing down her perception of time, or maybe the lack of visual cues while encased in a waterfall gave her no reference points, but as Hammett plummeted she had several distinct, complete thoughts.

First, if she lived she wanted to make sure Julie's dog, Kirk, was OK.

Second, she knew that if she died, Chandler and Fleming would probably be killed by The Instructor, but strangely that thought brought Hammett no satisfaction. Her sisters were her enemies, and she'd have to kill them both sooner or later, but the bigger enemy was The Instructor, and Hammett was pissed that asshole would get away.

Third, she felt some regret for trying to nuke London. Not because it would have killed a lot of people, but because of all the dogs that would have died.

And finally, if her last vestiges of humanity were wrapped up in caring more about dogs than human beings, it was probably best that she died when she struck—

*SMACK!*

Hammett had been knocked out a few times in her life. The brain just switches off consciousness, which fades out like a dimmer switch, making thoughts all dream-jumbly right before the blackness hit.

Hammett was also no stranger to having the air knocked out of her. The panic that ensued from not being able to draw a breath was similar to drowning.

Hitting the bottom of the falls gave her a great big wallop of each sensation. First, the little air she had left rushing out of her lungs as if squeezed like toothpaste, diaphragm contracting, ribs snapping, every tense muscle being slapped at once. That was joined by the hazy, about-to-fall-asleep feeling of oncoming unconsciousness, the shock of the long fall sucker-punching her with the strength of a mule kick.

Choking woke her up.

Hammett sucked in the cold murk of the Niagara River, her limbs feeling both frozen and on fire at the same time, her chest painfully screaming at her as her oxygen-starved brain went crazy with terror. She clawed at the water, not knowing which way was up, caught in some hellish undertow. The water beat on her face and shoulder like a flurry of fists, and she gasped again, coughing and sputtering, unable to focus on anything until a tiny bit of consciousness peeked through the encroaching darkness.

*The water is falling on me. I'm at the surface, but still under the waterfall.*

She pinwheeled her arms, scissor-kicking through the pain, the strap from the duffel bag full of weapons digging into her shoulder, then the current took her in the opposite direction and she was suddenly in calm water, alternating throwing up with gulping in air.

Squinting through the freezing mist, the wind whipping her hair and the roar of the falls deafening, Hammett sighted the shoreline to the northwest. Still coughing, she did a body inventory. Legs and arms were numb from the cold, but seemed to be working OK. Head ringing, and dizziness, perhaps a concussion. Several ribs very sore, perhaps broken or detached or both. Somehow she'd missed the rock and managed to survive a fifty-meter drop. Maybe the falling water broke the surface tension, making for a softer landing. Maybe she was indeed superhuman, which Hammett would admit she sometimes believed. Whatever the case, it was Hammett 1, Niagara Falls 0.

And her luck continued to improve. Twenty meters away was a boat. It had a rounded bow, almost like a ferry, and both decks were loaded with people in blue raincoats.

*The Maid of the Mist.* A sightseeing boat. It had ST. CATHA-RINES painted on the side, meaning it was Canadian.

Hammett swam for it. When she got within five meters she was spotted, an incredibly lucky event because all eyes were on the falls. With much shouting and activity, she was thrown a lifesaver and pulled aboard. People wrapped her in blankets and threw questions at her, and Hammett said, in French, how she'd leaned too far over the side of the boat and fell in but was OK.

When the boat went back to dock, she strongly refused all assistance, pulling away from those trying to help her, and hurried ashore, up the pier, through the gift shop, and into the parking lot, where she collapsed behind an SUV. The cold scents of pavement and exhaust folded over her. She couldn't stop shivering, and even more embarrassing, Hammett realized she was crying.

She sniffled, brushing away the tears, wondering what the hell was going on. Hammett certainly was *not* the pussy Chandler was, but she had been under similar stress. Was it survivor guilt? Doubtful. Hammett didn't have a guilt reflex. Relief she was still alive? Also doubtful. Hammett didn't view life as a gift. To her, it was more like a game to try and win, even though there was no real winning.

So what was with the dramatics? She was in pain, but managing it. She'd been close to death before, but hadn't reacted in this way. So what was it?

Hammett stopped pushing away the pain to allow her mind to focus on the problem. Not the easiest of tasks, because each breath was like being spiked in an iron maiden. But after a few moments of meditation, she was able to tune in to her tiny remaining nub of emotion, to focus on what she was crying about.

A man's face appeared in her mind.

The Instructor.

Hammett forced the image to go away, and then went back to dealing with her broken rib pain. But the image made complete sense. She was crying out of happiness, because she had a second chance at revenge.

And she wasn't going to let that chance get away.

# The White House

Ratzenberger finished a mediocre breakfast and thought about firing the entire mess staff and starting fresh.

A fresh start. It's what his administration, and this entire country, needed. But the people he had helping him were doing a piss-poor job. When was the last time he had an MD2 update?

His irritation rising, he picked up his phone and dialed the familiar number.

"Did you find them?"

"Not yet, Mr. President. But things are proceeding as planned."

"And Hydra? Have you corralled the three rogues?"

"Not yet, sir. But we're working on it."

The president looked around. He was alone, and the Secret Service swept twice a day for bugs, but he still didn't feel comfortable talking about this on the phone. Still, he was the goddamn president of the United States of America, the most powerful man in the world, and if he couldn't speak his mind in the Oval Office, what the hell was power for?

He gripped the phone tightly, snarling at the man known as The Instructor.

"I don't need to tell you how important this is—not only to me, but to this country."

"Yes, sir."

"We're changing the world, here. Making history."

"I understand that."

He said he did. But did he really? To Ratzenberger, The Instructor was just another one-note warmonger, polishing his gun and teaching kids how to kill. How could he understand what making history really was? All he knew how to do was fight.

"We got Alaska in 1867. Paid the Russkies two cents an acre. Even less than we paid for the Louisiana Purchase, sixty-three years earlier. You know I'm a big fan of Jefferson. The man had vision, like me. But his vision was limited. He should have taken more when he had the chance. But the world is changed now. You can't buy land to increase the size of your country. And in this current global climate, invasion is frowned upon. Hell, what has the US acquired recently? Hawaii, Puerto Rico, Guam, the Virgin Islands. Islands and atolls. A little bit of territory here and there. That's what it's all about, you know. Territory."

"I know, Mr. President."

"China. Those yellow bastards are a bigger threat than Russia ever was. A billion people. The have about the same amount of land as we do, but triple the population. And the industry they have. Those people are workers. We used to be an industrial nation. Now we import everything, including labor. Let me tell you, it isn't a war that will topple our country. It's the economy. That's why we're doing this."

"It's going forward as planned, Mr. President."

But Ratzenberger was on a roll now. The excitement, the passion, was taking over. He wasn't about to be placated.

"Forty million people in Canada. Another four hundred in Central and South America. We can't get bigger by going to war. No land grabs. No conquering territories. Those days are over. But this way we can almost triple our population, our landmass, our workforce and industry, our military. Manifest Destiny Two. The United States of Americas. That's plural, son. The Pacific to the Atlantic, the Artic to the Antarctic. A whole hemisphere of God-fearing democracy, from sea to shining sea, to shining sea, to shining sea."

"Yes, sir." Then a sigh.

The president stood up, his anger flaring.

"Look, that bullring in Mexico City, that music festival in Toronto, that's the spark that will set it all off. When Canada, Mexico, and Central and South America close their borders and declare martial law, they'll agree to anything to get our Ebola cure. They'll give us control. We save fifty percent of their populations, send in an occupying force to police them and maintain control, and within twenty years we'll all be one big country. By that time, other nations will have the vaccine. But they won't be able to produce it fast enough. Europe. Africa. India. China. Russia. They'll be weakened, and we'll have the largest army in the world. The last person to try to change the world in a dramatic way was Adolf Hitler. Say what you would about him, but that Nazi sumabitch had vision."

"As much I enjoy hearing your rants, Mr. President, was there another reason for this call?"

"Yes. I'm making you an offer. Screw the cabinet position. You get this done, I'll nominate you for vice president immediately. With your military record, the tenor of the country, I should be able pass it through Congress."

"An...interesting proposal."

"Do you accept?"

"I need to think it over."

"Think it over while you're getting the job done. I want Ebola outbreaks on both of our borders in the next seventy-two hours, and I want you to find your damn rogue operatives and terminate with extreme prejudice."

"Understood, Mr. President."

"Are the bodies in place at the borders? We don't want an outbreak in this country."

"Yes. Along with the autopsy reports, ready to be leaked. Once they are, you can seal the borders."

"And in Toronto and Mexico City, the virus will show up immediately after the infection?"

"This is a special strain, remember. People will be dying within hours."

Ratzenberger flinched a little, as any good Christian would. The whole thing was distasteful but necessary for the greater good. He had to remember that. "A virus that fast, won't it burn out before causing an epidemic?"

"Yes. But we don't want an epidemic. That would spiral out of control. We want the *appearance* of an epidemic. Let it flare up in a spot, then burn itself out. We can always make it flare up again."

"Yes, yes, of course." It all made sense, but he wasn't about to leave anything up to chance. "And my dose of vaccine?"

"Coming later today."

"Don't fail me. I'm not as forgiving as my predecessor was."

Ratzenberger hung up, then hit the intercom button to have his dishes removed. Making that offer to The Instructor was risky. That man was ambitious, devious, and had resources that were, quite frankly, frightening. But the rule about keeping friends close and enemies closer applied here. The carrot was a more valuable tool than the stick when it came to powerful, dangerous men. And with The Instructor as his successor, he'd help guarantee that MD2 continued after Ratzenberger left office.

Win-win.

A knock, and the Secret Service came in to do another damn bug sweep while the dishes were being cleared. The president left the Oval Office, heading for the bathroom, only to find some asshole had clogged the toilet.

# Fleming

*"Plans change," The Instructor said. "Adapt."*

As soon as the Secret Service walked in, Fleming killed the power to the bug so it no longer transmitted. Then she spent a moment trying to digest what she'd just heard.

The new guy in charge was batshit, bugfuck crazy. He wasn't trying to use Ebola to wipe out his enemies. He was using it to wipe out allies, then absorb them into the United States under the guise of protecting them.

A crazy plan. Or was it?

Occupying foreign countries hadn't worked out well for the United States in current history. The countries resented its presence, creating a growing animosity that often ended up in them hating America, and then plotting terrorist attacks.

But if those countries invited America in, to administer a vaccine and keep martial law, that might be a different story. Fleming still predicted resentment and rebellion from the natives, but if the virus devastated enough of the population, and the occupation was seen as beneficial, then Ratzenberger might actually be able to extend the US borders to the entire Western Hemisphere, from Cape Columbia, Canada, to Cape Horn, Chile.

Fleming immediately called Chandler, who was just south of San Antonio and still driving, and filled her in. Then she called Hammett, who sounded like she'd had better mornings.

"You OK, sis?"

"Why do you care?"

"Because the fate of the free world depends on you keeping your shit together."

"You're getting mushy on me."

"Seriously, Hammett. You sound like hell."

"Had a tiny bit of trouble getting into Canada. Still, it was better than being manhandled by TSA. Hey, do you have the phone number for that vet?"

"What vet?"

"Where we took Kirk."

Fleming gave it to her, wondering why one of the world's premier assassins cared so much about a dog she'd just met.

That reminded Fleming of her reaction when Sasha ran out into traffic. Her thoughts again drifted to Bradley, and her eyes drifted again to Scarlett's cell phone.

She grabbed it and rubbed her thumb over the power button.

A minute passed.

Fleming turned the phone on.

Five messages.

Don't listen to them.

Don't.

She pressed Play.

"Your friend Bradley ain't looking so well," Rhett said in a Southern drawl.

"I swear, I don't even know her name!"

Then Bradley screamed. A heart-wrenching, ear-bleeding scream.

Fleming shut off the cell phone. She'd heard a creaking sound, and realized it was her teeth grinding together.

"I told him not to come out of the shop."

Fleming closed her eyes. She turned the phone back on.

She listened to the other four messages.

They didn't get any better. And Bradley—poor, stupid, brave Bradley—kept quiet even as he screamed in pain.

He didn't know anything, and he was still trying to protect her.

Sasha sniffed the phone, perhaps recognizing her master's voice.

"The Instructor taught me that the mission always comes first," she told the fox. "To never jeopardize it for personal reasons. To never have close relationships with people, because they always ended badly. But you know what? I'm sick of following that asshole's orders."

Fleming accessed Hydra, tracking Rhett's and Scarlett's chips.

She'd find them. And kill them. And save Bradley.

Because when it came down to it, she wasn't just a tool, a weapon that the government could order around.

She was one of the good guys.

And dying doing the right thing sure beat living doing the wrong thing.

# Chandler

*"Every mission is risky," The Instructor said. "There are some risks you can see coming. Those you can prepare for, plan your way around. Those are easy. The real danger lies in the risks you never foresee. The ones that hit you like a bullet from the dark. If you want to go on living, prepare for the unexpected."*

It took a while to absorb everything Fleming had told me. Manifest Destiny Two?

In a warped way, it made sense. What was a little genocide if it made the nation stronger? The United States was expert at wiping out indigenous populations. Doing the same thing to the north and the south was par for the course.

But this upped the ante. Obviously, the pressure to stop this from happening had increased exponentially. This was no longer about clearing our names and killing The Instructor, or preventing a few Ebola outbreaks. This was real hero stuff. Not just saving London, but saving the whole world.

Thankfully, in light of my buzzing mind, the drive to Laredo, Texas, was blissfully boring, and keeping my speed at five miles an hour over the limit, I avoided police attention and made good time. I'd stopped once on the way, grabbing a few hours of sleep in a rest area outside Dallas, and I reached the town on the banks of the Rio Grande in twenty-four hours, and with enough sleep to keep me sharp.

Normally crossing the border from the United States into Mexico was easy. Long lines of cars dammed up at the checkpoint going north, but the fewer lanes leading south had just a trickle of traffic. A short drive down a frontage road near the crossing, however, told me things were different.

Lines a dozen deep snaked from the southbound checkpoint. Armed personnel checked interiors, undercarriages, and the cargo holds of trucks before allowing them to cross the Rio Grande, their uniforms both border patrol and Texas National Guard.

I continued driving, looping through narrow streets and back to the highway. As soon as The Instructor had released his evidence, I'd expected beefed-up security at the border. The development wasn't surprising. I just had to tweak my plan.

As I drove down the streets of Laredo, I found myself humming the song I'd learned to play on the guitar when I was eight, before my parents died, before I'd knocked around in foster care, before I'd been adopted by the man I still thought of as my evil stepfather. Strangely, I finally felt a touch of normal.

I didn't know if it was Hammett's beating and advice, Fleming's encouragement or the details she'd provided, or just the long drive and hot sun, but something had helped. This mission was easily both more important and more difficult than anything I'd done in the past, but it was a mission, and I was on my own. I knew what that was supposed to feel like, and as I exited the highway onto a palm-lined street in front of the Mall del Norte, the familiar icy resolve settled over me.

Emotionless.

Efficient.

Unstoppable.

I could do this. I had to.

I turned into the mall and parked, then loaded my shotgun and stuffed it into my bulging backpack with the rest of my gear, shoving my Jericho into my waistband.

As much as I wanted to trade my jeans and sweater for some new, climate-friendly duds, a trip to Macy's was too big a risk. Instead of entering the mall, I shouldered my backpack and skirted the building's perimeter until I came to a large alley-like opening reserved for delivery trucks and garbage removal. Each store in this section of the mall had a door that either opened to the area or joined with a long hall leading here. That resulted in trucks flowing in and out and a collection of Dumpsters lining the utilitarian courtyard.

Unfortunately, finding what I was looking for wasn't so easy. Or rather, whom.

I slid into the shadow of one of the largest Dumpsters, slung my backpack off my shoulder, and waited. Evening fell into night, and although the early autumn heat mercifully faded with the sun, I started to feel the hours that had passed since I'd last eaten, and the scents drifting from the food court made my stomach rumble.

As the retail day came to a close, employees from the mall's shops dumped the last of the day's garbage. The section of the mall I'd chosen was filled with stores selling clothing and accessories, electronics, and various personal items, and most of the garbage was cardboard packaging from their wares. The recycling Dumpsters were soon overflowing with cardboard boxes, broken down for disposal.

An hour after closing time, a vehicle finally entered the area.

The shabby blue pickup truck parked at one of the recycling Dumpsters out of my line of vision. I waited for the driver's door to slam before I slipped from my hiding spot.

By the time I walked up, the driver was nowhere to be seen, but box after box flew over the edge of the green receptacle and landed in the truck bed.

"Excuse me," I called.

No answer.

I tried again. "*Disculpe.*"

I spoke Spanish fluently, among a few other languages, but this time, I let my accent ring pure Texas.

Head popping up, he peered over the bin through narrowed eyes.

"*Por favor?*" I said.

His skin looked hard as leather. If he was an American, I'd peg him to be in his sixties. I suspected, however, that he was from the other side of the border, a *cartonero* from Nuevo Laredo, and as such he was likely to be fifteen or twenty years younger.

Shopping complexes like Mall del Norte were treasure troves of clean cardboard for anyone who could travel through the border checkpoint to claim it.

This guy had to be pretty successful to afford a truck, even though his left a lot to be desired, per US standards. But even a successful businessman might be interested in making a little extra money.

"Do you speak English?" I asked.

"Yes," he said.

"Oh, thank the Lord. I need your help, sir." I put a little tremble into my voice.

He watched me for a few more seconds, then grunted and ducked back to work in the Dumpster.

"I can pay. *Mucho dinero.*"

"For what?" He didn't even pause, just kept harvesting cardboard.

"I need a lift across the border."

This got his attention, and he returned to staring. "Into Mexico?"

"Yes. Please, I'm desperate. I'll give you a hundred dollars."

I could see his mind working. "Five."

Most *cartoneros* were working men scrambling to feed their families. But as much as I'd like to help him out, I didn't have five hundred dollars.

"I have a watch."

"Five."

I unzipped my backpack, looking for something I could spare to lose that might interest him. I pulled out the radar detector I'd used to prevent getting a ticket on the way down. It would be nice to have in Mexico, too, but I couldn't figure out what other item I might be willing to part with. "How about this? It's an Escort Passport 9500ix Radar Detector. Retails for around five hundred dollars."

"Five."

I was beginning to think five was the only word this guy knew in English. "The radar detector and my last hundred dollars?"

He climbed from the Dumpster, then pointed at my backpack. "How about that shotgun?"

Now *that* was an idea I was far less than crazy about. "Sorry."

"Then find another ride."

"I have other things. Night-vision monocular, binoculars…"

"The shotgun."

Time was ticking by, and I still had to procure a car on the Mexican side of the border and had hours of driving ahead of me. I couldn't afford to wander the mall looking for another lift. I could just pull the shotgun on him, but in order to get across the border, I needed the guy to be on my side, not fearing for his life and looking to tip off the border patrol.

I unwedged the shotgun from the pack. I was about to take out the shells I'd loaded when he snatched the weapon from my hands.

"OK," he said. "Sold."

Borrowed, I thought, growing less and less happy with my ride.

He stashed the shotgun in the truck's cab, then circled to the back and started shoving cardboard aside. He cleared the bottom of the truck bed, lifted out a panel to reveal a shallow box underneath, a space he likely used to smuggle drugs or people into the United States. Or maybe guns and cash back to Mexico.

I had to wonder if the beat-up nature of the pickup was just a cover. This guy seemed to be quite enterprising. All in all, that was a good sign, at least. He seemed to be as comfortable with smuggling as he was with driving a hard bargain, not the type who would show stress under the border patrol's suspicious gaze.

"You fit in there, I take you across."

I climbed into the truck bed and scrunched myself into the tiny space on my side, my knees pressed to my chest, my backpack with my remaining treasures wedged in beside me.

"Now I close and cover with cardboard, *si?*"

I took a deep breath of fresh air. "*Si.*"

He fitted the panel over me, and I was plunged into darkness.

I had a fear of drowning, and I wasn't fond of heights, but as luck would have it, claustrophobia had never been a particular weakness. I only hoped I could still say that by the time I climbed out.

It seemed to take forever for him to gather the rest of his cardboard haul, but finally the clanging and rustling over me stopped, and the truck started moving.

The border crossing wasn't far from the mall, and the truck wasn't moving long. As the hum of tires on concrete slowed, I could feel a surge of adrenaline. My focus became sharper, my senses honed. The vehicle moved, then stopped, inching closer as each car passed through. The line wouldn't be long. Even with the extra security looking for me, it would be our turn soon.

My pulse thumped in my ears, my breathing so loud in the tight space, it seemed the border guards must hear. Voices reached me, low and authoritative, but catching the words was impossible.

Cardboard shifted and scraped above, moving around the truck bed.

I reached for the Jericho, finding just enough room to slip it from my waistband. If they found the panel in the truck's bed, things would get messy. And while I hated the idea of shooting border agents, letting them take me was not only bad for me, it meant thousands of people in Mexico would die.

Maybe more.

Not much of a choice.

A round already in the chamber, I slid my finger along the outside of the trigger guard and waited. I smelled exhaust from the idling truck mixed with the scent of my sweat, listened to the shifting and voices from above, and there was something else.

A jingle.

The sound was distant, but still distinct. It would probably make Hammett shiver with glee. Me, not so much.

There were a lot of uses for dogs at border crossings, and at this checkpoint, canines were more likely to patrol the north-bound lanes, checking for drugs and undocumented workers, than the southbound. Still, with the entire country looking for the woman who assassinated the president, it was possible I was exactly why that dog was here.

I held my breath, listening for the jingle to grow louder, the sound of panting, anything that would warn me the animal was getting close. One minute dragged by, then another, then too many for me to count. The hum of male voices reached me, my smuggler's voice and that of border patrol, but I could only catch a word now and then.

I felt the transmission shift into gear, and the truck started moving.

I let out a long breath. Soon the hollow sound of tires moving over a bridge reverberated through the pickup's frame. Then solid ground.

I'd made it into Mexico.

The truck kept going for several miles, and I tried to note each upward grade, each turn, so I could find my way back to

Nuevo Loredo's center. Precisely what had made my impromptu coyote a good bet to sneak past border security might come back to bite me now that I was essentially his prisoner in his country, and I was on high alert. Judging from the uninterrupted speed and kidney-punching bumps in the road, we were on the outskirts of town, and as the truck finally slowed and then came to a stop, I slid my finger to the trigger. Breathing slowly, I waited.

Again the shifting of cardboard scraped and shuffled over me and then the murmur of men's voices speaking Spanish. Finally the panel covering me lifted, cold, fetid air washed over my sweaty skin, and I was staring up at a star-filled night.

And into the barrel of an AK-47.

# Julie

A knock sounded on the door.

Julie switched off the inane reality TV show she'd been watching, sank deeper into the love seat, and hugged the throw pillow to her chest. Since she'd been imprisoned in this room, the only people she'd seen were Derek Fossen, who brought her meals on a tray, and the nasty woman with the bug mole, who took her blood.

But she'd already had blood drawn, and Derek had brought dinner over an hour ago, and that meant this visit was different. And the thought of what it must be about made her feel sick to her stomach.

The knock came again. "Julie? Are you OK?"

Derek's voice, not The Instructor.

Julie let out a shaky breath. "Come in, Derek."

The door swung wide, and Derek stepped into the room. Dressed in his hazmat suit as usual, he looked at her for a moment without speaking, the concern on his face obvious even through his face shield.

She clutched the pillow tighter. "What is it?"

"The Instructor sent me."

She nodded. "I have to come with you?"

"He ordered me to deliver the invitation. You don't have to accept."

"But I will have to eventually."

"I suppose so. Yes."

Julie forced herself to stand. She gave the pillow one more hug, then tossed it into the chair. Since she'd been brought to this room, she'd been given real clothes to wear, not the hospital gown. Now she was dressed in a light sweater and jeans, comfortable, but not exactly date material.

If you could even call this a date.

She stretched her arms out from her sides. "Am I supposed to wear something specific? Or is this OK?"

"I don't think it matters."

Because she wouldn't be wearing anything. Of course. How stupid of her.

"All right," she managed to choke out. "Let's go."

"You don't have to do this, Julie."

"Yes, I do."

"I can tell him you're not ready yet."

Tears misted her eyes. She didn't know anything about Derek Fossen, but she'd seen the concern on his face and heard it in his voice, and it felt good to know someone besides Chandler cared about what happened to her.

"Thanks, Derek. But…"

"What is it?"

"He has my friend in custody. If I put him off too long…"

"You're afraid he'll take it out on her."

She nodded.

He frowned. "Who is your friend?"

"Her name is Chandler. If it wasn't for her, my life would have ended years ago."

"So you owe her?"

It was more than that. So much more. "She's like my big sister."

"You love her."

She nodded. "She's all I have."

The tears were flowing now, so many tears. She would think that one of these days her eyes would cry themselves dry, but the tears just kept coming.

Derek raised a gloved hand to her face and wiped her cheeks. "I'll tell him you aren't ready yet."

Julie shook her head. "But Chandler…"

"And I'll see what I can find out about your friend."

"Why…" Julie's voice broke. She cleared her throat and tried again. "Why are you being so nice to me?"

"Because you remind me of someone."

"The Instructor said that you needed extra persuasion to work on this…thing."

Derek shook his head, his bio suit crackling with the sudden movement. "That's not important."

"It must be important to you."

"You have enough to deal with right now. You don't need to take on my burdens, too."

"But, I want—"

"I'll tell The Instructor and see what I can find out about Chandler." He turned away, then stopped, his hand on the door-knob. "I'll be back as soon as I can."

# Fleming

*"The mission can't be personal," The Instructor said.*
*"Once it gets personal, abort."*

According to the chip tracker on Hydra's webpage, Rhett and Scarlett were in Worcester, Massachusetts. Fleming wasn't prepared to deal with them. Not yet. But the thought of them continuing to hurt Bradley made Fleming's stomach ache.

So she pulled over to the side of the road and made the call. Rhett answered.

"I was wondering if we'd be hearing from you. So has your boyfriend. A virgin, huh? You rascal."

"I'll make a trade. Me for Bradley. But you have to stop hurting him."

"Dunno if I can promise that. My partner is all riled up, itching to have a go at him."

"Then have fun with him, because you won't get me."

Fleming forced herself to hang up. Then she forced herself not to call back.

A very long ten minutes later, the cell rang.

"Tomorrow. One p.m.," Rhett said. "Boston."

"I can't get there fast enough."

"Every minute you're late, Bradley loses another body part."

"I don't have a vehicle, and I can't fly."

"You have sixteen hours to get it together and figure it out."

Rhett hung up.

Little did he know, Fleming had been driving all day and was already in Providence. Boston was a little over an hour away.

But that still might not be enough time for Fleming to prepare. She got on Google to look for a custom motorcycle shop, and after ten minutes of browsing found two likely candidates.

Hopefully at least one of them would be closed and unoccupied. Bradley's life, and hers as well, depended on it.

# Julie

This time, the knock woke Julie out of a deep sleep.

She had no idea what time it was. Propping herself up on the couch, she stared at the blank television screen, the movie she'd been streaming over.

"Julie? You awake?" Fossen called through the door.

She scrambled to her feet, smoothed her hair down, and tried to appear presentable. "Come in."

Derek stepped into the room and closed the door behind him.

"He wants to see me?" Julie said. It felt like she'd been living under The Instructor's threat for a long time, even though when she added up the hours it had to be only a couple of days. Still every hour grated, taking its toll. She was almost ready to just go to him and get it over with. She might have done that already, if not for Derek's insistence earlier in the evening that he tell The Instructor she wasn't yet ready.

"He's lying to you, Julie."

"The Instructor?"

"Yes." Circles cupped under Derek's eyes, and deep creases framed his mouth and lined his forehead. She knew he was under a lot of stress—"a bit of extra persuasion to do the right thing" is how The Instructor had put it. Even The Instructor had told her that much, although Derek had refused to explain the first time she'd asked him about it.

"What is The Instructor lying about?"

"A lot of things." Through the face shield, she could see Derek lick his lips, as if nervous, as if scared. "I looked for your friend, and I found out something."

"About Chandler?" Julie was afraid to ask what that meant, but she suspected she knew. "She's already dead?"

"Not that I know of." He put his hand on her shoulder, softly, gently. "I think you should sit down, though."

Julie didn't want to sit down. She'd been sitting for days. But the intensity in Derek's eyes and the wobble that already registered in her legs made her lower herself to the edge of the couch. "What is it?"

Derek sat beside her, the cushion dipping with his weight. "Your friend is in trouble."

Julie knew it. She clasped her hands together and pressed them between her knees. "Tell me."

"She killed the president, Julie."

She shook her head. His words didn't make sense, not one bit.

"It's true. The president was assassinated last week, and it was your friend Chandler who did it."

A hum rose in Julie's ears. It was impossible. Chandler had saved her, taken care of her. Chandler was a good person.

Memories of how they'd met raced through her mind. Chandler jumping out of a helicopter. Chandler shooting guns. Chandler killing.

But those had been bad guys she'd shot at, bad guys she'd killed. Not the president of the United States.

"I don't believe it."

"There's video of her doing it, Julie. Other proof, too."

She looked into Derek's eyes, searching for lies, but there was nothing that she could see. He seemed to be telling the truth.

She stared at the floor, her throat dry. "Then if she did it, she had good reason."

"There's a good reason to kill the president? I don't think so."

Julie braced her head with her hands. "Maybe not. I don't know. I just know Chandler. She's a good person. There's not a lot I know anymore, but I know that."

"She's the subject of the biggest manhunt in history, that's what they're saying on television."

"I've been watching TV all the time. I never saw anything."

"That's because yours is closed circuit. Just reality shows, sit-coms, dramas, and the movies you stream."

Of course. The Instructor had been controlling what she knew to gain her cooperation...and not only that. "There is a manhunt for Chandler?"

"Across the nation. Maybe across the world."

"But that means The Instructor doesn't have her."

"That's right. He was lying."

And if he didn't have Chandler...

"He can't hurt me." Relief poured over her in waves.

"He can, Julie. And he will."

He was right, of course. The Instructor could beat her and drug her and do all sorts of things short of killing her. But that wasn't what was keeping Julie in line. "You don't understand. He can't kill Chandler if he doesn't know where she is. The rest I don't care about."

Derek shook his head. "Don't talk that way. You need to hold on. Just a little longer. Give me a chance to get you out of here."

"You can do that?"

"Well, not on my own. But maybe if I have help."

"Help? What kind of help?" Julie wasn't sure there was any help for her.

He rested his hand on hers. "Listen, I'm not sure what's going to happen. But I know a reporter I can talk to. If what The Instructor is doing gets out, maybe the new president will shut him down."

He slipped an arm around her shoulder and squeezed her close, just for a moment.

It had been so long since Julie had been hugged by a man—a nice man—that once again she had to fight to keep from crying. "I don't want you to get in trouble, Derek."

"I won't. I'll make sure of it."

He was so kind, so sweet. Julie had never met a man like him. Of course, in the last few years, she hadn't met any men at all. "Why are you helping me like this?"

"Why do you keep asking me that?"

"Because I need you to answer."

"It's not right, what he's doing. Threatening you. Keeping you prisoner. Taking your blood and forcing you..." He looked away, as if he couldn't meet her eyes while thinking about The Instructor's plans.

"Please tell me."

He turned to her, his eyes glassy. "My sister. She's been sick a long time. Kidney disease. She's spent half her life in hospitals, being poked and prodded and treated like a thing, not a person. Her latest transplant...Well, she needs another one. But she's too far down the list."

"The Instructor can get her a kidney."

Derek nodded.

"And that's who I remind you of."

Another nod. "He'll keep you here. Forever. But maybe, if we tell someone, we can stop him, and get you some real medical help."

Julie's throat felt thick. She wished she could do more than hug Derek. She wished she could touch him, kiss him, but those things could never happen. Not with her. "Thank you."

"Don't thank me until you're free."

She would never be truly free, but she didn't have the heart to remind Derek of that. If he and his reporter friend managed to get her out of this, she would have what she needed.

The chance to make things right.

# Chandler

*"When you are faced with death, it is hard to look past the immediate threat," The Instructor said. "But to survive, you must train yourself to gather information about your enemy and your surroundings, recall what you've learned, and use logic to think through various solutions. The operative with the coolest head under threat is the operative who will come out alive."*

At first, the rifle barrel was all I could see, the thrum of my heart was all I could hear. I didn't have to do much thinking to know I was in deep shit. My problem was figuring out what I was facing and how to get out of it.

I forced myself to focus on the faces behind the gun. Three men in Kevlar vests stared at me, two young enough to show acne under their struggling goatees, one with a touch of gray working into the five o'clock shadow on his cheeks. All wore their hair short and had the hard eyes of men who could pull the trigger without thinking twice.

The Gulf drug cartel dominated this part of the border, and a *Z* tat on one's neck, combined with ink depicting *Santa*

*Muerta* dressed in military garb on another's bare upper arm suggested Los Zetas. Originally a group of former military men and police officers, Los Zetas functioned as an enforcement arm of the Gulf cartel, although rumor had it they were planning an attempt to take the territory for themselves. They were well armed and trained, and known for drug running, extortion, kidnapping, murder, and generally not messing around.

They sure didn't look like they intended to mess around tonight.

"Please don't hurt me!" I said, injecting desperation into my voice. I hugged my arms around my middle, using the movement to stuff the Jericho under my shirt and into the side of my waistband, so they wouldn't see that I was armed, at least for a few seconds.

"Get out." The graying soldier with the *Santa Muerta* tat waved the rifle at me and snatched my backpack from the compartment.

I unfolded my body from the cocoon, muscles stiff. No matter how much training I had, having a gun pointed in my face never felt good, and my body trembled a little, a result of a healthy amount of adrenaline dumping into my bloodstream.

I played up the shaking as I climbed from the truck bed. Keeping my eyes canted downward in a submissive angle, I sized the men up in order of threat. The leader was every bit as nasty as he looked. In addition to the tattoos, he boasted several scars, and I judged him to be in his later thirties, capable and lethal. The second was young, mid-twenties, and had a bottom-heavy face—twice as wide at the jaw as at the forehead. He'd probably been living the drug soldier life for a decade or more, and although the Zetas weren't as known for their skin art as many of the gangs south of the border, this guy had seen enough action to earn an impressive amount of ink. The third was a kid, fifteen if he was lucky, but as young as he was, his eyes already held the dead stare of a predator, and I'd bet he'd taken many lives.

The *cartonero* who'd acted as my coyote stood a distance away, smoking a cigarette and pretending as if he was casually surveying the land. Although the constant flick of his eyes suggested he wasn't feeling quite as relaxed as he pretended.

Greedy bastard.

Apparently he'd seen an opportunity to keep my shotgun in addition to whatever kind of cut the Zetas gave him, so he'd sold me. Nice.

Of course, I couldn't be too judgmental. I'd planned on taking the shotgun back once we'd crossed the border, after all.

I shifted my attention to my surroundings. A late-model Ford pickup in forest green was parked in front of the *cartonero's* truck, obviously belonging to my Zetas' entourage. Moonlight glowed on hill after hill of barren earth scattered with plastic bags, stained paper, scraps of cardboard and wood. From here, the lights of Nuevo Laredo twinkled dully over the hills of trash and rutted dirt, overtaken by the more brilliant light cascading from the American side of the river.

A landfill was a good place to bury a body, but I didn't think that's what these men had in mind. Killing me immediately wouldn't do them any good. Even rape would be amateurish, a few minutes of pleasure and little else. Some gangs might opt for a night of fun, but Los Zetas didn't have that kind of frivolous, undisciplined reputation. If everything I knew about them was accurate, they had bigger and more lucrative plans.

"You have family in the United States, no?"

I conjured up some tears and once again wrapped my arms around myself. "Yes."

"And they will pay?"

"My daddy. He has money. Please."

"How much money?"

"He's a businessman in Houston."

"How much?"

"I don't know. A lot."

The men exchanged glances and grins, congratulating themselves. None of them glanced the *cartonero's* way, as if he deserved no credit at all.

"You call him? Your papa?"

"I'll call. Anything you want. Please, don't shoot me."

Another chuckle.

"Oh, we won't shoot." The one in charge gave me a sly grin and lowered his pistol. "You the goose *and* the golden egg, American *puta*."

The others joined in both a suggestive chuckle and in lowering their guns.

Big mistake.

I brought the Jericho up, going for the leader first. A point-blank squeeze of the trigger and red exploded between his eyes.

To my surprise, the teen reacted faster than the second in command, firing a burst, missing by inches. I whipped back to him, just as he got it under control and the barrel of his AK zeroed in on me.

I kicked his weapon, throwing off his aim, and his shot went wide. Behind me, number two was finally getting his shit together, so I snapped my hips around, aiming a kick at his knee. My heel landed just under the kneecap, and I could feel the joint bend in a way it wasn't meant to.

"*Puta madre!*" He collapsed in the dirt, gushing a wave of Spanish obscenities.

Shifting my attention back to the kid, I reached into my tae kwon do arsenal and rotated into a spinning hook kick. My heel connected with his jaw, and he staggered backward but didn't drop his weapon.

A bullet screamed past my head.

Grabbing the straps of my backpack, I hit the ground and shoulder rolled, flipping my body around the truck's rear fender.

That last round hadn't come from the three I'd been dealing with, and in the dark mounds of dirt and garbage I couldn't immediately spot the shooter. The Jericho and Paragon Seal knife could only get me so far against a group of well-armed paramilitary drug cartel soldiers wearing body armor.

If I was going to come out of this alive, I needed my shotgun.

More gunfire erupted, pinging off the *cartonero*'s truck and throwing up dust from the dry earth.

I peered beneath the undercarriage of the truck. Senor Broken Knee levered himself up on an elbow, and squeezed off a few shots in my direction, but the kid was nowhere to be seen.

I heard a sound to the side of the truck, a magazine snicking into place.

Whirling around, I double-tapped, aiming high and ventilating his face with both rounds.

Somewhere in the darkness, an engine revved. Voices barked orders in Spanish. I counted eight, maybe nine.

I had to hurry. Despite the attempts of *número dos* to make up for his slow start by squeezing off rounds under the truck, I worked my way to the cab and yanked open the door.

The *cartonero* lay on the floorboards, my shotgun in his hands and aiming my way.

I pulled back just as the fléchette load blasted past me, exploding into the night. Shooting fléchettes, little pointed steel projectiles with veined tails, was akin to shooting a bunch of tiny arrows at a target with superspeed and velocity. I'd avoided being ripped apart, but that didn't prevent the *boom* from reverberating through my head and causing the buzzing to resume in my ears.

Damn it. By the time this mess was over, I wouldn't have any hearing left.

I whipped around with the Jericho, catching the cardboard collector mid-pump. One through the eye, blood spattering through the truck's cab, then I pulled my shotgun from his dead hands.

Now the odds were a little more even.

Hunkering low, I moved around the truck's front fender, peering at the spot where the leader's body lay in the dirt. *Número dos* stretched on the ground, rifle pointed in my direction. Behind him stood three new additions to the party, matching their compadres in tats, body armor, and weaponry.

They were peering in the other direction, as if watching...

I spun around and fired, the fléchettes tearing through the Kevlar of the first man and sending him stumbling backward. His partner ripped off a shot at me, digging up the dirt inches from my right leg.

I pumped and fired again, aiming higher, separating him from his face. He was dead before he hit the dirt.

Lead rained from the other side of the truck, giving me no choice but to fall back. I left the truck's shelter and raced for a mound of garbage-filled dirt. A better bullet barrier than the truck, I leaned my back to the mound, scooped in several good breaths, and tried to figure out my next move.

From my count, there were four Zetas still gunning for me, one injured, and a few I hadn't seen yet. They had vehicles at their disposal, and they knew the terrain.

I unzipped my pack and pulled out the night-vision monocular, slipping the strap over my head and flipping it on. Sight returned, green and hazy, and I reloaded my shotgun with more fléchette shells, then thrust myself upright and moved around the mini hill. A series of holes yawned on this side of the dirt pile, and wilted flowers were scattered over a low mound nearby. I'd heard stories of landfill operators leaving holes open in the garbage for the poor to use to bury their dead, a potter's field of sorts, but whether the holes were here as an act of charity or for Los Zetas to dispose of those who got in their way, I supposed it didn't matter.

I would do my best to provide some bodies to fill them.

I'd almost circled the pile when I spotted the pickup, a black Ford F-450 King Ranch with dual wheels in back. One man stood outside the vehicle, smoke from his cigarette drifting in the air, machine gun at the ready.

I took him out with one shot, then took cover at the side of a mound of refuse and waited.

Two soldiers came at me, one from the right, one from the left. They moved fast and sure, even though they didn't have night vision.

I blasted, swiveled and pumped at the same time, then blasted again, relieving them of the burden of breathing. Then I circled the dirt and returned to the *cartonero*'s pickup.

A shot whizzed past my ear, and I charged, running and gunning. A good marksman could pump and fire six shotgun rounds in less than three seconds. I did it in less than two, the last shot punching into the second-in-command's stomach.

When the dust cleared, I sized up the massacre through the monocular's greenish tinge. A slight rustle came from to the left of the *cartenaro*'s pickup, almost imperceptible under the lingering groans coming from *número dos*. Spinning toward the sound, I brought my gun up, ready to fire.

And aimed straight into a pair of sad brown eyes.

The boy couldn't be more than five. Crawling out from a hole covered with cardboard, he was filthy and wore little more than rags. He said nothing, only stared at my shotgun with a resigned look on his face, as if he was fully prepared to die.

I lowered my weapon.

"I won't hurt you," I told him in Spanish. "Everything's OK."

But of course, everything wasn't OK. A boy living in a hole. A small army of drug soldiers dead and one dying a stone's throw away. The threat of Ebola hanging over the people of Mexico City. None of it was OK.

Nausea pressed at the base of my throat. My body trembled, the sudden rush of adrenaline finally catching up with me. I forced my legs to carry me past the boy and in the direction of the trash-strewn dirt pile, controlling my heart rate, my breathing. When I gathered myself and turned back, the boy was gone.

"It's going to be OK," I whispered into the night, but this time it wasn't an empty reassurance. This time I was thinking of the children in Mexico City, and it was a promise I would damn well keep.

# Hammett

*"Use the downtime well," The Instructor said, "because it won't last long."*

The stolen credit card was declined at the Target Hammett visited, so she had to use almost all of her remaining cash to buy clothes—panties, a sports bra, gym shoes, jeans, a tee, a windbreaker—and three rolls of ace bandages.

She'd changed in the bathroom, taping up her broken ribs as tight as she could stand, threw away her old clothes, and had then walked to the Sheraton on Falls Avenue. She wasn't hungry, but in order to keep her energy up she'd forced down a burger in the Fallsview Restaurant at the top, charging it to a made-up name and room. Then she had gone to the business center and spent an hour researching Canadafest, the big music event happening the next day, and another hour researching the Ebola virus, complete with the requisite pics of people bleeding out of every orifice. Hammett had a stomach made of forged steel, but she winced at some of the images. Happily, though, the virus didn't kill dogs.

Afterward, the doorman called her a cab, which she'd taken to the Toronto Eaton shopping center and ditched without paying. Then she had cruised the mall for two hours, stealing three wallets from unsuspecting guys, and then trailed a lone woman with a casual resemblance to Hammett out to the parking lot and relieved her of her purse and her car using a well-timed punch to the side of the head.

Then it was on to the Homewood Suites near the airport, using the stolen ID but paying cash. The room wasn't as nice as the boutique hotel, but it was more than comfortable, and Hammett collapsed into a boiling hot bath while thinking about the best way to kill half a million people.

Ebola was normally spread via blood and other bodily fluids, but Hammett couldn't fathom how that kind of transmission would be effective at an outdoor music festival. It also would be near impossible to contaminate food or the water supply, because of the many different sources and vendors.

The Instructor had probably weaponized it somehow. There was published research that suggested the possibility the virus could mutate into an airborne pathogen. No evidence existed that it had, of course, but if Hammett were experimenting with turning Ebola into a weapon, she'd make damn sure her research didn't get out either. Chandler had said Julie's strain of the virus was already engineered to strike in hours rather than days, so why not take it a step further?

After all, that was the difference between an A and an A+.

So how would they spread it?

An airburst would disperse a good amount of an aerosolized virus but would be loud and attract attention. Maybe during a fireworks display? Or when the headliner took the stage? People would think it was part of the show.

Another possibility was to do something to the ground. Spraying the grass before the concert. People step on the virus and then touch their shoes or bare feet.

No. That wouldn't be very effective. The more Hammett considered it, the more she liked an airborne approach. Perhaps crop dusters. Or those helicopters used to douse forest fires.

She found the hotel's business center, got online, and Googled pictures of Canadafest, looking for aircraft. After only a few minutes, Hammett found her answer on YouTube.

She smiled at the genius of it. Say what you would about The Instructor, he was one crafty son of a bitch.

"But I'm craftier."

Then Hammett began to plot her next moves. And they weren't moves Fleming and Chandler would approve of.

# Isolde

*"It often takes time to earn a man's respect,"* The Instructor said. *"Killing him is quicker."*

"Tell me about your children," Izzy said.

The pilot had a bad case of the flop sweats, possibly because of the gun she was holding to his head, possibly because of the razor she pressed to his crotch, possibly because he'd just watched Tristan slit the throat of his copilot. It also might have been a combination of all the above.

"They're b-babies," he stuttered. "Two and a half, and seven months."

"What are their names?"

"Clarissa and Matthew."

Izzy ran the back of the blade up his jawline, collecting a bead of sweat. "I bet, more than anything, you want to see them grow up. Am I right?"

He nodded.

"And it would be such a tragedy if they grew up without a father, don't you think?"

"I'll do anything you want."

Of course he would. They always did. "Do you have life insurance? To take care of Clarissa and Matthew if something bad happens to Daddy?"

Another nod, sweat dripping off his chin.

"That's very responsible of you. Because bad things do happen. I bet, when you got up this morning, you didn't imagine this scenario here. But it is happening. Now reach into your pocket, give me your wallet. Move slowly, because this razor is really sharp."

He adjusted his hips in the chair he sat in, and gingerly removed the wallet from the back of his slacks.

"Take out your driver's license. Read me your address."

His voice was faint, but he followed orders.

"Now I know where Clarissa and Matthew live. And let me share something with you. I really, really hate small children. You see these black marks on my arms? The full-length lines are people I've killed. The ones half the length are preteens. So I'm going to give you a chance to show me how much you love your babies."

She pressed the razor's handle in the pilot's hand. "Slit your own throat, or I'm going to visit your house, tie up your children, and set them on fire."

"Oh…Jesus…please…"

"Don't pray. That pisses me off. You have five seconds to do it. And let me tell you, I really enjoy a good marshmallow roast over screaming babies. Five…"

"I have money. Stocks and some CDs."

"Four…"

"I'll do anything you want. Please."

"Three…"

He raised the razor to his Adam's apple, his hand shaking so bad he nicked himself in several places.

"Two…"

"You…you promise you won't hurt them?"

"You have my word."

The pilot closed his eyes, then dug the razor into his own neck.

Izzy stepped away, impressed. In her experience, less than ten percent of the people she tried that on actually went through with it, and the majority of those were mothers. Most fathers usually tried to lunge at her with the razor.

He began to choke and gag, coughing blood through the new hole in his neck, aspirating it, eyes wide with panic and disbelief.

Izzy took a step back and raised her hand, the one not holding the gun.

"Fingers crossed," she said, showing him. "I lied to you. I'm going to kill your kids, and your wife."

His eyes got really wide, and he finally swung at her with the blade, but she easily dodged it, lashing out with her combat boot and breaking his knee, then watching as he flopped around on the floor like a landed fish. When he finally stopped moving, Izzy took the razor from his bloody hand, went to the sink next to the coffee machine, then carefully cleaned it off. She added one more cut to her arm, shuddering from the sensation. Then she dabbed on some ink and peered out the window of the office.

They were in one of the giant hangars at Downsview Airport, adjacent to the park where Canadafest was being held. Even though it was barely six a.m., there were already tens of thousands of people milling about among the great expanse of food tents and Porta-Johns. Izzy could see the stage in the distance where more than a dozen bands, including several she liked, would be playing later that day. Hopefully they were doing live recordings, because it would be the last performance for all of them.

Tristan began the process of dragging the pilots back to the truck. They'd be disposed of later. Before coming to the airport, they had dropped the Ebola-decimated corpse they'd had on ice in the parking lot of a local hospital. The autopsy report—already completed—would be leaked later that morning. As soon as Izzy and Tristan sprayed the crowd, they would drive back to the United States, the president would close the borders, and it would be mission accomplished. This strain of Ebola, enhanced by scientific tinkering, was incredibly hot. First exposure to hemorrhaging took hours rather than days, and the fatality rate was over ninety percent.

Canada was screwed.

Izzy planned to celebrate the mission's success by forcing herself to eat a cracker. Maybe she'd even put some cheese on it.

In the hangar, there was a man atop the aircraft, doing some patchwork. Izzy climbed the rope ladder hanging off the side, and snuck up on him without being noticed. Her balance was excellent, but her hand-to-hand combat skills were mediocre, so she ended him with a suppressed shot to the back of the head, taking careful aim so she didn't breach the aircraft's shell.

At the same time, Tristan crept up on the driver of the movable mooring tower and snapped his neck with less effort than it took Izzy to remove a screwtop beer bottle cap. That put the current death toll at eight, counting two crew members in the rear part of the hangar, and the two guards they'd shot by the fence. You'd think, with a festival so large, there would be better security.

Then again, this was Canada, one of the safest countries in the world. Izzy planned to move here one day, after the virus killed forty percent of the population and housing was cheap.

It took a half hour to rig the aerosol tank beneath the craft with heavy-duty chains, which Tristan did while Izzy familiarized herself with the cockpit and began the preflight check. There were more switches and knobs than in the simulator, but everything was clearly marked. She quickly located the throttle, the prop pitch and reverse levers, elevator wheel, and rudder pedals. Then she began going over the gauges, memorizing the layout.

Tristan opened the massive hangar doors, letting in the morning sun, which hit Izzy in the face and made her squint. She fished out her Ray-Bans, stuck them on her face, and watched her partner climb into the mooring tower vehicle.

Easiest op ever. Izzy could almost taste her victory cracker.

The thought of it made her stomach turn.

# Julie

This time there was no knock.

The door flew open, and The Instructor himself stepped into Julie's room. He was dressed in blue scrubs this time, looking like a doctor, although she didn't think he was one. His face looked tight, his skin flushed, and he stood with his shoulders shoved back and hands balled to fists by his sides.

Julie scrambled to her feet, heart pounding. She'd been watching TV, a singing competition reality show, and the music warbled on about lost love and heartbreak.

"You're coming with me," The Instructor said.

She didn't want to, especially when anger was rolling off of him like heat waves. She stepped back, her calves pressing against the love seat. "Why? What happened?"

He shot her a glare, as if she should know damn well.

"Is it Chandler?"

"Now."

Julie clenched her hands, her palms damp, fingers trembling. The only reason she'd agreed to give him what he wanted was to protect Chandler. Now that she knew Chandler wasn't under his control, he could go screw himself. "You can't hurt me. Not any more than you already have."

"I most certainly can. Young lady, you have no idea how bad life can get. But why should I hurt you, when I can hurt your friends?" He made *friends* sound like a dirty word.

"I know you don't have Chandler. You don't even know where she is."

A muscle along his jaw clenched.

"And how do you know that?"

Oh God, she shouldn't have said anything. The only person she had talked to in days was Derek, and she'd just given him away. "If you knew where she was, you would have told me more than you have."

He looked down at the floor, relaxed his hands, letting them hang at his sides. When he looked back up, his face was different. No longer angry. A picture of patient calm.

Eerie.

Had he believed her excuse? She couldn't tell. His face gave away nothing at all.

"Now, come with me, Julie," he said in a soft voice. "I have something you need to see. Then we can talk about Chandler."

Julie wrapped her arms around her middle. She didn't want to go, but if she didn't cooperate, nothing would stop him from forcing her. "Will I be coming back to this room?"

"That depends entirely on you."

Julie stepped toward him, swallowing into a parched throat. She didn't want him to hit her, but if he did, she'd deal with it.

The Instructor studied her with those blank eyes until the hair rose on the back of her neck. He raised his hand to her face and skimmed his fingers down her cheek. "It's really too bad you didn't take me up on my offer. But after this, I'm hoping you'll see things in a different light and realize how important it is to keep me happy."

Revulsion crawled over Julie's skin, but she forced herself not to react. "You wanted me to see something?"

"Follow me."

He led her out of the room and down the hall. She had only walked the halls twice, but she recognized they were heading in a different direction. Not toward The Instructor's office. And while she wasn't convinced that should make her feel relieved, it did.

They came to a sally port: two doors separated by a short hall. When The Instructor opened the first door, it made a sucking sound, and Julie felt like she was walking against the wind. They entered, the door closing behind. Then a buzzer sounded, and The Instructor opened the door on the other side to similar effect.

An effort to keep the virus isolated. To keep her isolated.

They passed several doors then came to a *T*. Julie glanced through another set of doors to see three security guards, before The Instructor whisked her in the other direction.

The place was a maze of halls and doors, but she could guess their purpose. There were two parts of this building, her part and the one everyone else occupied. As if they couldn't get far enough away from her for their liking.

She didn't blame them.

A woman stood at the end of the hall, watching them. She wore no protective gear. Hair smooth and chic in a blond bob, she looked like she'd stepped out of a New York fashion magazine—not one of the models, but an editor or executive. Like she had some power and wasn't afraid to wield it like a sharp sword.

Her leg was wrapped in bandages, a crutch under her arm, and she watched Julie with bored, bitchy eyes.

"Where's Rhett?" The Instructor asked the woman.

"How should I know?"

"Find him. I'm going to need assistance."

Giving a huff, the woman turned and limped down the hall.

They turned a corner, and The Instructor led her into yet another hall, this one looking exactly like the last: a maze of tile, blank walls, and closed doors.

"Here we are," The Instructor said, stopping at a door at the end of the hall. He opened it and ushered Julie inside.

The space looked like some sort of locker room, lockers lining the walls with benches in front of them. He led her through that area and through an air-locked door. This room was tiled and looked like a shower, but the most striking thing about it was the purple light. It flooded every square inch, making her hair glow lavender where it curled along her collarbone.

During all those lonely evenings at the lighthouse, she'd read up on viruses. At least enough to know that ultraviolet light made them unable to replicate. She wasn't sure if that was the case with her virus. Her virus was engineered to be a weapon, and it was possible many of the rules she read about didn't apply.

Another air-locked door, and the next room was filled with supplies. Tape, latex gloves, and receptacles marked with biohazard signs. Hazmat suits hung on the wall flanking yet another door.

"We don't need any of this gear, do we Julie?"

Julie wasn't sure why he was taunting her. Maybe to remind her that he was inoculated, that he was invincible, that she was powerless to hurt him.

She didn't need the reminder.

The Instructor crossed to the door and peered through the small window in its center. "Looks like they're ready for us."

He opened this door and led her into a sally port like the one near her room. Once the first door was closed, he opened the second.

Like the others, the door gave a sucking sound as it opened, and although the air currents felt like they were sucking her into the room, a bad smell washed over her in a wave. Earthy and feral and almost overpowering, the smell made Julie feel sick. She covered her mouth and nose with a hand, but she could still taste it as if it had already coated her tongue.

The Instructor waved Julie inside.

The room looked just like the first room he'd kept her in, only instead of one bed in the empty space there were two. The first held a woman, or what was left of her. She was Julie's age, with shoulder-length, black hair, and her mouth was open, as if it was difficult for her to breathe. Her wrists were fastened to the bed rails with thick Velcro straps, but the arms themselves were so covered with red and purple bruises, there wasn't an inch of normal skin. She watched Julie with sunken, bloodshot eyes, staring blankly as if she was barely conscious of her surroundings.

Julie stepped back in horror. She could sense others in the room, but she couldn't pull her eyes away from the sight. She'd seen something like it before, back in the lab on Plum Island, before she knew she was infected. And it had haunted her nightmares ever since.

"Julie."

She turned toward the voice, to the second bed…

*Oh God.*

"Derek!"

Secured to the bed just like the woman, Derek's face was bruised, one eye almost closed and lip swollen. But the bruising appeared natural, like he'd been beaten up, not like the woman. She'd never seen him without his hazmat suit. She'd also never seen him as frightened, desperate, and angry as he looked now.

She spun to face The Instructor. "What is going on? Why is Derek here?"

"Dr. Fossen was planning to sell out his country, Julie."

She shook her head. This was wrong. God, this was so wrong.

"He was caught leaking important information. Information vital to our nation's security."

So she hadn't given Derek away. The Instructor already knew. "That's not what he was doing."

"He's a traitor."

"A traitor because I wanted people to know you're kidnapping citizens? Holding them prisoner?" Derek's voice cracked. "Killing people?"

Julie looked at the woman. Nausea swamped her, not because of the sight, but because she knew what was wrong with her.

"It was me. It was my blood."

"It's not your fault, Julie."

"It is. They took my blood. They..." And if The Instructor had done this to the woman, did he intend to do the same to Derek?

"It's my fault. If he was trying to tell someone, that's only because I asked him to."

"He chose his path, Julie."

He chose his path? "You said earlier that Derek needed extra persuasion to work on this project."

The Instructor smiled. "Even that didn't prove enough. And maybe that is your fault."

"Don't listen to him, Julie," Derek said. "Nothing is your fault. It's this sick bastard. This Instructor. He likes hurting people, Julie. He likes killing them. This would have happened whether you were here or not."

The Instructor spoke first. "This woman in the bed beside him is Derek's sister."

His sister?

"She won't be getting her kidney transplant. We gave her something else instead. A bit of your blood."

Julie felt dizzy. She looked to Derek, wanting him to say The Instructor was lying. Wanting him to say anything but what she'd just heard. "This is her?"

Derek looked away, his cheeks wet with tears.

Julie wanted to go to him, to hold him, to make everything OK. But she couldn't make it OK. It would never be OK again. "Oh God, Derek. I'm so sorry."

"You should have told me Dr. Fossen was planning to talk to a reporter, Julie. I wish you would have. It didn't have to come to this. But this country is too important, and it's my job to make sure it's safe."

Pressure built at the bottom of Julie's throat. Vomit, a scream, she didn't know which. "What are you…"

The door sucked open, and a man wearing jeans, boots, and a button-down shirt strolled inside like it was nothing. "What I miss?"

Julie recognized him from the boat the night they'd taken her from the lighthouse. This must be Rhett.

The Instructor nodded to the cowboy, and in a streak of motion too fast for Julie to follow, Rhett was by her side, one hand on her elbow, one bending her wrist back just enough to control her.

Julie stared at Derek. She didn't know what was coming next. She was afraid to know.

"It's not a surprise, really," said The Instructor. "A pretty girl like you, a damsel in distress, what kind of red-blooded male would be loyal to his sister when he might have a shot at you?"

"A romance, huh?" Rhett drawled in Julie's ear. "Hot damn."

"The pity is, they never even got to kiss."

"Like two star-crossed lovers, huh?"

"Maybe you could help them fix that, Rhett."

"It'd be a pleasure."

Rhett forced Julie to step forward. She twisted and fought, but that just made him move behind her, pin her arm behind her back, and raise it up to her shoulder blades, until she couldn't take the pain, couldn't control her body.

The cowboy had pushed Julie's face an inch from Derek's when he met her eyes. "Not your fault," Derek said. Then she got another press from behind and their lips were sealed.

"Just call me goddamn Cupid," Rhett said.

Julie began to cry and couldn't make herself stop.

# Chandler

*"The secret to success is to clear your mind of side mat-
ters and focus on the mission," The Instructor said.
"Emotion is the strongest motivator there is, but it's also
dangerous. Passion can cloud the mind and cause desperation where there needs to be control. Don't feel, do."*

Unable to find a sign of the boy, I'd returned to the *cartonero*'s truck, dragged his body from the floor of the cab, threw it
into one of the holes, and buried it. Then I placed cardboard over
the floor and seats and cleaned up the rest as best I could. I would
have preferred driving the late-model green Ford, of course, but I
didn't wanted Los Zetas on my tail if I could help it. With the *cartonero*'s body buried, it would take them a while to realize he was
involved in the massacre at all. And the longer it took them to tie
the mess to him, the longer I would have to freely use his truck.

I discovered an extra thousand pesos in the *cartonero*'s glove
compartment, along with a tied bundle of twigs that I recognized,
and a pack of Doublemint gum. I found my way to Highway 85
out of town, switching to Highway 75 near Monterrey. With the
window open to disperse the smell, I opened the bundle of khat
and began to strip off the epidermis of a stem with my teeth, which
I then chewed. It was astringent and sour, sort of like chewing an
aspirin, and soon dried up all the saliva in my mouth. I added a
stick of gum, and drove as the drug took effect.

Khat was popular in the Middle East, and gaining favor in
Latin America. Chewing it provided euphoric and stimulant
effects, the perfect companion for a *cartonero* driving long dis-
tances every day. It tasted like gnawing on a Christmas tree, but
with my lack of sleep I needed the boost, and it also helped me
focus.

Dawn started to pink the sky, and my drive was mountainous and quite beautiful. The combination of my successful escape from sure disaster and the khat fueled me into the next day.

Self-doubt, my ass.

I thought a lot about the little boy I'd seen in the landfill during the entire drive. Like most Americans, I'd heard about the poverty in Mexico, but seeing it up close and in the form of an innocent child was different.

I'd known some horrible people: my abusive adoptive father being the first, my homicidal boyfriend Cory the next, and of course, The Instructor. But I'd never teetered on the edge of starvation, and I'd never lived in a hole in the dirt.

The Instructor's Ebola attack might start in the bullfighting ring, but it would spread. Through the streets of Mexico City, out along the highways and airways, until it brought an already struggling country to its knees. And the thought that the new president and The Instructor would slaughter the people of Mexico, children like the boy I'd seen in the garbage, for political power, didn't make me sad or panicked or doubtful.

It made me furious.

And I was going to make damn well sure it didn't happen.

I puzzled over the delivery system, ruling out food and water contamination because Ebola was spread via bodily fluids. They probably tinkered with it, but even if people could get infected through swallowing the virus, that seemed like a sporadic way to distribute. Maybe it was Vaccination Day at the bullring, each attendee getting what they thought was a DTaP shot. Sort of like getting a free cap when you go to a ballgame. Or maybe that was the khat talking.

Ruling out ingestion and injection left inhalation. Ebola wasn't aerosolized, but I wouldn't put it past The Instructor to figure out how to do it. That meant I would be looking for a reservoir that could spray virus. The ventilation system would be the way to do it for an indoor event—that was how Legionnaires' disease was spread. So what would be the equivalent for outdoors? Did Mexico have cooling stations like US theme parks did, spraying cool mist when people walked beneath them? A possibility…

Thanks to the radar detector and the stimulant, I made record time via the toll roads, and by the time the sun rose above the mountains, I was heading into the city.

Mexico City was a jumbled-up cross between rich and poor, sophistication and chaos, the aroma of five-star cuisine and the stench of rot. Fresh-air food markets and world-class museums met squalor and hopelessness. The city itself sat high above sea level in the caldera of a dead volcano, the peaks holding a fog of hot smog over the city. At a population of more than eight million and a surrounding metropolitan area well over twenty, that was a lot of smog, a lot of noise, a lot of heat.

By the time I arrived, I was exhausted, hungry, and stiff. My nerves were also totally unprepared for the tangle of buses and cars driving to and fro with little heed for any rules of any road. But after a few close calls, I fell into the familiar suicidal groove like slipping into a favorite pair of shoes.

Unfortunately in this traffic, it was impossible to tell if I was being followed. So once I closed in on my destination, I stashed the *cartonero*'s pickup in a small private lot in a less than affluent neighborhood. The back still jammed with cardboard, I left the keys in the ignition. I was betting the truck would be gone within minutes, blood and all, making it impossible for Los Zetas to tie me to the murders in the landfill. The last thing I needed was more people after me.

I flagged down one of the green VW bugs that served as taxicabs in the city. Hailing a cab on the street was considered a somewhat risky thing to do in Mexico City, since taxi robberies happened disturbingly often. But since a garden-variety robber was several notches down on my list of threats, I figured I was safe enough. My biggest concern at the moment was sweating to death.

I directed the cab to take me to the nearest shopping area, and there I bought a lightweight top, cargo pants, and sunglasses to obscure the lines of my face and my injuries, then flagged down a different cab.

Closing in on El Plaza de Toros México, I spotted a bike pulling a cart, commonly called a pedicab in the United States. I'd once hijacked one of these and raced through the streets of New York, pulling a mother-son duo who'd refused to vacate. I'd been trying to save Julie, and seeing one of the contraptions now made me think of her.

What was she going through?

What was in store for her?

Heaving a breath of sour smog, I found a compartment deep in my heart and locked my concerns safely inside. Fleming would find Julie. I had to trust that. And if I'd proven anything over the past days, tangling my personal feelings with work led to disaster.

I was in control.

I was unemotional.

I was ice.

The bullfighting ring was adjacent to the Estadio Azul, the soccer stadium named after its brilliant blue exterior and seats, but it was no less spectacular.

The ring's grandstand rose in the center of the grounds, a big cone surrounded by pens for the bulls, stables for horses, parking for service vehicles, and stands offering concessions. A concrete wall surrounded that, encompassing a city block. About four meters high and painted two shades of chipped orange, the wall had entrance gates on each side, five in total. Every few meters a column interrupted the flow, each topped with a statue of man and bull in various phases of the fight.

El Plaza de Toros México was the largest bullfighting ring in the world. And looking at the way the walls of the grandstand itself inclined up and out on all sides, it was no wonder The Instructor had chosen this location for his strike.

A big bowl of a stadium within a bowl of a city, the structure wouldn't allow airborne Ebola to escape easily, and that had to be part of his plan. The pathogen would linger, giving spectators plenty of time to breathe it into their lungs. And once they were carrying the virus, the burgeoning population, close quarters, and rampant poverty would ensure the infection's spread. It would balloon into a national crisis in a matter of hours.

I scanned the structure, focusing on the advertisement for a bank rimming the bowl's edge, and another at the top that proclaimed LA VICTORIA ES TUYA. Victory is yours.

I hoped it was speaking to me.

Directing my driver to pass the plaza, I let him take me several blocks down the street. There I paid him and climbed out. I then took a circuitous route back to the bullring. I focused on adopting the walk and posture of a local—not too fast, a slight shuffle of the feet. One of the most important skills of a spy is being able to blend in, to still the mind, to adopt the mannerisms of the populace, and the more I concentrated on these details, the calmer and more invisible I felt. If Heath was one of the operatives here, and I was pretty sure he would be, I wanted to do whatever I could to spot him before he recognized me.

An exhibition prior to the official start of the season, this afternoon's event had the area buzzing. Concession stands lined a shady park in the adjacent block. The exhibition was set at an earlier time than customary for a bullfight, but it still wouldn't begin for several hours. Scores of people were getting an early jump on the festival, and as I got closer, a brass band started warming up on a *paso doble*. I could smell tortillas and varieties of chili-spiced meat combined with the scents of hot pavement, car exhaust, and manure. As in all big cities, birds fluttered in the streets, mostly pigeons, fighting for crumbs of food, and a constant racket of vehicles and sirens and horns and the endless whistles of traffic cops filled the air. Gate number one seemed to be the only one open. It was still hours from the start of the event, and only those readying the plaza for today's exhibition were allowed past the uniformed guards.

I stopped at a corner *taqueria*, one of the sources of the tortilla-and-meat smell. Looking much like a college sports bar with exposed pipes, fluorescent lights, and streamers hanging from the ceiling, the place was cheap and relatively clean. A handful of patrons loitered in the place, eating breakfast. A couple who only had eyes for each other took up one table, two men who looked me up and down stood in line, and a teenager served food behind the counter. None of them seemed out of place.

I ordered two cheese and chili quesadillas and two bottles of water at the counter, then positioned myself at a corner standing table with a view of the stadium gate. I slipped a water into my backpack, then ate slowly, savoring the food while I surveyed the plaza gate and watched the festival crowd grow.

To figure out how the attack would take place and stop it, I needed to get into the plaza. After watching the guards stop people at the front gate and allow only those with identification badges through, I started looking for alternative routes.

I noted that trees reached over the concrete wall at several points. Buses transporting festivalgoers lined the streets. It was tough to jump the gate in broad daylight without being seen, but with this combination of elements, I might be able to manage.

When he finally showed up, I almost missed him.

Dressed in jeans and a light blue *guayabera*, the short-sleeved, button-down shirt common to the area, Heath looked like dozens of men I'd seen coming and going all day. A straw cowboy hat covered his head, shielding the eye patch from my notice. But his walk—that arrogant, rolling amble that had drawn me from the first time I met him—gave him away.

He entered the gate, chatted with the guards as if he knew them, then strolled in, as if it was something he did every day. I had to wonder if it was and how long he'd been preparing in order to pull off an inside attack.

As soon as Heath disappeared through the gates, I waited a few beats, looking for signs of the big woman, Earnshaw, who I assumed was his partner, or any of the other Hydra Deux members in case I had that wrong. When none of them showed, I tossed the wrappers from my meal and left the restaurant.

I passed the gate on the other side of the street and continued down the block. At the corner, I crossed, following the curve of the wall to the spot were three buses lined the curb. Hidden behind buses and camouflaged by trees, I shimmied up one trunk, climbed out on a branch, and dropped onto the plaza's outer concrete wall, flattening my belly to the top. It didn't take longer than five seconds.

Inside, a small parking lot spread beneath me, a groundskeeper's truck, two stock trailers, and a smattering of cars filling the spaces. From there, a ramp led underground and presumably into the bowl-shaped arena itself. In the corner to my left, bulls stood in corrals, swiping at flies and pawing at the dirt. Closer to fight time, each would be herded into the individual stall called the *chiquero*, where he would wait to enter the *anillo* and fight for his life.

I was about to lower myself to the pavement when I heard voices below. Two men who looked barely old enough to drive walked up the ramp, and I recognized their faces from the poster out front. The matadors.

Heath emerged behind them, driving a small pickup truck up the ramp to the parking lot area. The truck, whose bed was filled with rakes and a large tank for watering down dust in the arena, was hitched to an arena drag, a plow-like apparatus designed to break up clumps and smooth the arena for optimal footing.

It made sense. Posing as a groundskeeper and *arenero*, he would have free rein of the entire place.

The truck door slammed, and I flattened my cheek to the concrete, listening to his boot heels drum the pavement, closer with each step. The tree over me offered some camouflage, but while I hadn't been worried about the matadors spotting me, Heath was a different story.

The footsteps stopped.

I brought my hand around my back and pulled the Jericho, fitting it snug in my hand, finger on the trigger.

He started moving again, this time away. When his steps started to blend with the city sounds, I raised my head and peered inside. He reached the main gate, and after a few words with the security guards, he left the plaza.

I had another decision to make: take a look around the plaza or follow.

The Plaza Mexico wasn't going anywhere. I could always come back and play needle-in-the-haystack. If I let Heath go, I might not catch up with him again until it was too late.

I jumped to the outside of the wall, hung off the edge, and absorbed the ten-foot drop with my knees. Adjusting my backpack and checking to make sure my pistol was secure and out of sight under my baggy T-shirt, I walked down the sidewalk and peered around the corner.

Heath was just outside the gate...and heading straight at me.

I slipped back behind the wall. The shadows under the trees were dark. There was a good chance he hadn't seen me, at least not well enough to recognize my face. I had a few seconds lead time, but I had to move fast.

I crossed the street and blended into the outer edges of the festival crowd.

Music bounced through the park, the brass *paso doble* replaced with a Cuban salsa equally at home in nightclub or daytime festival. Booth after booth swayed with T-shirts, bullfighting capes—the pink *capote* and red *muleta*—and *bota*, the sides of the wineskins stamped with pictures of matadors and bulls. Carts sold tortillas and nearly every imaginable foodstuff to fill them, and the air smelled of spice and sun and felt sweaty and alive.

Peering through a chink in the crowd, I watched a light blue *guayabera* and cowboy hat move toward the park. Pulling out the Jericho, I kept it low and in front of me, hidden among the folds of my T-shirt. Firing in a crowd as thick as this was dangerous, the chance of hitting an innocent far too great, but I couldn't let Heath get the drop on me, either. He hadn't killed me in Maine, but that didn't mean he wouldn't now.

The hat bobbed closer. I slipped behind a display of pint-size *chaquetillas*, the ornate waistcoats that are part of the matador's suit of lights, and waited for him to pass so I could slip in behind. He cleared the stand, and I got my first clear look.

Not Heath.

Shorter and more heavily muscled, the man I'd been watching was a regular Mexican version of Tequila.

Damn.

In a city of millions, finding Heath was less likely than locating the needle in the haystack. Unless I located him in the next few minutes, I'd have to move to plan B.

I flowed through the crowd in the direction of the music. I'd search a few minutes longer, then circle around and return to the plaza and scour every inch inside those walls before the stands filled.

Heath must have spotted me, otherwise I wouldn't have lost him, despite the fact that seeing him had rattled me more than I wanted to think about. As with my glimpse of him at the lighthouse, I felt jangled and off-balance. Only this time, I didn't have tear gas and flashbangs to blame.

A hand pressed against the small of my back.

I started to turn, expecting a pickpocket or some asshole trying to cop a feel, but before I could, the hand clamped mine, hyperflexing and twisting it into a wrist lock.

"Going somewhere so fast, *bonita*?"

I wanted to strike, to whirl around and plug a few rounds into his belly. But with all the people around me, I didn't dare.

Applying pressure to my wrist, Heath took my gun and pressed the barrel into my side, angling upward to do maximum damage. He leaned close, and his lips brushed the back of my left ear. He was no longer wearing the hat, a wifebeater had replaced his blue *guayabera*, and I realized he must have traded with the hombre I'd been tracking.

"This is our secret, but I'm glad you didn't get barbecued back in Maine."

"Feeling you this close makes me wish I had."

"Oh, you can't mean that. I would be so hurt."

"I just bet."

"You don't understand what you do to me, Chandler."

"I'm Hammett."

He laughed his breath warm on my cheek. "I can't say it didn't throw me a little to see three of you in Maine, even though I was briefed that you had identical sisters. But I know you. And no matter where you are or what disguise you wear, it makes no difference. We're connected, you and me. I feel you in my heart."

He fitted me hard against him and swayed his hips, the move so sexy I wanted to punch him.

"Trying to fight me wouldn't be smart. There are so many civilians in this place. I'd hate to see them get hurt."

"Reading my mind now?"

"No, *mamacita*. I'm reading your body, like always."

"Go to hell, Heath."

"Oh, *querida*, you have no idea how much I've missed you. You are just what I need. In fact, I have a little treat for you."

I angled my body ever so slightly. A broken wrist and possible bullet wound would be better than letting him take me. I just needed an opening.

"Look around you, Chandler. All these people. All these children. If you try to fight me, many of them will die. Many more will trample each other trying to get away. Are you willing to be responsible for that?"

My stomach clenched. As much as I hated this bastard, he did know me. And every time I turned around, he used that knowledge to beat me at my own game.

I was sick of it.

But not sick enough to cause these people harm. And of course, he knew that, too.

I nodded. He released my wrist, the gun still stabbing into my side. But before I could even think about moving to disarm him, I felt the sting of a needle in my arm. I pulled away, sending the syringe flying, but I knew I was too late.

"What did you give me?"

"Something you'll adore."

"What?"

"Just a little Special K, *bonita*. Lean back against me and enjoy the ride."

# Fleming

*"The best defense is a good offense," The Instructor said.*
*"And the best offense leaves no survivors."*

Using the lock picks that Harry McGlade had thoughtfully provided, Fleming had made good use of the fabrication tools the custom motorcycle shop had offered. Using sheets of steel, pneumatic machines, a blowtorch, and good old sweat equity, Fleming had been up all night building what might have been her finest creation.

It had some problems. Weight, for one, though the two-stroke engine helped. And ventilation. Fleming had sacrificed keeping cool for bulletproofing. But the biggest problem was mobility. Turning was tough. Stairs, or bumps, or even steep grades, were impossible.

She used ramps and a winch to load it into the back of her van, kept the ramps for later, and got out of the shop before it opened for the day. It was still five hours before the supposed rendezvous at noon, but Fleming wasn't waiting until then. She was going to bring the fight to Rhett and Scarlett.

The odds weren't good. In fact, the outcome could be downright pathetic. Fleming was outnumbered, outgunned by who knew how many, and crippled. Chances were high she wouldn't even be able to save herself, let alone Bradley.

But she sure as hell was going to try.

# Hammett

*"Hindsight is twenty-twenty," The Instructor said. "But in the heat of the moment, doing stupid things often seems preferable to doing nothing at all."*

Hammett got there early, and she was almost too late.

Downsview was a private airport, and Hammett hoped she'd have time to anticipate Tristan and Isolde's arrival, giving her enough time to search through twelve hangars on site for the right one. After a nightmare-filled forty winks at the Homewood Suites, she'd gotten up sore and stiff at four a.m., forced down a gas station breakfast burrito, and purchased a new TracFone to replace the one she'd lost in the river. But by the time the cab dropped her off and she'd cut through the fencing on the west side, Hammett saw the aircraft was already out on the runway and ready to launch.

It was three hundred meters away, bright red, and massive. CANADAFEST was emblazoned on the side, underneath the obligatory maple leaf of the national flag. The same zeppelin she'd seen on YouTube.

Except this wasn't technically a zeppelin. Zeppelins were made by a specific German company and were rigid airships, keeping their recognizable shape via an internal metal frame even when not filled with helium. Hammett's research revealed the Canadafest dirigible was a blimp; it had a tough outer skin called an envelope and no internal structure apart from suspension cables and the two ballonets—large inflatable rectangles that functioned as ballasts.

The airship was being towed by a truck with a tower attached to the flatbed—the mooring tower—a cable at the top hooked to the craft's nose and keeping it on the ground. Once the cable was released, the airship would launch, and once launched it would infect the festival with Ebola from that funky-looking tank attached to the rear of the gondola.

Hammett couldn't let that happen. So she set her jaw and ran for it.

In perfect health and gym shoes, she could sprint two hundred meters in under twenty-five seconds. In boots and a vest, carrying a bag of gear, with at least four broken ribs, it was less of a sprint and more like a pain-wracked jog, and as Hammett halved the distance she saw the mooring line fall away and a large man— Tristan—enter the gondola door just as the ship began to rise.

Hammett's first inclination was to yank out her shotgun and try to punch some holes in the craft, preventing it from liftoff. But the dirigible was just so damn *huge*—at least sixty meters long and more than fifteen meters wide in the middle. Hammett didn't believe anything smaller than a howitzer would deflate it. Plus, the air pressure inside the envelope would be much lower than the air surrounding the craft, which meant helium wouldn't leak out; rather, outside air would leak in. Even with big holes, it would fly for hours.

So Hammett kept running, and when the blimp rose to a height of two meters—too high to reach—she jumped onto the truck, took two steps up the mooring tower, and launched herself at the rope ladder hanging off the blimp's side as it passed overhead.

Her hands slipped, but Hammett got her armpit in the rung, and then the twin engines attached to the gondola kicked on and the blimp began to ascend more rapidly. Wind whipped in her ears, blotting out most sound and making her ears and throat ache. Within a few seconds, they were fifty meters up.

Hammett grabbed the rung above her. Not eager to fall again after Niagara, she pulled herself up and managed to get her feet on the ladder. She was hanging too far away from the gondola to reach it but could see inside the cockpit. That little emo bitch, Isolde, was flying. The hulk, Tristan, was pointing a gun at Hammett's head.

He fired, a high-powered round punching through the reinforced window, missing.

Hammett climbed as fast as she could—not very fast because the wind was smacking her around and the blimp was moving a lot quicker than she expected. Not airplane quick, but at least forty miles an hour and accelerating.

The airfield, and the park below, got smaller and smaller as they climbed to three hundred meters, and Hammett wondered, even if she got to the top of the damn aircraft, what the hell she was supposed to do once she got there.

She supposed she'd figure it out.

Once she reached the midpoint on the ladder, where it rested against the side of the blimp, it was much easier to climb than when it was flopping around in midair, and her pace improved. It took another painful, gasping minute to get to the apex. She sat down, holding onto the ladder, and spent a moment getting her heart rate and breathing under control. In the distance to the south, she could see the CN Tower poking up through downtown Toronto, and beyond that, the vast blue-green expanse of Lake Ontario. To the east, Canadafest, the gathering people looking like a sprinkling of multicolored sand against the green park. The outside air was cold and getting colder, and the aircraft was turning back toward the festival. Hammett assumed Isolde would buzz the crowd low to the ground, like a crop duster, but she seemed to still be ascending.

Hammett hadn't dressed for blimp-surfing. Her boots were slick and a bit bouncy on the rubber and fabric surface of the envelope, and her sweater wasn't warm enough in the high winds. It was about fifty-five degrees Fahrenheit on the ground. If they climbed to ten thousand feet—and perhaps the airship could—it would drop to around thirty-five. She wouldn't live long at that temperature. Which, perhaps, was why Isolde was still ascending.

In hindsight, climbing onto a blimp may not have been the smartest decision.

Wrapping one leg around the rope ladder, Hammett dug into the duffel bag for something she might be able to use. Her fingers brushed her karambit knife, and she decided to cut a large hole in the blimp, forcing a slow descent. But it was a short blade, and even when she pushed it into the envelope all the way to the hilt—which took considerable straining and grunting—it still didn't puncture the thick catenary curtain on the blimp's top.

OK. New plan. A big hole wouldn't work, but maybe a smaller hole could still be useful.

Taking out the shotgun, Hammett aimed downward. She fired, fléchette rounds blowing a fist-size hole in the envelope.

That was a start. But she needed a bigger opening than that if she was going to climb inside the blimp, lower herself to the gondola, and kill those assholes flying this thing. It was a crazy plan, and one with a very limited chance of success, but she couldn't think of anything better.

Hammett jacked another round into the chamber and fired again, wishing she'd traded places with Chandler and gone to Mexico instead, because so far this op sucked balls.

# Chandler

*"When up against forces you know," said The Instructor, "remember they may also know you."*

Special K, or ketamine, is a dissociative anesthetic, and I felt the effects quickly. My heartbeat increased first, the thrum in my ears even louder than the music. Then the aches and pains I had collected over the past days began to feel distant, and my body felt weightless, like I was floating above the ground.

"*Bonita?* Good, no?"

Heath spoke in my ear, but he sounded far away. "I don't know about you, but I'm in no condition to drive home."

"Oh, I will take care of you."

"I was afraid of that."

We wove through the crowd, the surreal sensation growing, of being outside of myself. I felt as if I wasn't walking with
Heath at all, but was instead a bystander watching Heath guide
me through bull masks and bright pink *capotes* and load me into
one of the green-and-white VW bugs.

On the street, lights were brighter than they should be,
sun sparking off chrome and glaring off the windows of buildings, pulsing when I stared. We wove through traffic at break-
neck speed, but instead of gripping the seat in front of me, I just
watched people and trees whip by in time with the patter of my
heart. Every little while, it occurred to me that I should get away
from Heath, or better yet, kill him.

I tried to go for his good eye, then watched as my hands
didn't quite reach his face. And what seemed like a second later, I
wasn't sure any of it had happened at all.

I found myself staring out the window at a little girl, dressed
in a half shirt and miniskirt. Her face looked exaggerated, made
up like a hooker. A man stood near her, soliciting the driver of a
car pulled to the curb. Her father? Her pimp? I wasn't sure there
was a difference. She looked seductively at the cars around her
one minute, and the next she appeared to be ready to cry.

I tried to hold on to her, to my surroundings, but then she
was gone, and I wasn't sure if the girl was real or if I was thinking
of Hammett's story of when she was a girl. I felt like I was floating
from the car, or maybe I was dead.

I wasn't clear on anything else until gradually I realized I was
sitting in a chair, as if I was slowly descending back into my body
or waking from a dream. I didn't have to check my wrists and
ankles to know I was bound, but I did it anyway. Plastic zip ties
dug into my arms, pinned behind me. My feet were bound to the
legs of the chair.

The wall in front of me was in desperate need of paint, decorated with an oil portrait of *La Virgen de Guadalupe* in rich
greens, golds, and reds and a small shelf underneath to hold votive
candles. I smelled the faint scent of tamales and heard a distant
announcer speaking Spanish, his voice filtered through thin walls.

Mexico City, the little girl in the streets, the Plaza Mexico, the festival where Heath...

I felt him watching me before I saw him. And when I focused on his face, the mix of hallucinations, reality, and old memories came rushing back, and for a moment I couldn't tell one from the other.

He had changed into black pants and a long-sleeve, white shirt. "You're back, no?"

"No thanks to you." I remembered the sting in my arm and would have rubbed it had I not been bound. "Ketamine?"

He canted his head to the side in a half shrug. "It made you... compliant."

"You like that, don't you?"

"Compliant women? No. You should know that about me by now, *bonita*. A real man prefers his woman full of fire. But a real man also prefers his woman doesn't try to kill him with her bare hands."

Unable to hold his gaze, I glanced around the room. I was still under the effects of the drug and wasn't myself. At least that's what I wanted to believe. If I was honest, I had to admit Heath confused me. He conveyed so many mixed signals, body language, and voice inflections that I'd found him hard to read since the first day we met. Although I'd always rolled my eyes at his overtly sexual comments and stupid endearments, before I knew he was an operative, I believed the intensity between us was real. Now I realized he was playing me, he had to be, but the intensity was still there, still so natural, that it continued to throw me.

I needed time to sort imagination from memory and figure out where I was and how I was going to get out of here.

"So now that you have me, Heath, what comes next?"

"We kill you. Like Heath should have done out on the street."

The voice was rough as number three–grade steel wool, and, apparently, female. Sort of.

I turned my head in its direction and caught a glimpse of the amazon who'd broken into the lightkeeper's house at Heath's side. She was even bigger than I remembered, her biceps stretching the cap sleeves of her T-shirt tight, her breasts firm even though she wasn't wearing a bra.

I glanced at Heath. "She's Catherine Earnshaw to your Heathcliff?"

"Just Earnshaw," he said. "Fits her better."

"I never figured you for a tragic lover wandering out on the moors pining for his soul mate."

His lips crooked up on one side. "You'd be surprised."

I met his smirk with a bored expression.

"Come on, can't we get rid of her? I have much more entertaining things I'd like to be doing." Earnshaw's voice deepened, getting downright husky. A blatant come-on if I'd ever heard one. A come-on directed at Heath.

The lips that were so cocky a moment ago tensed up in reaction to his partner, and I could see that despite her suggestive tone, he didn't like her very much.

Of course, I doubted Heath would let simple dislike get in the way of sex. To any operative, sex was a tool, a way to manipulate. But I had to wonder if his partner understood that.

And if she didn't, maybe I could use it to my advantage.

"What do you want, Heath?"

My words were simple, not necessarily suggestive. But as I said them, I met his gaze and held it, my eyes carrying the heat my words didn't.

His lips twitched upward at the corners. "Tell me your secrets, *bonita*."

"To you, I'm an open book." Feeling the woman watching us, I matched his smile. As much as I hated this man, he didn't suffer from a shortage of hotness. Playing up to him was easy, disturbingly so. Exactly what had gotten me in trouble the first time. Call it chemistry or stupidity, but liking him was as easy as breathing.

Only this time, I knew who he was, and I was ready for him. I wouldn't let him win.

"How did you find me?" he asked.

"You're an open book to me, too."

"So you sensed where I would go? Mexico City, in all of the world? The Plaza Mexico, in all of Mexico City?"

"I know you like bullfighting. And, if I remember, cockfighting."

He smiled.

Earnshaw looked from him to me and back again, then pulled out a cell phone. "I'm going to call The Instructor, ask him what he wants us to do with her."

"Wait," Heath said. "I have a few more questions."

She folded her massive arms over her massive chest, her biceps popping. "Well, you better hurry."

"Tell me about your sisters."

One subject I didn't want to discuss, especially not with him. "Not much to tell. I only learned I had sisters a few days ago."

"Where are they now?"

"I don't know."

"I don't believe you."

"Then I guess we've reached an impasse."

"The Instructor said you were close with the one in the wheelchair, that she had been your handler."

"A voice on the phone."

"That's not what The Instructor seemed to think."

"The Instructor also seemed to think he could blackmail the three of us into working for him, and he was wrong. If I were you, Heath, I'd watch my back. He might need someone to blame this on, or something to hold over your head, and I'll bet there's video of you at the bullring."

Heath's expression didn't change. Not surprising. He'd probably considered this possibility. "What do you know about The Instructor's plans?"

I didn't answer.

"Give me a minute with her, and she'll tell us all about where her sisters are and what they know." Earnshaw circled the room and stopped in front of me, looking like she couldn't wait to kick my ass.

Maybe making her jealous while I was cuffed to a chair wasn't the best idea I'd ever had.

"Should I do that, Chandler? Should I turn you over to Earnshaw? I must warn you, she would probably have a gold medal in Olympic wrestling if she hadn't been thrown off the team for crippling her practice partners. Twice."

"Funny. I would have guessed she'd been ousted for steroids. Or maybe they found male genitalia."

Earnshaw lunged, but Heath stuck out his palm, holding her back.

"What do you think, Chandler? Would you like a demonstration?"

"Up to you. You need a woman to do your torturing for you, who am I to judge?"

Earnshaw's mouth formed an ugly smile. She stepped toward me, the floorboards creaking under her bulk.

When she snaked a forearm under my chin, I wasn't ready. Her second arm pressed down from above, and she lifted me straight out of the chair by my neck.

It was a guillotine choke, known in judo as *mae hadaka jime*. It could be applied two different ways: as a wind choke, that prevented air from reaching the lungs, or a blood choke, cutting off blood flow to the brain. Earnshaw opted for the wind choke, and the familiar feeling of not being able to breathe overtook me in a panicky wave.

The only thing I was missing was the water.

I wasn't sure how Hammett's technique would work on not breathing, but I tried it anyway.

It was a horrible failure. I squirmed and kicked, but the plastic ties kept me firmly in place. All I could do was wait to die.

"That's enough."

She didn't release me.

"Earnshaw, let her go."

She still didn't comply.

My ears started ringing. Darkness shaded the edges of my vision. I was vaguely aware of Heath extending a pistol, pointing above my head.

Earnshaw dropped me.

The chair's legs hit the floor with a *crack*. I sputtered and coughed but still couldn't get air, and for a moment I thought she might have crushed my trachea.

"It doesn't matter if you tell us about your sisters, Chandler. Our people already know where they are."

It took me several of seconds of coughing before I could croak out an answer. "Then why waste time asking?"

"I just wanted an excuse to talk to you."

Earnshaw circled me, her heavy steps creaking through the floorboards. "Kill her or I will."

"We're not going to kill her."

If I wasn't mistaken, I thought I actually heard a growl coming from deep in her throat.

"I'm calling The Instructor," she said.

"No, you're not. Chandler is our insurance policy, Earnshaw."

"Insurance?"

"Chandler is right about The Instructor. After today, he'll own us, and while that might not bother you, it's not happening to me."

Earnshaw looked from him to me, as if struggling to follow.

"Who better to blame for a terrorist act than a terrorist? Chandler already assassinated POTUS. After that, killing thousands of Mexicans is nothing."

Earnshaw frowned, as if she was still unconvinced, but at least she didn't give my neck another one of her bear hugs.

"You want to keep her here?" she asked.

"I think it's wise. Go get ready."

Once Earnshaw left the room, Heath leaned close, his breath tickling my ear. "The day I met you, I knew you were the only one who could keep up with me."

Unable to hit him or kick him or even give him a head-butt, I settled for spitting. I hit him in the neck, my dispatch sliding down over his collarbone.

He gave me a smile, totally unfazed, then lowered his lid in a wink.

Earnshaw clomped back into the room, carrying two loaded-down duffels and my backpack. "You're not going to just leave her zip-tied to the chair, are you?"

"No, I have something special planned."

He handed his pistol to Earnshaw, then pulled a knife from his belt and sliced through the ties binding my ankles to the chair.

"Stand up."

I hesitated, getting the feeling I wasn't going to like this one bit.

"Don't give Earnshaw a reason to shoot you."

I wasn't sure she would require much of a reason, but I decided to keep that comment to myself. Instead I pushed to my feet, my wrists still secured behind my back.

Heath shoved the chair clear, unzipped one of Earnshaw's duffels, and produced a bundle of the long, nylon ties. "Now let me see you demonstrate *vriksasana.*"

"Yoga?"

"What's the matter, Chandler? Not feeling Zen?"

I shifted my balance to my left foot, raised my right, and rested the sole against my inner thigh, toes pointing downward to my knee. I raised my chest and focused forward, my arms bound behind my back.

"Very nice."

Heath encircled my raised leg with one of the zip ties, tightening it until my calf and thigh were bound closely together, my knee at a sharp angle. Using another, he fastened my ankle to my thigh as well, locking me into a tree pose I couldn't escape. Then he dipped his hand back into the bag and pushed something into my hands.

Most of the object was composed of a sphere, a little over six centimeters in diameter and weighing approximately four hundred grams. I knew what it was before my fingers brushed the fuse mechanism at the top.

"Now get a good grip," Heath said. He gave the M67 grenade one last little tug and held up the pin for Earnshaw to see. "Think she'll get away so easily now?"

Earnshaw grunted and handed back his pistol.

"If you have stamina and strong muscles, *bonita*, you'll live long enough to take the blame for infecting Mexico City with the Ebola virus."

"And if I don't, I blow myself up."

Heath smiled. "You are used to risking your own life. That isn't enough to keep you in line. But apartment walls in Mexico are thin. I wouldn't be surprised if some of the neighbors joined you."

"You really are a heartless bastard," I said.

He leaned closer, his smile fading. "You hurt me."

"Not as much as I want to."

"And what if The Instructor keeps to his word, and we don't need someone to pin this on?" Earnshaw asked.

"Then I imagine, after some time, even the most hearty of stamina will run out." He ran a finger down the side of my face. "*Adios, querida.* Maybe I will see you again."

Arms already starting to cramp, I silently cursed the day he was born.

# Heath

*"Part of any operation is recognizing that every player has his or her own agenda," said The Instructor. "The better you are at discerning the aims of others, the better your chances of using them to get exactly what you want."*

"I know you want to fuck her," Earnshaw said the moment the apartment door closed behind them. She carried two bags, one filled with weapons and equipment, the other with her disguise for today, and despite the obvious weight of the former, she hefted it as if it were nothing.

Heath groaned inwardly. "Earnshaw. Such language coming from a lady."

"I know you do. I could break her over my knee like a stick."

"You are indeed a formidable woman."

"But you don't look at me like you look at her."

Of course he didn't. No one was that good an actor.

"I am but a man, with a man's weaknesses."

"Meaning you're a pig."

Heath wasn't going to argue with that.

He slipped on a baseball cap and sunglasses, and Earnshaw did the same. Then they caught a cab and ordered it to drop them at Benito Juárez International Airport, where Earnshaw stashed everything they didn't immediately need in a secure metal locker in the baggage storage area. Heath kept few things beyond his Sig Sauer, Chandler's backpack, and cash, then he paid for a month's rental on the locker, the maximum allowed. He and Earnshaw wouldn't go near the equipment again. But better to let the authorities find it eventually, than for weapons to get into the hands of children by discarding it in the street.

After grabbing a coffee in silence, they caught another cab, and Heath directed the cabbie to take them to the Plaza de Toros México.

Earnshaw hadn't said a word since her accusation, and the last thing Heath needed was for her to be feeling all angry and resentful toward him going into this operation. He had to say something to smooth things over.

The trick was figuring out what.

"Chandler doesn't have anything to do with what I feel for you."

It was true enough. Where Heath found Chandler unspeakably hot, he barely tolerated Earnshaw, and on some days, not even that.

She knotted up her lips and stared out the window.

"I simply knew her in the past."

She turned to look at him. "I know."

He raised a brow.

"The Instructor told me."

"Did he?"

"After you didn't kill her in Maine…" Earnshaw shook her head, the beads decorating the ends of her braids clicking against one another. "I had to know what that was about."

"So you checked up on me."

"You'd do the same."

He might, but he wouldn't go through The Instructor. "He told you to keep an eye on me?"

"Yes."

"And report back to him?"

She nodded.

"And take me out if I got out of line?"

"Yes."

"And have I done anything out of line, Earnshaw?"

"Not until now."

"And what did I do now that was so bad?"

"You should have killed her."

"Then we wouldn't know what we know now."

"And what is that? That she knew where to find us? What good does that do?"

"It's always good to know what your enemy knows. Especially if it involves a breach in your security. You learned that the first day of training."

"Bullshit. You didn't have the cojones to kill Chandler, so you left her death up to chance like some damn movie villain."

"I left nothing to chance."

She shook her head, sending her braids flying. "I care for you, Heath. I think you know that. But I know who butters my bread here, and it's not you. It's The Instructor."

"I've never doubted your loyalty. Why are you doubting mine?"

"Because I saw how you look at her."

"And how is that?"

"Exactly the way I want you to look at me."

"Perhaps I would, if you trusted me."

Earnshaw turned away from him and stared out the window.

Heath looked ahead, over the cabbie's shoulder, but hardly noticed the swerving cars or heard the traffic cops' whistles and salsa music blaring through the open window of the next car. He didn't like being so transparent, especially not to a *bruta* like Earnshaw, and in the back of his mind he worried that seeing Chandler had thrown him off his game.

"I will play my role. You will spy on me for The Instructor. Chandler will take care of herself. I promise."

She answered with another grunt.

"We're almost there. You'd better get ready."

She heaved a sigh and then pulled her top over her head. She wasn't wearing a bra, and the cabbie swerved a little, too busy watching her bare breasts to pay attention to traffic. She stripped off her pants as well, then dressed in a long, full skirt in red, orange, and dark green and covered in sequins. A white peasant blouse completed the outfit. In addition to a tourist look that would blend right in at the bullfight, the full skirt gave Earnshaw plenty of fabric to conceal a .44 Magnum and the Ka-Bar knife she always carried, a lucky charm she'd won by beating a Marine at arm wrestling.

Heath pulled on his black vest and red sash, and they were both dressed by the time they reached the Plaza de Toros México. While he paid the driver, she drifted into the crowd spilling from the festival and lining up at the ticket windows.

He took Chandler's backpack and made straight for the gate, ready to put the final touches on the bullring and wait for his chance to put the plan in motion.

So The Instructor was suspicious. But the old man didn't see everything. If he had, he'd have given Earnshaw the order to kill Heath long ago. Because by the time either of them had figured out what Heath really had in mind, it would be too late.

# Julie

The end came quickly for Derek's sister, and Derek and Julie witnessed it all. The mottled bruises covered nearly every inch of her skin. The whites of her eyes turned bright red, and she started coughing. In minutes the spittle was blood, and she was vomiting. The blood kept coming, blood pooling between muscle and skin, filling like a water balloon.

And finally her eyes grew dark, blank, and Julie could sense she was gone.

Mercifully gone.

Derek cried, and his tears were pink with blood.

Julie pounded on the locked laboratory door, begging The Instructor, someone, anyone, for something to help with Derek's pain.

No one came.

So Julie did the only thing she could; she held his hand, held it until he passed, only letting go when his skin began to slough off.

By the time Derek finally died, Julie's heart felt hard as a stone block. She swore, if it was within her power, to never let this happen to anyone else.

Never.

# Fleming

*"War is about casualties, not prisoners," The Instructor said. "Spare no one."*

Fleming parked on a side street a block away from where Rhett, Scarlett, and Bradley were holed up. She closed the Hydra window on her laptop where their tracker dots blinked, and tied Sasha to the van's outside door handle, taking a measure of solace that if she didn't return, someone would find the fox.

She figured, with the element of surprise, and a lot of luck, she had a nine percent chance of getting out of there alive, with Bradley.

But nine percent was a chance worth taking.

Fleming placed the five-pound bag of ice she'd gotten at a fast-food drive-through on her lap, and used a series of pneumatic pulleys to lower the boxlike steel enclosure around her reinforced wheelchair, snapped it into place atop motorcycle shocks, and rolled down the ramps and into the empty parking lot.

The chair weighed three times as much as it once did, due to the quarter-inch steel enclosure that now surrounded it. A two-stroke engine, geared to her right wheel and venting out the rear, was attached to a throttle on her armrest. She saw through a thin, eye-level slit. Her shotgun barrel fit through a small hole on the left, her Skorpion a hole on the right.

Fleming had fashioned her wheelchair into a tank, capable of withstanding small-arms fire and buckshot and speeds up to twenty kilometers per hour. It had a few other bells and whistles as well, including a compressed air mortar packed with metal screws. She was ready to kick some ass.

As long as there weren't any stairs.

Fortunately, Fleming's research revealed the address didn't seem to have stairs. It was an abandoned factory in an industrial strip, situated between Perkins Farm and the west bank of Lake Quinsigamond. Surrounded by trees, the property was formerly owned by an abrasives and ceramics manufacturer that went bankrupt years earlier. Twenty thousand square feet, with thirty-foot ceilings, it seemed like an odd place to stash a hostage.

She rolled up Atlas Street, approaching from the south, passing a lot filled with a dozen old freight containers, and coming to a tall fence cordoning off the property. Through the narrow view of her eye slit, the factory looked neglected, complete with a rusty gate and weeds growing through the cracks in the parking lot. But the chain and lock on the gate were shiny and new, and steam billowed out of one of the smokestacks near the back of the building.

For facing certain death, Fleming was surprisingly calm. In control of her heart rate, her breathing. Her mind focused. Her senses on full alert. Technically, this was the first mission she'd been on since Milan. So many times, she'd dreamed of going into the field again, both figuratively and literally. At the top of her game, she'd been as good as Chandler and Hammett. Capable. Resourceful. Deadly. When that was taken away from her, she'd remained relevant. Using brainpower instead of firepower—to a degree none of her sisters could match. But the desire to go on an actual operation, rather than coach from the sidelines, had always been on her mind.

*We lament what we've lost, not what we still have.*

Now was her chance. A slim chance, but more than she thought she'd ever get. And this was a mission she actually cared about. Fleming wasn't trying to silence some diplomat or kill a despot.

This was Operation Save Bradley. Something that mattered.

Her days of being a mindless weapon were over. So were her days of using her brain to assist shady people who worked for shady organizations with shady goals.

Fleming was about to do something simply because it was the right thing to do.

It felt good. Damn good.

Even if it was pretty much guaranteed to kill her.

She opened the hinged front flap of her steel enclosure, leaning forward through the opening and using a lock pick and tension wrench on the padlock. Thirty seconds later she was heading for the loading bay behind the warehouse, keeping an eye out for surveillance cams. She found one, top corner of the building under the gutter, and shredded it with a fléchette round.

Now they knew she was here. It was on.

Fleming racked the shotgun, and put it in its holding clamp, barrel pointing out through the balistraria, and waited for Rhett and Scarlett to appear.

The problem was, they didn't.

But a dozen guards armed with submachine guns did.

# Isolde

*"Sending others to die in combat isn't easy," The Instructor said. "But it beats dying yourself."*

"She's shooting," Izzy said to Tristan. Her thin legs were burning from working the rudders, and she was pissed off that one of those bitch sisters had hitched a ride on her airship. Her hope had been to rise high enough to freeze their unwelcome guest, but that plan changed when faced with shotguns.

"What do you want me to do about it? Yell at her to stop?"

"Go out and get her," she said.

Tristan stared at her like a dog who didn't understand a command. He was sitting behind Izzy in the first of eight passenger seats, his oversize frame barely fitting. Behind him, blocking the rear window view, was the Ebola tank, attached to the outside of the gondola via lift bolts and three thick chains.

The shotgun blasts continued.

"Shouldn't we land first?" Tristan said.

"We won't be able to land if she crashes us. You're not afraid, are you?"

Tristan shrugged, then walked to the cabin door. He opened it up, looking at the rope ladder twisting in the wind, hanging at least two meters away.

"When I kill her, how do I get back in?"

"I'm landing right now," Izzy said. "But you need to take her out before she does too much damage."

Tristan nodded, then crouched at the cabin entrance and leaped out into open air, grabbing the ladder with one hand.

Izzy offered a rare smile. She would have bet even odds he'd miss. But that big bastard had some slick moves.

She hit the air intake, filling the ballonets, beginning their descent. This little detour was a pain in the ass, but not that big of an inconvenience. They still had plenty of time to kill a half million people.

Ground zero for a pandemic. Someone would write books about this day.

That is, if there was anyone left.

# Hammett

*"Always remember to look behind you," The Instructor said.*

These blimps were made of some seriously tough shit, thick rubber and polyester fabric, stronger than steel. It took Hammett all of her fléchette rounds, and all but three of her piranha rounds, to make a hole in the top of the envelope big enough to climb into. That left her the armor-piercing shells to blast through the bottom, into the gondola. She also had the fire-spitting dragon's breath rounds left, some regular shells, and her Mateba autorevolver. No doubt her opponents were armed, but probably not as well armed as she was.

Hammett got on her knees, took a big breath, and stuck her head into the hole, using the flashlight to check out what the inside of a blimp looked like. Not surprisingly, there was a lot of empty space. A fall straight down to the bottom—a twenty-meter drop—would break her legs, if not kill her. Luckily, there were several thick suspension cables that hooked into the catenary curtain at the top of the envelope, and extended down to where the gondola was. The nearest was a few feet away, on a steep angle. If Hammett could reach it, she'd be able to slide down and—

The first bullet hit her in the back, right over her heart, and was followed in rapid succession by three others before her body reacted and she rolled over. Unable to take a breath, Hammett flattened her belly against the top of the blimp and watched, horrified, as her duffel bag fell into the hole and disappeared into the darkness.

# Chandler

*"Sometimes the motives of others are not clear," said The Instructor. "And that's when you have to see past the obfuscation of their words and judge purely on actions."*

The opposite of a fail-safe, a fail-deadly system is designed to be lethal in the case of a failure. But even as the time ticked by and the cramp in my arms spread to my spine and my legs and my feet, something nagged at the back of my mind and wouldn't let go.

Operatives in the Hydra program were trained to perform their duties quickly, efficiently, and without moral confusion. I'd been a great example of that clarity of thinking my entire career, until recent events turned my life upside down. From that point, I'd struggled. I'd been erratic. I'd let my emotions take over at times.

But what was Heath's excuse?

Since I'd met him, he'd enjoyed talking about how we were alike, and I'd mostly chalked that up to his desire to get in my pants. But today, Earnshaw had been right. He should have killed me in the street. Instead he pretended to question me, then rigged me in this position with a grenade and left. It didn't make sense. If Heath had confused me before, he totally discombobulated me now.

Unless there was a reason he didn't want me to die. A reason that went far beyond sexual attraction. And if he didn't want me to die for some reason, he would know I'd never wait patiently for his return while holding this damn M67.

What in the hell was he up to?

I concentrated on the pain seizing my muscles, imagining it flowing out through my elbow, visualizing each muscle group relaxing, staying perfectly balanced, mind over matter. This time, Hammett's trick worked, and as the pain abated, my breathing slowed, my mind cleared.

I could still hear the television next door and smell tamales. Pigeons fluttered outside the window, and I almost felt like I was back in my old apartment in Chicago, the city where I'd first seen Heath, although at that time, I hadn't caught a glimpse of his face.

In fact, I hadn't realized at first that he was a threat. He had all the body language down. The small movements and attitudes that had convinced me he was a civilian, that he was doing exactly what he seemed to be doing. In that case, shopping on Michigan Avenue.

In this case...

I skimmed my fingers over the grenade, up the fuse mechanism, until...

There it was. The grenade's pin and safety clip. Both still in place. The pin he'd brandished to convince Earnshaw hadn't belonged to this grenade at all.

Focusing on the portrait of *La Virgen de Guadalupe*, I hopped across the floor, then turned around, back to the wall, and eased the grenade onto the votive shelf beneath the painting.

Once free of the explosive, I lowered myself to a sitting position on the floor and worked my leg and foot until, little by little, the zip ties slid toward my knee, then off completely. Without the tie binding my thigh and calf, the ankle fastener was easier to escape, and once I had my feet, all that was left was locating a sharp edge on the windowsill and sawing my wrist binding across it until it was thin enough to break.

They'd left nothing in the apartment, not even a used tissue, so I picked up the grenade and slipped it into one of the thigh pockets in my cargo pants, then I was out the door and down five flights of rickety wooden stairs. Outside, I ran five blocks before I was able to flag down a green-and-white Beetle. I yanked open the door and barked out, "Plaza Mexico," before my butt hit the seat, adding, "*Rápidamente*," for good measure.

Traffic was crazy, as always, and as we threaded through the streets and merged and switched lanes while zooming around roundabouts, I tried to picture what I knew of the plaza in my mind's eye and plan the best gate to enter. It took me a few blocks to notice my cabbie was slowing down, and he'd taken a detour.

"Le Plaza," I repeated, although I knew it wouldn't do any good.

He turned around to face me with a little snub-nose revolver in one trembling fist. "Your money," he said in decent English.

"Really? Now?"

"Money or I shoot."

Heath and Earnshaw had left far too long ago, and the bullfight was already starting. I *did not* have the patience for this. "Sure, anything you want."

I dipped my head down as if pulling out my cash, then moving fast, I shot my left hand up, grabbed his, twisted the barrel to the side, and jabbed the fingers of my right hand straight into his eyes.

He released the gun and bellowed. Clutching his face with one hand, he clawed with the other, trying to get ahold of me over the seat.

"Na-uh," I said and focused the gun on him. "Out of the car. Now."

He didn't move. "*Puta.* There are no bullets."

"No bullets?"

"They are *muy expensivo.*"

I didn't know if he was bluffing or not, but I didn't want to chance a look, not while I was within his reach.

So I drew back the gun and hit him.

His head snapped back, and he let loose with a flood of obscenities. I hit him again, and he slumped against the seat. Convinced he was no longer in shape to quickly drive away, I climbed out of the backseat, opened the driver's door, and dragged him out onto the pavement. Then I slipped behind the wheel, shifted into gear, and accelerated into traffic.

Weaving through a gaggle of crazy drivers, I checked the revolver, but he had been telling the truth. No bullets.

Maybe that's why he was robbing me: to buy some.

The fake cabbie had cost me time, but at least I had wheels, and in the ashtray he had a small roll of cash he'd probably stolen from some poor tourists. I stuffed it into my pocket and focused on the road.

Getting anywhere in Mexico City was easier said than done, and the rest of the drive was an endless string of frustrations. Finally the Plaza Mexico rose ahead. I screeched around a sharp turn into a side street flanking the stadium and stopped.

I sprinted out of the cab, leaving it in the street, and raced toward the bowl-shaped ring. Amid honking horns, a trumpet sounded, high and clear, the signal for the beginning of the fight itself or one of the three stages within. Since Heath was working as an *arenero*, I had to assume the attack would come between bulls, when the *areneros* would be tending the ring.

Ironically, or perhaps not, much of what I knew about bullfighting, I'd learned from Heath himself before I became aware he was an operative.

There are three stages in a bullfight. In the first the *picadors*, men mounted on padded and blindfolded horses, wear down the bull by inciting him to attack them and plunging their lances into the bull's neck.

The second stage belongs to the *banderillero*, who runs toward the bull on foot and plunges barbed darts decorated with colorful ribbons into the bull's neck.

It isn't until the *tercio de muerte* or third of death, that the matador takes center ring and performs a series of passes with his cape. That's when the chants of olé would start, the countdown to the bull's death. Today that death would be followed by many, many more, if I failed to stop it.

I had to hurry.

The entire area around the bullfighting ring was vibrating with energy. Concession carts lined every available space. Smells of food mixed with heavy exhaust. Cheers exploded from the arena.

I bought a ticket at the window using cash from the cabbie's stash. I didn't want to draw attention to myself, and I figured security would be watching the walls much more closely than earlier today when the plaza was closed.

Chants of olé started before I could get through the gate.

The matador was clearly in the ring and had started his passes. The *tercio de muerte* had begun, and once the bull was dead, the *areneros* would make their entrance.

I made it through the gate and the metal detector that spectators were required to pass through. Rushing by signs directing spectators to *de sombra* and *de sol*, the shade and the sun sections of the grandstands, and past statues of notable men and portraits of the sport, I wound my way back to the business areas of the plaza, the entrances to the bulls' pens and the ring itself. A security guard stood in my way, guarding against the matador's groupies, no doubt. But if American rock stars taught us anything at all, it was that not all groupies were kept away from their idols.

"*¡Olé!*"

I sidled up to the guard. He was younger than ideal, and it occurred to me that he'd probably see me more as a desperate cougar than anything else, especially since many matadors would be still in high school if they lived in the States. But maybe that in itself gave me something to work with.

And if manipulation didn't do the trick, I had other ways of dealing with him.

"*¡Olé!*"

Again I spoke in serviceable Spanish, but let a Texas accent bleed through and my voice lilt as if with a touch of too much tequila. "I was wondering if you could help me."

He shot me a look of obvious skepticism, but he didn't seem uninterested. "I will try."

"I want to meet a real matador. Are they down there?" I pointed down the ramp.

"I'm sorry. That area is restricted. You must go back to your seat."

I toyed with the sleeve of his uniform with my fingertips. "But it would be the highlight of my vacation. Please. It would mean a lot."

"I'm sorry."

Just my luck. I found a man who couldn't be seduced, at least not easily. Problem was, I didn't have the time to do it properly. With each shouted *olé*, the crowd counted down to their own deaths.

Time to try a different tack.

I slipped the rest of the cabbie's cash from my pocket and flashed a few hundred pesos. "I won't cause trouble. I promise."

He eyed the cash, his face hard. For a long moment, I thought he was going to refuse and force me to kill him. Then he plucked the *dinero* from my fingers. "You sneaked in. I never saw you."

"Thanks." I ran down the ramp before he could have an attack of conscience.

The bowels of the bullring were cramped and hot. Even before I reached the bottom of the ramp, sweat had slicked my back, and I longed for fresh air.

The ramp ended at a small, empty garage-like area. The odor of exhaust lingered, and I scanned the area twice before spotting the chute leading up to the arena.

"¡*Olé!*"

The crowd erupted into frenzied cheers, the stands thundering overhead. I could only guess, but my money said the matador had made his fatal strike. The celebration of a good kill seemed to be exploding overhead, and that meant as soon as all the roses and hats thrown into the ring were removed, Heath would be smoothing and spraying down the surface to control dust.

Spraying, that was the key.

I still didn't know what part he intended me to play, but I had my own objective, and if his didn't fit with mine, I wouldn't hesitate to take him out.

I moved up the chute toward sunlight, finding myself in an area surrounding the ring itself. To my right, the bull corrals. Horses claimed the other side of the ring, but many of them were already in the ring, the *picadors'* mounts dressed in padding that resembled quilted mattress covers.

In the ring the *picadors* and *banderilleros* carried the matador in a victory lap, their huge sombreros bobbing into view. I scanned the area, looking for a tractor, a truck, or an ATV that might be used to smooth and water the ring.

Then I spotted it, on the other side of the bulls, a small pickup idling at a gate, waiting for the celebration to close. It was the truck Heath had been driving earlier, the tank still filling the truck bed and the drag harrow trailing from the back. As the vehicle drove around the arena, it would spray a mist of water to control dust and rake the surface smooth.

Only I had a strong feeling it wasn't water in that tank.

I sprinted through the walkway between the ring and the first-row seats. The celebration passed me on the inside of the ring, the crowd roaring around me, sombreros, roses, and upstretched arms blocking my view of the truck. I dodged my way through groups of people, running as fast as I could. Almost there.

A large man wearing a huge hat, and for some odd reason, a red-sequined skirt, jutted out in front of me, blocking my path.

"*Disculpa.*"

He didn't move. I put my hand on the small of his back, giving him a shove. He turned around, and I realized it wasn't a man.

I was staring into the brutal face of Earnshaw.

Honest mistake. And holy shit.

I leaped for the wall, caught the top with my hands, and pulled myself up until my hips balanced on the edge.

She went for my legs, and I knew if she grabbed me, I was dead.

I twisted and kicked, stomping her in the jaw just as her hands hit my ankles. Blood gushed from her nose and slicked her face, and I flipped over the wall before she could get a hold and landed on my feet in the dirt.

The truck had just passed, and I launched into a run after it. The sandy surface churned beneath the scarifying blades and smoothed under the finishing bars dragging behind, but I couldn't see any spray coming from the tank. Not yet.

A startled *arenero* looked up from his rake, then stared past me, eyes wide. Behind, I could hear a low bellow, and I didn't have to look over my shoulder to know that Earnshaw had made it over the wall and was in pursuit. I could only hope her broken nose and battered face would slow her down.

But I damn well wouldn't bet on it.

Willing my legs to move faster, I caught up to the drag harrow and leaped onto the finishing bars. Keeping my feet moving, I scrambled up the drag and onto the framework of blades. One slip, and I'd be shredded, my flesh left in bloody ribbons. The tank peered down at me from the truck's bed, ready to spray at Heath's command. I was immune to the virus, but with the flick of a switch, he could make the tines too slick for me to keep my balance.

Yet he didn't.

Pushing aside a barrage of questions, I climbed up the rig, hand over hand, foot beside foot, until I reached the truck bed. Stealing a glance over my shoulder, I saw that Earnshaw had reached the rear of the drag and was pulling herself up on it and toward me.

The Ebola tank took up the entire space, so draping my body over the smooth curve, I tiptoed along the edge of the truck box. The pickup swerved. My right foot slipped. Pulse thumping in my ears at the close call, I managed to pull myself back up and make it to the cab.

Struggling to balance, I kicked the driver's window. The impact shuddered up my leg, but the glass remained intact. I kicked it again. And once more.

Glass shattered, falling from the window frame in pebbles.

I reached through the space, meaning to rake my fingers across Heath's face, disabling him long enough to slip into the truck. But I grasped nothing but air.

The vehicle swerved toward the wall, and suddenly I was flying forward. I hit the dirt, breath whooshing from my lungs before my mind caught up to the realization that Heath had hit the wall.

No, not the wall. A gate.

The wooden *burladero*, meant to shield the gate, wasn't strong enough to stand up to a truck, and it splintered in front of the truck's left fender, the gate behind bent inward, off its hinges.

The truck revved, and I could sense it backing up, or at least trying to, but just as I struggled to my feet, Earnshaw slammed into me.

I flew forward. Somehow keeping my legs under me, I outpaced her momentum like a star running back, leaving her falling to the ground, grasping but not gripping. Her skirt fell down around her legs, binding them like shackles, and revealing a pink thong that on her looked downright wrong.

The truck door slammed behind me, and for a second I assumed Heath would join in our fight, or simply pull a gun and end me. Instead, he circled to the drag and started unhitching it from the truck.

Not that I could worry about him long, because Earnshaw was coming at me once again.

After getting a taste of her strength back at the apartment, I was not eager to let her get a hold of me. As strong as I was, she was stronger, and I believed every bit of Heath's comment about crippling being the only thing that had kept her out of the Olympics.

I danced backward like a featherweight boxer trying to fight Tyson. I hit her in the side of the head with a quick snap kick, too fast for her to respond, yet what I gained in quickness, I lost in power.

She didn't blink, just hunkered in low, ready to grab my foot if I tried the same trick again.

A large mass moved to my right. Not Earnshaw. There was something else in the ring with us.

Earnshaw's eyes flicked to the side. "Oh, shit."

At first I thought it might be a trick, a way to throw me off my guard. Then the mass moved closer, and I gave in and took a peek just in time to see a gray-and-white-dappled bull stop along the fence and turn in our direction.

His horns spread from his head, hooking at the end to point their sharp tips at us. Shoulders as tall as mine, the animal was massive, easily bigger than the two of us combined. Hell, he was bigger than two of the two of us combined, maybe three.

"That's a lot of bull," I said.

The beast lowered his head and charged.

# Hammett

*"In a fight to the death," The Instructor said, "don't be the one who dies."*

*Oh, shit*, Hammett thought as she watched Tristan finish climbing the rope ladder up the blimp. He stood to his full height and shrugged his shoulders in his armless T-shirt, the best muscles money could buy popping and undulating in his arms and chest. That was scary enough on its own. But it was especially scary a thousand feet in the air when Hammett had no weapon other than a tactical flashlight.

*I survived Niagara Falls, only to be killed by some musclehead on top of a blimp.*

Hammett undulated her diaphragm, forcing in a breath, her ribs screaming. She didn't think the bullets had penetrated her Kevlar, but it felt like the shots had broken a few more ribs, and perhaps her scapula. Wincing at the pain, she forced herself onto all fours, and then her feet, lifting her hands above her head in surrender. She quickly formulated a plan, which was easily the worst plan she ever hatched, but she really had no other options.

Above the roar of the bitterly cold wind, she yelled, "I'm unarmed!"

She turned a slow circle, showing she had no hidden weapons, feeling at any moment the head shot would end her.

Oddly, it didn't. So far so good.

"You need a gun to take me, big man?" she called.

He didn't answer, didn't drop the gun, and continued to close the distance until he stood a meter away.

"I get it," Hammett said. "You've taken so many steroids, the only way you can handle a woman is with a gun. Cock doesn't work anymore?"

Tristan had been trained by The Instructor and should be impervious to taunts. Even though he was easily twice Hammett's weight, he had to know how dangerous she was. He wasn't going to risk fighting her. The smart thing to do was put two in her head and then kick her to the earth below.

But then he gave Hammett the biggest surprise of her life and holstered his pistol.

"Never raped anyone on a blimp before," he said. "Maybe I'll give it to you as I break your neck."

Hammett almost laughed. He was giving her a chance. Granted, the chance was slim, but it was a better deal than she'd had a few seconds earlier.

"Promises, promises," she said, and winked. "Come get me, big boy."

He rolled his shoulders, looking a lot like a CG version of the Hulk minus the green skin, and then stepped forward and lashed out with his right leg.

For a huge man, Tristan was extremely fast. Hammett couldn't dodge the kick in time, and blocking it full-on meant broken bones, so she turned and stepped away, absorbing a glancing impact on her shoulder. Her arm instantly went numb, and she was knocked onto her back. She managed to use the momentum to roll to her feet again, standing on wobbly tiptoes against the curving slope of the blimp's edge. One more step back and she'd slide off and make a big spot on Toronto.

Tristan advanced, a smirk on his face, his Asian eyes narrowing to slits and making him look like a homicidal Buddha. If Buddha had spent his life in a gym instead of meditating.

Hammett buried the pain, the fear, and launched herself at the giant.

He raised an arm to block, and Hammett dropped to one knee under it, swinging an uppercut between his legs, connecting with everything she had. She immediately followed by dropping to a push-up position, then donkey kicking her left leg up and planting her boot into Tristan's face.

He was a tree, not budging at all, but Hammett heard him grunt and knew she'd hurt him. Reaching up, she grabbed for his holster.

He caught her left wrist, twisted, and snapped her arm as easily as if it were a pencil.

Hammett screamed, anticipating the pain, howling as it came on and hit like a locomotive. She gritted her teeth as Tristan pulled her to her feet by her broken appendage and dangled her in front of him. A cat toying with a mouse.

His nose was bleeding, and his amused expression had turned sour.

"Did I miss your balls?" Hammett said through her clenched jaw. "Tough to hit such a small target."

Then she struck with the tactical flashlight, aiming for his eye. He flinched in time, lowering his head, but the flashlight was heavy and solid and ripped a nice gash in his forehead.

He roared, throwing Hammett to the side.

She rolled twice over the top of the blimp, and then she went over the edge and was sliding, face-first, into Canada.

# Chandler

*"When it comes to fighting, there's more to it than brute force," said The Instructor. "But if brute force gets ahold of you, make sure you're slippery."*

As the bull started toward us, Earnshaw stepped backward, as if she was going to run for the wall. I was about to do the same, when her left knee snapped up and drilled the inside of my thigh, just missing the grenade in my pocket, but hitting my femoral nerve.

Hits and kicks aren't common in grappling, and I wasn't expecting the move. My mistake. Pain shot up my leg, the limb collapsed under me, and for a few seconds, I was unable to react. Hell, I was unable to think. All I could do was lie there and wait for the deathblow.

But instead of finishing me off, Earnshaw whirled around and stepped to the side just as the bull lowered his head. His horn caught the side of her skirt. The fabric ripped, and he continued past, missing her and me.

The bull's pass gave me time to recover, and I struggled to my feet before either he or Earnshaw could come at me again. Good thing I did. In seconds, Earnshaw was back to hunkering low, focused on me, as if the bull wasn't a factor. Beyond her, I could see Heath unhooking the drag and returning to the truck cab, not lifting a finger to help defend his partner from the bull or from me.

Again I wondered what he was up to, why he seemed so content to let me live to cause trouble. Not that I could ponder long, as Earnshaw started toward me, looking for an opening.

I gave her a shifting target, relying on speed and footwork to keep my distance. Although I wasn't in Earnshaw's league, I had trained in judo. As a result, I could read her position and had enough of a feel for the way she would attack that I could avoid the traps she set.

Still, I was fighting from a totally defensive position. I needed to find a way to attack, or I wouldn't last long. Since with each strike, I was offering her a foot or hand, kicks and hits were risky. I had to find a way to beat her at her own game.

The bull turned back around and lowered his head again, pawing at the ground.

She came at me executing *morote-gari*, going for my legs. My every impulse said to back away. Instead, I shifted to the side, stepping my right leg back and out of her grasp. At the same time I pushed her head down, drilled my full weight down on her shoulders, planting her on hands and knees in the dirt, only one of my legs encircled by her beefy arms.

The bull started his charge.

With Earnshaw holding my left leg, I had nowhere to go. "Bull!" I yelled.

She glanced up at me. Blood covered her mouth and chin, and when she smiled, her teeth glistened red.

If I released my downward pressure on her shoulders, she would be able to spring to her feet. But that didn't mean she would try to escape the oncoming bull. In fact, she didn't seem to care about the bull at all.

If I let her up, she would kill me. If I stayed I would be gored.

For a second, I thought about pulling out the grenade. The only problem was the explosion wouldn't just kill Earnshaw and the bull, it would kill me, too, and maybe others. And once I was dead, there would be no one left to stop Heath.

My fingers closed over the bright red, orange, and green fabric of her skirt. I gave it a yank. The tear the bull had started widened and the seam gave. With one more mighty tug, I tore the garment from Earnshaw's body.

Spotted gray-and-white barreled toward us, those sharp horns leading the way. A few steps more and…

I fumbled the fabric, gripping the waistband and holding the skirt out to the side.

The bull's focus shifted toward the bright colors, and he plowed straight through, coming close enough for me to feel the radiant glow of his body heat.

"*¡Olé!*"

The cheer rippled through the crowd.

I hardly had time to notice, as I was soaring through the air from an Earnshaw toss. I landed on my back, hitting the dirt hard, then scrambling back to my feet. Just as I did, Earnshaw came at me again. Naked but for a peasant blouse and pink lace thong, she reached for the ceramic knife strapped to one thigh and charged.

I stepped to the side, avoiding her at the last moment, but this time pain ripped along my forearm followed by icy cold.

Shit. I was cut.

Letting the pain flow wherever the hell it wanted, I didn't spare my arm a glance but kept all my attention on Earnshaw and the bull. If I couldn't figure out a way to fend off both of the beasts and stop Heath, a cut on my arm would be the least of my problems.

Grasping the skirt in both hands, I whipped the heavy fabric around in front of me like a matador wielding his *capote* in a serpentine motion, my left arm compensating for the weakness in my right.

Earnshaw danced back and forth, looking for a window of attack through the whirling cloth. The bull stared at us and lowered his head for another charge, and in my peripheral vision, I could see the truck moving away from us, circling the perimeter of the ring.

Earnshaw struck first, charging with the blade, and I stepped to the side, letting her thrust behind me into the skirt.

"*¡Olé!*" the crowd cheered. And just for the hell of it I executed a *rebolera*—a flourish where I swished the skirt behind my back.

Now it was the bull's turn. I kept the skirt at chest height, performing a *pase de pecho* as the bull breezed underneath. He bucked his head upward as he passed through the skirt and barely missed Earnshaw on the other side.

"*¡Olé!*"

Earnshaw circled me, her center of gravity low, the knife ready. I kept the makeshift *capa* moving, fabric whirling between us as my shield.

Voices erupted, not just cheers this time, but menacing yells, and I saw uniforms gathering on the other side of the main gate into the ring, and the bull doing a rollback and heading our way.

Earnshaw struck high this time, her hand finding my shoulder, her hip turning into me, as if she intended to use a *harai goshi* throw to take me down. I grasped her shoulder in an attempt to stay on my feet, still gripping the skirt, the colorful fabric billowing over her shoulder.

The bull lowered his head and plunged his horns into the skirt.

Breath exploded from Earnshaw's lungs and she was ripped away from me and thrown to the dirt. I flew to the side, falling to a knee before recovering to see the bull bucking his head, drilling his horns into her, then under her, tossing her in the air as if she weighed no more than a supermodel. She landed on her side, her head twisted and looking up at the sky, her eyelids fluttering, still alive.

The bull raced a few meters before turning for another pass.

Launching into a dead run, I scooped Earnshaw's knife from the arena floor. In one motion, I slashed her throat, severing carotid, trachea, and esophagus.

The bull started his next charge, and this time, his target was me.

The truck lurched to a stop in front of me, barely missing Earnshaw's body. Heath flung open the passenger door. "Get in!"

I leaped into the truck.

The bull slammed into the door, making the vehicle shudder.

"Go, go, go!" I yelled, but I needn't have bothered. Heath was already stomping the accelerator. The wheels spun and swerved, dirt spraying behind us. The truck shot for the gate.

We hit the barrier without slowing down, slamming it open. Security officers and police who had gathered outside jumped to the side, a few squeezing off shots after us, apparently unconcerned about hitting the crowd.

I hoped none of those bullets had penetrated the tank in back.

Rubber screeching pavement, Heath raced through the plaza and rocketed out onto the street. He wove between traffic like a racecar driver suffering from dementia, making me grip the door and dashboard, willing the truck to not roll and cover the streets with Ebola. Amazingly we didn't suffer even a fender bender, and by the time the cops had a chance to get to their cars, we were long gone.

We hit the highway, the fastest track out of the city and into the surrounding mountains.

"You…" I struggled to catch my breath. "You came back for me."

"Of course."

"Why not kill me? Or let the authorities deal with me?"

"I don't want to kill you, Chandler. Haven't you figured that out yet?"

Of course I had. I just hadn't nailed down why. Or maybe the question wasn't why. Maybe it was more about what. Namely what he wanted me to do for him.

Now that made sense.

"You used me to kill your partner."

"It was convenient."

I thought about my warning to him that The Instructor might be setting him up. "And you needed a fall guy."

"Yes."

The last piece slid into place in my mind. It was so obvious; I didn't know why I hadn't seen it before.

"Because if I got my hands on the virus, I would destroy it. If The Instructor believes I took it, you think you're home free."

A smile curved his lips, wind from the broken driver's window playing with his hair.

"I don't think I've ever met anyone so arrogant. Except maybe my sister Hammett."

"She must be a lovely girl."

"She's a psychopath," I said. "He'll find out eventually, you know."

He shrugged a shoulder. "By the time he does, I'll have my boot on his throat and it will be too late."

"Too late for what?"

"Him and his power grab. The power will be all mine."

"Heath, what are you planning?"

His smile grew until it was an all-out beam. "*Querida*, I am going to change the world."

# Hammett

*"Sometimes anger is the only thing keeping you alive,"*
*The Instructor said.*

Hammett slid on her chest over the side of the blimp, caught a glimpse of the rope ladder as she fell, and managed to snag it with her good hand.

She dangled there, unable to pull herself up, barely able to take a breath with so many broken ribs. Her arm hurt as bad as anything she'd ever felt, and there was so much adrenaline buzzing in her system, she couldn't concentrate enough to push the pain away.

Hammett considered letting go. It would be a quick, certain death. She'd have failed the mission, but the more she thought about it, the more an Ebola outbreak appealed to her. Human beings didn't deserve this world. Let the dogs have it.

She peered down at the ground, ready to drop, but she couldn't force her hand to open. Her will to live was too strong, her training too ingrained.

Before she could try again, she was being lifted. That asshole, Tristan, was hauling her up the side of the blimp.

"I'm not done with you yet," he said, blood from his forehead gash dribbling into his closed eye.

Hammett smiled. "That just sweet talk, or can you man up and show me?"

He put his hands around her throat, and she lashed out with her good hand, slapping his head, smearing blood into his other eye and trying to blind him. He continued to squeeze, cutting off her air and the blood supply to her brain.

Hammett blacked out.

When she woke up some undetermined time later, she was on her back and Tristan was tugging at her belt.

Seriously? This moron was actually going to try to rape her on top of a blimp? It was so ridiculous it was almost funny. It was also a serious mistake. Tristan had forgotten who he was dealing with.

Hammett was happy to remind him.

She chopped at his neck, which was like hitting a tree, and then caught his left ear and pulled with all she had.

Hammett was strong. So was Tristan. But you didn't lift weights with your ears, and she managed to tear part of it off.

That seemed to dampen his ardor, and bellowing, Tristan punched Hammett in the face.

She managed to lift her head up in time, his hard knuckles meeting her hard skull. Her skull fared slightly better, and through the disorientation she tried again for his holster, locking her fingers around the butt of his .45, pulling—

—only to discover his holster was snapped closed.

She quickly changed targets, finding his groin, squeezing hard enough to crush walnuts, and even with all his training, he made the male mistake of lowering his hands to protect his junk.

Hammett jammed her finger up into his bloody nose, punching the tip through the cartilage and hooking her knuckle around Tristan's septum. Then she yanked his face to the side, pulling herself up by his nose, and bit into the bastard's neck, going for the jugular.

Hammett's mouth filled with blood, but she didn't get much more than skin. Her bite had the desired effect, though. When someone was chomping on your throat, the natural tendency was to push them away, and Tristan shoved himself off of Hammett and fell onto his ass.

Free of his weight, Hammett kipped up to her feet, snapped her hips, and reverse-kicked Tristan in the jaw. Then she leap-frogged his kneeling form, twisted around behind him, and unsnapped his holster, removing his .45.

"On second thought," Hammett said into his remaining ear, "I'm not in the mood."

She flicked off the safety and emptied the gun into the back of Tristan's head.

For a moment, Hammett knelt there, almost expecting him to get back up even though most of his skull was gone. But he was dead, a fatal victim of his ego and the little dude in his pants.

Men. What idiots.

She fought an overwhelming wave of pain from her injuries, got it under control, then patted him down with her functioning hand. Hammett found a wallet with a few hundred in cash, fake ID, and a condom he'd never had the chance to use. He also had a radio, keys, a Swiss Army knife, and, as she'd hoped, a tactical flashlight.

Hammett pocketed the knife, and walked, on her knees, over to the hole she'd made in the blimp. Using her new flashlight, she once again peered inside. Grabbing the suspension cable would be tough, especially with only one arm and no real handholds.

*Handholds. Hmm...*

Hammett crawled back over to Tristan's corpse, then labori-ously dragged him to the hole, scooting on her butt, pulling with her legs and back. When she got him there, Hammett let his arm dangle into the opening. Then she put the flashlight in her teeth, took a deep breath and held it, and locked her legs around his biceps, shimmying down his arm as if it was a rope.

When she ran out of arm length, her handhold literally became a handhold, and she clutched his dead fingers and swung for the cable like Tarzan on a very thick vine.

She touched it with her heel on the first attempt, but couldn't reach. On the second try, she locked her legs around it.

*Here we go...*

Hammett released Tristan's hand and began to rapidly slide down the cable.

Friction burned through her pants, making her thighs feel like she was holding coals between them, and when Hammett reached up with her good hand to slow her descent, she got a nice tear across her palm. But she managed to slow herself down enough to not die or break anything else when she reached the bottom. Unfortunately, she did knock the wind out of herself, the flashlight popping from her mouth and spinning off into the envelope.

Hammett had a lot of practice being without air, but the body's desire to breathe trumped every other need it had. She managed to get on her knees, seeking the fallen light, but only crawled a meter before her reflexes overrode her wishes and she sucked in a breath of pure helium.

Her oxygen-deprived brain began to immediately shut down, and Hammett figured, if she was lucky, she had fifteen seconds before she was unconscious, death following shortly thereafter.

# Fleming

*"If you're outnumbered," The Instructor said, "don't be outgunned."*

Submachine gun fire pinged off of her steel enclosure, and Fleming had been unprepared for the noise, like being inside a bell during a hailstorm. She shut out the pain in her ears and aimed at the first group rushing at her, emptying a Skorpion magazine, killing four men before they knew what was happening. Turning manually with her hands, Fleming then motored toward the entrance ramp, near one of the loading docks.

The others had taken quick cover, in doorways, around metal Dumpsters, one poor sap who hid behind a Loading Zone sign no wider than his wrist.

Fleming took the guy unaware of his own girth out first with a fresh burst from the Skorpion, shooting him a dozen times and completely missing the sign. Then she used fléchettes to punch through the Dumpster, grouping her shots to ventilate any target behind it bigger than a jackrabbit. Since the men behind it were many times bigger than rabbits, Fleming witnessed proof of her success by the copious amount of blood that ran in rivulets from the Dumpster corner into the sewage drain.

She reached for the piranha rounds, loading them by feel, squinting through her eye slit and watching the guards return fire from the doorway, and more from another door a hundred meters north. Fleming pegged them as private contractors based on their ages—older—and group dynamic—every man for himself. She unleashed another torrent of piranha rounds, which ate away their hiding spot until they were exposed, and then ate away at them until they were dead.

Fleming hoped that was the last of them. If not, she crossed her fingers that they wouldn't have anything stronger or higher caliber than what they currently used, because her armor was working just—

A high-velocity round pinged through the top of her enclosure, penetrating the steel as easily as a wet finger through a slice of white bread, missing her face by a few inches.

Sniper rifle. And Fleming didn't see where the shot came from.

She gunned the engine, no choice but to go forward, needing to close the distance because she was too far away to hit him with her guns. Her eyes were focused on trying to find the sniper's position, and the only way that would happen was if he fired again.

He did, the slug piercing her armor and stripping off the outer layer of skin from her neck, leaving her feeling as if she'd been burned with a hot iron.

Fleming opened the hatch, and unloaded the rest of her Skorpion mag at the doorway the shot came from, still barreling forward. Out of ammo, she switched to the shotgun, shooting round after round as the sniper returned fire, turning her steel plating into Swiss cheese.

She finally caught him in the leg, and he dropped the rifle and pitched forward, howling and trying to scramble away on three limbs until she finally rolled up and ended him.

Since he conveniently left the door open, Fleming rolled inside, her modified chair barely fitting through the doorway. No other guards attacked her, but she got a big surprise just the same.

The factory was no longer abandoned. Fleming saw men and women in lab coats running around, heading for a dozen cars parked inside on the south side of the warehouse, hidden from prying eyes outside. On the north side was a gigantic blue plastic tarp, which looked a lot like those children's bouncy castles, complete with several industrial-size blower fans. But Fleming knew it wasn't a trampoline inside the plastic. Instead, it was an enormous positive airflow chamber.

She had found the lab where they were manufacturing the Ebola virus.

# Scarlett

*"Always fight back, even when you're injured," The Instructor said. "Especially when you're injured."*

The Instructor had done a very good job setting up the laboratory. It had all the safeguards of a P4 containment lab, ensuring the virus wouldn't get out. But the security—four cameras and a dozen private sector half-wits—was severely lacking. Granted, no one ever expected this location to be breeched, but they could have at least had a plan in place if it was.

With The Instructor gone for the day, and Scarlett and Rhett guests of the facility, they had no authorization to order them around, and could only watch the monitors as one after another died senselessly.

It wasn't until the little armored vehicle opened up its front hatch that they knew who was driving it.

"It's the cripple," Scarlett said, amazed. "How did she find us?"

Rhett frowned, uncharacteristic of him. "Keep an eye on the boy. I'll take care of this little filly. I owe her one."

# Isolde

*"Remember the mission," The Instructor said. "Plans may change, but always keep the objective in mind."*

Izzy had no idea what was taking Tristan so long. She'd once seen him take on an entire motorcycle gang. One of those first-round Hydra whores shouldn't have been a problem. Even if he was having some fun with the girl and getting his freak on, Izzy knew from experience he finished pretty fast. Something had to be up. She unclipped her walkie-talkie and spoke.

"What's the situation, over?"

No response.

"We're ready to land. I need you to grab the mooring line, over."

Nothing but static.

"Fine, if you like riding up there, I'm going to make a pass over the festival. Looks like about fifty thousand people have shown up so far. I'm going to give them a little spray."

Tristan stayed silent. Izzy wondered if somehow the woman had gotten the better of him. But she instantly dismissed the notion and headed for the crowd.

Let the big lug screw around up there. She had people to kill.

# Hammett

*"Sometimes the will to live might be all you have left," The Instructor said. "And sometimes it is all you need."*

Hammett groped in the darkness for the flashlight, gripped it, and swept it around the envelope interior looking for the ballonets. There was one a few meters away, half inflated, and she lunged at it, dropping the light, opening Tristan's pocketknife with her teeth, and attacking the rubber as her senses began to fade to blackness.

Faintly aware she made a slit and seconds away from passing out, Hammett pressed her face to the hole and sucked in cold air.

Good old oxygen, used as ballast in the ballonets to control the ascent and decent of the airship. She gulped in the air greedily, clearing her head, gaining control over her body once again.

Hammett smiled, despite the pain still racking every inch of her body. If she'd been born a cat, she would have to wonder how many of her nine lives she'd already used up. At least six. But there was still work left to do.

She filled her lungs, pulled herself away, picked up the flashlight, and began to search for her dropped duffel bag. She found it quickly, looped it over her shoulder, filled her pockets with supplies, pulled out the shotgun, and emptied it beneath her feet where she guessed the gondola to be.

The piranhas punched through easily, and Hammett quickly reloaded with armor-piercing rounds, shooting in a circle around her feet, connecting the holes until she fell through and into the passenger compartment.

She landed on top of a chair, stood there for an instant, and immediately collapsed as Izzy pumped bullets into both of Hammett's legs.

# Heath

*"You are smart and lethal and have had the best training in the world," said The Instructor. "But there will come a point when you've met your match."*

Chandler scrunched up her nose ever so slightly, and a crease dug between her eyebrows. "Change the world, Heath? How?"

Heath took his eyes off the highway and glanced her way. He found it hard to take his eyes off her. Just riding in the truck with her fired his blood. Add that to the adrenaline rush of escaping the bullring, and he could barely keep his hands to himself.

She must have put some kind of love hex on him.

Heath smiled, chuckling to himself at the idea.

"Is something funny?"

He eyed her bloody arm and motioned to the space behind the seat. "Your backpack. You should take care of that arm. You'll find everything there, except the weapons, of course."

She fished out the pack and started cleaning and bandaging the knife wound on her forearm. As she worked, he noted her pull something from one of the pockets of her cargo pants and slip it into the pack, but he didn't say a word.

She pulled a bottle of water from the pack, drank about half, and offered the rest to him.

"*Gracias.*" He downed the rest.

"Answer me, Heath. How do you expect to change the world? With the stuff in that tank? It can change the world, all right. It can cause a pandemic."

"You're not thinking creatively enough, *bonita.*"

"You're going to use it for leverage."

"Of course."

"To do what?"

"To restore justice. So few people have so much, and do you know why? Because they take it. They buy politicians and change laws to benefit themselves. All the while, others starve."

"And you're going to reverse this."

"I have the power now, so I call the shots."

"And who are you planning to shake down?"

"The United States government, the Mexican government, the cartels and crime bosses and billionaire bankers."

"So where do you think you're going to hide while you threaten the most powerful man in the world?"

"Most powerful?"

"President Ratzenberger."

He made a face, as if he'd just eaten something rotten. "Most powerful? I think not."

"OK then, where are you going to hide while you threaten The Instructor?"

Heath couldn't help but smile. His Chandler was smart, all right. Just one more thing that made her irresistible. "Where I grew up. A place where a man can get lost."

"And where is that?"

"Tijuana."

"I thought you were American."

"My father was, and I was born in the USA. But my spirit, and *madre*, are *Mexicano*. When my father left, and my mother was deported, she brought me to the only place she could find a living. *El dompe*."

"The landfill?"

"My American blood gave me a way out. But others, they have no way out. Poverty crushes their souls, kills them every day, steals their dignity. This"—he gestured to the back of the truck—"will let me change that."

"Have you ever seen someone die from the virus?"

"Have you ever spent time along the Mexican border?"

"You won't be able to hide, Heath."

"You'd be surprised."

"No, you're the one who will be surprised."

Heath glanced Chandler's way. It had occurred to him that she would make a play for the virus, try to remove him, even in the face of the many times he'd spared her. Assassins were unpredictable that way.

Just one more reason they were made for one another.

"And why will I be surprised, *bonita*?"

"Remember asking me how I found you?"

"You mean it wasn't my love of the bullfight?" Not that he'd ever believed that line.

"You have a tracking chip right below your belly button. So does Earnshaw. So did I."

He frowned. It sounded like something The Instructor would do. "Tell me about this chip."

"Hydra training. The Instructor implanted it on my duodenum when I was being waterboarded. I assume that's where yours is, too."

"And how did you use it to track me?"

"Fleming gave herself a back door into Hydra's computer system. Once we knew Hydra Deux existed, she used it to see where the six of you were."

He brightened again. "So you came to Mexico to be with me. I knew you felt the same."

"I'm serious, Heath. You should be, too. The Instructor is tracking you right now."

That was one thing Chandler never understood. He was always serious. "What makes you think he isn't tracking you?"

"I removed mine, and I can remove yours, too, if you'll let me."

"And why would you do that?"

"The Instructor will know precisely where we are if I don't."

"I mean, why would you do that when killing me would be much more convenient?"

Her lips tensed ever so slightly, betraying her thoughts. "I can't let you keep the virus, Heath."

"I know. And I can't let you take it, *bonita*. So where does that leave us?"

# Isolde

*"When you have to shoot, shoot," The Instructor said. "Don't talk."*

Izzy's first indication something was wrong was hearing the *thump* above her. It was followed by the bellow of a shotgun. By the time the woman fell into the cockpit, Izzy was waiting with her 9mm, and shot her legs out from under her.

"Shotgun. Drop it."

The operative tossed the shotgun aside.

"Which one are you? Chandler or Hammett?"

The woman looked like shit, but still managed a smirk. "Does it matter?"

"I like to know who I'm killing."

"Betsy."

"Excuse me?"

"My name is Betsy. But I go by Rebecca. She's the strong one."

Izzy had no idea what that meant, but she didn't really care. Chandler or Hammett or Betsy or Rebecca, whoever this was didn't have long to live. And Izzy wanted to make sure her last moments were memorable.

"How did you get past Tristan?"

"My sex appeal. It was like he'd never seen boobs before. And looking at you, that might be the case."

Izzy scowled. She'd never really liked Tristan, but he was her partner, and he knew how to hurt a girl, which she'd miss.

"Doesn't matter. You still lose. I'm about to spray the festival right now. With Ebola."

"Lame," the woman said. "I almost nuked London."

"So, you're Hammett. I heard you were a real badass. You don't look so bad now."

"And you look like a preteen boy who needs a sandwich."

Izzy bared her forearm. "Do you know what these marks are?"

"Men who have rejected you?"

"People I've killed. I'm going to add you in just a few minutes."

Hammett sighed. "By shooting me? Lame. I've got bullets in both legs, my arm is broken, and you still need a gun."

Izzy offered one of her rare smiles. "Oh, I'm not going to use a gun. I'm going to do you with this."

She pulled out her razor with her other hand.

Hammett laughed. "What are you going to do with that, little girl? Give me a Brazilian?"

"I'm going to cut your face off."

"Cut my tits off, too. You could use a pair."

Izzy walked slowly over to Hammett, savoring the moment. Supposedly, this woman was The Instructor's favorite. The one all others were measured against. And although Izzy had to give her credit for talking trash while facing certain, painful death, it was going to be a delight killing her. Maybe she'd use a different color ink for this one, since she was so special. Perhaps blue. Or red.

She pressed the gun to Hammett's forehead, then lowered the razor to the woman's chin.

Hammett's smile didn't waver. Even as Izzy began to cut.

# Fleming

*"When opportunities arise,"* The Instructor said, *"improvise."*

Looking around the makeshift laboratory, Fleming realized her mission had just gotten a whole lot more important. She needed to raze this place, making sure nothing survived. And the best tool for that was fire.

Much of the equipment in the lab was metal or glass, immune to flames, so Fleming headed for the indoor parking lot. On her way, Fleming reached into the bag she had resting on her feet and took out the jar of goop she'd concocted earlier by dissolving Styrofoam pellets in gasoline. Homemade napalm. Sticks to anything, and burns hot, even underwater. She reached the first line of cars, opened her hatch, and dumped a gooey blob onto the hood of a Volkswagen. As she did the same with a Honda, a stocky, older woman ran up to her. Dressed in scrubs, she had an orange-tinted mole on her face that resembled an Asian beetle. Her expression was sour.

"That's my car, you bitch!"

Bug lady threw something. It hit the side of Fleming's tank, the sound of shattering glass and a splash of liquid. Fleming glanced down at the shell of her enclosure. Blood—probably infected with Ebola—dripped down the side, the glass of the broken test tube sparkling from the concrete.

While these scientists and lab folks were unarmed, Fleming had no sympathy for people who created biological weapons. Especially when they threw them around like infectious water balloons. Fleming shot the woman with an armor-piercing round, which punched through her and the car she was trying to protect.

Speeding past the body, Fleming began shooting other cars in their gas tanks, creating a huge gasoline slick across the floor that reached the plastic of the inflatable containment lab. After wheeling a safe distance away, she reloaded with dragon's breath and fired at the puddle of fuel.

It ignited with a *whump!* that damn near knocked her chair over.

Fleming's lap was cold and wet, due to the bag of melting ice, but sweat still broke out on her face and shoulders. She hadn't had time to install proper ventilation in her enclosed vehicle, and with the engine and her own body heat she'd anticipated things to get toasty.

But now that she'd set the place on fire, raising the ambient temperature, her tank was quickly becoming an oven.

She continued to cross the warehouse, another guard appearing in front of her, more interested in finding the exit than fighting back. Fleming would need to consider that option herself, and soon.

But not without Bradley. She'd come here to find him, and even though it was paramount to destroy the virus, she wasn't leaving without her recently deflowered nerd.

She wheeled through a burning tear in the plastic tarp, and saw the interior had been designed like a hospital. Rooms and hallway and offices and lab, complete with tile floor and overhead lighting.

"Bradley!" she called out.

Then someone attacked from the side, leaping out from behind a water cooler and wrenching the shotgun from her hands. All Fleming saw was a blur in a cowboy hat.

Rhett.

And he'd taken Fleming's last gun.

# Hammett

*"Pain is temporary," The Instructor said. "Death is forever. At least, when in pain, you know you're still alive."*

The hard part was not flinching when the razor blade bit into her cheek. Hammett had to wait for Isolde to let her guard down, and not moving while she was being cut would be something the skinny little emo had never seen before. She'd be expecting screaming and begging and flinching and fighting. Defiance would be alien to her, and hopefully Isolde would be so surprised she'd give Hammett an opening.

So as the girl worked the razor around Hammett's jawline, Hammett kept perfectly still, the smile frozen on her face, her eyes locked to Isolde's. Part of Hammett's mind forced the pain away. The other part made her good hand creep toward the karambit knife she'd tucked into her pocket.

"I've got to admit, I'm impressed," Isolde said. "You have amazing control over your body. But tell me, Hammett, can you stay completely still when I carve out one of your eyes?"

Hammett winked.

Then, in a fluid motion, she thrust her broken arm upward, knocking away the suppressed pistol, while her right hand brought up the karambit and ripped Isolde from crotch to sternum, opening her up like a zipper.

The emo looked down, her face pure shock as her insides came out.

Isolde dropped the gun, then fell to her knees, making a squishy sound as she knelt on top of internal parts that were no longer internal.

"I'm sorry," Hammett said, reaching to the side and opening the cockpit door, "but you're not big enough to ride this attraction. I'm afraid you're going to have to get off."

The blimp continued its quick descent, ready to crash into an approaching golf course. Hammett grabbed Isolde by the hair and jerked her out of the aircraft, watching as she splashed into a water hazard, her intestines trailing behind her. Then Hammett quickly located the ballast compartment in the rear of the gondola and began throwing out twenty-five pound bags of lead shot.

The blimp came within ten meters of hitting land and then quickly rose. Which was good, because Hammett couldn't let the authorities get ahold of the virus. That wasn't part of the plan.

She began to crawl to the instrument panel, but her legs wouldn't cooperate. Hammett gave them a cursory glance, and saw the bright red blood pumping out of her left thigh.

Shit. An artery. Bad, too.

It never rains but it pours.

Her vision blurring, Hammett looked around for something to make a tourniquet. She cut a seat belt off one of the seats, and tied that above the wound as tight as she could. Then, with some inner reservoir of strength Hammett didn't know she had left, she managed to pull herself into the pilot's seat.

*Just a little longer. I can do this.*

She'd flown many aircraft before, but never a blimp. But the controls weren't too hard to figure out. The pedals moved the rudder, which steered port and starboard. A wheel on either side of the chair controlled the angle of descent. The throttle controlled the twin engines. And the various buttons were self-explanatory.

Hammett shook off the encroaching drowsiness, then checked her direction, leveled off her altitude at five hundred meters, and then headed south toward Lake Ontario, using the famous CN

Tower piercing the clouds in the distance as a compass point. She
needed to make it to the water. Once she did…

That's when she passed out from loss of blood.

# The White House

"The op went sour in Mexico," The Instructor told him.

Raztenberger felt his blood pressure surge. He gripped the
phone so tightly his knuckles turned ghost white.

"How?"

"Chandler."

"Goddammit! I told you to corral those bitches."

"They had help, sir."

"Help? Who could possibly be helping them?"

"According to the security cameras at Plaza de Toros, it was
Heathcliff."

The president wasn't sure how to respond. Disbelief?
Rage? Disappointment? "You gave me assurances concerning
Heathcliff."

"I had another operative covering him," The Instructor said.
"She was killed. But I know their location. I'll have another team
in place shortly."

"Black ops?"

"Locals. But they're good."

"And the Canadian theater?"

"Satellite photos show the blimp is…off course."

Ratzenberger closed his eyes, seeing red. "These are your
rogue operatives. If you want that vice presidency, you'll fix this."

The Instructor hung up. The president set the phone down,
almost tenderly.

Chaz rubbed up against his leg, purring, and Ratzenberger
scooped the cat up into his lap. Then his eyes scanned the Resolute
desk, locking on a Montblanc pen he didn't recognize.

He picked it up—

—holding it to the kitty's neck.

It was tempting. So tempting. He could vent his frustrations, while also getting rid of something he hated. And then…

Then, what? Dump it in the waste bin? Hide it under his coat and try to smuggle it out of the White House? And how would he explain the bloodstains?

Ratzenberger pushed the damn cat off his lap, unharmed. He was the most powerful man in the world, but he couldn't even get away with killing a stupid animal.

He absently tucked the pen into his jacket pocket, and then said a short prayer, asking God to help The Instructor make this right.

# Chandler

*"In any operation, it's important to have a clear objective going in," The Instructor said. "As long as you know the ends, you can improvise on the means. It's when you allow black and white to blend into gray that you are in danger of losing your way."*

We drove for miles through mountains and skirted the coastal plains of the Gulf of California, one hour stretching into the next, and the entire time, all I could think about was the little boy I'd seen climb out from under the cardboard box in Nuevo Laredo. I'd thought about Heath over the years, mostly about how much I hated him, how he'd managed to beat me at my own game, but I'd never given much consideration to who he was or where he'd come from.

I shouldn't be letting myself think about that now.

My mission was clear. I had to destroy the virus. If that meant I needed to destroy Heath first, then that was what must be done. He was right: killing him and dumping his body would be a convenient solution to all my problems. Unfortunately, it wouldn't be easy for a multitude of reasons.

We stopped for gas at a Pemex station along Highway 15, close enough to the gulf to smell salt riding the air. The station was fairly modern. A bright green canopy stretched over the pumps, a concrete apron beneath. On the other side of an empty dirt lot sat a convenience store, still open. A single rig parked in the back, probably some *camionero* getting a few hours of shut-eye before again hitting the road. Save for him, the gas station attendant, and the young man behind the convenience store cash register, Heath and I were alone.

After the attendant filled the tank, Heath paid and pulled the truck into the dirt lot and out of the bright, overhead light. He slipped the keys from the ignition and into his pocket and then got out. "Stay here. I will get us something to eat."

I got out, too.

"You know I have a gun, *querida*."

"Just stretching my legs."

"And what fine legs they are. I would hate for anything to happen to them."

I'd expected a warning or a threat, but despite his words, the lilt in his voice didn't suggest either. "Do you flirt with every woman you see?"

"Only the ones who want to kill me. It turns me on."

"So every woman wants to kill you?"

He gave me a grin. "Just you, *mamacita*. That must be why only you can truly turn me on."

I shook my head. The man had a line for every occasion.

We entered the store and picked up a couple of *tortas*. We reached the counter, and Heath pulled a wad of pesos from his pocket, peeling off the appropriate amount, the whole time never taking his eyes from me.

Upon leaving the store, we walked side by side, watching each other, our steps synchronized as if part of a dance.

I thought of the short dossiers Fleming had obtained on Hydra Deux. Heath had many skills, but the one I was reminded of now was his prowess in the martial art capoeira. Brazilian in origin, the fighting style began as a means for African slaves to train in combat without their Portuguese masters' knowledge. A combination of attacks, defense, and mobility, capoeira resembles a dance, a careful orchestration of movement flowing with precision and speed. It was actually about outsmarting your opponent with tricks, feints, and deception. Once you realized it was no dance, it was usually too late.

I'd trained in capoeira as well, and as I fell in beside him and matched my steps to his, it felt as if we were participating in a *roda*, training disguised as a game. In a *roda*, the combat starts with the *chamada* or call, where a more experienced *capoeirista* tests an opponent through a side-by-side walk. It's a test of awareness, where each is vulnerable to attack, and each attempts to read the other's hidden intentions. Any breach of focus and you leave yourself open to a takedown or a strike.

Ten meters from the truck, I attacked.

I extended my right leg behind him while striking my right arm back into the center of his chest. Execution of the move, called a *vingativa*, was critical, and mine was a touch off. Instead of being knocked off his feet and laid out on his back, he was able to flip backward onto his hands and cartwheel out of range with an *au compasso*.

Movement fluid, he tossed our sandwiches to the ground and settled into a *ginga*, the swinging footwork of capoeira. The smile on his face was broad and irritating.

"You want to play, *bonita*?"

"Playing isn't foremost on my mind, no."

"Then you aren't enjoying your work as much as you should."

He threw a *queixada* at me, a high, fast kick aiming at my chin. I lunged to the side—a lateral *esquiva*—then launched an answering kick.

He ducked, my kick flowing over his head, then from his position close to the ground, he countered with a *tessoura*, standing on his hands and scissoring me with his legs, pushing my feet out from underneath. I escaped with an *au compasso*, cartwheeling as he had, but by the time I was back on my feet, he was too. And we shifted and rolled in the *ginga*, sizing each other up, looking for the next opportunity to strike.

Capoeira in *roda* is performed to music. But although we had only swirls of dust and sounds of the night, and the stakes of our game were higher than most, we settled into effortless rhythm, not a constant barrage of attack, but footwork, moves, and feints intended to test the other's weaknesses, to deceive, and to trap.

He would try my defenses with a kick, and I would evade with an *esquiva*. I would throw a series of high strikes at him, and he would counter by moving low, going for my feet. We landed some blows, but both of us were skilled at countering the moves, at ducking and rolling away from the force, and the strikes didn't fully connect. He focused on my every move, even when he didn't appear to be looking at me, and I did the same with him, trying to read his body as well as his mind.

"We are evenly matched, *querida*," he said, "though you possess a sexiness I lack."

I doubted that. Serious as our fight was, I had to admit he looked disturbingly good, and I wasn't just talking about his capoeira skills.

Heath launched at me with an *armada*, a fast, spinning kick. I evaded the kick, but before I had a chance to counterstrike, he came at me again, this time with one *meia lua de compasso* after another, a rotating kick that packed a huge wallop.

Caught unbalanced, I bent backward into a *ponte* to avoid his attack, then walked over onto my feet.

"*Maravilloso.*"

"You expected less?"

"From you?" He shot me one of his smirks. "I expect nothing but the best."

I tied a series of kicks together, *quiexada* to *armada* to *meia lua de compasso*, but he evaded them smoothly, turning on his hands. I moved back into the sway of *ginga* before trying one more kick, a roundhouse off my back foot. The kick is called *martelo de estalo*, or cracking hammer, and until it's delivered, it's a hard kick to read, especially when hidden among the more dramatic spinning kicks. The top of my foot connected with Heath's ribs, and I could hear the breath rush from his lungs.

Heath dropped to the ground, and for a second, I thought I had him. I shot out with another *martelo de estalo*, this time going for his head, but as soon as I was on one leg, he countered with a *rasteira*, cutting my legs out from under me like wheat surrendering to the blade of a scythe.

I hit the ground, now my turn to gasp for air, and before I could spring to my feet, Heath was on top of me, pinning me to the dirt.

He leaned in close, his breath tickling my ear. "You are so hot, *bonita*. You're on fire." He nibbled on my ear, his body bearing down on mine, hard and unyielding.

I decided to play along until he let down his guard, then turn the tables. If sex was on the menu, it was difficult for the male of the species to pay attention to anything else. As soon as he lost his focus, I'd put him down.

He shifted on top of me, fitting the evidence of his arousal snug between my thighs. He kissed my ear, then trailed along my hairline to the side of my neck, then my throat.

I could feel his heart thumping against my ribs, echoing through my chest. He smelled of leather and sweat, earthy and real, and before I knew what I was doing, I was kissing him back. It started with a brush of my lips against his cheek, the light rasp of stubble sending chills over my skin. He tilted his face toward me and then brought his mouth to mine.

The kiss wasn't tender, but hard and urgent, and what he gave me, I gave back. Our tongues tangled, stroking in time with our lips one moment, struggling for dominance the next. I pulled my right hand free of his grip and tangled my fingers in his hair, forcing his mouth harder against mine.

And all thoughts of me kicking his ass melted away.

I couldn't remember a time I'd needed anything so desperately, his kiss, his heat, his touch. Still pinning my left wrist to the dirt, he slipped his free hand under my shirt and clawed one cup of my bra aside. His fingers found my nipple, and I gasped as he pinched and teased.

I spread my legs apart, and he nestled deeper, denim against denim, moving in time with our kiss, the friction building until I was breathless with it, my back arching and hips bucking, beyond my control.

God help me, I wanted him, needed him, skin against skin.

I skimmed my hand down his shoulder, his back, until I reached his belt. Working my fingers between our bodies, I fumbled with the buckle.

A chuckle rumbled through his chest and tickled my lips.

"Right now, *querida*? Here in the dirt?"

I answered with a tug, pulling the belt loose. Another few yanks and the button fly of his jeans was open. I thrust my hand inside.

Heath was hot and hard, and he surged into my palm. I slid my fingers down his length, and his chuckle turned to a moan.

He deepened the kiss, devouring me, and even though his erection was no longer rubbing against me, I felt the delicious pressure again building between my legs. I ripped my left hand free of his and shoved his jeans farther down his hips, but it wasn't enough. I wanted to be naked. I wanted him inside me.

More than wanted. Craved. An aching and mindless need.

"I have a better idea," he said.

He lifted himself off me, hitched up his pants a touch, then offered me a hand.

I could have flipped him right then, thrown him to the ground, and judging by the smirk curling one side of his lips, he knew it. But I couldn't make myself care about that now.

I grasped his hand and let him pull me to my feet. A few steps, and we were beside the truck, but instead of opening the door, Heath pressed my back against the warm steel, grasped my shirt, and pulled it over my head. My bra came next, and then he unfastened my jeans. I pushed his jeans back down his thighs and took him in both hands, cradling him from below.

In the back of my mind, I realized the attendant in the gas station was likely watching in the light bleeding from the gas pump canopy, but I didn't care about that either. Let him gawk. All I could focus on was Heath. The smell of his skin, the feel of him in my hands, his urgency as he stripped off my cargo pants and pushed them down to my ankles.

After guiding the fabric over my feet, he skimmed back up my body, littering hot kisses until he reached the apex of my thighs. He parted my legs, moving his mouth between them, giving me sucking kisses and long, fat licks until I thought I'd go insane.

Tremors rippled through me again, but it wasn't enough. I grasped his shoulders, lifting him to his feet.

"Now," I said, my voice sounding hoarse and desperate.

For once in his life, Heath didn't throw me a *querida* or *bonita* or even a *mamacita*. In fact, he said nothing at all. He grasped my hips and lifted me, then leaning me back against the truck, he fitted me onto his length.

I took him inside, wrapping my legs around his waist, holding tight to his shoulders as he thrust into me. He buried his face in my breasts, first claiming one nipple then the other with lips, tongue, and teeth. Again a wave built and crashed over me in pleasure so acute it bordered on pain. I threw my head back, gasping for air, crying out, and Heath met me, bucking and shuddering as he bellowed my name.

*¡Dios Mío!*

We clung to each other for several moments, sweating, breathing hard, still joined, Heath holding me up. I couldn't quite understand what I was feeling. It wasn't love. It was no longer simple lust. Instead, I felt strangely whole. As if a part of me had been missing for a very long time, and I'd finally found it.

Eventually, too soon, he lowered me down, and we dressed and recovered the *tortas*, neither of us saying a word.

When we climbed back into the truck, Heath handed me the Paragon Seal knife he'd taken from me in Mexico City, along with my cell phone.

"We are equally matched, *querida*. In more ways than one."

I nodded, but although he'd just handed me the means to kill him, I no longer wanted to. In fact, I was beginning to think he was right. Maybe I had met my match.

And although I knew it couldn't last, not with that tank of Ebola on the back of the truck, maybe I wanted to hold on as long as I could.

# Hammett

*"Don't go down with a sinking ship,"* The Instructor said.

When Hammett opened her bleary eyes, the needle of the CN Tower was a hundred meters away, and the blimp was heading straight for it in a collision course.

Shot through with adrenaline, she pressed her numb leg against the rudder pedal, pushing on her knee with her good hand, while simultaneously throttling down and changing the prop pitch.

It was going to be close. Damn close.

The blimp got so close to the tower, Hammett could see a wide-eyed man standing on the upper observation deck, a mop in his hand and his jaw hanging open. She waved at him as the airship floated past, narrowly missing the building by a few meters.

Sighting Lake Ontario ahead of her, Hammett began a rapid descent. No doubt being watched by thousands of people, she'd have to execute this next part perfectly for her plan to work.

She left the captain's chair and inched her way to the passenger area of the gondola. After finding her bag, Hammett went through it and pulled out her Mateba autorevolver. She raised the rear window, and fired four times at the chains holding the aerosol tank, careful not to hit the tank itself. The armor-piercing rounds cut through the heavy chain as advertised, and the tank dropped away from the gondola, splashing into the lake only fifty meters above the waves. She threw the Mateba, her shotgun, and the duffel back out the window and fished the TracFone out of her pocket.

Hammett called two numbers from memory. The first one, she got a machine, and she quickly spit out, "It's done." She got a machine the second time as well, and had time to blurt, "Toronto Inukshuk. I need you to—"

Then the blimp crashed into Lake Ontario.

The impact knocked Hammett off her feet, and water rushed into the gondola, assaulting her with a freezing, bracing slap. She managed to pull up a seat cushion, finding the strap underneath that told her it could be used as a floatation device, then waited for the cockpit to fill up. Once it did, she kicked feebly out the window, popping to the surface alongside the collapsing blimp envelope.

The shore was five hundred meters to the north.

Hammett was pretty sure she wouldn't make it.

But she tried her damnedest.

# Chandler

*"Secrets are power," The Instructor said. "Convince others to reveal theirs, but guard yours with your life. Sometimes they're worth more."*

We didn't stop again until we'd left the salt air of the Gulf of California behind and reached the town of Caborca, on the edge of the Sonoran Desert. We chose a motel just off the highway and next to yet another OXXO convenience store. It had thirty rooms, outside walkways, and a courtyard complete with rusted, greasy barbecues and stall-like picnic areas. We pulled the truck up to one of the grill spots and nestled it among several other pickups and RVs, hidden in plain sight.

I tried to call Fleming, got voice mail. Left a coded message, explaining the situation.

A king-size bed, a bistro table with two scarred chairs, and an ancient television were the only things in the room, but it was free of bedbugs and had a private bathroom, and that was all I needed.

When we'd decided to stop, it had been with the idea of getting a couple of hours' rest, a little food, and then getting back on our way. As it turned out, we skipped the sleeping and the food, and got straight to the sex.

We explored each other with hands and mouths, taking time and paying attention to details we hadn't had patience for back at the gas station. Heath had a talented tongue, as did I, and each time I attempted to bring him to release with my mouth, he pulled away and turned it on me, until an honest-to-God whimper issued from my throat.

"More?" he asked, looking up from between my legs with a glistening smile.

I nodded, not sure my voice would function.

He gave me more, refusing to let me return the favor, and finally out of trembling frustration I pulled his hand back in a judo hold, forced him onto his back to straddle him, and rode him until I made him whimper as well.

After a mission, my sex drive often spiked. There was something about close brushes with death that made life—and sex—precious, and the celebration of both essential. In the past, I would visit bars and pick up strangers. It had done the job on a superficial level, but I'd never felt truly satisfied.

Lund had been different, but he'd also been a disaster. He'd made me see my life, recognize finally what I was, the shortcomings my stepfather had identified so many years ago.

Tough to fully let go with someone judging you, especially when it led you to judging yourself.

I climbed off and stretched out, leaning my head back on the pillow, beginning to wonder if I'd fallen for Lund because I really loved him, or because I liked the way he saw me...before he really knew what I was.

"I thought we were having fun. Where did this broodiness come from?"

Of course, Heath had been reading me.

He moved up my body and stretched out beside me. After pulling the sheet over the two of us, he began playing with one of my nipples. "No answer?"

"It's a pain in the ass to be around spies."

He raised his brows. "They are some of my favorite people."

"Favorite? You mean the most despicable."

"Now, if you're talking about The Instructor, then I agree. But…"

"We lie and kill for a living, Heath."

"There are worse things."

"Name one."

"Politician? Lawyer? Movie critic?"

"Oh, I hate those guys."

"Don't you, now?"

"But I'm serious, Heath."

"Having a crisis of conscience, *bonita*?"

I didn't know what I was having. A few days ago, I'd broken down. A blithering mess on the pavement, filled with self-hatred. But now, I seemed to be OK. And that bothered me. Even my sex drive was so tangled up in violence that I couldn't seem to separate the two.

"We are what we are. We have done what we have done."

Again I didn't have to say anything for Heath to read my thoughts. "It's not that easy."

"Why do you think about it so hard?" He leaned over and took my nipple between his lips, sucking and flicking with this tongue. "Why not just relax and have fun?"

We'd been having fun for over an hour, and although I'd tried, I could no longer push back the thoughts. "What are you saying? That if I don't think about it, it will be OK?"

"If you accept who you are, where you came from."

"I can't do that."

He returned to leaning on an elbow, studying me. "Why not?"

"Because…" My throat felt thick, like I couldn't quite push the words through. Although I didn't know what I would say, even if I could speak.

"You don't like where you came from? What made you? You think any of us would be in this business if we did?"

He had a point. I supposed Fleming was the closest thing to well-adjusted of anyone I knew, and even she had some issues.

"The difference is that you blame yourself for the past, *querida*. You beat yourself up."

"And you don't?"

"I accept myself. You need to do the same. But instead, you think, and think, and since you can't change the past, it always turns out the same."

It was what Hammett had said to me, in her own way, both with words and blows. After her impromptu counseling session, I'd regained my focus in the field, but I was still at a loss of how to deal with the rest of my life.

"I've done a lot of bad things, Heath. How do I accept that?"

"There has been bad in your life, but there also has been good. Consider the good as least as much as the bad."

"Good?"

"You can't think of anything good?"

I shook my head, not wanting to dig too deep, to scrape too close to the nerve. In the Chicago alley, I'd let down that protective wall, and I'd been overwhelmed. I wasn't going to make that mistake again. Especially with Heath watching. "Can you?"

"Find something good in my life? Right this minute?"

"Yes."

"That's easy. All I have to do is look at you."

I rolled my eyes. "We're killers."

"That is what we do. But it is not what we are. We are more than that. This bond we have, I know you feel it, too. You are more than just an assassin, *bonita*."

"Our bond is because we're both amoral, highly trained, and like to fuck each other."

"And it's good, no?" He smiled, so wide I wanted to either punch him or kiss him, I couldn't tell.

Maybe both.

"You're no help," I said.

He shrugged, his smile not fading even the tiniest bit. "My mother was the sweetest, most nurturing, most gentle person I've ever known. Like *La Virgen de Guadalupe*, you know?" He added a wink.

I was sure some sort of trick was coming, although I wasn't sure what. But when Heath brought up the *La Virgen*, I figured I'd better watch out.

"What does your mother have to do with this?"

"When I was ten years of age, I was approached by a *cabrón* who called himself *El Sol*. He saw that I could work, saw I could fight, heard my father was American, and wanted to recruit me into the *Cártel de Guadalajara.*"

"What did you do?"

"I did what any smart boy at that time would. I said I'd consider it."

"You said yes."

He tilted his head to the side in acknowledgment. "But when my mother found out, she was not so agreeable. She went to see him."

I raised my eyebrows. "So what happened?"

"Two days later, his body was uncovered by a bulldozer in *el dompe*."

So much for sweet and gentle. "She killed him?"

"Mama never admitted it, but I know it to be true. She did it to save me."

"Blessed be the Virgin."

"When tending a garden, you must care for the seeds you plant, and be ruthless with the weeds."

"So why are you telling me this story?"

"Because you are like my mother."

I shook my head. "If that story was true, and if your mother really did kill *El Sol*, she did it to protect you. I'm not a shield. I'm a sword."

"Really? How about the girl from the lighthouse? You haven't been protecting her for years?"

"Trying."

"Sometimes trying is the best you can do. And it doesn't have to be someone you care for. You could have fought back outside the Plaza Mexico, but you chose not to. All I had to do was threaten the civilians. And look at how hard you worked to keep me from spreading The Instructor's virus."

"So your mother tried to keep you from a life of crime, but you wound up being a killer anyway."

"How could I not? I am her son. And like her, I am good at pulling weeds."

I wasn't sure if Heath was completely self-aware or completely oblivious. "So tell me about your father."

"Trying to change the subject?"

"I'm interested. Did you know him?"

He looked away. "I don't talk about my father."

"So you aren't as open as you want me to be."

"We all have bad people in our lives. That doesn't make us bad, understand?"

I let his words hang in the air unanswered, my mind too knotted and exhausted to come up with a response. Instead, I thought again about the tank of Ebola. As a minute passed, then two, I listened to the rhythm of Heath's breathing, hearing it slow down, the snores starting to come.

"You're faking it," I said.

He peeked his eye open and stared at me. "So full of mistrust."

"I don't trust you, because you're trying to fool me."

"I must fool you to get you to trust me."

"That makes no sense."

"If I can convince you to sleep, it will allow me to sleep. Neither of us can run out if we are both sleeping."

I didn't correct him, preferring to let him think my silence was strategy instead of—as he called it—thinking too hard once again.

Minutes ticked by.

"So what are we going to do?" I said. "Each pretend to sleep until one of us tries to sneak out and steal the truck?"

"I was hoping to induce a mindless stupor in you through multiple orgasms."

"And I appreciate the effort, but the mindless stupor is not happening."

"What about more psychoanalysis?"

"Not if you ever want to get laid again."

He propped himself up on his elbow to look at me. "How about I tie you to the bed and pleasure you until you can no longer stand it? Imagine: lying there, helpless, exposed, as I teased you beyond endurance."

"And then left me there while you took the truck."

"Perhaps. But the offer stands. It is preferable to shooting you, no?"

"How about I poke out your other eye?"

"That's cold. Did you know they are selling 3-D televisions now? A whole world of entertainment, lost to me."

"I could shoot you in the leg."

"Here, my gun is closer. You can use it. Just give me a few minutes, and it will be ready again." He pulled up the sheet to show me the evidence.

"I'm serious about this, Heath."

"I'm serious, too, *querida*. Look."

"Seen it already."

"Ouch. So cold." He lowered the sheet.

"Where are my guns?"

"I should tell you this so you can threaten me with them? I thought we were beyond that."

"I can't let you have the virus, Heath."

"It's for the greater good."

"No good can come from biological warfare."

"It's the threat of warfare that's good. Think about it. We can manipulate governments. Change policies."

"We? Sleep with the devil, and he includes you in his plans."

"I'm *el diablo* now? A moment ago I was *el ángel del orgasmo.*"

"It's terrorism."

"It's a tool against widespread government corruption."

Heath was right about one thing. I wasn't going to shoot him. Not just because I had feelings for him, but because part of me trusted him to do the right thing. At the same time, I wasn't entirely sure he was above shooting me, so I couldn't let him know I wouldn't shoot him. So maybe I would shoot him.

Shit. This was precisely the reason I didn't get close to guys.

"How about we get dressed, get something to eat, and discuss it?"

"So you can slip something in my food?"

He smiled. "You were thinking the same thing, eh? Did you have anything I could borrow? I'm out of Special K."

"You want me to give you something to slip in my food?"

"What if I promise I won't use it on you?"

"Why don't I just slip it in my own food?"

"Why don't you just let me have the Ebola?"

"If you threaten with Ebola, you'll have to show them what it can do."

"So a few bad people die. The world can do without weeds."

"But it won't be just the weeds. It will destroy your whole stupid allegorical garden. You haven't seen what it can do. It's a thousand times worse than *el dompe.* Trust me, it's awful."

"Is there any biological weapon that isn't?"

I rubbed my face, my eyes. Maybe just running for it was the smart move. We were both naked. If he was self-conscious and looked for pants, I'd have a ten-second head start.

Then again, how far would I get driving a truck naked? And what would I do once I destroyed the virus? Hitchhike to the border?

"Please don't make me chase you naked," Heath said.

I groaned. "Reading my mind again?"

"I considered it myself. But I know you would run right after me."

"How about rock-paper-scissors?" I suggested.

"Rock-paper-scissors for the future of the world?"

"Or we could go back to you trying to subdue me with orgasms."

"And psychoanalysis?"

"No, save that for yourself."

He resumed playing with my nipple. "We could flip a coin."

"If I won, would you really let me have it?"

"Probably not."

"Back to square one."

The problem was that in our brief history together, Heath had outsmarted me more times than I had him. I couldn't let it happen again. Especially not when the stakes were so high.

"So we're not going to eat, drink, sleep, or take our eyes off each other," I said.

Heath smiled. "Sounds like love."

"Love requires trust."

He laughed. "I've been in love many times, and trust has never been part of the equation."

I thought about Lund. I realized now that I hadn't known him long enough to call it love. Yet I had trusted him. I felt affection for Heath, and God knew, I felt lust, but the trust was noticeably lacking.

Maybe shooting him was the way to go.

"I see that look in your eyes, *bonita*. You're thinking about finding your guns again."

"If you keep doing that mind reading thing, I might."

"Just reading your body."

"Like always," I finished for him.

"You win. No eating, drinking, sleeping, or clothes." Heath's eye twinkled. "It really is love."

He leaned over to kiss me just as I heard a footfall on the walkway and spotted the shadow pause outside the window of our room.

# Julie

Julie sat on her bed in her locked room, staring at the wall, thinking about Derek Fossen and his poor sister. Dead. Because of the monster in Julie's blood.

When the popping sound began, Julie had no idea what it was.

Then she saw people running past her room, obviously panicked.

More pops. Her heart felt like it was stuttering in her chest.

Gunshots? Had the police found this place?

Had Chandler?

She needed to get out of her room. Now.

The door was locked, as expected. But now that no one was paying attention to her, escape wouldn't be that difficult.

She went to her bed, unlocked the wheels, and with a running start, rammed it against her door.

Once. Twice. Thrice. Four times was a charm, the knob coming off and the door swinging open. She hurried into the deserted hallway, her vision hazy.

No, not her vision. The hall was smoky. It stung her eyes and singed the back of her throat. A fire?

That's what it smelled like. But she knew the police had smoke grenades. Maybe Chandler would have them, too. She needed to get out of there, to find—

"Help! Help me!"

A man's voice, accompanied by a pounding sound. She followed it, came to a door with a dead bolt.

"Who's there?" Julie yelled at the door.

"Please help me! They locked me in here, and I smell smoke!"

Julie turned the dead bolt and opened the door to face a man her age, a bloody bandage covering his ear. His face flushed with relief when he saw her.

"Thanks, I—"

"Stay back!" Julie warned, almost tripping to stay out of his reach.

He immediately halted, spreading out his palms. "It's OK. I'm not going to hurt you."

That wasn't what Julie was worried about. "No, you don't understand."

"I'm Bradley. I was grabbed and taken here. Where are we?"

"I don't know," Julie said. "I was grabbed, too. But…I'm sick. You need to keep away from me."

Bradley nodded at her, like she was a slow child. "OK. Do you have a name?"

"Julie."

"Do you know where the exit is, Julie?"

She shook her head.

"OK. I'm going to go look for it. Stay with me. There are some very bad people here."

*You have no idea*, Julie thought. But when Bradley headed down the hallway, she followed him.


# Heath


*"Everyone has their weaknesses," said The Instructor.*
*"Be mindful of yours at all times, because you can be certain others will be."*


Heath could feel the ripple of Chandler's muscles tensing, and he knew his were coiled as well. Whoever had come to visit didn't have their health in mind.

"My Mossberg," Chandler whispered.

Heath hesitated only a moment, then reached alongside the bed for the bag he'd brought into the room. Chandler reached inside, taking her shotgun. Heath palmed his Sig Sauer. Then he

THREE

tossed back the sheets and eyed the crumpled ball of denim lying on the floor beneath the front window.

"No time," Chandler whispered. "Just shoes."

She was right, of course. They wouldn't get far barefoot. But the thought of his *huevos* flapping free with lead flying all around didn't please him. He slipped into his cowboy boots.

Chandler climbed out of bed, naked except for footwear and backpack. She held her shotgun at waist level. Above it, her perfect breasts. Below, an area of her he liked just as much.

Life was too short for Heath not to take a second to stare. Was there anything hotter than a naked woman with a lethal weapon?

The doorknob began to jiggle, slowly, the lock preventing it from opening. Chandler backed up against the wall, drawing a bead, and Heath crouched behind the bed.

There was a chance, however slim, that it was the motel owner, or a drunk guest thinking it was their room, or some other harmless possibility.

That thought was wiped from Heath's mind when the door burst inward, revealing a Mexican dressed in black from his boots to his hat, a pistol in each hand.

Heath aimed for his head, shooting just as Chandler's shotgun boomed. The explosion was deafening in the tiny room. They both hit their mark, but hers ripped through his chest, and through the wall behind him.

Three more men stormed the room in rapid succession with their guns blazing, but against Chandler's shotgun they might as well have been bees in a hurricane. She cut them down as fast as she could pump the weapon, which was ridiculously fast.

"What kind of rounds do you have in that thing?" Heath yelled, barely able to hear his own voice over the ringing in his head.

"Fléchette. Steel darts."

Years ago, Chandler had taken his eye, but Heath was angrier at himself for letting her get away from him. "I really am in love," he said to himself.

— 389 —

"What?"

He smiled. "We've got to get out of here."

"No shit."

Keeping low, Heath stepped toward the front of the room, making a last-ditch grab for his pants. The front windowpane shattered, glass and lead flying and peppering the wall behind him.

He dove for cover behind the bed and then scrambled to the side window.

They'd chosen an end room so they'd have multiple avenues of egress, not that he believed they would need them since they'd only planned to stay a couple of hours. But he'd learned years ago that a little planning could save your ass. Keeping low, Heath peered down at the parking lot.

Hombres dotted the parking lot below, several dressed all in black and wearing Stetsons and boots like some sort of damn cowboy convention, all of them carrying AK-47s.

"The situation is not encouraging," he said.

"How many?"

"A dozen that I can see from here. Probably more in front."

"Who are they?"

"*El Cártel de Sinaloa*," Heath said. "They like to dress as *rancheros*."

"So why does the cartel care about us?" Chandler asked. "You piss these boys off somehow?"

"Me? Of course not. Everybody loves me. You?"

"As far as I know, the only cartel that would like to see me dead is Los Zetas."

Heath pulled his eyes from the men in the lot to shoot her a glance.

Chandler shrugged. "It's a long story."

"Well, it's safe to say these *cabróns* are not doing favors for Los Zetas. They aren't amigos."

"I'm betting they have a financial arrangement with The Instructor."

"No one followed us from Mexico City."

"Your chip, Heath."

Of course. They hadn't followed the truck, they'd tracked him. Chandler had warned him, and he hadn't taken her seriously.

Heath shook his head. They never should have stopped, even for a couple of hours. But at least, if he had to die, he would do it with a smile on his face and the smell of Chandler on his skin.

"If we jump out the window, we'll be dead before our feet hit the ground."

"So we go through the door."

She zipped open her backpack, pulled out a box of shells, and began loading.

Heath aimed his Sig at the window, watching for movement behind the flapping curtain. The breeze from outside was oven-hot already and smelled like dust, exhaust from the highway, and gunpowder.

"What this time?" he asked, noting her rounds were a different color.

"Piranha."

"I am unfamiliar. It fires scary little fish?"

"Sharpened steel tacks."

"Perfecto."

She slid the box of shells inside the pack and slung it back over her shoulder.

"Ready?"

"As I'll ever be, *bonita*."

"On me." She stood and advanced to the door, which had swung closed.

Heath followed, the soles of his boots crunching over glass. He spotted his jeans under the window, sunlight sparkling on the shards covering them.

Chandler stepped to the side of the doorframe, her shotgun pointed to the ceiling, she nodded, and Heath yanked the door open.

Two bodies slumped on the threshold, three more in the hall. They wore body armor over their western shirts, not that it had done them any good against fléchette shells. Chandler stepped over the corpses, then crouched low, staying in the right angle between building and air-conditioning unit.

Heath moved in behind her, stopping to wrestle an AK-47 from one of the dead men. He slipped the strap over his head, the webbing wet and warm and sticky against his bare skin. The smell of blood and gunpowder hung thick in the back of his throat.

He checked the weapon and then brought it to his shoulder, peering through the scope and getting an up-close view of Chandler's ass.

"Tell me you aren't looking as my ass through the scope," Chandler said without turning around.

"If I did, I would be lying to you, and we are working on building trust. Besides, it was your call to not get dressed."

"I don't want to get shot because you're preoccupied being the horndog."

"I can't think of a better reason to get shot. And you need not worry, I've got your ass covered."

"I bet."

They moved slowly, expertly, falling into a well-rehearsed stealth mode. The hotel formed a right angle, the walkway elbowing where one wing met the other, then ending at a slanted roof, clay tiles angling down over the hotel's main office. The picnic areas backed by a tall fence flanked the other side of the lot, and judging from the lack of activity around the spot where they'd nestled the truck, the men below either hadn't located it or didn't know its value.

Only one staircase served this wing of the hotel, about four doors down angling in two sections with a landing in between. A second staircase spilled out near the office.

"The office," Heath said.

Chandler nodded. "On me when we're ready."

"Just give the word."

Male voices shouted below, whoever was in charge of this assault directing men up to the second floor.

Chandler aimed the shotgun at the spot where staircase met balcony. A vine climbed up the stairs and clung to the railing, spreading in both directions. The vine's leaves trembled with the vibrations of feet climbing steps.

Three men appeared, running up the stairs, rifles ready. One wore a black cowboy hat like others Heath had noticed. The other two were dressed less cowboy and a little more military. All wore body armor.

Chandler took out the first man just as his foot hit the walkway. He flew backward, his red hat tumbling onto the balcony.

While she pumped another shell into the chamber, Heath hit the next two with clean headshots. Their bodies fell back down the steps, metal clanging.

"Move! Move! Move!" Chandler yelled. She rose to her feet, blasting at the steps and men beneath.

Heath raced down the walkway, keeping low and close to the wall. At the top of the stairs, he dropped to a knee and fired at the handful of *cabróns* lurking at the bottom. He caught one in the neck, the others ducking back and out of the way. Stepping toward the walkway's edge, he laid down a steady stream of fire and called to Chandler, "On me! Go!"

"Coming to ya!"

She ran, low and fast, passing behind Heath and then taking up position at the intersection of the second wing.

"I got you! Go, go, go!"

He met her at the angle. Positioning themselves back to back, they each covered one of the wings.

A pickup idled in the parking lot, a group of men gathered around it, some squeezing off a round now and then, some standing around watching as if this was some kind of spectator sport.

"*Yo quiero tu panocha,*" one of the men yelled, thrusting with his hips. Several others laughed.

"I have to reload," Chandler said, her expression neutral.

"Go ahead."

"*Yo quiero tu panocha,*" the man repeated, others joining in.

"*Yo tengo hambre mamasota, mucha hambre!*"

The come-ons might not bother Chandler, but they bothered Heath. He fired, taking off the top of the man's head.

"At least he's not hungry anymore."

Several rounds flew back their way.

"Ready to move?" he asked Chandler.

"On me, OK?"

"I like it when you say *on me*. It makes me remember being on you."

She stood in all her naked and armed glory and blasted several shots. Heath was already in motion. A man emerged from the second staircase, heading straight for him. Heath hit him on the run, then took a knee.

Lead flew up at him from the staircase, and he leaned flat against an angle in the wall to stay out of the stream. He couldn't tell how many men remained below, but judging from the rain of bullets, there were many. He and Chandler wouldn't be able to make it down this staircase either.

He eyed the roof of the office, still ten meters away, then swung back to Chandler.

"On me! Move!"

Then Chandler was running, and he was shooting. When she reached the protected angle, she hunkered down beside him.

"I'm out." He dropped the rifle, letting it swing from his shoulder on its strap. Then he pulled his Sig from his pack. "Stairs are no good. We need to keep going."

"OK," Chandler yelled back. "On me! Go!"

Gunfire popped and pinged around them. Just as Heath cleared the second staircase, a *ranchero* in black stepped out, obviously lying in wait, rifle in hand.

Shit. A pistol was no good. Not from here. Not without armor-piercing rounds. Heath fired anyway, the bullet hitting the man in the body armor.

The drug soldier stumbled forward, then Chandler pivoted and pumped a load of razor-sharp tacks into him from the other side.

Heath let out a whoop as she turned back to the men below, pumped, and fired. "Go! Go! Go!"

Heath made it to the end of the walkway. "I got you! Go!"

She ran, covering the last stretch of walkway as he fired. When she reached him, she knelt down beside him, chest heaving.

"You're giving me a hard-on, *bonita*."

"You better watch out. You'll get it shot off."

"Now that would be a shame. But with you looking like that, I don't stand a chance."

"How many are left?"

"At least ten. And those remaining will be better. The young ones, trying to make their bones on our blood, went first. The rest will be old pros."

Chandler glanced back at the man soaking the concrete. "You might want to take advantage."

"Of you?"

Chandler gave him a wicked smile. "Of his ammo."

"Good idea." While she gave him cover, he raced back and searched the body for extra magazines. Finding two, he returned to Chandler's side.

Beautiful Chandler.

She could turn right now, bust one of those piranha shells through him, and be free and clear. No tracker. No way for The Instructor to find her once she got away. She would be able to destroy the virus and be on her way home.

"Why didn't you do it?" he asked.

"Kill you just now?" She fired two blasts in the hostiles' direction. "I thought about it."

"But you didn't."

"Tried to at the gas station."

"You weren't trying. Not unless you intended to fuck me to death."

"That was my plan this morning, until these guys showed up."

His Chandler. She was something, all right.

Heath took a deep breath, the air foul with gunpowder and the odor of blood. "You said you removed your chip."

"Yes."

He'd noticed the wound, just under her belly button, while they were making love. Skimming his gaze down her body, he could see the red line, the black stitches right now.

"I am thinking removing mine might be a smart idea."

"You'd trust me to?"

"You're not planning to kill me, right?"

"Not today. You?"

"Couldn't do it, *bonita*, even if I wanted to."

*Even if he had to.*

And that was not a good position for a spy to find himself in.

# Hammett

*"Die on your time," The Instructor said. "I forbid you to die while on my clock."*

The last two hours were a blur.

Somehow Hammett had managed to reach the harbor on her floating chair cushion, haul herself out of the water, and limp a kilometer west.

The cold water had numbed a lot of her pain, and her blood loss made the whole journey almost an out-of-body experience.

She finally laid down in a large patch of bushes near the shore, hidden from passersby by their height, too cold to even shiver, blithely wondering what would kill her first, hypothermia or hypovolemic shock.

Ultimately, it didn't matter. She'd completed her mission. Stopped the threat. Saved a half-million lives. Not too shabby for a few days' work.

Her only regret was not finding a good home for Kirk. Which was an interesting regret, considering all of the terrible things Hammett had done in her life.

During her walk, she'd ignored several people who asked if she needed help. Even now, Hammett could probably sit up, let out a yell or two, and be in a hospital within a few minutes.

And from there, a public trial, jail, and execution. Or worse, no trial at all, swept away to a black site where she'd be tortured the remainder of her life.

This way was better. At least she'd die on her terms.

A gull appeared overhead, riding a thermal so it seemed to hover.

For some reason, Hammett's mind flitted to an earlier conversation with Chandler.

Did saving all those lives make her a hero?

Probably. But no one would ever know about it. Or care.

Truth was, Hammett didn't care either. Life didn't matter, hers included.

Still, dying a hero was something she never could have predicted. Hammett was the epitome of the phrase *born to lose*. Destined to make the world a worse place for everyone.

And yet, as she cashed in her chips, shuffled off her mortal coil, the balance books told otherwise.

Hundreds killed. Hundreds of thousands saved.

Hero?

Maybe she was.

The gull changed directions, flying away.

Hammett took a breath. A shallow one.

Her heart fluttered. Arrhythmia.

Her systems were shutting down.

It wouldn't be long now.

Hammett wondered, under better circumstances, if her life could have turned out differently.

What if her birth mother had lived, and she'd grown up with her six sisters?

A mother and a father, in a nice, suburban household.

Grandparents who baked cookies.

As many dogs as she wanted.

She imagined a family vacation. Disneyland. Pictures hugging Mickey Mouse.

Skinning a knee and having someone kiss it to make it better.

Dad pushing her on a bike. Mom pushing her on a swing.

Doing her sisters' hair because that's what sisters did, not because they were on the run.

What if…

The two cruelest words in the English language, *what if*. But Hammett let the fantasy play out.

Growing up, safe and secure.

No hurt. No abuse.

Losing her virginity to an adorable boy who cared about her.

A college, studying something normal.

A job that didn't involve killing.

A marriage in a big white dress, cutting a big white cake.

A baby growing inside her.

Hearing a child, *her* child, call her mama.

Spending holidays with the family. Catching up with her sisters. Trading pictures and stories and recipes.

Watching her kid grow.

Baking cookies with her grandchildren, in a big house with as many dogs as she wanted.

Being loved.

Hammett had never known what it felt like to be loved.

But that wasn't a regret. It was impossible to regret something you had no control over.

Hammett had been dealt a bad hand. She played it as best she could, with bluff and bluster and maybe even a bit of courage.

But bad hands don't win. It was finally time to fold.

Another breath, even weaker.

Such a strange thought, knowing that her next breath could be her last. Everyone had a last breath. Hammett's was coming soon.

Was it worth keeping track of how many breaths she had left?

Was anything worth it? Any of it?

Hammett considered, for the first time since she was a child begging the universe for help that never came, if there was a God, a heaven.

If so, God was in for a surprise. The world he created sucked, and when she showed up, she was going to smack some regret into him for doing such a crummy job.

A smile creased her lips at the thought.

*Ready or not, God, here I come.*

And then an unlikely hero, codename Hammett, aka Betsy, aka Rebecca, closed her eyes for what she knew to be the very last time.

# Chandler

*"Your body is a tool," said The Instructor. "Using it, either to overpower or to seduce, means no more than using a shovel to dig a hole or a hammer to drive a nail. Nudity is an instrument for distraction. Sex is a trap to ensnare. Your tits, your pussy: they make you strong, give you power over others. It's your feelings that make you weak. Eliminate them."*

The implications of what Heath had asked of me swirled in my mind. To let himself be that vulnerable around me was a big step, and ultimately a foolish one. Of course, if we didn't get out of this mess, we wouldn't have to worry about Heath's tracking chip. He wouldn't be going anywhere but a shallow grave, and neither would I.

"What are you thinking? Over the roof?"

"Beautiful and smart." He pointed at the boulevard running in front of the hotel's entrance. "We circle around, approach the truck from the other direction. Good?"

"And what's to keep our friends from meeting us in the street?"

"I'll take care of our friends." He grinned. He let his rifle hang from the strap and started digging in his duffel. "It's a surprise."

Footsteps clanged up the stairs. A gunman emerged onto the walkway, then tried to reverse his direction.

Too slow.

I blasted him, his head and torso flashing red before collapsing on top of the first man, then I turned back to Heath. "Now would be a good time for that surprise."

Heath held up two M67 fragmentation grenades like the one he'd left me holding in the Mexico City apartment, the one that was now in my backpack.

"Nice."

"This should be enough," he said. "You can save yours for later."

So he knew I had it. Not that it mattered since at the moment we were on the same side. "Planning to pull the pin this time?" I asked.

"I just might. Ready?"

I eyed the clay tile. "Not really, but let's do it anyway."

He pulled the first pin and lobbed the grenade over the rail. Then he ducked back, shielding me with his body as we both crouched. The explosion shook the building. And once again, I couldn't hear a thing except that incessant ringing.

Heath stood up, leaving me with a view of his body that made my mouth feel a little dry. Strong shoulders, washboard abs, his V-shaped torso angling down to his cock, positioned right at eye level.

"Don't look at me like that," he said. "I need my blood to stay in my brain."

I smiled, soaking in another second of the view before I pulled my attention away and stood alongside him.

The clay was slippery, some of the tiles that were in disrepair breaking under the soles of my boots as I climbed. Gunfire spat below. I was about four meters up when the second explosion went off. I flattened to the tile, holding on to keep from sliding back the way I'd come.

"Hurry, *bonita*."

I scrambled, feeling Heath behind me even though I wasn't able to hear the sound of his movement. I crested the top of the roof, then flipping over, I half slid, half scrambled down the other side.

The streets were still clear, as far as I could see, and when I hit the eave, I let my body keep going.

The fall was only about three meters, but it felt like ten. I took the impact with my knees, bending deep, but then stopped before flowing into a shoulder roll. The road was paved, a boulevard with cactus lining the median in the center instead of the bushes or small trees you might see in the Midwest, but the pavement was rough and littered with gravel and dirt from the surrounding roads and lots. The thought of road rash all along my naked back was less than pleasant.

Heath landed behind me, also forgoing the shoulder roll. He waved in the direction of the OXXO convenience store, and I fell into a run behind him, keeping my shotgun ready. Heath was fast, even faster than me, and he crept into the lead.

I watched his cute little butt and pushed to keep up. The only thing worse than running without a bra was riding horses without one, and I'd done both in the past week. My breasts bounced and jolted with each stride, and for the first time since I'd seen Hammett naked, I was grateful to be a cup size smaller.

A car swerved toward the median and stopped in the street. I swung my weapon toward it, but instead of the armed men I expected, an older man stepped out, craning his neck as if to catch a better view of the well-armed streakers.

Shouting erupted behind me, followed by shots fired.

Ahead, Heath reached the convenience store. He dropped to a knee and fired at the men behind me, providing cover.

I reached the store's door, yanked it open, and rushed inside, Heath right behind me.

A clerk stood behind the register, his phone to his ear. Upon seeing us, he raised his hands and started backing away. "*No disparar! No disparar!*"

"Get down!" I ordered in Spanish, but the man only cowered more, his whole body shaking. The scent of urine tinged the air.

"Here." Heath grabbed my arm, pulling me behind a shelf of candy just as the door chime sounded and footsteps thundered inside.

"*¿Dónde están?*" a gruff voice said.

The clerk stammered, his words unintelligible.

"*¿Dónde están?*"

I thought I heard weeping. Then a gunshot shook the small store.

The clerk cried out, in pain but still alive.

"*¿Dónde están?*"

Heath and I exchanged looks. He reached into his duffel and pulled out a small canister I recognized all too well. I held up my hand, asking him to wait while I reached into my backpack. My fingers closed over the item I was looking for. I pulled out the gas mask Harry had provided and put it on.

Hell if I was going to risk breathing in tear gas again.

Smiling, Heath pulled the pin on the gas grenade and tossed it to the front of the store.

Gas hissed, and bullets flew, shattering the glass cases at the rear of the store. As soon as the first wave of gunfire ended and the coughing began, we made our move.

I shot first, blasting into the smoke, pumping the shotgun, then blasting again. It was hard to say if the clerk was dying, dead, or just injured, but I had to assume he was on the ground, which gave me free rein.

Heath fired by my side, and soon we realized the return fire had ceased. Grabbing my arm, Heath pulled me toward the door, not saying a word, not that I could have heard if he'd shouted.

I stumbled over one body, then another. The third reached up to grab my leg, and I shot him in the head. Glass crunched under my boots, the tile slick as ice underneath. By the time we reached the shattered door, I was shaking, the adrenaline finally catching up to me.

We circled the outside of the store. A tall corrugated steel fence loomed behind the OXXO, separating the Dumpsters in the back from the hotel picnic areas.

Heath bent down, his hands joined together, palms up, offering me a leg up. His eyes were red and tears wet his cheeks, and I had to admit, I felt a certain amount of satisfaction as I pulled off my gas mask.

"Too bad you forgot yours this time."

He smirked. "I thought all women liked a sensitive man who wasn't afraid to cry."

I gave him a quick kiss. "That's bullshit. We like bad boys."

I stepped into his hands, and he gave me a boost, throwing me high enough to grasp the edge of the fence and pull myself up.

He took a run at the fence and leaped, then pulled himself up, and we both dropped down into a picnic area adjacent to our truck.

From here we could see a handful of men near the entrance, and somewhere in the distance, a siren screamed.

"We can wait. They won't want to be around for the police."

"I don't want to be around for the police, either."

"One second."

As if on cue, the Sinaloa troops clambered into a pickup. Heath and I crossed the picnic area and slipped into our truck, then eased out onto the street and wound our way out onto the highway, only meters behind the men who were hunting us.

"Where to?"

"A safe house, but not for Hydra Deux. I know the woman who lives there."

"Old girlfriend?"

He tilted his head to the side, not committing to yes or to no. "She makes her money from the *polleros*."

I nodded. I'd heard some use the term—literally chicken herders—to describe coyotes who led people across the border into Arizona. "So she works for the Sinaloa cartel, too."

"All this area is controlled by them."

"Do you trust her?"

"Are you kidding? She'd just as soon slit my throat as look at me, but I don't intend to give her the chance."

We continued north and then angled west, just two heavily armed, stark-naked spies out for an afternoon drive.

"I'll need to find some shade soon," I said, wiping sweat off my brow with the back of my arm. "I definitely don't want to get sunburn where the sun doesn't normally shine."

"If you like, I can shade those sensitive parts of you with my hands."

"You're so gallant."

"But then, my sensitive areas will be exposed. I will need you to return the favor."

"Quid pro quo. An entirely reasonable request."

"How forgetful of me. I noticed some sunblock in the glove compartment. Perhaps we should rub some on right now."

"Do you ever stop thinking about sex?"

"Only when I am sleeping. And then, I dream about sex. With you."

"Right."

"Would I lie to you?"

We managed to keep our hands off of each other until we reached the Mexican border town of Sonoita and the area ironically called Hombres Blancos, or White Men. The town looked like so many others along the border: dry, dusty, a patched-together jumble of recycled building materials and a few more conventional-style buildings.

Heath swung onto a dirt road veering off the dirt road we were on. Shacks built from cinderblocks, corrugated steel scrap, and bits of wood flanked the road. The neighborhood was poor, but here and there, a pot of flowers sat on a carefully swept step or a colorful bit of fabric framed a glass window. People cared, even if they didn't have much money to show it.

Heath parked the truck at the end of the road, behind a tangle of mesquite. "Filena should have some clothes to fit you," he said as we climbed from the pickup.

Filena? Pretty name.

I hated her already.

"That would be appreciated," I said.

"But I don't know. I could get used to this nude thing. Maybe we should buy some land on the Sea of Cortez, build a private resort. No clothes allowed. Just you and me, *bonita*, naked all the time."

I gave him a smile. I wanted to tell him it sounded lovely. It did sound lovely, but all I could think about was Heath's chip, the Ebola, and what I needed to do next.

He led me back to our destination. Merchants pulling carts filled with ice cream, newspapers, and cheap corn liquor stopped to stare. Faces peered from windows, wide eyes watching the naked people brazenly walking the street. There was still no sign of the cartel's men. We'd lost them for the time being, but now that we were stationary, they would be coming, as soon as The Instructor told them where to find us. Or more accurately, where to find Heath.

We had to hurry.

He led me to a house that was half cinderblock and quite a bit larger than those around it and knocked on the worn door.

A lizard darted up the whitewashed wall. A truck that had lost its muffler roared by on the street. The floorboards creaked inside, and although I couldn't see anyone peering out the covered windows, I was certain someone was.

The lock rattled, the knob turned, and the door inched open, a privacy chain spanning the gap. A dark eye with long lashes peered through, then a face, beautiful enough to be a movie star. "Armando?"

I glanced at Heath. So that was his real name. Interesting.

"Filena." Heath offered his hands, palms up, asking for help. "*Necesito tu ayuda.*"

Filena scowled at Heath, then at me. "Why should I help you? Where are your clothes?" she rattled off in rapid Spanish.

I watched Heath, waiting to see what he'd come up with to explain the situation.

"We were having sex when some men with guns interrupted."

I almost laughed. The truth: I hadn't seen that coming.

— 405 —

"What men?"

"*El Cártel de Sinaloa.*"

Her eyes narrowed. "*Un momento.*"

She closed the door.

Heath shifted to the side.

I had a feeling that I knew what was coming next, and his reaction confirmed my suspicions. A few seconds later, the privacy chain rattled. Then the door opened and the nose of a Rossi .38 snub emerged from the dark interior.

Already positioned to the side, Heath grabbed Filena's gun hand at the wrist and yanked her forward. She stumbled, off-balance, and let out a shriek. He stepped behind her and brought his left down hard just above her elbow. Then he jerked her hand up and back, forcing her elbow up to her ear and ripping the gun down and out of her grasp without a shot fired.

It was like a dance, effortless and beautiful, a thrust upward and a little pivot of the feet, and Heath was holding the gun, leaving Filena cradling her own arm and grimacing with pain. "Inside," he ordered in Spanish.

"*Pinche buey!*"

He ordered her to sit and then handed me her revolver. "Need to find something to tie her with."

I gave it back. "I have something." Dipping a hand in my backpack, I located the paracord Harry had provided. I secured Filena's hands and ankles and then tied her to a wooden chair.

The interior looked much like the house had looked from outside. Modest to the extreme. A washbasin and wood slab countertop lined one cinderblock wall, a cupboard on the other. Stacks of bottles and boxes and plastic tubing filled the corner, and the place smelled like chilies mixed with dirty cat box.

Heath made for the cupboard and rummaged inside, and as Filena continued the flood of profanity, I longed for a roll of duct tape to use on her mouth.

"Oh, I think we need this." Heath held up a bottle of Herradura Seleccion Suprema. "No *tejuino* for you, eh Filena?" he said, referring to the fermented maize brew common in the area.

"*Pinche culero!*"

"But you don't drink this yourself, do you? You have this for keeping the gangsters happy. You give them your body and your booze, you make their meth and help them rip off the *polleros*, and they let you live, obviously in high style."

"*Tu eres la venida que tu madre se olvido de tragar.*"

Heath shot her a disgusted look. "How can you say something like that? So sad, what you have become."

Leaving Filena shouting curses down the hall after us, Heath and I found her bedroom. The room smelled like body odor, and was furnished with a mattress, a chest for clothing, and a bucket in lieu of a toilet.

"Charming, no?" Heath said.

"She probably has to spend whatever money she makes on expensive tequila." I pulled most of the remaining pesos from my backpack and set them on the chest.

"You feel sorry for Filena?"

I wanted to protest, but there would be no point. "Who is she? Why do you two seem to hate each other so much?"

He brushed my question aside, as if it was a cobweb he wished to clear.

"You see how it is here, Chandler? How people are forced to live? Corruption. Poverty. Their higher ideals wiped away by basic need. And then there's Filena, who threw away her ideals with both hands out of selfishness and lack of honor. You and me, we can do more good than leave a few pesos so Filena can buy tequila for cartel gangsters. We can force real change for people who deserve it."

It was obvious where he wanted this conversation to go. Exactly the direction I didn't. I shook my head, opened the chest of drawers, and picked through the neatly folded clothing inside.

Her jeans fit me, and I added panties, a T-shirt, and socks. Unfortunately, I still had no bra, but as long as I wasn't riding horses or engaged in more foot races, I figured I'd survive.

Heath located a pair of men's jeans and a shirt that fit him perfectly, and since I saw no other evidence of a man in the room,

I had to wonder if the clothing actually belonged to him. He didn't dress, but sat naked on the mattress with his bottle. And once again I found myself looking at him, a touch of longing, or at least lust, in the pit of my stomach.

He splashed a little of the tequila on his belly, then I threw him some alcohol wipes, and he finished sterilizing his skin.

"You sure have a way with women, Heath," I finally said, pulling the syringe of Demerol from the first-aid supplies. "Seems every one you've slept with wants to kill you."

"I don't care about the women of the past. The only one who has the power to kill me, *querida*, is you. And the only way to kill me is to break my heart."

I tried my best to give him a smile, but my lips wobbled.

"I know your secret," he said.

"What's that?"

"You put me under a love spell, didn't you? *La Santisima Muerte.*" He gave me a wink. "From now on you might as well just cut it off and wear it like a rabbit's foot around your neck, because it belongs to you anyway."

I supposed him teasing me with Mexican folklore about spells of fidelity was a sign of his trust. It made me feel worse than I already did.

"We're running out of time," I said, approaching with the syringe. "It's Demerol. Just a local."

"Save your anesthetic, *bonita*." Heath raised his bottle. "This is all I need." He winked. "Besides you."

"I don't think you realize how painful this is going to be."

"I don't think you realize that I'm not planning to let you steal the truck keys."

"What happened to trying to trust each other?"

"Would you trust me if you were in my place?"

A quote from *Wuthering Heights* popped into my head. Catherine describing her bond with Heathcliff. I hadn't read the book since I was fourteen, but I could still see the words as clearly as if I had eidetic memory after all.

*"Whatever our souls are made of, his and mine are the same..."*

I blew a derisive laugh through my nose. We were the same, and that I was entertaining the possibility of a relationship with Heath at all suggested I was delusional. And yet I felt more myself than I had in what seemed like a very long time. Maybe Hammett was right. Maybe I was out of my mind. Or maybe I was finally coming to grips with who I really was, and maybe someday, I would be able to quit thinking so hard and accept it.

Maybe…someday…

"What is so funny?" Heath's cheeks held a flush, the tequila starting to work its magic.

"I think you might be right. I think we might actually be made for each other."

"You think, *querida*? You think too much."

"So I've heard."

"Stop with the thinking. You need to *feel*. You need to *do*."

I ripped open the sterile package and brandished the scalpel. "I need to cut. You really think you can tough it out?"

"I know I can."

So had I when my chip was removed. Only it hadn't worked out the way I'd expected.

"Take another drink, Heath."

He did, and he'd just lowered the bottle when I made the first incision, slicing through skin and the first layer of subcutaneous fat.

He grunted, gritting his teeth.

"It gets worse."

"Just do it."

I slipped my fingers between the strands of muscle, searching for the telltale lump of the tracking chip, just around the size of a quarter. Probing underneath the striations, I sought out his duodenum.

Heath grasped my wrist, hard enough to hurt.

"On second thought, I think the Demerol might be a good idea."

I already had a shot prepared, and gave him a few quick jabs. After only a few seconds, his face relaxed.

"Demerol, eh?" His voice had lost its edge.

"I mixed in a little morphine."

"You tricked me, *bonita*."

"You can believe that. Or you can believe I didn't want to see you in pain."

He closed his eyes, his breathing slowing down. I went deeper, finding the chip quickly. I took hold of it with a clamp and removed it as gently as I could. Then I closed up the incision with sturdy, if not fancy, sutures.

I bandaged him and gave him a shot of penicillin. The bottles of Demerol and morphine I left on the mattress next to him, just in case the pain was too much for even a man of his machismo to handle. Then I fished the keys from his duffel and slipped them into my pocket and the Jericho into my back waistband. I set his Sig Sauer a short distance away, close enough for him to retrieve it, but far enough that I would be long gone by the time he did.

"Leaving?"

I hadn't realized he was conscious, and I wondered how long he'd been watching. "I have to get rid of the chip, or they'll be knocking on our door."

"Then you will be back?"

I swallowed, my throat dry, and said nothing at all.

"You say nothing, because you don't want to lie to me. Even with this betrayal, the seeds of our mutual trust are sewn."

"OK, I won't lie. I won't be back."

"And I won't lie. You placed my gun too close to me, and even through this drug haze I could grab it now and shoot you." He smiled sadly. "But I won't."

"It's better this way. The virus would spread, and kill innocents."

"Innocents are already being killed. The people of Mexico need someone to stand up for them, to champion them. You would destroy that?"

"I'm not destroying the champion, only this particular weapon."

He struggled to sit up and then fell back to the mattress. Although I'd done my best to avoid cutting his abdominal muscles, I'd had to separate and stretch them to extract the chip. They didn't work the same way after that, at least not right away, and it took a little while to figure out how to compensate. Add that to the booze and narcotics, and he would be worthless, at least for a little while.

"I'm sorry, Heath."

"Why? It's what I would do."

"I know."

He stared at me, not answering for a long time; the only sounds were whistles and merchants' carts outside.

Finally I turned toward the door.

"Be careful on El Camino del Diablo," he said. "*La Migra* are watching, but they aren't alone. *La Muerta* waits there as well."

# Fleming

"*Once you give up hope, you give up everything,*" The Instructor said.

"Well, howdy there, sweet thing." Rhett smiled, holding Fleming's shotgun at his waist, pointed her way. "That's quite the contraption you're riding around in."

Fleming didn't move. She didn't even breathe. She didn't want to give Rhett any more reason to shoot her than he already had.

"And what's in your lap, there? Ice? Gets hot in there, I bet."

"Where's Bradley?"

"Missy, he's not your concern anymore. You queered that deal when you broke in and started shooting up the place."

"You still have some oil under your fingernails."

Rhett held up his hand, showing Fleming the bandage. "Oh, I owe you for that. And I'll pay you back, with interest. The

Instructor wants you alive, but that doesn't mean we can't have a little fun first. Now get out of the wheelchair."

"I can't walk. Remember?"

"Little lady, I do not give a shit. You can drag yourself across the floor like a beached mermaid, for all I care. Now get out of the goddamn chair."

Fleming grabbed her armrest—

—and hit the button.

The homemade air-compressor mortar concealed beneath the wheelchair seat was packed with a kilogram of three-quarter-inch metal screws, which Fleming estimated flew at a speed of four hundred meters per second.

Rhett's good ol' boy smile was shredded right off his face, along with his eyes, ears, and any other distinguishing features. It happened so fast that Fleming saw the skull beneath the flesh before the blood began to flow.

He dropped to his knees, his hands clutching what used to be a face, with an anguished, well-earned scream.

The blood fell around him like red rain, and he had enough of a tongue and throat left to yell a garbled, "Help me!"

"Sorry, Rhett," Fleming said. "You're screwed."

Actually, she wasn't sorry at all. In fact, Fleming was secretly pleased she got to use the *screwed* line. She wouldn't ever admit it to anyone, but that was the reason she'd loaded the mortar with screws instead of heavier lug nuts. "You're nuts" wouldn't have been nearly as cool.

He dropped dead a moment later, and Fleming wheeled over. Bypassing her trashed shotgun, she reached down for Rhett's pistol and shoved into the back of her pants.

"Hold it."

Fleming turned her head.

Scarlett stared at her through the sights of a 9mm.

"Keep your hands there," Scarlett said, limping over. "I think we'll go with Rhett's original plan."

She grabbed Fleming's wrist and yanked, pulling her out of the front hatch in the chair, tossing her onto the blood-slicked floor.

Fleming landed on her belly, immediately flipping over to face Scarlett.

"I underestimated you," Scarlett said. "I thought, after your accident, all the fight would have gone out of you. But you've proven yourself to be a big pain in the ass, even without the use of your legs."

Fleming kept her voice even. "Where's Bradley?"

"He's waiting for us. We're going to get out of here, go someplace nice and private, and you'll get to watch while I use a blowtorch on his face. Maybe I'll say something snappy, like you did. 'You're fired.' Or, 'Is this your old flame? I think I carry a torch for him.'"

"You should kill me now," Fleming said. "Because you'll regret it if you don't."

Scarlett laughed. "Kill you? It's never been the goal to kill you. Haven't you figured that out yet?"

"What the hell are you talking about?"

Scarlett moved a step closer, almost within reach. She stared down at Fleming and smiled. "I can't believe it. You still don't know how you got injured in Milan, do you? And who did it to you."

# Chandler

*"Facing death is part of the job," said The Instructor. "Don't blink."*

*La Muerta.* Death.

I wasn't sure how Heath had guessed I would cross the border via the brutal stretch of desert known as the Devil's Highway, but I wasn't surprised. He seemed to know my thoughts and feelings better than I did.

He drifted off, and I left and closed the door behind me. In the adjacent room, Filena narrowed her dark eyes. "You kill him?" she said in English.

"No."

"Too bad."

"You're a real charmer. I see why he likes you so much."

"Who cares what you think? You are just another of his whores."

"You're one to talk."

She stuck out her chin, defiant. "Armando sells his body, same as me. But I sell it to make men happy. He kills with his. I'd rather be a whore than a murderer."

She knew Heath was an operative? Interesting. And a bit troubling.

Several gallon jugs of water lined the side of the cupboard where Heath had found his tequila, along with a jumble of empty bottles and rubber tubing, equipment often used in meth production.

I opened my backpack and took out my body armor and slipped it on. It was incredibly lightweight, a relief since the temperature was already close to one hundred degrees Fahrenheit. I'd used a good number of my shells, so in removing the body armor, I was able to fit a length of tubing and a gallon of water inside my backpack. I took another jug of water just in case. All the equipment in the world would be worthless if I didn't have enough water.

"You are dead, you know. Both of you."

"It's been a lot of fun," I told her, "but I have to get going."

She raised an eyebrow, and I was again struck by how pretty she was. "You're Chandler, aren't you? Armando told me about you."

I was a spy, but I was a woman, too. And what woman could walk away from that?

"He did?"

"Don't think you're special. You're just another notch on Armando's belt."

"Not like you, huh?"

She laughed, and it was ugly. "He has talked about you. But he never told you about me. And you think you know him."

"I think," I said, "that you're a small-minded, jealous little tramp who hates her life and herself."

"Why should I be jealous? When he was in trouble, he came to me, *puta*."

Questions crowed the back of my mind, things I wanted to ask about Heath, about her, about what had gone so wrong between them. But no matter what answers she gave, no matter how much I learned about Heath, no matter how I would like to let myself feel about him, he and I had very different aims, and neither of us would back down.

At least this time, I'd come out on top.

"They'll track you down."

Hand on the knob of the front door, I paused. In the end, as much as I was beginning to care for Heath, all I could really give him was a fighting chance. "I'm counting on it."

The streets looked the same as when we'd arrived, children playing, merchants selling, dogs barking, eyes watching from windows, but the very pressure of the air seemed to have changed, like a storm coming in, only there wasn't a cloud in the sky.

I oriented myself using the area's mountains and then launched into a fast walk, taking a different route back to the lot where we'd left the truck. The air smelled hot and dusty, tinged with the sweet stench of garbage. A pickup thundered behind me, the bed filled with watermelon to sell, and as I crossed one of the more central, paved streets, I passed a man hawking meter-high carvings of Jesus on the cross and *Santa Muerta*, skulls and angels, and *La Virgen de Guadalupe*. An old woman spotted me and launched into a torrent of Spanish, trying to sell me some local culture.

I held up a hand and kept moving.

I'd plunged into another group of ramshackle houses, painted turquoise and white and orange, when I felt the familiar *whump whump whump* of helicopter blades beating the air above.

Shit. I hadn't counted on a helicopter.

I turned from one dirt road onto another, sticking close to the cinderblock walls of houses and cover of mesquite and banana trees. With Heath's tracking chip in my pocket, I couldn't hope to disappear, but to shoot me they would have to spot me, and I intended to delay that moment as long as possible.

The chopper's buzz grew louder, drowning out the whistles of children and accordion-driven *norteño* music blasting from a tinny car radio.

I reached the dry open lot, our truck with its tank of death visible through the waves of heat rising from the dirt. I stopped, trying to pinpoint the chopper's location.

In this town, like many others, electric lines crisscrossed from pole to building, a supplemental web of wires branching off in all directions from the authorized and unauthorized tapping of electricity. A fire hazard and eyesore, in this case it also provided a shield, porous to be sure, but enough to prevent the helicopter from hovering too close. Once I broke from the ramshackle cover of buildings and electric wires, I'd be easy to spot. And easy to approach.

I scooped in a deep breath and stepped into the street.

As if on cue, the silver Eurocopter EC 120B zoomed in above me, its blades stirring up dust and beating the scraggly leaves of a palm. Judging from the corporate look of the craft and the pair of *ranchero* gunmen peering out the open door, it was my Sinaloa cartel friends. When they spotted me, they raised their rifles.

AK-47s again. Maybe they got a deal buying in bulk.

I dashed along the rutted street and then ducked under a steel sheet propped up like an awning just as bullets sprayed the path I'd just walked.

People screamed, children ran.

Bastards.

I might be able to avoid getting killed, but if these guys kept it up, innocents wouldn't be so lucky.

I dropped my extra water and brought my shotgun up, firing, pumping, and firing again, until I was out of shells. The chopper pulled up, hovering just out of my shotgun's effective range, and although I was sure at least some of the shot had hit the bird, it didn't seem to have an effect.

I was getting low on shells. The fléchette and piranha now gone. I slung my pack off my back, digging for the dragon's breath.

A slug whizzed past my face, too close.

Shit.

I pulled up the zipper. No time to find the shells, no point in firing again until my friends came in closer. Unfortunately, an AK-47 could pack a wallop even from their current position. That left only two options, continue to draw fire while using children and old women as cover, or run for it.

I ran.

Springing into the road, I pushed my legs and pumped my arms, racing in a zigzag like some crazy sprinter who'd lost sight of the finish. I gripped my empty shotgun in my right hand, my pack flopping in my left, and sweat dripping salty into my eyes. I reached the other side of the road, the open lot stretching in front of me, my boots skidding on the loose gravel.

The helicopter thundered right behind, buzzing over the remaining power lines and then dipping low. Shots cracked, some close enough for me to feel the pop as they broke the sound barrier.

I kept going, running, zagging, pushing for the truck at the far side of the lot. Almost there, only a few yards to go.

Gravel pinged and danced around my feet. A slug thunked into my back, slamming me into the dirt. I couldn't move, couldn't think. Opening my mouth, I strained to breathe, but all I inhaled was dust, chalky and gritty on my tongue. Another slam caught my side, like a baseball bat to the rib cage.

The chopper roared above me, and I waited for the next bullet, this one to my skull, ending it all. A second passed. Two. But although all I could hear was the beating blades, the headshot never came.

I glanced up and back, spotting the helicopter turning around, getting ready to make another pass.

Gritting my teeth against the pain ripping my back and lungs, I willed myself to my feet. Thinking I might even have to kiss

Harry for the Level III-A ballistics body armor, I spit dirt from my mouth and stumbled on to the truck.

I yanked the door open, but by then, the helicopter was back on top of my position. Bullets rained down, shattering the windshield, puncturing the roof. I shoved myself away from the door and raced down the embankment and into the arroyo. The helicopter pulled up enough to clear the trees, then roared after me.

Every stride sent a stab of pain down my side. Each breath I took wrapped my ribs in agony. I stumbled, fell to my knees, then pushed myself up and kept going. I needed to find cover, needed to locate a place where I could double back, but all I could see in front of me was parched, open ground.

Tugging open the zipper, I fished out the last of my shells. My hand trembled as I dropped the pack and loaded the shotgun.

The chopper swooped in low and fast, blades beating, guns firing.

I pumped.

I fired.

The dragon's breath peppered the helicopter, engulfing it in flames. One man jerked back into the interior, the other lurched as the shot hit, then caught fire. The chopper bobbled in the air, and he fell, tumbling to the ground like a meteor entering the atmosphere.

I went into the pack again and grabbed the grenade, removed the safety clip, pulled the pin, and pitched it up and through the open door. Then I took several strides, dove to the ground, and covered my head.

The explosion flattened me to the dirt with the force of a giant fist. The helicopter wheeled to the side, its blade catching the earth and sending it cartwheeling straight at me.

I scrambled to my feet, slipping and sliding, unable to get traction. Something whizzed past my ear, and I let myself fall back to the ground just as the tail rotor cartwheeled over my head. An explosion pounded the air followed by a hot *whoosh* of an inferno.

I wasn't sure how long I lay there. Ten seconds? Twenty? But eventually I found the strength, wherewithal, and balance to lift my head and push myself to my knees and then to my feet. The chopper lay in a silver heap of contorted metal, black smoke carrying the stench of burning fuel, plastic, and human remains.

With at least two broken ribs, maybe more, and extensive bruising, I was the lucky one in this fight. But I knew my luck wouldn't hold. The Instructor would be offering the cartel a lot for them to put in this much effort. They wouldn't give up.

Grabbing my pack, I noticed the canvas was not only gnawed apart by bullets, it was also wet. I unzipped it the rest of the way, and pulled out the water jug, the plastic at the top punctured and more than half the water gone.

"Great," I said, choking back a hysterical mixture of laughter and tears. "Holy water."

No time to assess what other damage there might be, I carried the jug by hand to protect what I had left, plodded through the rock-strewn arroyo, and climbed back up to the truck. Cresting the bank, I spotted two pickups. Late models with dual wheels in back. It didn't take much to guess they were cartel reinforcements.

One of the trucks continued down the road. My guess was that he aimed to circle the arroyo, see what had become of the chopper. The other split off in the opposite direction, heading through town.

I had to get rid of Heath's chip and disappear.

I made it to the truck and slipped inside. Glass from the side windows littered the seats, and cracks spiderwebbed the windshield. I slipped the key in the ignition and prayed—to Jesus, to Allah, to the Virgin of Guadalupe, to *Santa Muerta*, to anyone I could think of—for it to start.

The engine fired to life.

I drove through the lot and pulled out onto the dirt road. The highway led in three directions, north to the border crossing into Lukesville, Arizona, and south where it split at the Plutarco E. Calles Monument, one fork leading into Sonoita and farther south, the other through La Botella and then angling back north and west along the border.

I opted for La Botella, hitting open highway and driving west. Heat burned through the windshield, the cracks making it hard to see the road. The temperature was soaring into triple digits. Not having had a drink since we'd been interrupted at the hotel, I was starting to feel ravenously thirsty, and I took a swig of the water I had left, not bothering to waste a drop washing the remnants of sand from my mouth, swallowing every bit.

With who-knew-how-many cartel soldiers hunting for me, my first priority was to get rid of the chip. My second was to destroy the virus. I still had a good amount of water left in the jug, and unless my situation changed, it would have to be enough.

I left La Botella and continued west. The border between the United States and Mexico is a long one, and although it was fenced and heavily patrolled at some points, like the lines between Tijuana and Chula Vista, Ciudad Juarez and El Paso, Nuevo Laredo and Laredo, there were other stretches where the barriers were made by nature. Rivers, mountains, and deserts.

Such was El Camino del Diablo, or the Devil's Highway.

The area of the Sonoran Desert stretching between the border and Highway 8 that connected Phoenix and Yuma, the Devil's Highway was crossed by thousands of illegals every year. But desert and mountains weren't the only features of the area. The Barry M. Goldwater Air Force Range stretched between the Gila Mountains to the west and the Sand Tank Mountains to the east. The land was also used for training by Marines and flown over by the Air National Guard.

And of course, there was *La Migra*: the US Border Patrol.

But even for all this, the area was so vast and desolate I figured it was my best bet.

Through the open passenger window, I could see the border fence only yards away, running parallel to the road. Once I was clear of the more populated area, the fence became little more than nothing; some staggered posts running with barbed wire mixed in among tall saguaro cactus, creosote bush, and bur sage.

Up ahead a pickup trundled along the road, moving west, its bed filled with a jumble of cardboard and other discarded goods, probably heading to be recycled and sold. I accelerated, pulling along his right side, my tires kicking up a cloud of dust on the shoulder of the highway. Dipping my hand into the pocket of Filena's jeans, I found Heath's chip and pulled it out, then I lofted it into the back of the truck.

So much for providing The Instructor someone to track. Now I needed to disappear.

I followed the truck another mile, then turned off to the north, following a set of ruts that led to the border fence. Up close the fence was even less impressive, its wires easily ducked under or climbed over. Of course, this wasn't much of a defense, but what border security pundits on American cable news didn't mention was that the desert itself was a more formidable barrier than any fence.

Mountain ranges and blistering sun, and air so dry you could feel it leach the moisture from your skin, greeted anyone desperate enough to cross this section of the border. I stopped near the fence, safely out of eyeshot of the highway, to call Fleming. Once on the other side of the border, I would head for Highway 8, stretching between Tucson and Yuma. I planned to hitch a ride at that point, or hijack a car, if it came to that, but if Fleming had ideas of how to get me back to wherever she was, I was open.

My phone searched and searched for a signal but found none. I gave up after a minute of waving my hand around. Why people did that, myself included, I had no idea. As if those extra few inches would bring you close enough to a cell tower to get a connection. Once I was back in the USA and clear of the desert, it would be easy to find a phone signal. I could call Fleming then.

I plowed straight through the fence, taking out posts and flattening wire, then jolting and lurching, I pushed the bullet-riddled truck into the wilderness.

My path was dictated by the convergence of many mountain ranges, but eventually I twisted and turned my way into a sweep of utter desolation.

Now the hard part began.

I parked the truck near a jut of rock and tangled mesquite and climbed out, carrying my shotgun, my backpack, and my holy water with me. With the side windows shattered, the air conditioner hadn't done much to cool me on the drive, but now that the wind was no longer streaming in, I realized just how high the desert temperature was.

I peeled off my body armor. Pain wrapped my rib cage, a sharp jab with every breath, amplified by a continuous, deep ache. I almost put the vest back on for support and then thought better of it. The air outside was well over my body temperature, and I still had hours to go before sundown. If my body couldn't cool itself, I would be finished.

Steeling myself, I pulled out my Paragon Seal knife and got to work hacking the branches off the mesquite bushes and piling them in the back of the truck. Once it was full, I stacked more branches underneath the vehicle until I had myself a bonfire.

Sweat poured from my skin, barely surfacing before evaporating into the dry air, and I stopped to take another long drink from my plastic jug.

Opening the pickup's gas cap, I pulled the section of hose I'd taken from Filena and fed one end into the gas tank. The other end I stretched downhill and took between my lips. Luckily the tubing was transparent, and as I sucked, the gas fumes making me want to retch, I could see the light yellowish cast of the fuel moving toward me. As the gasoline reached my end, I took the tube out of my mouth and let the accelerant flow onto the brush I had stuffed around the tank.

The gas flowed well, finally petering off after I'd given the dry wood a good soaking. Leaving the tube in the tank, I moved my gear a good distance away and picked up my shotgun.

I pumped a shell into the chamber and let the dragon breathe fire.

The gasoline erupted into flame with a *whoosh!* that I could feel even at this distance. And with the fire, came more heat.

Eyeing the burning tank, I let out a small laugh, thinking of Harry's stupid comment. I would never tell him I'd actually ended up destroying the Ebola by shooting it.

Provided I lived to ever see the annoying bastard again.

# Years Ago…

Her codename was Scarlett, and she couldn't wait to get the hell out of Milan.

It wasn't that the city itself was so bad. She supposed it was all right on some days, but the entire country of Italy annoyed her. The men were too forward, the climate too hot, and she preferred a nice French Bordeaux over cheap-ass Chianti.

When she'd taken the job, she'd liked the idea of traveling. She'd failed to take into account that not all destinations were created equal. In fact, some were shitty.

A burst of static sounded in Scarlett's ear.

It was about damn time.

"Ready?" she asked.

"Go," came the voice in her earpiece. "They're expecting you."

Scarlett pushed the gurney-like massage table into the hall. Already on the fourth floor, she took the elevator to the fifth and started for the end of the corridor.

Two bodyguards stood outside the ambassador's suite, and they watched her approach with blank stares. The larger one was particularly stupid-looking, built like a retired football player, just slightly on the fat side of fit. Despite a mustache that needed trimming, the smaller of the two looked sharp enough, at least physically, but Scarlett could take him if the need arose.

"So you're the masseuse, huh?" said the big brute. Not waiting for an answer, he started giving her table the once-over, looking through the folded towels, robes, and scented sheets for anything that might be used to hurt the VIP he was paid to protect.

Of course, by now he was already too late.

Mustache man grinned. "And I'll need to check you."

"Lovely," said Scarlett, not meaning it.

He skimmed his hands down Scarlett's sides, his fingers molding over her breasts on the way. "Do you give naked massages?"

"Massage is usually done that way," the man's brutish partner said. "You strip down, lay on a table and—"

"I mean where she's naked. You know. Happy endings and all the trimmings?"

Reaching her ankles, he reversed direction, moving up the insides of her legs. His check of her inner thighs rose a bit higher than it had to, but instead of saying a word, Scarlett thought about all the ways she could kill him.

"You're clear," said toothbrush 'stache, winking at her. "You have extra time and want to make extra cash, maybe we can arrange something."

She gave him a deadpan stare. "You couldn't afford me."

Chuckling, the big one knocked twice, opened the door, and let her into the room. "Set up in the sitting room."

Scarlett gave a curt nod, and when the door closed behind her, she moved on to more important things.

Rolling the massage table to the center of the room, she folded back the top sheet and moved quickly into the bedroom. The ambassador was stretched out on the bed, and judging from his lack of breathing, he'd already gotten the hell out of Milan.

But Scarlett wasn't here for the ambassador.

Fresh air wafted from the far window bank—if the jumble of odors riding the hot currents could be considered fresh—and Scarlett could see the wire stretching between the two open panes.

Unbuttoning her uniform shirt to expose her bra, Scarlett crossed to the window, focusing on the wire stretching between the two open panes. She glanced out the window at the figure climbing down in the dark, fitting her fingertips under her breasts and gripping the edge of the bra's underwire. Prying upward, she freed the piece of metal, not underwire at all, and folded it into its true form.

Wire cutters.

Scarlett placed the blades on the wire.

"Waiting for your signal," she said into her mike.

"Hold. We don't want her dead. Just crippled. Give her another few meters…now!"

She didn't wait to see the damage. That would be verified from below, and frankly she didn't care about the woman at the end of that wire either way. Scarlett was here to do her job and move on to the next op. So with thoughts of a return to Paris or New York in her future, she closed and locked both windows, returned to the entrance to the bedroom, and screamed for the bodyguards.

# Fleming

*"Revenge can be served at any temperature," The Instructor said.*

Fleming stared at Scarlett, not sure how to react to the story she'd just told. It had enough details to be true.

If so, this woman was responsible for the greatest tragedy of Fleming's life.

"Why?" Fleming finally asked. "We were both on the same side."

"He wanted you sidelined. He had your IQ tests, or some other aptitude bullshit like that. Knew you'd be more valuable riding a desk than doing fieldwork. But he also knew you wouldn't do it willingly. That fall was just supposed to cripple you. And I gotta say, I did a spectacular job."

Fleming knew who the *he* was. The Instructor.

During rehab, he'd visited with her. Got her working on integrated circuits and encryption codes, eventually leading to the device that launched a nuclear attack on London and blew up the president.

He, and Scarlett, had done this to her, just because The Instructor decided her mind was more valuable than her legs.

"You're angry, I bet. I'd be. You merely shot my leg, and I'm ready to set a box of kittens on fire. I can't image the pain you went through. All the surgeries. All the rehabilitation. Years of it. And for what? You're still a freak who can't walk."

Fleming kept her tone neutral. "I set the warehouse on fire."

"Indeed you did. The Instructor is going to be irritated."

"Since I can't walk, and neither can you, how do you think you'll be able to get us out of here?"

Scarlett's brow furrowed. She obviously hadn't thought things through.

"There's something else you haven't considered," Fleming said. "Obviously, The Instructor has gone through great lengths to keep me alive. That means you can't shoot me."

Scarlett's eyes became wide, and Fleming's hand shot out and grabbed her good ankle. She yanked, putting all Scarlett's weight on her bad leg, and the woman crumpled like a house of cards.

Once on the floor, Scarlett didn't have a chance. Fleming was all upper-body strength, and grappling, even for her life, was one of Scarlett's weaknesses according to her dossier.

She quickly disarmed Scarlett, breaking her arm in the process. As Scarlett screamed, scrambling to get away, Fleming grabbed her ankle, applied some simple leverage, and broke her leg. Then Fleming put Scarlett in a full nelson, holding the gun to the back of her head.

"What do you think, Scarlett?" Fleming whispered through clenched teeth. "You think turnabout is fair play? I break your legs in fifteen places each. Maybe your arms as well. Think about all the surgeries. All the rehabilitation. Years of pain, Scarlett, just for you to end up in a wheelchair anyway."

"Please," Scarlett whimpered. "Anything you want."

"Where's Bradley?"

"Room 17, Corridor C."

"What did you do to him?"

"Shot him in the ear. That's all. I swear."

Unless Scarlett was the best actor of all time, Fleming believed her. "Do you want to spend the rest of your life in a wheelchair?"

"No. Please God no."

"I don't want that either, Scarlett. You'd give the rest of us cripples a bad name."

Fleming fired, blowing the back of Scarlett's head out through her face. Scarlett slumped over, and Fleming released her and sat up, staring at the body. She'd done the right thing, for both Scarlett and the handicapped community. No one liked a whiner.

"Fleming?"

Fleming brought up the gun, and saw Bradley standing there. Her relief was short-lived when she noticed someone following him.

Julie.

Fleming swung the sights from Bradley to her.

Julie was an Ebola carrier. Too dangerous to live.

The smart thing to do was kill her right now.

"Fleming?" Bradley's smile dropped off his face. "It's OK. This is Julie. She isn't one of them."

Fleming didn't take her finger off the trigger. She watched Julie's eyes flare in fear.

"Sorry," Fleming said.

Then she did the right thing, even though it was hard.


# Heath

*"Forget about your family," The Instructor said. "They've already forgotten about you."*


Heath wasn't sure how long he'd been in the drug and alcohol haze when he finally regained his senses, the muscles of his belly screaming. He rolled to his side, grabbed the tequila, and raised it to his lips. The delicious burn down his throat and into his stomach wouldn't be enough to stem the pain, not of the surgery or of losing to Chandler. But the Herradura Seleccion

Suprema was damn good, and he might as well drink while he had the chance.

He supposed he should be angry that Chandler had betrayed him, but he knew that wasn't the whole story. By taking the tracking chip, she was making herself a target, drawing the cartel soldiers away from him, giving him time to get his sorry ass together and disappear. A noble and gracious act.

But she'd also stolen the virus. If she made it out of town without being killed, she would destroy it, and along with it, the opportunity he'd been working toward since that day in his father's house when he'd made a deal with *El Diablo*.

A crash came from the outer room, then voices, Filena and two men, the hum of their voices drifting through the walls.

He set down the bottle and rolled from his side onto his hands and knees, the mattress shifting under him. Shuffling to the edge of the bed, he eased onto the floor, focusing on his breathing to mitigate the pain.

His hand touched the Sig just as the door clanged open.

Gripping the pistol, he swung around, his finger squeezing the trigger just as he lined up the barrel on a *cabrón* with an AK.

Two shots and the man staggered back against the wall and then slid to the floor.

Heath wasn't so lucky with the second man. The *ranchero* wannabe ditched to one side, taking cover. Also armed with an AK-47, he wouldn't be easy to get around. Heath had to make his move before the man regrouped.

He forced himself to his feet and grabbed the pair of jeans he hadn't yet slipped on. Sig in his left hand and pants in the right, he moved behind the door.

It only took a few seconds until the barrel of the assault rifle poked through the opening, shooting a few rounds at the bed. The bottle of tequila shattered.

*Pinche buey!*

Shooting some of the best tequila Heath had ever had. Obviously he lacked the cojones to poke his head far enough inside to see what he was shooting.

*Gran error, cabrón.*

Heath whipped the denim around the door, trapping the rifle barrel between the pant legs. Yanking it to the side, he plowed into the door with his shoulder at the same time, trapping the man against the jamb.

The rifle fired two more times, the rounds flying wide, the blasts ringing in Heath's head. Keeping up the pressure on the door and his hold of the rifle, he brought his pistol around and squeezed off three rounds.

The man's body sagged. Heath let him fall to the floor. Up-close kills were messy, and up close with a firearm was even worse.

He gave the man only a cursory glance to verify he was dead, focusing instead on the rest of the room. Filena sat on the chair in the mess she called a kitchen, still tied. She was the only one in the small space, the door securely closed.

"Chandler left?" he asked in Spanish, even though he knew the answer.

"A while ago. I heard shooting." She had the gall to smile.

Heath focused on lowering his gun before he did something rash.

Ducking back in the bedroom, he pulled on the jeans and shirt, shoved his Sig into his waistband, and slung his duffel over one shoulder. He knelt beside the men, grabbing one of their rifles and finding a set of keys in the first man's pocket. Then he stepped back into the room and untied her, trying not to show Filena how much pain he was in now that the drugs Chandler had given him were wearing off.

"What am I supposed to do now?" Filena said, rubbing her wrists and gesturing to the pair of men messing up the floor.

"What you always do," Heath said. "Sell out your dignity."

He knew he shouldn't be so harsh, but the fact that she'd gotten involved with the cartel still grated on him like a rasp against an exposed nerve.

"You're bleeding," Filena said.

Heath expected to find her staring at his gut, but instead she focused on his forehead. Reaching up, he found sticky heat along his hairline. "*Chinga'o.*"

He must have been hit by a sliver of stucco or concrete chipped off by one of the cartel hombre's bullets. He felt the wound; it was bloody, as most head wounds were, but the cut itself was superficial.

"Are you going to tend to it?"

The concern coming from Filena was surprising. "No time."

"Chandler left too long ago. You're not going to catch her."

"Maybe not. But I have an idea of how I might find her." He rifled in his duffel, pulled out a thick wad of pesos, and tossed them Filena's way.

She let them fall to the floor at her feet. "I can make my own money."

Heath frowned. "I see how you make your money."

"You are no better. I fuck. I make drugs. I help smuggle people. But you kill. And you look down your nose at me?"

"You don't have to do any of those things. I've sent you thousands of dollars, and what do you do with it? Buy expensive tequila for gangsters?"

"I use it. But not for me."

He wanted to demand to know exactly what she used it for, but he knew she wouldn't tell him. She'd refused every time he'd asked. He couldn't even fault her for that. Long ago he'd told her to find her own money, and she had. Now that he had money to give, she wouldn't let him take back his words.

"Take it now. Use it to leave this place. The cartel won't believe a word you tell them, not with two dead *cabróns* lying on your floor."

"So you finally care?"

"Take it and clear out. I'm serious, Filena." He grabbed a pen from the countertop and took ahold of her wrist.

She pulled against him. "Let me go!"

"Be still." He flipped her hand up and wrote an address on the heel of her palm, and then he released her.

She glanced at what he'd written. "I am not going back to Tijuana."

"You'll be safe there, *mi hermana*."

"I am only your half-sister, American bastard. And I haven't been your sister at all since you abandoned me all those years ago, without a peso to my name."

He could remind her he'd needed the money to bury their mother, that he hadn't a peso left for himself either, but what was the point?

"Fine. You don't like *mi hermana*? I will call you *puta* then. Something you're more accustomed to hearing from the scum you hang around with. But hate me or not, go to that address anyway. People will be looking for me, Filena. Powerful people. And they might be so desperate they will try to reach me through you. You need to disappear, whether you want to take your big brother's advice or not."

He opened the door, then pausing on the threshold, he glanced back.

"Please," he said, then closed the door behind him and headed for the Sinaloa soldiers' sweet black Ford dually parked outside the house.

Heath could never control Filena, not since she was born, and that wasn't going to change now. But she was always good at saving her own skin, so he had to trust she would do so.

He had to focus on finding Chandler. Now that she'd destroyed the virus, he needed her more than ever if he was going to continue with his plan.

# Chandler

*"Survival in the wilderness depends on your knowledge of your surroundings," said The Instructor. "And when that isn't enough, you'll have to rely on sheer doggedness."*

I watched the fire burn for several minutes, throwing on more wood as the first turned to ash.

If I'd thought the desert was hot earlier, I'd been mistaken. Sun beating down from a cloudless sky combined with the fire, wrapping me in sweaty misery. After the fire had raged for over an hour, I pulled out my phaser-like thermometer gun and checked the temp.

The tank itself was well over one hundred degrees Celsius, more than enough to do the job. But still, I checked every fifteen minutes for the next two hours, keeping the fire stocked with brush.

I kept checking even as the fire died down, until I was sure there was no chance a single cell of Ebola was left alive.

By the time the flame was spent, tires melted and burned, only smoldering wreckage left of what used to be the truck, the sun was dipping close to the horizon. I stepped away from the fire, and the air actually felt cool in comparison; although my thermometer gun read thirty-nine degrees Celsius, still above one hundred degrees Fahrenheit.

It was hard to cool off at that kind of temp. Hopefully when the sun went down, the heat would follow.

I tucked the thermometer in my tattered backpack and pulled out my night-vision monocular, staring at the shattered lens.

Damn.

Throwing the worthless equipment into the dirt, I fished out my flashlight and my compass. Then I stuffed my shotgun in the pack and strapped it on my shoulders. I carried the jug of water in one hand, not wanting to risk the last of the precious liquid leaking out in the backpack, then I started to walk.

The hike was difficult from the first step. My body was so battered, every muscle and joint and bone hurt, my cracked ribs screaming with each breath, and all I could think about was how much I wished I was still lying in bed next to Heath.

Sunset splashed red, orange, and pink across the western sky, dramatic behind the spindly arms of saguaro cactus and the mountains' rugged outline. The colors faded to twilight, then twilight gave way to darkness.

The air temperature continued to hover around body temperature, not giving me much relief. Sweat pooled under my armpits and slicked my back. I walked on.

When most people think of the desert, they picture sand dunes and dry rock. The Sonoran Desert had its share of both, but this time of year, just after the end of monsoon season, plants abound. Cactus and creosote bush. Desert broom and ocotillo. In spots, the plants make walking difficult to impossible. But even though rain falls during monsoon season, once the dry winds of fall start flowing from the west, the earth grows parched quickly.

I cursed that hot wind now, but kept trudging.

Now and then I encountered evidence of the people who had traveled this path before me. Bits of trash, plastic bottles drained of water, food wrappers, a pair of threadbare underwear that must have been chafing its owner.

I could see no lights twinkling save for the stars above. I heard nothing but the normal desert night sounds: the chirping and buzzing of bugs swarming around me, the scratching of rodents in the stony soil, the howl of coyotes.

Eventually I came to a streak of desert so smooth that barely a track showed in the earth. Stopping at the swath's edge, I surveyed the area in my flashlight beam.

This was a trap, laid by the border patrol. Simple, but effective.

Every few days, agents would chain a set of tires to the back of a truck and drag the ground smooth. The drags would be arranged in parallel stripes, each cutting east and west, forcing walkers moving north to cross the path. Much too wide to jump over, wire crossers would leave prints that were easy for the sign cutters—those experienced in tracking—to read.

And the drags weren't the only traps waiting for me.

Inground sensors called Oscars were also buried through this stretch of desert, transmitting a radio signal whenever something of size came within its range. Although I hadn't spotted any of their telltale antennas among the bramble of creosote bushes, I suspected they were here somewhere.

If my footprints were discovered or the Oscars were tripped, the border patrol would follow up, radioing other units to check at the next drag and the next, trying to head me off. Once they had me trapped between one drag and the next, they would close in.

I pulled out my knife and cut a branch from a creosote bush. Walking across the drag path, I swept it back and forth over the ground behind me, erasing my tracks. With the US government searching for me, the footprints of a female traveling alone might attract attention. Even with my brush-out trick the sign cutters would know someone had passed this way, but at least they wouldn't have reason to believe it might be me.

Better safe than caught.

Regardless of my precautions, though, the border patrol would follow up. I had to get away from the drags.

Which meant I had to head for the mountains and cross the most brutal terrain of all.

# Fleming

*"If you want to be invisible, stay solo," said The Instructor. "Trying to take others with you, for any reason, will only give you away. Better they die than you fail your mission."*

When they reached the van, Sasha was still tied outside.

"Sasha!" Bradley fell to his knees beside the wiggling fox and gathered her into his arms.

"Inside," Fleming directed. "Hurry."

Smoke billowed into the sky, the air around them hazy and hard to breathe. They'd stayed long enough to ensure the warehouse was completely destroyed, and luckily the local first responders had been slow to intervene in this area of the city. Whether that was due to abandoned warehouses being low on the priority list or a special arrangement The Instructor had made to keep them out of his business, Fleming couldn't say. But although smoke was still heavy, the fire was already dying down when the first sound of sirens ricocheted off the boarded-up buildings surrounding them.

Fleming loaded her passengers into the van, Bradley in the front seat with Sasha curled on his lap. Julie far in the back, a safe distance away. Then Fleming loaded her chair and settled behind the wheel.

"You OK back there?" Fleming asked.

Julie nodded.

Bradley petted the little vixen. He still looked as if he was in pain, even after the shot Fleming had given him, but with his hand stroking the little fox's fur, he seemed to be on the mend. "Where are we going?"

"I haven't figured that out yet."

"You both could stay at my condo," Bradley said.

Fleming couldn't help but smile. Even after all he'd been through, Bradley was ready to invite them into his home—Ebola girl and all. His generosity humbled her.

"The Instructor will be watching your condo. We need to find a place that he can't tie to any of us. Any ideas welcome, at this point."

"I'm sorry," Julie said. "The lighthouse is the only place I know, and..."

"It's OK." Fleming still wondered if she was crazy to not kill the girl and burn her with the lab. All of her training dictated that was exactly what she should do. But although it might come down to that, she couldn't tie up that loose end until she knew if Chandler was still alive.

Good thing she was no longer listening to that damned Instructor voice in her head. He would be squealing all sorts of reasons why waiting was a bad idea.

She shifted into gear and started down the road. She'd stick to side roads until she could figure out which direction would be the best bet.

"We're looking for something secluded?" Bradley asked.

Fleming nodded. "This time of year, a beach house might be a good bet. Know of anything on Cape Cod?"

"We're in Massachusetts?" Julie said.

"How about the Hamptons?"

Fleming glanced at Bradley. "That might work. We can't have the location lead back to you, though."

"It won't. It shouldn't, anyway. It belongs to friends of my aunt, who is really my second cousin once removed, or something like that. They let me stay there one summer back when my uncle was still alive."

"How long ago?"

"Six or seven years? But my aunt goes there all the time. She and her friend are both widowed, and…"

"You're sure the place is vacant?"

"My aunt is with the owner in Paris right now. They travel together now that both their husbands have passed. If you want, I can call, ask if it's OK to stay there."

"I'd rather you didn't."

He looked disappointed. "It's a really nice place. I think you'd like it."

"It's not that I don't want to stay there, Bradley, I just don't want you to let anyone know that's where we're going."

Bradley nodded. "Yeah, right. Sorry. I'm not thinking like a spy, am I?"

"I like the way you think just fine."

He grinned, and Fleming wanted to kiss him so badly she almost stopped the van. How she resisted, she wasn't sure, but she managed to turn around, hop on I-90, then take I-395 south into Connecticut.

Bradley fell asleep in the seat beside her with Sasha curled on his lap.

They reached New London in good time, with no one on their heels. Fleming bought tickets to the Cross Sound Ferry, running to Orient Point on Long Island's tip, and when the Cape Henlopen Ferry was ready to depart, they drove aboard.

Fleming checked Bradley, still sleeping soundly after his ordeal, then glanced into the back. "Julie? Want to take a walk to the upper deck with me? Get some air?"

"Sure."

After scribbling a note telling Bradley where they were in case he woke up, Fleming and Julie climbed out. Afraid her chair would gain unwanted attention in its current state, Fleming resorted to her crutches and leg braces.

The ship was old, World War II era, fitted with new diesel engines and modified for its current use, now accommodating ninety cars and nine hundred passengers. Fleming would wager that in the summer, the fleet of ferries had all they could handle, shuttling passengers back and forth to the Hamptons. But now, cool weather and fall winds had chased many summer tourists from the island, and the ship was only using a fraction of its capacity.

Fine with her. She could use a little alone time.

After a painfully slow walk, she and Julie reached the deck. The sound stretched around them, steely waves tipped with the reflected orange of sunset. They stood on the side facing east, and Fleming noticed an island looming ahead.

"Do you know what that is?" Fleming asked, pointing.

Julie shook her head.

"Plum Island."

Almost a minute passed before Julie replied. "That's the lab where I was the first time. When all this started."

"Yes."

"Is that why you drove this way?"

"This is the fastest route."

"Then why are you showing this to me?"

Why *was* she doing this to the poor girl? Did she hope Julie suddenly felt inspired to dive into the sound, erasing any need for Fleming to take action to protect the world's population?

"What is it? You might as well be honest."

"I'm worried about you, Julie."

"Don't be. I'll stay away from Bradley. Believe me, I don't want to be the cause of any more death."

"I know."

"But that might not be in my control."

The girl got it. She understood exactly what she was, what destruction her blood could cause. Fleming wasn't sure why she ever thought Julie needed a reminder.

"I know you're doing the best you can, Julie."

The girl stared out at the waves, her hair tossed by the breeze. "Do you think Chandler is still alive?"

"Chandler is particularly hard to kill."

It was a lame answer, but that seemed to be all that was currently in supply. Fleming stared into the waves, leaning against the cold rail, and wished she could come up with better assurances than that, for Julie and for herself.

"I'd like to say good-bye to her, if that's possible."

Chills rose over Fleming's skin. Julie really did understand.

Nothing Fleming could say in response would be adequate, so she turned to the girl and took her into her arms.

Fleming held her for a long time, and when Julie finally pulled away, they walked back to the van in silence. When Fleming opened her door, Sasha gave a little trill of a purr, then closed her eyes like her still-sleeping master.

After reaching the other side of the sound, the rest of the trip was blessedly uneventful. Bradley woke as they circled Flanders Bay and directed the rest of the way, until they turned off a back road and into a long, straight, concrete drive flanked by trees.

The house rose at the end. It was huge, turrets spiking into the sky like some kind of fairy-tale castle.

"Bradley, I want to kiss you."

He beamed. "You like it?"

"It couldn't be more perfect."

"There is a fence around the property. This drive is the only approach to the house. Well, this and the waterfront. But there are security cameras all along here. We should be able to see anyone's approach long before they get here."

"And here I was just thinking that it's beautiful."

"I'm a quick study, aren't I? I mean with the spy thing?" He winked at her.

"I'll say," she said, not thinking of spycraft at all.

Fleming pulled the van to the side of the house, climbed into her chair, and lowered it to the pavement. Bradley walked to the side door, Sasha in his arms, and punched the lock code into the number pad. Like clockwork, the door buzzed and unlocked, and he opened the door and stood there grinning.

Julie waited for Fleming, then walked behind her to the house, as if staying close in case Fleming needed help.

"Pick out a room," Fleming said. "It looks like there are plenty."

"I'd like to face the ocean. Is that OK?"

"I think that will be nice."

"Once we settle in, then what do we do?"

"We wait to hear from Chandler."

And Hammett. She'd gotten a voice mail saying, "It's done," but nothing since.

Fleming couldn't help but wonder if Hammett was done as well.


# Hammett


*"Celebrate life when you can," The Instructor said. "It doesn't last long."*


Hammett opened her eyes, expecting to see the face of God. She didn't expect God to look like Harry McGlade.

"Hiya, hottie. Thought I'd lost you."

She was in bed, an IV in her right arm, her left in a cast. But this wasn't a hospital. It looked like a hotel suite.

"You're in a hotel suite," he said. "Been here for about sixteen hours."

"Who patched me up?" she asked, surprised by how strong her voice was.

"Hospitals have to report gunshot wounds, and you've got a famous face. But I have friends in low places, and lots of money to pay them. Doctors, concierges, paramedics. Believe it or not, when I got your call I was already on the way to Toronto."

"How?"

"I planted a tracker in your bag. When I realized you were in Canada, I drove up from DC, planned on surprising you. But I didn't expect to find you in the bushes by that stone thing, the Inupchuck."

"Inukshuk. It's a Toronto landmark on the shoreline."

"I know. I had to Google it."

"You saved me," Hammett said.

"Yeah."

"Thanks."

"No prob. Why'd you call me, of all people?"

Hammett answered honestly. "I didn't have anyone else."

McGlade reached out and squeezed her hand. "Funny thing. I don't, either."

"I trashed your 'Vette," Hammett said, staring into his eyes. "And lost all your gear."

"Sounds like you owe me a lot."

"Also, I gotta tell you, I think you're fun in a sleazy kind of way, but you aren't my type at all."

Harry grinned. "You aren't my type, either. I've got a thing for hot psychos, but it usually doesn't work out well for me. So I think we should keep our relationship purely physical."

"I'm OK with that. Also, I have another favor to ask. I'm going to need a ride back to the states, and ID to cross the border."

"And how are you paying me for all of this?"

"How about a combination of money and sex?"

"That's my favorite combination."

"And can we stop and pick up a friend of mine? His name is Kirk."

"Kirk? I'm jealous."

"Kirk's a dog."

"Now I'm aroused. Are you too weak for a blow job?"

Hammett laughed. "Hell no. Bring it on, McGlade."

# Chandler

*"My training has made you who you are,"* The Instructor
said. *"You are nothing without me."*

When dawn finally started chewing on the eastern edge of
the sky, I had cleared the trap of drags and was heading into the
mountains. It was the tail end of monsoon season, but although
bushes, cactus, and some scrubby grass sprang up everywhere,
the gritty soil was already bone dry. Unfortunately, the arid con-
ditions hadn't stopped the insects. They'd been after me all night,
swarming around my face, buzzing in my ear, and leaving every
bit of exposed skin itchy with welts.

Pain wrapped my rib cage, making each breath torture. I kept
going, pushing one foot forward then the next, picturing the pain
moving up my spine, and when it reached my shoulders, blasting out into the air like a laser. I wasn't sure if Hammett's trick
helped or not anymore, but I did keep moving, and at this point,
that was something.

I'd checked my GPS tracker many times during the night,
keeping myself moving predominantly north. Now with the day's
light, I shoved my flashlight into my backpack.

With the sun came the heat, and although the desert hadn't
cooled off overnight as much as I'd hoped, the difference the sun
made was dramatic. In hindsight, I should have kept some of the
gasoline from the truck. Wiping gas on exposed skin cooled it as
it evaporated, much better than sweat did. But I'd been so intent
on destroying the Ebola I'd missed that trick.

With sunrise, I faced another problem as well. I would be visible to helicopters and planes flying overhead.

I had to stay alert.

By the time the sun was fully over the eastern horizon, the temperature was well into the hundreds, and I could already feel sunburn tightening the skin on my face. My fingers were swollen as well, clumsy and hard to bend, and I felt as if an ice pick was lodged in the inside corner of my right eyebrow.

My last conversation with Hammett drifted through my mind. About being a hero. About how it felt. By now she must have her answer. Either that or she was dead.

I guess I had my answer, too. With Heath's help I'd stopped the plan to infect Mexico City, and now that I'd destroyed the virus, I suppose I could be considered a hero. But I didn't feel valiant or strong. I didn't feel vindicated.

All I felt was alone.

And thirsty.

The air stirred, sending dust devils whirling around rock and brush, rising toward the cloudless sky. Birds came awake, quail cooing from the arroyos, a cactus wren belting out its raspy call, staccato as a machine gun. A Gila woodpecker poked its head from the hole it had made in one of the fat saguaros. Cicadas started their chant, crescendoing until I could hear nothing else, and then dying out only to begin the song all over again.

By the time the sun climbed to midmorning, I could feel stored heat radiating from the rock, nature's pizza stone. I took one of my last sips of water, but it had grown so hot, I could barely feel it in my mouth. It did little to soothe the dryness of my throat and tongue, nothing at all to slake my building thirst.

My legs felt heavy, the pain of my injuries increasing, each step fast becoming torture. My toe plowed into a rock, sending it bouncing, and a scorpion skittered beneath my feet.

I had to watch the path in front of me. A misplaced foot might send me rolling down the rocky slope, never to get up again. An unaware step might land on a snake as it slithered from its night-time hidey-hole to soak up the rays.

By high noon, I could feel the heat of the rock through my boots. My back was no longer wet, my sweat evaporating into the dry desert air as soon as it squeezed from my pores. I drank the last drops of water and let the plastic jug drop to the desert floor.

The beat of a helicopter sounded overhead. I peered into the sky, but I saw nothing but the lazy wheeling of turkey vultures, following, waiting for my death.

The helicopter could be a trick of my water-starved mind, but I couldn't risk that it was real. I headed farther into the mountain, keeping close to juts of rock and clumps of creosote bush and mesquite. Branches ripped at my arms and snagged my backpack. Rocks skidded under my boots, and twice I nearly fell.

Soon I was no longer able to focus on the threat of aircraft or whirling vultures, instead directing every ounce of focus into putting one foot in front of the other.

One of the side effects of dehydration was going crazy. I'd heard stories about people stuck in the desert losing their way, wandering in circles until they fell prey to heat stroke or burrowed into the ground to escape the heat only to roast like a pig at a luau.

My mind wandered to Fleming, the sister I'd always wanted. She'd saved me many times before, by being my lifeline during missions when I'd known her as Jacob, and by pulling me from Lake Michigan after I'd drowned.

I sure hoped I'd see her again.

I stumbled on, down one rocky peak then up another. Checking my GPS. Moving north. Always north.

My breath came in a shallow pant, my heartbeat's patter impossible to control, even with all the techniques for regulating my body. My concentration was fast becoming shot. Thoughts wandering.

A sound rattled in my ears, mixing with the rapid thrum of my heartbeat. I had to have water. Any kind of water.

A movement caught my eye, and simultaneously the sound fit into place. A rattlesnake, right in front of me, its tail raised, warning me off, threatening to attack.

Without thinking, I stepped forward in a stomp, landing right on the rattler's head. Its body writhed for a few seconds, and I ground my boot into the dirt until it stopped moving.

Damn. Maybe I still had something left.

Hammett's stupid story flitted along the edges of my mind. The urine. The snake.

I had to admit that right then if I'd been able to urinate, I'd drink it without a thought. So would drinking snake's blood be so bad?

I fumbled with my pocket, my fingers too clumsy to pull my knife from tight denim. It took three tries, but I finally extracted it. It only took one to slice off the snake's head. Then I lifted the limp body to my lips.

The blood was warm, and my mouth was too dried out to taste, but I could feel the wetness, and that alone made me want to cry with gratitude, if only I could spare the tears.

Chalk up another point in Hammett's favor.

After draining every drop I could from the snake, I tossed its body to the ground, folded my knife, slipped it in my pocket, and continued my walk. By the next peak, I'd forgotten all about the feel of liquid in my mouth. The need for water was again throbbing in my head, as if the snake's blood was nothing but a mirage.

My mind wandered to Julie, how I'd left her on the island alone for years, and how I'd let her down when it really mattered. If I ever saw her again, I would hug her tight and never let her go. I would gladly kill anyone who tried to hurt her. I'd gladly die for her.

I thought of how my stepfather had blamed me for everything, how I knew that in some cases, he was right. In others, he was a pure, unadulterated asshole, and I felt as if I might be starting to understand the difference.

I hadn't really thought about my birth since I'd found out I was one of seven identical sisters, all sculpted from a young age to be spies. But now I had nothing to do but think. And it was easier to let random ideas scroll through my mind than focus on the predicament I was in or what I really wanted: water.

I imagined what it would have been like to grow up together. To know Fleming from childhood. To fight with Hammett over Barbie dolls and Nerf guns. I wondered what the others were like as well. What their lives were like. If any of us would have gotten along if we hadn't been enemies from the moment we met.

A muscle in my calf seized, and I lurched forward, struggling to keep my footing, trying to stretch out the cramp so I could walk, knowing I was in for much more as my muscles begged for moisture and were denied.

And still I walked on, shuffling up to one rocky and brush-crowned peak only to be presented with another.

I thought of Kaufmann, my parole officer, my savior when I was fourteen. Hammett hadn't killed him, but she might as well have. She was there. She had a hand in making it happen. And yet I was pretty sure I no longer hated her.

As disturbing as that realization was, I had a feeling Murray Kaufmann would be proud. If he were here, he would probably believe Hammett could be rehabilitated. After all, he'd believed in me.

He was a better person than I was.

So was Lund.

I'd never thought about how alike the two men were. How every time either one looked at me, I could sense they saw the person I wished to be, not the one I actually was. How that was the thing that I loved most about them.

Kaufmann had looked at me that way up to the moment he died. Kindness and hope and forgiveness in his eyes.

Lund had eventually recognized what I really was, and for the first time since he'd left me in that farmhouse, I didn't feel pain at the thought. I felt relief.

Or maybe that was just delirium.

I was growing dizzy now, and Filena's jeans and T-shirt chafed against my skin. I'd seen a man die from dehydration once in Tunisia. A gun dealer I was sent to kill, he'd escaped into the countryside when my attempt to ambush him on his way to his remote estate had fallen apart. I was waiting at his property when he'd made it back a day later, mumbling gibberish and vomiting blood through blackened lips. He'd collapsed less than fifty meters from his home, and I'd left him where he'd fallen, not even offering him a bullet to ease his passing.

If there was such a thing as an afterlife, I bet he was watching me now and laughing.

I couldn't help a little chuckle myself. Not about dying of dehydration and heat stroke, but at how ironic it was that I'd spent most of my life with a fear of drowning. Never had it occurred to me that I'd die begging for water with each step. Just as it had never occurred I would end up killing four of my sisters after a lifetime of longing for siblings. Or that I would feel anything but animosity toward Heath.

I plodded on, thoughts mixing with thoughts until they no longer made sense. Tired, so tired. My muscles cramped. My throat rasped. My will to live ebbed with each step.

*Water.*

I'd fallen into training with The Instructor, because it would let me become somebody worthwhile. I'd stayed because I was good at it, but I had to wonder if there wasn't more to it than that.

I did bad things to bad people. Made myself inhuman, unfeeling. And although there were only a handful of people in this world who cared about me, I'd managed to hurt most of them and let the others down.

And for what?

A shadow whirled around me. Glancing up I spotted four turkey vultures now, soaring in circles, their naked heads and necks sticking like spindles from their bulky, feathered bodies.

I didn't want to punish those who cared about me. I didn't want to punish myself anymore. This spy bullshit was for the birds.

I let out a laugh, the sound rasping in my throat.

"I quit."

My tongue felt swollen and stuck to the inside of my mouth, making my words sound more like an indiscriminate bellow than any kind of bold statement. But the idea had taken hold of me, an idea I'd toyed with before and ultimately pushed away. But this time, I was done pushing. This time I was embracing it with both arms.

"I quit."

I disintegrated into a fit of coughs.

Regaining my breath, I gathered what little saliva I could, sucked in a breath of parched air, and shouted into the sky. "You hear that, you fucking vultures? I quit."

No more Hydra. No more killing. No more having to abandon and betray and be despised by those who loved me. I no longer wanted to wish I was someone I wasn't. I wanted to be proud of the person I was.

It was a little anticlimactic, perhaps. I'd been disowned by the government I'd served and now topped their Most Wanted list. But now the breakup was coming from my side, too, and it was the most glorious, out-of-body experience I'd ever had.

Whether I made it to Highway 8 or died trying, I was free.

I staggered another hundred feet before I recognized what was up ahead. A road. An SUV parked on the shoulder. The figure of a man standing outside the driver's door.

Border patrol?

At this distance and through eyes so parched I could hardly keep them open, it was hard to tell.

I didn't care.

Stumbling toward the vehicle, I prayed it wasn't a mirage. I'd done my part, saved the people of Mexico City. I was finished. Imprison me, put me on death row, make an example of me for the world—nothing the government could do mattered anymore.

*Water.*

The agent would have some.

*Water.*

It was all I could think of.

*Water.*

I should have recognized him right away, his posture, his rolling gait as he crossed the road and dodged through brush and scrub and cactus toward me. He hunched forward slightly, as if in pain, and that might have been what threw me off, but when he looked up and I saw his eye patch and his gorgeous, scarred face, I cried out.

Stumbling forward, my foot hit a rock, but instead of kicking it out of the way, my toe jammed and I spilled forward onto my hands and knees.

Heath reached me, fell to his own knees beside me. "Oh, *bonita.*"

He cupped my cheek with a cool hand. Then he was fitting something between my lips, and water, sweet water, flooded my mouth.

When I'd sucked down as much as I could, I forced myself to focus on his face. He was pale, his eye patch askew, a cut along his forehead bleeding sticky into black hair. I reached a hand up and wiped away some of the blood, then straightened the patch, my fingers lingering on its edge.

"I'm sorry."

"For what?"

"Your eye."

He smiled. "Not for destroying my Ebola?"

"No. Not sorry for that."

His smile grew wider. "You won this time. You bested me."

I shook my head. "I'm done playing."

"Altogether? Or by someone else's rules?"

"Altogether."

He narrowed his gaze on me, and I had to think that maybe for the first time, he hadn't known what I was going to say before I said it.

"I can't picture you settled down in small-town America, living in a house with a picket fence."

"You're right. I'm more of a city girl."

"I'm serious."

"I am, too. I quit, Heath. For good."

"How about you think about it, and when you decide, you let me know?"

"I've decided."

"Not so fast, *querida.* I have something coming up, something big, and I need your help."

"Is that a euphemism? Because I'm a bit under the weather."

He chuckled. "You're right. We'll talk about it later. For now, you come with me. I have one thing I must do, and then I will spend all my time taking care of you."

I shook my head. As much as I wanted to hole up with Heath, I couldn't. "I have to get to Fleming. I have things to do, too."

"Where is she?"

"I don't know. But if you can get me out of this desert, I can call her."

"I'll do that. And I'll take you to her."

"It will be a long drive."

"We aren't going to drive. I have systems in place. I have been planning my move against the powers that be for a long time."

"A plane?"

"*Sí.*"

I liked the sound of that. "Is that how you found me in this huge desert? These systems?"

He tilted his head to the side. "That and hacking into the satellite surveillance system to locate your heat signature. You stood out against the hot ground. The cool spot along El Camino del Diablo."

The cool spot. I liked the sound of that, too.

He helped me to the truck, air-conditioning blasting on my skin. And although I wasn't sure what was in store for Heath and me, or if anything was in store at all, we understood each other, we were the same.

And for now that was good enough for me.

# Fleming

*"Pay attention to the world," said The Instructor. "It will tell you everything you need to know."*

Fleming didn't have to wait for calls from Hammett or Chandler to hear the news of their operations. The big plasma television in the master bedroom suite told her all she needed to know.

The blimp crash at Canadafest dominated the news cycle on all the major cable stations. A hijacking, the whole crew dead. The airship was recovered from Lake Ontario, along with two unidentified bodies of the supposed hijackers.

News of Mexico City was harder to come by, but finally she located a report on a Mexican television station sandwiched between a variety show and Spanish-dubbed reruns of *Dallas*. The report of the scene at the bullring was dramatic, the news anchor's voice cracking with excitement as he reported. Fleming wasn't certain if he was exaggerating or not, but in the end it didn't matter. There were no reports of Ebola deaths. Both Chandler and Hammett had succeeded in diverting The Instructor's plans, and that brought Fleming to the next phase of this particular game.

She was going to enjoy this.

# The White House

Ratzenberger hung up the Oval Office phone, so angry he was trembling.

Canada and Mexico, failed.

The Ebola lab, destroyed.

The girl, taken.

Manifest Destiny Two, going from a certainty to a pipe dream.

It had taken everything in his power not to scream at The Instructor when he got the news. The man had botched things, terribly. But he still wielded power, still commanded respect. He also assured Ratzenberger that this was just a minor setback. They'd be up and running again soon enough. How, the president had no idea. But he had to take The Instructor at his word.

He had no other choice.

"Angry, Mr. President?"

Ratzenberger jerked, startled by the female voice. Who was talking? Where had it come from?

"The pen."

He patted his jacket pocket, taking out the Montblanc he'd found on his desk.

"I'm a bug," said the pen. "And I've recorded all of your conversations for the past few days."

There was a click, and then Ratzenberger heard himself ranting about MD2.

"Do I have your attention?" the pen asked.

"Yes," the president mumbled.

"We own you now, Mr. President. Unless you want to be impeached, thrown in jail, and executed for treason. Do you want that?"

"No."

"Good. We're willing to allow you to stay in office, provided you stop all the take-over-the-hemisphere nonsense. But we want something in return."

"You think you can blackmail the most powerful man in the world?"

"Yes. Because I've got safeguards in place. You go after me, or my sisters, and the tapes automatically get sent to CNN, among other media outlets. Is that what you want your legacy to be?"

"No." Ratzenberger nervously itched at his nostril.

"And stop picking your nose. It's disgusting."

He pulled his hand back, shocked. They could see him, too?

"We have bugs planted all throughout the White House, among other places," said the pen. "If you go beyond regular measures to try to find them, we release the tapes. For this relationship to work out for everyone concerned, we need to keep a close eye on you. Understood?"

"Yes."

"Our first demand is easy. In fact, we'll be doing you a favor."

"What is it?"

"All we want is a simple name and address."

# Chandler

*"Sometimes when you think it's over,"* said *The Instructor, "it isn't over."*

Heath hadn't been lying about the plane. He kept it in Calexico, an hour west of Yuma. Using a pilot's license under the name Emilio Rodriguez, he had us in the air in record time. The craft wasn't quite as luxurious as a corporate jet, but it was cool and stocked with plenty of water, all I cared about.

I wasn't sure when I'd decided to trust Heath, but I had. Even to the point where I slept through much of the flight.

Fleming was on Long Island, and after landing at a private airstrip in Connecticut, Heath rented a car under another of his assumed names and drove me to the address in Easthampton Fleming had given me.

I was still weak when he helped me out of the car in the castle-like mansion's drive.

"Want to come in?" I asked.

"The last time I saw your sisters, one of them tried to kill me."

"You have that effect on women, don't you?"

He lowered his lid in a wink. "Story of my life. I will see you again, no?"

I hesitated, but only for a second. "Call me."

"How about we meet? In three days. Chicago. Dinner at the restaurant where I first saw your beautiful face."

It took me a beat to figure out the place he meant. "You saw me that night. Unfortunately, I didn't spot you."

"Wear something sexy?"

I nodded. "It's a date."

Judging from his smile, and from the kiss he then laid on me, I'd better get some rest before those three days were up.

Fleming opened the door before I reached it. "I guess you came up with your own way of beating Hydra Deux."

"I have my ways."

She nodded, watching me through narrowed eyes. "Sure you brought him over to our side?"

"He was never on theirs. Heath's on his own side. And at least for now, we want the same things."

I leaned against the doorjamb, my legs shaking.

"As long as you're sure."

"I'm sure."

"Then get in here before I have to carry you in."

I gave Fleming a hug, whether it was spy protocol or not, and she introduced me to Bradley Milton.

"You're probably aware your name is Milton Bradley backward."

He glanced from me to Fleming then back again. "You two really are identical, aren't you?"

"Nah," I said. "She's the crazy one."

Fleming nodded. "And she's the boring one."

As soon as Bradley left the room, Fleming's smile faded. "You look terrible."

"Thanks, sis."

"Really. You'd better lie down. We're not out of this yet."

"Hammett on her way?"

"She's picking up Kirk."

"And Julie?" Fleming had told me she'd rescued Julie, and from the sound of it, the girl had been through even more hell in the already hellish life she'd led.

"She's been waiting to see you. Lie down in the first bedroom." She pointed down a hall on the main level. "I'll tell her you're here."

"And you'll fill me in on Bradley?" I raised my brows.

"Sister talk can wait until after you get a nap."

"Yes, Doctor." I enjoyed giving Fleming a hard time, but the truth was, I couldn't wait to lie down.

The room was dark and safe and comfortable. That, plus the bottle of Gatorade and aloe vera gel Bradley brought me, was everything I needed.

Almost everything.

A silhouette filled the doorway, and tears filled my eyes.

"Oh, sweetheart."

She raced across the room and was in my arms hugging me, and I didn't even care about my epic sunburn. She smelled of shampoo, and after all Fleming had told me on the phone of her ordeal, I figured it must have taken a four-hour shower to wash her experience away.

"Fleming told me about what happened."

"I know."

"And you're OK?"

"A lot of people had it much worse than me. A lot of people died. I try not to think about it too much."

"We'll fix this, Julie. Fleming and Hammett and I will fix this." Strange how I was getting used to including Hammett in my declarations. "I promise you that."

"I know you will." She sat on the edge of the bed and smiled. "You saved the people in Mexico City. Fleming told me about it. How does it feel to be, like, a superhero?"

With all that she'd been through, she was still so fresh and real and young. I thought of my last conversation about heroism and couldn't help but laugh.

"What's so funny?"

"A chat I had with my sister Hammett. About saving people. About what being a hero would feel like."

"So what does it feel like?"

I shook my head.

"You are a hero, Chandler."

I kept shaking. Back and forth. "You're amazing, Julie."

"You are!"

"I used to think so. That I was one of the good guys, even if I did bad things."

"And now?"

"Now things are complicated."

"You destroyed the virus."

"I don't know if that makes me a hero."

"You saved people. You saved me back in New York."

"But not in Maine."

She waved it away with a hand, as if the truth were as easy to fan away as a bad smell.

"I'm an assassin, Julie. That's what I was trained for. That's what I do." I wasn't sure if I should tell her, if I should destroy her vision of me. But I'd always tried to be honest with Julie. I couldn't betray that now. "I killed the president. You must have heard about it."

I thought it would feel better to say it. Instead I felt tired, as hopeless as before. My near-death euphoria in the desert aside, I was as shackled by the reality of what I was as I ever had been.

"I know you must have had a good reason."

"Did I? I thought so at the time. Now I don't know. I'm sure of one thing, though. I'm not a hero."

"You are to me."

I shook my head. "If I really was, I would have kept The Instructor from taking you back at the lighthouse. I would have kept him from knowing about you in the first place. I failed, Julie. I failed you."

"You've never failed me, Chandler. But maybe saving me isn't the most important thing."

"Then what is?"

"I don't know. But maybe saving others isn't the only thing heroes do."

I shook my head. Whether it was due to the dehydration or my lingering exhaustion or the beating my body had taken over the past couple of weeks, I wasn't following.

Julie took my hand, folding it between hers. "Maybe saving people is only part of it. Maybe inspiring others to be heroes counts, too."

"Inspiring?" I thought of Fleming, who'd been heroic long before I knew her and steady as a rock ever since. Maybe Hammett, although I still had trouble imagining that nutjob doing anything altruistic, and if she accidently did, I'd doubt it was because of anything I had said. Heath had a certain heroism about him, but while I might have inspired him in certain sexual ways, I hadn't been able to talk him out of keeping the Ebola. I'd had to take it. "Who have I inspired?"

"Me."

I looked into her beautiful face, so sweet and yet worn with cares far beyond her years. Far beyond *anyone's* years.

Tears flooded my vision. I tilted my chin up and opened my eyes wide, trying to keep them from streaming down my cheeks. "You were always a hero, honey."

Julie gave me a little smile and shook her head. "That's nice of you to say, but it's not true. Knowing you made me who I am. And you know what? For the first time in my life, I'm really proud of myself."

I reached out for her and took her in my arms. For a long time, we just sat there, holding each other, and when she finally pulled away, my eyes were dry, and I felt calm.

"Get some sleep, will you?" Julie said. "And don't worry about anything. It's all going to be OK. I promise."

I smiled, remembering when I'd said to her the same things she was now saying to me.

Julie pushed up from the bed and stepped toward the door. Pausing, she looked back at me, a smile fit for an angel curving her lips.

"Thanks, Chandler," she said. "I love you so much. And I'm proud of you."

"I love you, too, sweetie. And I'm proud of you, too. So proud."

Then I closed my eyes, and a few seconds later I heard the door close behind her.

# Julie

Julie pulled the door tightly closed and leaned back against it. When she'd imagined seeing Chandler again, talking to her, she'd assumed she would break down and blubber like an idiot.

But somehow, for the first time in what felt like forever, she'd had no need for tears.

The doorbell chimed, and she heard voices in the foyer.

She needed to sneak out of here, to go upstairs. As a threat to anyone except the few who were inoculated against her virus, she was walking death.

She stepped into the hall and was about to turn the corner and make a run for the back staircase when she heard the bark.

*Oh my God.*

She stopped, unable to walk one more step, unable to move.

The click of canine toenails on marble echoed down the hall.

Tears sprang to Julie's eyes. Happy ones.

Another bark.

Julie craned her neck around the corner, peering into the foyer. A woman and a man stood with Fleming and Bradley, but she didn't look at any of them. She only had eyes for her sweet, loyal, brave, brave Kirk.

The woman noticed Julie. She nodded, then dropped the leash.

Feet slipping, Kirk went nowhere for several strides, like some kind of cartoon. Then his nails finally grabbed purchase and he bolted into Julie's arms.

She gathered Kirk to her, ruffling his ears as he licked her face. "I thought you were dead, buddy. How..."

"He's a great dog."

Julie looked up at the woman who'd been holding Kirk's leash. Her face was so much like Chandler's, except for the different placement of her cuts, scrapes, and bruises and the fact that she had wildly colored hair. "Hammett?"

The woman nodded.

Julie remembered seeing Hammett after The Instructor's people had dragged her through the lighthouse window. "You saved him?"

She nodded. "And I gutted the emo bitch who shot him."

Julie remembered the girl. How could she not? And although she probably shouldn't be glad to hear about someone's death, she couldn't manage even a hint of regret. "Good."

Kirk pulled away from her, wagged his way over to Hammett as if to check on her, then wagged back to Julie.

Julie ran her fingers over his soft head. Her stomach clenched, her eyes misting. A second ago, she'd had everything figured out. Now that she knew Kirk was alive, she wasn't sure what to do.

She peered up at Hammett. "He seems to really like you."

Hammett looked confused, as if she had no idea what to say. "He's a great dog," she repeated.

"Could you..." Julie's voice cracked, and for the first time since she'd made her decision, she wasn't sure if she could go through with it.

She looked down at Kirk's smiley, panty face, and listened to him beat his tail on the floor. *Thump. Thump. Thump.* Lowering her lips to his head, she kissed him and ruffled his ears one last time. Then she pushed herself to her feet. "I want you to have him," she said to Hammett.

"Me? Why?"

"He likes you. And you seem to appreciate him."

"I do." Hammett stared at her for a good long while, only Kirk's happy tail *thump* marking the time. Finally she spoke again. "Did you tell Chandler?"

Julie knew they were no longer talking about Kirk, that Hammett understood what her gift of Kirk meant, what Julie was about to do. Although she'd just talked to Chandler, Julie wasn't sure her friend would ever consciously accept what had to happen.

"No. She wouldn't understand."

Julie already felt her resolve slipping, and what she was about to do was too important to let herself back down now.

"I'll give him a good home," Hammett said.

Julie was just about to walk away when Hammett drew in a breath.

"You know, when I first met you," Hammett said, "I thought you were worthless and whiny. I'm never wrong. But I was about you."

Julie had the feeling this was as close to a compliment that Hammett ever gave. She pressed her lips together in something she hoped Hammett would interpret as a thank you. "Take care of Kirk, OK?"

"Anyone tries to hurt him, they're dead."

Julie nodded. She'd made the right decision. And although she felt sad about leaving Kirk, she had a sense that she could trust Hammett with him. That as strange and abrupt and unlikable as Hammett was, she wouldn't see Kirk as a burden, but would appreciate the unconditional love and companionship he offered.

She picked up her sweet dog's leash and handed it to Hammett, and without another glance back, she walked away.

The house was quiet, only the chimes from a grandfather clock in the study breaking the stillness. Julie climbed the stairs and continued down the hall, her footsteps so light she almost felt like she was dancing.

She wondered if she should feel sad about what she was going to do. But instead she felt peace, a full-body calm that she hadn't experienced in a long time. Maybe ever.

Julie ducked into the room she'd claimed as hers, a large guest suite with a sitting area and a private bath. The window was set in a little alcove with a window seat and had a gorgeous view of the ocean, the crash of the waves as soothing as a lullaby. The Atlantic Double Dunes Preserve on one side of the property and the Amagansett National Wildlife Refuge on the other made for a serene setting. Natural. Peaceful. Julie couldn't ask for anything more.

She walked into the bathroom and ran a glass of water, then took the bottle of codeine she'd stashed in the back of the vanity, behind the towels.

Staring at herself in the mirror for a few seconds, she thought about the note. After all, a note was mandatory. Julie had told Chandler thanks, but she wasn't sure her friend really understood that Julie was most proud not of what she'd done, but of what she was about to do.

The most heroic thing she'd ever done in her life.

She carried the pill bottle and the glass back to the window seat and set them on the sill. Grabbing a notebook and pen, she stared at a blank page. And stared. Seconds ticked into minutes, but nothing poignant or witty came. Whatever words popped into her mind didn't seem enough.

Setting the notebook on her lap, she picked up the bottle, opened the cap, and dumped several pills into her palm.

Might as well begin.

She gagged a little on the first handful, chasing them down with the water. After that, it became easier. Another handful. Then another.

It only took a few minutes to register the effects. Sleepy. And, ironically, she felt like giggling.

All the loneliness of the past years faded away. The burden of knowing what she was, the lives that her blood had taken, the inability to change her future—one by one all the pressures and frustrations and fears melted into the rhythmic crash of the waves.

Julie laid back, closing her eyes, wondering what she should be thinking about. Was there more than just this life? A heaven? Would God understand why she was doing this?

He must. She was saving lives.

Blurry from the codeine, she reached for the notebook. The pen was tough to hold, the room starting to spin and fade at the same time, but she managed to write her suicide note. And as she set the notebook on her lap and let the pen fall from her hand, her last thought was that though the note was brief, it was certainly apt.

THIS IS MY GIFT TO THE WORLD.

Death took her gently, leaving a small smile curving her lips.

# Chandler

*"Listen to your instincts," said The Instructor. "They will recognize the truths your mind refuses."*

I had no idea how many hours I slept, but when I finally opened my eyes, light slanted through the west-facing window. Almost sunset.

My stomach felt tight. After all the rest I'd finally gotten, I wasn't sure why I felt so uneasy, but I couldn't ignore it. Something wasn't right.

I found my sisters, Bradley, and Kirk in the expansive great room in front of a bank of windows overlooking the ocean. The dog raised his head and thumped his tail. Hammett was asleep on a couch, and I didn't see a sign of Harry—a good thing, as far as I was concerned.

"Harry gone?" I asked Fleming.

She nodded. The gesture was natural enough, but I could sense a tightness in her movement, and little lines of tension bracketed her mouth.

The sense of unease that I'd awoken with clamped down on the back of my neck. "What is it?"

Bradley glanced at Fleming. He looked as if he was about to cry.

"Fleming?" My voice rose with panic, and it wasn't until that moment I realized who else was not in that room.

And then I knew.

"Where is she?"

My throat closed, making it hard to breathe, and I felt like I was choking...drowning.

"Where's Julie?"

Kirk lowered his head and whined.

Hammett opened an eye, but didn't say a word.

Bradley glanced at the staircase.

"Chandler..." Fleming started.

I didn't let her finish.

Spinning around, I went for the staircase, grabbing the banister and propelling myself up the steps two at a time. Julie loved the ocean, and if she was up here, she would be in a room with an ocean view.

I reached the landing, ran down the hall, and threw open the first door.

Empty.

I did the same with the next bedroom and the next. Finally I focused on the farthest door, a room set off by itself, and my whole body started to tremble.

The hall blurred, tears welling, overflowing, coursing down my cheeks. I didn't want to go near that closed door, and yet I had to. I had to see her.

I heard a creak on the stairs behind me, but I didn't turn back to see who was following. Instead I forced one foot to move, then the next, until I was standing with my hand on the doorknob.

I thought back to all the difficult things I'd done in the past couple of weeks. None compared to turning that knob, pushing the door open, forcing my eyes to focus on the window seat.

Julie lay back against the cushions, her blond hair spread over damask, the orange sparkle of sunset on cresting waves her backdrop. She looked as if she was asleep. Her lashes half-moons on pale cheeks, her cheeks relaxed, a slight smile on her lips.

A piece of paper rested on her lap. I picked it up, the page shaking so badly I could barely read it.

*Julie's gift to the world.*

My breath jammed in my throat, caught in a stuttering sob. I knelt beside her, touched her forehead, already starting to cool. Then I lowered my face to hers and kissed her cheek.

How long I stayed there, I wasn't sure. But I was aware of Fleming coming into the room long before I finally spoke. I looked at her, leaning on her crutches, her face pinched.

"She thanked me, you know. She said I helped her to be brave. I didn't understand."

"It was for the best, Chandler."

"How can you say that?"

"You know Julie couldn't live. You knew it the night you flew her to that island."

I shook my head. "I should have been able to change things."

"I don't know how you can say that. You did everything you could to save her. But the threat was in her blood. She knew it. She took care of it."

I looked back down at the note. *Her gift. Julie's gift.* A gift I didn't want her to have to give.

"I thought about killing myself," Fleming said in a hushed voice.

I sat back on the carpet and turned to look at my sister, my *strong* sister, far stronger than me. "When?"

"The first time? After I fell. I dragged myself to the street, to get help. But after they patched me together, and the real pain started, I thought about it. Every damn day."

"But you didn't."

"No. Because somehow I knew that it would be selfish. That I would be doing it to save myself pain, to save myself the humiliation of being in this chair the rest of my life."

I had no idea what point she was trying to make, so I said nothing and waited for her to continue.

"I thought about it another time, too. Almost did it."

"When?"

"In the prison, under the Badger Ammunition plant."

I swallowed, my throat as parched as it had been in the Sonoran Desert. "The pain?"

"The pain was bad. And if I'd done it, if I'd slit my throat, no one would have known the transceiver's self-destruct code. The president would still be alive. Ratzenberger wouldn't have succeeded a good man, and The Instructor would still be on a leash. So I probably should have killed myself. But I had a selfish reason for staying alive."

Fleming was the most unselfish person I'd ever known. "What?"

"I thought they had you. And I wasn't going to let them hurt my sister."

I let that sink into my brain. The irony of it—how I had then given The Instructor the code to save our skins—must have been bitter for Fleming indeed. "You must hate me."

"No."

"I hate me."

Fleming shook her head. "I'd do it again. But Julie didn't kill herself for a selfish reason, Chandler. By doing what she did, she saved millions of lives. Maybe billions."

I looked back at Julie. As much as I wanted her in my life, as selfish as my need was, I knew she was right to do what she did. I wanted to hug her once again, pull her close, tell her how amazing she was.

Instead I turned back to Fleming. "Julie was a hero."

Fleming looked at me and nodded, and although I'd never spoken to her about heroes, I could tell she understood the significance of my statement.

"She sure as hell was."

I wasn't sure how long Hammett had been listening, but now she stepped into the doorway behind Fleming.

None of us spoke for a long time, the sound of the waves outside and the ticking of a grandfather clock the only noise in the house. Finally Fleming broke the stillness.

"None of us measure up to Julie in the hero department, but we can contribute to the security of the world in another way."

Hammett frowned. "And what would that be?"

"I have The Instructor's home address."

"Hot damn," Hammett said. "How did you pull that off?"

"Seems POTUS would like to keep recent events under wrap."

"I'll bet," Hammett said. "You up for settling the score, Chandler? And remember, he's mine."

Once upon a time, I would have felt as elated at the prospect of paying The Instructor a visit as Hammett did, but now all I could manage was a somber nod.

"We have something to do first."

The smile fell from Hammett's lips. I hadn't known my psycho sister to give a rat's ass about any human being, but even she seemed to recognize that Julie deserved respect.

All the respect in the world.

We wrapped her body in sheets, and the blanket from her bed. Even as I worked, I didn't have a sense that this physical flesh was Julie anymore. The spark that was the real her was gone. To a better place, I hoped. If anyone deserved to be in a better place it was Julie.

Fleming located a crematorium for pets twenty minutes east, much easier to break into than one devoted to humans. I suppose some people might think taking Julie to a place for animals was disrespectful, but that was only because they didn't know Julie. I was certain she would like the idea.

The crematorium was joined with a cemetery and funeral chapel. It had closed at five p.m., and by the time we arrived, after nightfall, the place was deserted. The crematorium housed two furnaces, and one was still warm. We slid Julie inside and, in silence, turned the heat to high.

After her body was ash, we put her into an urn and sprinkled her off the Long Island coast.

Our last errand was dropping off Bradley. He'd bought a carrier for his fox and insisted on taking the late train out of New York. Fleming had let him, deciding it was best he not be any part of what we were about to do. He stood on the curb, giving Fleming a long kiss through the open door.

"Come on, you two. Get a room," Hammett said. "Or let us join in. A threesome with triplets, Brad. What do you say?"

Bradley's cheeks turned red.

"I'll call you," Fleming told him.

Bradley closed Fleming's door, gazing at her the way Kirk used to look at Julie, the way the dog was looking at Hammett now.

Fleming waved.

I stared at the city lights through the windshield, folding my feelings and memories and putting them gently back into that compartment in my heart. I would never be the selfless hero Julie was, but there was something my sisters and I could do to make the world a better place. "Let's go."

# Chandler

*"Eliminate enemies when you can," said The Instructor. "You don't want to be looking over your shoulder the rest of your life."*

We left New York and drove west, stopping to drop Kirk off at a dog boarding kennel and stealing plastic sheets from a construction site for the back of the van. At the Hamptons house, Bradley had discovered a bundle of clothing including coats waiting to be donated to charity, and the three of us now had new, warm threads.

Finally after a long drive we came to a nondescript house in a nondescript suburb, practically identical to every other one on the block. Upper middle class, but far from a gated community. The only swimming pools were aboveground, the cars in the driveways Hondas and Chevys.

"This is it?" Hammett asked.

Fleming frowned. "Unless the president is lying to us. And I don't think he would. He understood that we could ruin him, even if he killed us."

"But it's so…ordinary," Hammett said.

I agreed. Two stories tall and covered in beige vinyl siding, the house had a garage facing the road, a bank of windows overlooking the street, a row of Japanese yew underneath. Just looking at the front, I could see the entire floor plan in my mind's eye. Ordinary upon ordinary. The Instructor had loomed large in my life—in all of our lives—and ordinary was the last thing I'd been expecting.

Fleming passed the house and continued up the street, coming to a cul-de-sac rimmed with similar houses in varying shades of beige. "Do you think he has bodyguards?"

I shrugged. "I dunno. Maybe he thinks anonymity is enough."

Hammett opened the side door of the van. "I'll go around back. You cover the front." She pressed her earpiece, the radios left over from supplies Harry had provided to Fleming. "Check, check one."

I heard the delayed echo of Hammett in real life and in her radio.

"Check two," I said.

"Check three." Fleming nodded at me. "Be careful, ladies."

Hammett hobbled out, a crutch under one arm, her bag in the other, fading into the darkness across the street.

I went behind her. The night was chilly, and I was glad Bradley had discovered the coats. As I walked down the street, I slipped into the mind-set of a suburban girl walking home from a day at the office. Tired, oblivious to the surroundings, anxious to get home and have a glass of Pinot Grigio and watch a little TV. I approached the front of the houses slowly, casually, as if I belonged there.

"He's there, in the dining room, eating," Hammett said.

Damn she was quick, even with a crutch.

"No signs of any guards, or even an alarm system. And check this out—there's a woman and two kids eating with him. I think it's his family."

I wasn't sure how to take that information. It was all so incongruous to what I was expecting. All The Instructor's preaching about avoiding personal ties, and yet the man had a wife and children? Could that be legit?

"Hold position, one," Fleming said. "Two, what's your twenty?"

"At the driveway," I answered.

"Plan?"

"I'm going to ring the doorbell." It was a simple plan, ordinary, and it seemed to fit the situation.

"Copy. Proceed. Over."

I stuck my hand in the pocket of my trench, gripping the 9mm. A flutter moved through my stomach, my palms as sweaty as if this was my first hit. Then, summoning up more courage than I'd ever needed to on any other mission, I rang the bell.

A few seconds later, The Instructor opened the door.

"Well," he said, a dab of red sauce on his chin. "This is a surprise."

It hadn't been long since I'd last seen him, and he looked the same, despite the house and kids. At least the familiarity of those steel-blue eyes and hard face made this experience feel a little less surreal.

"Follow me," I told him.

"Can I tell my family good-bye?"

"No. Keep your hands at your sides and walk out the door. Anything else, and they watch you die. Then I let Hammett go in and shoot them all."

"She's here, too?"

"Step outside. Now."

He followed orders. I shut the door behind him and gave him a quick pat down, finding him weapon-free. Then I marched him back toward the van.

"Package picked up. Heading home."

"On your three o'clock," Hammett said, limping alongside the opposite sidewalk.

The Instructor's face looked pale in the streetlights' glow. "How'd you find me?" he asked.

"We bugged the Oval Office. The president gave you up."

"Never trusted that one. But then, as I've said many times, you can't really trust anyone, can you?"

The van pulled up.

"Open the side door. Get in."

He did, facing Fleming holding her Skorpion. "Back of the van," she told him. "Handcuffs on the mat. Kneel down and cuff your hands in front of you, then lie on your stomach."

He complied. I climbed in after him, followed by Hammett. A perfect abduction.

"So what now?" The Instructor asked. "You take me some-place secluded? Torture me? Get all my secrets? All my contacts?

Run Hydra yourself? Let me tell you something about being a patriot, ladies. It's about loving your country more than you love anything. Including its people. This nation is great because folks like me are willing to do what it takes to make it great."

"I am so fucking sick of your platitudes," Hammett said, pulling out a knife and scraping it back and forth against the stubble under his chin.

"Wait," I said.

Cheek pressed against dirty plastic, the bastard smiled. "I knew you wouldn't throw away this opportunity."

"Opportunity?" I repeated.

"Knowledge is power, and power is irresistible."

Power? Running Hydra? Manipulating people? Ordering death and ruining lives in the name of the good ol' US of A? The whole idea made me more than sick. It made me angry.

"There's only one thing I want to know," I said.

"Ask away."

"What happened to our biological parents?"

The Instructor's shrug was as emotionless as his stare. "I don't know. It might be in a file somewhere. But I never cared to get that personal."

An animal growl rumbled deep in Hammett's throat.

"Your biological parents aren't important. They didn't have anything to do with what you've become. Credit for that is mine alone. Look at how much you've done," he said. "You three are my greatest accomplishment. Better than any of the others."

"I'm done listening to him," Fleming said. "Chandler?"

I stared down at the man who'd turned me into what I was, what I no longer wanted to be.

"Punch his clock," I said to Hammett.

"With pleasure."

She jabbed him in the back with the knife, up under his shoulder blade, penetrating his heart.

"Even with all my experience," The Instructor said, "I didn't see that coming."

And then the son of a bitch died.

We drove him to a vacant lot, relieved him of his wallet, and dumped his body and the plastic sheet there. The cops, and the world, would think it was a robbery.

Afterward, none of us talked for several minutes. Hammett broke the silence.

"I want a Slurpee. You guys up for a Slurpee?"

"I could use some coffee," Fleming said.

"Find a 7-Eleven. My treat."

Being the suburbs, we found one within a few blocks.

"Park along the side," Hammett said. "No need for all of us to appear on their cameras."

Fleming parked several car lengths down. Hammett turned to me. "Need anything?"

"I'm OK."

"You sure?"

I looked at my sister, unsure of what she was really asking.

But ultimately it didn't matter. The answer was the same.

"Yeah. I'm sure."

She winked at me, gave me a playful punch in the shoulder, then limped out of the van's side door.

"So," I said. "What are we going to do about her?"

Fleming turned to look at me, fatigue shadowing her eyes. "You mean, do we need to kill her?"

I nodded.

"We should," Fleming said, sounding more tired than she looked. "But the bitch is kinda growing on me. What do you think?"

"We got The Instructor. Mission is over. All that's left is to clear our names."

"Kill Hammett, let them find her body. Presidential assassin is dead, case closed."

I nodded. "But..."

"But it doesn't feel right?"

"Yeah."

"We would be doing the world a favor, Chandler. She's dangerous."

"So are we."

"Dangerously psychotic. Who knows what she'll do in the future?"

I let out a heavy breath. "I agree."

"And she's probably thinking the same thing about us. How do we know, when she comes back, she isn't going to try for us both?"

"I'm thinking the same thing." I dipped my hand in my trench pocket and took the 9mm snug in my hand. It didn't hurt to be prepared.

"So...?"

I wasn't sure what to say. On one hand, I didn't want to be looking over my shoulder for the rest of my life, wondering if Hammett was behind me. On the other, my feelings toward her had mellowed considerably. Plus, there was something else. Something even more important.

"I don't want to be this person anymore, Fleming. A cold-blooded killer. I want a new life, a different future. Could you look Hammett in the eye, after all we've been through, and pull the trigger?"

She turned her head away, staring straight out the windshield. "The eye? What's wrong with shooting her in the back?"

"Answer the question."

"She needs to be taken out, Chandler."

"That's not my job anymore. Is it yours?"

Fleming didn't answer.

"Do you want to do what The Instructor said?" I pressed. "Start up Hydra again? Create another kill squad?"

"No."

"So when does this end?"

"With Hammett."

"Are you going to do it?"

"I dunno." She leaned her head back against the headrest.

"I'm not," I said, pulling my hand from my pocket and folding my arms.

"So what do we do?"

"We drive away."

"We might regret it later."

"I'm sure we will. But if neither one of us is going to kill her, and Hammett might come back and try to kill us, it seems like the only option we have."

Fleming frowned. "What about my coffee?"

"Drive away, sis."

Fleming started the van and cruised through the parking lot. But as we passed the 7-Eleven storefront window, I realized our decision had been unnecessary. The only person in the store was the clerk behind the counter.

Hammett had disappeared.

# Fleming

"Three beers!" McGlade said over his shoulder. Then he looked at Fleming and Chandler, seated next to him. "You girls want anything?"

Fleming laughed. They were in Harry's box at the United Center in Chicago—a premier suite that came equipped with a private hostess, a fridge, leather sofas, and a flat-screen television, the latter necessary because the seats were located on the top row of the stadium, so high up and far away from the basketball court Fleming feared a nosebleed.

Chandler sat on one of the sofas, her legs tucked under her. She looked good, having finally gotten some rest. They'd arrived in Chicago yesterday, and Chandler had retrieved some of the money she had stashed at various drop points around the city and elsewhere. After emerging from the health club with a duffel filled with ten thousand cash, identification, and a few weapons, the two of them had checked into a hotel and gone shopping, just like regular sisters.

Now Chandler was dressed casual in jeans, a cute top, and boots. Fleming had spent more time on her appearance, and wore, for the first time since the accident, high heels and a skirt. Which, in the wheelchair she'd just bought, rode up high enough to make eye contact with McGlade impossible. Every time his head turned her way, he talked directly to her lap.

Not to her chair. Not to her scarred legs. All Harry cared about was catching a glimpse of her thong.

It made her feel wonderfully normal. But she hadn't dressed up for Harry. She'd dressed up for someone else.

The hostess brought them each a beer, and Harry gulped down half of his, then licked off his foam mustache.

"So, ladies, how are we going to start this?"

"Start what?" Chandler asked.

McGlade put his feet up on the table, crossing his ankles. "I was thinking you two begin with some kissing action while you rub baby oil on each other. I'll join in when I'm done taking pictures."

Fleming laughed again, and it came out as a very unladylike snort. Chandler rolled her eyes.

"Come on," McGlade said, almost whining. "Think about all I've done for you."

"We paid you back for that."

"What about the morgue? I just saved both your asses."

McGlade had made his way into Cook County morgue, and through a combination of stealth and bribery, managed to steal the body of one of the dead Hydra sisters Chandler had put there. When her body was discovered yesterday, along with a note confessing to the assassination, the manhunt ended.

"That was a favor you did for Hammett," Chandler said. "And I recall she already paid you in full."

Chandler had told Fleming about Hammett's special deal with McGlade, which had turned out to be a very smart solution for all involved. Fleming was sort of disappointed she hadn't thought of it herself. Though she was pleased she didn't have to pay Harry with her body, as Hammett had.

They hadn't seen Hammett since her disappearance after killing The Instructor. Fleming had followed up with the kennel

Kirk had been in, only to find out he'd already been picked up. Hammett had disappeared without a trace.

But Fleming had a feeling they'd be seeing her again. Probably much sooner than they wanted to.

"You two promised you'd double-date me."

Fleming sipped some beer. "And here we are. As promised."

"Perhaps your definition of *date* is different than mine. Mine includes oral-genital contact."

"I'd love to see that," Chandler said.

"Really?"

She nodded. "If you want, I can push on your back while you bend down and try to blow yourself."

Harry seemed to be actually considering it. The Bulls scored, the crowd erupting into cheers.

"OK, how about this," Harry said. "We go back to my place, jump in the hot tub, take a bunch of Rohypnol, and just let nature take its course."

"Nature would probably involve me killing you," Chandler said.

"So cold. Tell me, did you give your last lover's dick frostbite?"

Chandler laughed. "The opposite, actually. We both got sunburned."

"He should have been a gentleman and shaded your parts."

"That's what he said."

"How about you, Wheels? My spa is equipped with handicapped railings and a ramp."

For some reason, this tickled Fleming. "Really?"

"Absolutely. I'm fully equipped to accommodate the physically challenged. I even have a love swing over my bed. Once I strap you in, it's like sex on the space shuttle. Totally weightless."

"I've never tried one of those."

Chandler shot her sister a look. "You're not really considering it."

"Have you tried a love swing?"

"No. But I haven't tried eating broken glass, either."

"It's sharp," Harry said. "And hurts worse coming out."

"Here's the thing, McGlade," Fleming said. "I'm seeing someone."

"Serious?" he asked.

Fleming thought about it, then smiled. "It might be."

"Is it that nerdy guy? From the house in the Hamptons?"

"Bradley. Yes."

McGlade shrugged. "Invite him along. He's not too hairy, and I'm open-minded. Every guy has some experimental years, when they're bi-curious. Mine lasted from seventeen, up until forty-four."

Fleming couldn't tell if he was kidding or not. "Really?"

"Sure. If he's not into it, you guys can still use the swing without me."

Chandler shook her head. "While you watch from the closet."

"The closet?" Harry sneered. "Ridiculous! That's what the closed-circuit cameras are for."

Fleming knew the likelihood of her and Bradley visiting Chateau McGlade was zero, but Harry was growing on her. Sort of like a fungus.

The beer kept flowing, along with some terrific Chicago-style deep-dish pizza, and in between the innuendos, rude comments, and blatant come-ons, McGlade turned out to be a pretty good host and everyone had fun.

When the game ended, Bulls winning by eight, he made one last attempt at getting his wick dipped.

"Just thirty seconds in the women's bathroom stall," he said. "C'mon. I helped you guys out. Return the favor. Throw a dog a bone."

Maybe it was the beer, or her good spirits, but Fleming didn't think that the request was unreasonable, for all he'd done for them. They were all consenting, slightly drunk adults. Why the hell not?

"I'll play you for it," Fleming said to Chandler. "Rock-paper-scissors."

"Ick. Hell no."

"Come on. Throw him a bone. Loser goes."

"You're insane."

"It's thirty seconds. How far can he get in thirty seconds?"

"Too far."

"He won't even have time to get the condom on."

"Actually," McGlade said, "I'm already wearing one."

"You walked through the desert, and you're a chicken when it comes to a quickie in the bathroom?"

Chandler blew out her cheeks. "You seem to be pushing this hard, sis."

"The lady knows what she wants," McGlade said.

Fleming gave a little shudder, despite her brave talk. This whole thing was crazy, and she wasn't sure she'd go through with it even if she lost. But before she could call it off, Chandler piped up.

"Fine. But Harry's playing, too."

He shrugged and balled his hand into a fist. "If I win, I get both of you."

Fleming eyed Chandler, who shrugged. "Why not? Then we each do half the work."

She agreed. "OK. Rock-paper-scissors. On three. One…two…three!"

When they saw who lost, neither Chandler nor Fleming could stop laughing.

# Chandler

After Fleming and I left Harry, we said our good-byes, at least for the time being, her off to meet Bradley at the Museum of Science and Industry and me to a solo room in a small, comfortable hotel on Ontario. I checked in with my new suitcase filled with goodies Fleming and I had purchased the day before and took a long, hot shower. I can't say I didn't think of Julie. She was on my mind nonstop, as were Hammett and Kaufmann, and now and then, even Lund. But tonight, my thoughts were mostly focused on Heath. On sex. On a new beginning.

I dried my hair and put on a little makeup, then dressed in my new lingerie and a killer Robert Rodriguez sheath dress. I'd even bought heels, albeit only two inches, and once I'd put on my new outfit, I hoped to feel like a new woman.

Not an assassin.

Not a target.

Not even a hero.

Just a woman. One who was about to go on a date with a man who was so like her in many ways.

I swiped on lipstick, checking my appearance in the mirror next to the door. Then I eyed the knife lying on the pile of clothes I'd changed out of. A woman going on a date didn't usually wear a nine-inch knife.

Turning away, I ripped the tag off my new evening clutch and filled it with a few bills, lipstick, and the hotel key, then I walked out the door.

A second later, I walked back in, picked up the knife, hiked up my dress, and strapped it to my thigh.

I wasn't a spy anymore, but that didn't mean I had to be stupid.

# Heath

The Capital Grille on St. Clair, a block off the Magnificent Mile, was just as Heath remembered: rich mahogany and brass decor, portraits of racehorses, hunting scenes, and powerful men, soft music, white linen, exceptional wine, and the most beautiful woman in the world walking through the door.

He stood to get a good look. He still thought Chandler was at her most *magnífico* naked, whether armed with deadly weapons or not. But the formfitting black sheath in leather and suede was a nice second choice.

They shared a kiss and sat, then Heath poured her a glass of wine, the bottle from his private wine cellar at the restaurant, a perk for regular guests of the establishment.

They raised their glasses and took a sip.

"Delicious," Chandler said.

"Not as delicious as you in that dress."

"Thank you. So what are we toasting?"

"Our partnership."

"I hope you're referring to what we'll be doing in bed later."

"Always, *querida.*"

"But there's more to it, isn't there?"

"Yes. Feelings are deep between us."

"That's not what I'm referring to, Heath, and you know it."

He couldn't keep the touch of a smile from his lips. "See? You understand me. As if our hearts beat as one."

She rolled her eyes. "You're talking about this plan of yours, aren't you?"

"I know you've quit, *bonita.* I respect that. But I believe we can help each other."

"Each other? I don't need help with anything except finding a new apartment, so unless you've recently taken up real estate, I don't see how—"

"The president won't stop chasing you. You think you have ways of controlling him, but it won't last. He isn't the type of man who will be controlled for long. He must be stopped."

"Stopped how?"

Heath stared at her, watching the realization come to her eyes. She leaned in closer, lowered her voice.

"You're saying we kill the president?"

"Yes."

Chandler frowned. She brought her glass to her lips, sipped, then stared over the rim, as if waiting for the Bordeaux to provide wisdom.

"I understand why I'd be interested in that, but how does it help you?"

"Back in Mexico, you asked me about my father."

She nodded, silently waiting for him to continue.

"The first time I remember meeting him face-to-face, I was fifteen. I took a bus to Phoenix and broke into his home with the mind to kill him. I failed then, but I've spent these many years since both discovering new reasons I must do it and making sure I don't fail again."

Chandler was good at controlling her expressions. Maybe the best, next to him. But her eyebrows arched and her lips tightened, and Heath could see his declaration and the truth behind the words surprised her.

She took another taste of wine before she spoke.

"And what does this have to do with the president?"

"Why are you asking, *bonita*? I can see you have already figured it out."

"Ratzenberger is your father."

Just at that simple statement, Heath could feel the determination harden inside all over again.

"*Si*. And I cannot take him down alone."

# The White House

Ratzenberger stared at the pen on his desk, but didn't dare move it.

He'd play along, for now.

But this wasn't over.

Not by a long shot.

If it was his last act as commander-in-chief, he would make those Hydra bitches pay.

Them, and his goddamn illegitimate son, Armando. He rued the day that little bastard came to his house and he sent him to The Instructor rather than killing him.

But his time would come. All their times would come.

Like all great leaders, Ratzenberger had a backup plan.

One that made Manifest Destiny Two look like a kindergarten Christmas pageant.

# Toronto

Lyle Gerard had only started working in greens maintenance at the Oakdale Golf and Country Club last week, but he was already convinced it was the greatest job on earth. He was outside all day, trimming the greens, fertilizing the turf, raking sand traps until they were smooth as a baby's bottom. And if he was lucky, someday he might play on one of the course's twenty-seven holes.

He'd parked his cart at the eighth green and circled to the trailer to unload the mower when he saw her on the shore of the water hazard. A girl, spindly creature, with short black hair draped over one eye and black marks all up and down her arms. She was cradling something pink and red to her belly. It wasn't until he got closer that Lyle could see it was her own insides.

*What the hell?*

She tossed her head, flipping her hair out of her eyes.

"Don't just stare, you stupid hick. Get me a fucking doctor."

# EPILOGUE

# Hammett

The rented tugboat ate diesel fuel like a freighter, and the sonar equipment was outdated and subpar, but on the second day of searching Hammett found the submerged tank of Ebola thirty-five meters down, roughly two hundred meters offshore.

She anchored, lowered the winch, and got into her dry suit. It was bitterly cold, terrible weather for boating, let alone diving, so she had this part of Lake Ontario to herself, away from prying eyes. In the harbor, she had a truck waiting, and a crew of laborers on standby.

As she'd hoped, no one had seen the tank fall off the blimp, and when the blimp was recovered it had floated a good distance away from the drop site. She'd spent the last six weeks waiting for her broken arm to heal and anxiously surfing the Internet for news about the tank being discovered. But it hadn't been, and there hadn't been any Ebola outbreaks anywhere in the world.

Yet.

Kirk came over, licked her face. She gave the dog a pat on the head.

"What do you think, Kirk? Sell it to the highest bidder? Or unleash it upon the world? You'd like a world without human beings, wouldn't you, boy?"

He wagged his tail, agreeing.

Hammett smiled.

*Armageddon, here I come.*

The End

# CAST OF CHARACTERS

**CHANDLER** is an elite spy, working for an agency so secret only three people know it exists. Trained by the best of the best, she has honed her body, her instincts, and her intellect to become the perfect weapon.

**FLEMING** used to be a field operative like Chandler, until she was paralyzed on a mission. A genius, Fleming turned her attention to miraculous inventions and being Chandler's handler, but she's always longed to return to the field.

**HAMMETT** is a dangerous psychopath with all the training of Chandler and none of the moral fiber. She's a super-assassin, and she loves it. Unsympathetic to her fellow human beings, she has a soft spot only for animals.

**TEQUILA ABERNATHY** was once an Olympic gymnast before he became an enforcer for the Chicago mob. Now semiretired, he does favors for friends and those who can pay his rates. He is featured in the thriller *Shot of Tequila*.

**DAVID LUND** works as a firefighter in central Wisconsin. The picture of an everyday hero, he is incapable of turning down a person in need of help. He is featured in the thriller *Pushed Too Far*.

**PRESIDENT J. PHILLIP RATZENBERGER** took over the Oval Office when his predecessor was assassinated in *Spree*.

**JULIE** has been hiding on a remote island off the coast of Maine since Chandler first rescued her. Read how that happened in the Chandler novella *Exposed*.

**HEATHCLIFF** is a member of Hydra Deux. Heath first runs into Chandler in the novella *Hit*. His Hydra Deux partner is former Olympic wrestler Earnshaw.

**SCARLETT** is also from Hydra Deux. Her Hydra Deux partner is charmer and cowboy Rhett.

**ISOLDE** is another assassin for Hydra Deux. Izzy's partner is the gargantuan Tristan.

**BRADLEY MILTON** is a robotics expert who lives and works outside of Baltimore.

**JACQUELINE "JACK" DANIELS** is a Chicago cop who appears in *Shot of Tequila*, *Whiskey Sour*, *Bloody Mary*, *Rusty Nail*, *Dirty Martini*, *Fuzzy Navel*, *Cherry Bomb*, *Shaken*, and *Stirred*. *Flee*, *Spree*, and *Three* take place in the time span between *Dirty Martini* and *Fuzzy Navel*.

**HARRY MCGLADE** runs a private investigations firm in Chicago. McGlade is possibly the most offensive human being of all time.

**THE INSTRUCTOR** is the man behind the top-secret Hydra super-assassin program as well as Hydra Deux. He trained superspies Chandler, Fleming, and Hammett as well as their now-deceased sisters Ludlum, Clancy, LeCarre, and Follett. He also trained Scarlett, Rhett, Isolde, Tristan, Earnshaw, Heathcliff, and the deceased Rochester.

# AUTHORS' NOTE

We truly hoped you enjoyed *Three*. While it can be read as a standalone thriller, this is the third part of a series featuring Chandler, Hammett, and Fleming. If you like to read things in order, it is: *Flee, Spree, Three*. Chandler also appears in the short novels *Exposed* and *Hit*, and Hammett appears in the short novel *Naughty*, all of which take place prior to *Flee*.

The characters of Jack Daniels and Harry McGlade appear in *Whiskey Sour, Bloody Mary, Rusty Nail, Dirty Martini, Fuzzy Navel, Cherry Bomb*, and *Shaken*, written by J.A. Konrath. They also appear in *Stirred* and *Serial Killers Uncut* written by J.A. Konrath and Blake Crouch. Harry McGlade also appears in *Babe on Board*, written by J.A. Konrath and Ann Voss Peterson.

# THE CODENAME: CHANDLER SERIES

## By J.A. Konrath and Ann Voss Peterson
### *In chronological order*

*Hit*
*Exposed*
*Naughty*
*Flee*
*Spree*
*Three*

The events in *Three* occur after *Pushed Too Far* by Ann Voss Peterson and *Shot of Tequila* by J.A. Konrath, and in between *Dirty Martini* and *Fuzzy Navel* by J.A. Konrath.

## J.A. Konrath's/Jack Kilborn's Works Available on Kindle

JACK DANIELS THRILLERS
*Whiskey Sour*
*Bloody Mary*
*Rusty Nail*
*Dirty Martini*
*Fuzzy Navel*
*Cherry Bomb*
*Shaken*
*Stirred*
*Killers Uncut* with Blake Crouch
*Serial Killers Uncut* with Blake Crouch
*Birds of Prey* with Blake Crouch
*Shot of Tequila*
*Banana Hammock*
*Jack Daniels Stories* (collected stories)
*Serial Uncut* with Blake Crouch
*Killers* with Blake Crouch
*Suckers* with Jeff Strand
*Planter's Punch* with Tom Schreck
*Floaters* with Henry Perez
*Truck Stop*
*Symbios* (writing as Joe Kimball)
*Babe on Board* (with Ann Voss Peterson)

OTHER WORKS
*Afraid* (writing as Jack Kilborn)
*Endurance* (writing as Jack Kilborn)
*Trapped* (writing as Jack Kilborn)
*Draculas* with J.A. Konrath, Jeff Strand, and F. Paul Wilson
*Origin*
*The List*
*Disturb*
*65 Proof* (short story omnibus)

**Ann Voss Peterson's Works Available on Kindle**

THRILLERS
*Pushed Too Far*

SHORT STORIES
*Babe on Board* (with J.A. Konrath)
*Wild Night Is Calling* (with J.A. Konrath)

ROMANTIC SUSPENSE NOVELS
*Gypsy Magic* (with Rebecca York and Patricia Rosemoor)
*Claiming His Family*
*Incriminating Passion*
*Boys in Blue* (with Rebecca York and Patricia Rosemoor)
*Legally Binding*
*Desert Sons* (with Rebecca York and Patricia Rosemoor)
*Marital Privilege*
*Serial Bride* (Wedding Mission series)
*Evidence of Marriage* (Wedding Mission series)
*Vow to Protect* (Wedding Mission series)
*Critical Exposure*
*Special Assignment*
*Wyoming Manhunt*
*Christmas Awakening*
*Priceless Newborn Prince*
*Covert Cootchie-Cootchie-Coo*
*Rocky Mountain Fugitive*
*A Rancher's Brand of Justice*
*A Cop in Her Stocking*
*Seized by the Sheik*
*Secret Protector*

Visit the author at annvosspeterson.com.

# ABOUT THE AUTHORS

Award-winning author Ann Voss Peterson wrote her first story at seven years old and hasn't stopped since. To pursue her love of creative writing, she's worked as a bartender, horse groomer, and window washer. Now known for her adrenaline-fueled thrillers and Harlequin Intrigue romances, Ann draws on her wide variety of life experiences to fill her fictional worlds with compelling energy and undeniable emotion. She lives near Madison, Wisconsin, with her family and their border collie.

J.A. Konrath broke into the writing scene with his cocktail-themed mystery series, including *Whiskey Sour*, *Bloody Mary*, and *Rusty Nail*—stories that combine uproarious humor with spine-tingling suspense. Since then, Konrath has gone on to become an award-winning and best-selling author known for thriller and horror novels. He is also a pioneer of self-publishing models and posts industry insights on his world-famous blog, *A Newbie's Guide to Publishing*. He lives in Chicago with his family and three dogs.

Made in the USA
Charleston, SC
20 May 2013